Praise for PAUL GARRISON's previous novel

FIRE AND ICE

"HEART-STOPPING SUSPENSE . . .
ONE OF THE BEST THRILLERS TO
STEAM INTO VIEW FOR SOME TIME."

People

"A FINELY CRAFTED THRILLER BY
A MASTER STORYTELLER."

Clive Cussler

"AN OCEAN OF ACTION . . .
EXPECT TO LOSE SLEEP READING THIS BOOK."

Denver Rocky Mountain News

"SUPERIOR WORK . . .
PAUL GARRISON HAS HIT THE JACKPOT."

Houston Chronicle

"THE STORY LEAPS INTO ACTION
FROM THE FIRST PAGE . . .
I LIKE EVERYTHING ABOUT *FIRE AND ICE*."

San Jose Mercury News

Also by Paul Garrison

FIRE AND ICE

PAUL GARRISON

RED SKY AT MORNING

HarperTorch
An Imprint of HarperCollins*Publishers*

This is a work of fiction. Names, characters, places, and incidents are products of the author's imagination or are used fictitiously and are not to be construed as real. Any resemblance to actual events, locales, organizations, or persons, living or dead, is entirely coincidental.

HARPERTORCH
An Imprint of HarperCollins *Publishers*
10 East 53rd Street
New York, New York 10022-5299

Copyright © 2000 by Paul Garrison
ISBN: 0-380-80220-1

First HarperTorch paperback printing: January 2001
First Avon Books hardcover printing: March 2000

HarperCollins ®, HarperTorch™, and ◈ ™ are trademarks of HarperCollins Publishers Inc.

Printed in the United States of America

Visit HarperTorch on the World Wide Web at http://www.harpercollins.com

10 9 8 7 6 5 4 3 2 1

For my old pal, John M—a Prince of New York.
Thanks for your name, your title, and your take on the town.

1

A TORPEDO TRACK streaked the moon-silvered Atlantic.

"This is so beautiful," said Rita. She was entranced by the swirling ocean surface. A heavy moon had risen ahead of the giant cruise liner. Behind them, hours after Manhattan's skyscrapers had sunk beneath the ship's snow-white wake, New York City's night glow still haloed the western sky.

The night was so lovely, so full of stars, that she and Jack kept breaking off from the dancing to run out on deck. They paused for one last look on the way "home" to their incredible cabin. Cool breaths of the sea mingled with warm shifts from the land.

"What are you staring at?"

Jack was leaning on the ship's rail gazing at his beautiful bride and thinking, Sometimes you get lucky. Just when you're sure you'll end up alone wandering Greenwich Village muttering to yourself, your boss introduces you to Rita.

You stop smoking and start running. A year later your best man toasts the luckiest guy in town. Champagne wedding breakfast at Gramercy Tavern, on Rita's boss; upgrade to honeymoon stateroom, thanks to yours. And you're sailing to Italy on the *Sovereign Princess* with a woman who's so proud to be with you that she hangs onto her bride's bouquet until the ship's out of range of her girlfriends waving from the pier. Then all of a sudden, in the middle of the river, she goes, "Look, they're happy, too!" and throws her flowers to some woman kissing a tugboat captain. Only in New York.

"What?" Rita asked softly.

He felt his eyes get warm. What right turn had he made, what wrong turn had he missed, that got the two of them together for that first look that made everything else happen? Overwhelmed by joy, embarrassed by tears, he looked down at the rushing waves.

"Jesus H!"

"What?"

"Look!"

It was racing toward the ship.

"That's a torpedo."

"Like from a submarine? It is not."

"Rita, before we met I spent a lotta nights watching *World at War*. That's a torpedo."

"It can't be."

It streamed close by, angling behind the ship, disappeared in the white wake, and emerged to hurry on in the distance, arcing little rooster tails of spray.

"Couldn't have been." He watched it disappear.

"Oh, here comes another one."

A second bubble track, straight at them and this time a lot closer. Jack took her hand instinctively, but it was still so unlikely that instead of backing away, he leaned over the rail to see what it really was. They never looked so fast on The History Channel. He thought this one would miss, too. But it changed course at the last second and smacked into the hull right under where they were standing.

The night exploded brilliant white. He felt something hard as a fist in his face. When he heard the thunder he was already flying through the air with the awful realization that Rita's hand had been torn from his.

"Admiral Tang!"

Sonar's urgent warning jolted every man in the submarine's cramped control room. "Small craft nine hundred yards astern, sir."

Tang Li whirled back to the periscope, alarm sweeping the triumph from his face.

Ahead, a mile across the water, he saw flame pillaring from the liner he had torpedoed. They still hadn't launched any lifeboats. Thousands of passengers were milling on the dark decks.

Tang spun a half circle to scan the moonlit sea behind the submarine. "Radar?"

"Wood or fiberglass hull," answered Shi Deng, the submarine's surface eyes. "Or I'd have picked it up on my pre-attack sweep." Shi Deng's blunt farm-boy's fingers darted like dazzled moths between knobs and keypad as he tried desperately to locate the enemy he had failed to detect.

In ordinary units of the People's Liberation Army, sailors were shot for less. In Admiral Tang's elite Submarine Expeditionary Force—his crews said with only half a smile—a bullet in the back of the head was preferred to a look of disappointment clouding the admiral's determined face. For Admiral Tang had, like some Mandarin of old, plucked only the best from the deep sea of Chinese poverty to give them proud places in his fleet.

He was a sailor's sailor, a first-rate seaman, and they loved him for it. Born to all the privileges accorded the *gaogan zidi* by a society obsessed with station, he was shockingly democratic, having inherited from his grandfather the

Revolutionary's belief that great leaders led from the front. Thus he berthed in the submarine like the lowest machinist's mate. Thus he had personally fired a torpedo into the hapless cruise liner to draw New York's defenders out of their harbor.

It was Fleet Week in New York, the annual late-spring port call by U.S. and foreign naval vessels. Admiral Tang had fought hard to convince his cautious superiors in Beijing that the presence of so many warships would serve as a smoke screen. Churning the coastal waters, cluttering the channels, and congesting the airwaves with their radios and radar, the peaceful visitors had unknowingly camouflaged the approach of his submarines.

"Closing, Admiral." It was Sonar again—Junhaoi Hong, a fisherman's son, who could hear on his passive receivers the stealthy hiss of movement on the water—while Radar still struggled to piece a target out of sea clutter. Hong was proud to outdo Shi, but as fearful as every man on the boat that somehow the enemy had penetrated their security zone.

The lives of ten thousand men were in their hands. For tomorrow at high tide—thirteen minutes before noon on Tuesday—the People's Liberation Army's Submarine Expeditionary Force was going to raid the city of New York.

Admiral Tang laid a mental gridwork over the sea surface and searched for the menace yard by yard through his periscope's night lens. If he was victorious, the attack on New York would set into motion a plan that would, ultimately, unseat his Beijing bosses and make Tang Li emperor of a unified China.

But if the Americans discovered Tang's flagship before the attack, his fleet was doomed. Total surprise was his only hope of victory. His submarines had to penetrate the harbor unseen and shelter in the shadows of New York's skyscrapers before American forces could retaliate. In the heart of the city, the U.S. military would have to muzzle their firepower or slaughter their own people.

With Tang's boats shielded from air and missile attacks, his commando shock troops would storm ashore to rout the lightly armed police. Years of defense cuts had stripped nearby Forts Monmouth, Drum, and Dix of active-duty troops, and the Americans would have to wait precious hours for soldiers from distant Southern bases.

But if whatever was creeping up behind his submarine betrayed his presence, U.S. ships, planes, and helicopters would destroy his frail boats in the open ocean.

McGuire Air Force Base was only twenty minutes fighter time from his present position; Groton Submarine Base, a hundred miles; Naval Combat Logistics currently had two cruisers at Colts Neck, New Jersey; Brunswick, Maine, four air patrol squadrons; and how long before the Reserve Anti-submarine squadrons at Willow Grove scrambled their A-6s?

"Only reservists," Commissar Wong had scoffed. Tang had referred Wong Tsu to American reservists' combat records in the Gulf War. He despised Commissar Wong. But he couldn't dismiss the political officer whom the Communist Party and the Army had attached to his armada. Though Tang had no doubt that Commissar Wong was a Trojan horse with secret orders to drown the victorious admiral before he returned home a dangerously popular hero. Red flags would still fly over Tiananmen Square. But it would be a martyr's welcome accorded by the Beijing leadership with whom he had worked hand in glove preparing this invasion.

"Still closing, Admiral," said Sonar.

After the planes and the helicopters, nuclear-attack submarines would come hunting his boats—big-eared foxes pouncing silently on mice. And when the mighty East Coast Atlantic Fleet emerged from the world's largest naval base in tidewater Virginia, fire and steel would rain down on the panicked survivors.

A tiny sailboat crept into the powerful night glass, nosing toward them like a curious duck.

An old man was at the tiller—his shock of snowy hair rendered lime green by the low-light enhancer. Beside him, a boy of ten or twelve.

Grandfather in a wooden boat on a magic night that his grandson would remember forever—if the sharp-eyed boy weren't eagerly focusing binoculars at Tang's periscope standing out of the Atlantic like a fence post.

Tang's hand strayed toward his scarred right ear. A policeman's club had pulverized the cartilage and crushed the rim of his eye socket. Abrupt air-pressure changes in the submarine were torture; tension seemed to pierce the damaged drum like a needle. He thought of his own grandfather—a swashbuckling veteran of the Long March. He'd been as exciting as Tang's father was dull, and outings like these two shared in their sailboat had lighted Tang's childhood.

Tang weighed their fate against China's fate. Chaos was about to destroy her. The Communists had squandered their Revolutionary heritage until all they had left was the power to obstruct. The coastal cities were rich on foreign money, the vast interior poor. Banks were bankrupt, state companies foundering, and hundreds of millions of poor people wandered the country begging for work. At any second, envy and class hatred would explode in civil war.

Tang had seen the waste firsthand, while building his fleet and recruiting his men. He had heard the pleas of the hopeless, and had smelled the stink of corruption. But no change came easily in China. The princeling *gaogan zidi* sons and daughters of Party leaders and PLA generals cared only for wealth.

"Helm! Turn right one hundred and eighty degrees."

As the submarine circled, Tang rotated the periscope to keep the sailboat in his sights.

In China, the bold were feared, innovators despised. So Tang had looked to the past, when the Middle Kingdom's greatest emperors had ruled. By modeling himself after those clear-eyed Sons of Heaven, he would forge an industrial titan where one billion Chinese would be proud again. He would destroy the Party and restore the Middle Kingdom.

First, reunify the people with military action: conquest. The target: Taiwan. Recapturing the renegade island would recapture Imperial China's dignity and honor.

The key was to stop the Americans from interfering, as they meddled all over the world. To block them, Tang had devised a second strategic initiative—a parallel action that would hold the United States at bay while China's army invaded Taiwan. He would take Manhattan hostage.

Tang's armada was poised to achieve all of his goals: paralyze the potential meddler, restore his nation's pride, and guarantee his own ascension to the throne of the Forbidden City. And finally—as a small personal bonus—exact vengeance for an old injury. His ear throbbed and he rubbed it again.

Montauk Point Coast Guard station was well within range of the handheld VHF radio likely carried on the sailboat. This near the coast, even a cellphone could do them in.

"Full ahead."

Propelled by electric motors, the submarine lunged in silence.

"Planesmen—surface the bow."

The elderly American stood in astonishment as the curling white bone of the submarine's bow wave broke the dark water directly in front of his sailboat. A big old man, tall and stoop-shouldered, he shoved his tiller hard over with one long arm and drew the boy to him with the other.

The little boat turned awkwardly, losing way as the wind spilled from its flapping sail.

"Helm, right two degrees—steady!"

The submarine displaced one thousand eight hundred tons, the sailboat less than two. So Tang felt nothing of the impact through the double-steel hull, while the rearing bow blocked his view of all but the toppling sail.

In his wake swirled scraps of wood and cloth. But in the unlikely event that man or boy survived the initial collision and the rush of the one-hundred-and-seventy-foot hull and the seven thrashing blades of her propeller, Admiral Tang ordered another one-eight-zero turn and drove back through the wreckage like a blunt knife.

2

AT THAT MOMENT in New York, on a tugboat tied to a Tribeca pier, Ken Hughes and Kate Ross were wrapped in each other's arms—thirty-seven hours into the blind date from Heaven.

Kate hadn't really considered it a date at first. She had sworn off dating, recently—blind dates in particular—and besides, the tugboat captain was way too old for her.

Julia, who had set them up, had insisted. "He's a pretty young fifty-three. If you were Chinese you'd be almost perfect for him—perfect's supposed to be half the guy's age plus seven."

"I'm not Chinese."

"But you're both into boats," argued Julia, who hadn't a clue that sailboaters and tugboatmen got on like mice and elephants.

When Kate protested that she was not in the market for the nautical version of a truck driver, Julia, who had slept with more men than Kate could even fantasize about, said, "Rule of life: all tugboat captains are great-looking. He calls himself a wharf rat, but he's really a romantic. And he's a reader. You can talk books. Trust me."

Kate had agreed to meet the tug captain for Sunday brunch, mostly because—like many New Yorkers—she made a point of overscheduling her life rather than risk a quiet moment peering into a pool of lonely think-time. But she hadn't bothered to make a reservation and she found the Grange Hall doors blocked by people waiting for tables: software coders blinking in the sunlight and T-shirted Internet lawyers spilling onto the sidewalk. Then down Commerce Street had come this stocky guy with a weathered face, a lively smile, huge hands, and sky-blue eyes.

Couldn't be him: he was wearing clean khakis and a polo shirt, and if he was a nautical truck driver, he had neither visible tattoos nor dirty fingernails; not even, she thought— forming, with little hope, a tentative smile—a Popeye pipe in his mouth. But he walked right up to her and stuck out his hand and said, "You must be Kate. Julia described you well."

Kate shook his hand and smiled back, thinking, Thank you, Julia; what did you say to make him come?

She said, nodding toward the line, "I should have made a res. It's at least an hour."

As she turned back to him the sun filled her eyes. Ken Hughes, who'd been suckered by Julia into hoping for nothing more than a pleasant afternoon with an intelligent woman, thought, They're green, she's got a smile like a bonfire, and I'm a goner.

He said, "Want to try the White Horse?"

But around the corner on Hudson, the White Horse sidewalk was loud with Fleet Week sailors in shore-leave whites—and twice as loud inside.

The Perry Bistro took them in. And there, among sleepy Frenchmen and their cheerful dogs, the Yalie and the wharf rat began to talk.

Kate was a book editor. Ken, like many mariners, always had a book in his hand for the long, empty hours off watch. He had never met someone who actually edited them and he announced, on their second glass of wine, that he had read *Moby Dick* eight times.

Kate laughed.

"Wha'd I say?"

"If Herman Melville had brought *Moby Dick* to my publishing house, my boss would make me take Herman and his agent to lunch: 'Herman, we've got two books here. A neat little whaling how-to, which would be better served by a New England small press, and then this 'thing' that the captain—Ahab?—has for the white whale. I have to warn you that Marketing feels it's a trifle phallocentric, and Publicity says it's anti-animal. I think I can deal with that, I hope, but I have to ask you, Herman, how wedded are you to the Calvinist stuff?' "

Ken laughed. But he wondered if he sounded as uneducated as he was. You could learn a lot reading alone; almost anything—except the long view from all the big and little things that an educated woman like Kate had absorbed in college.

Kate was taken with Ken's enthusiasm, which reminded her how she had loved to read when she was a kid. When she saw that she had made him a little cautious with her joke, she hastened to admit her worst nightmare. "The way the business is these days, I'd probably pass on the next Melville, or Thomas Wolfe, or Pynchon, because I'm expected to lure a Mary Higgins Clark clone with a trillion-dollar offer. Anyhow, that's what I do. What do you do? All I know about tugboats is that they look scary from a sailboat."

"Scary? Didn't you ever read *The Little Red Tugboat*? I feel like a minnow when I come alongside an eighty-thousand-ton ship."

"It's my day off. Why read about it when I have you here to tell me the inside scoop?"

Ken still looked reluctant to go into detail. Kate said, "I've been sailing my whole life, but I don't know a thing about ships and tugboats. I've never met a tugboat captain before. Who knows when I'll meet another?"

Not soon, if I can help it, thought Ken.

While not exactly cheerfully resigned to ending up alone, he had stopped hoping for the kind of deep connection he'd occasionally seen couples share. He had taught himself to use work and books—and hanging around friendly bars—to fend off loneliness. Not a bad life; he sure as hell wasn't complaining—and he knew from personal experience that it beat a lonely marriage hands down. But Kate Ross had an unsettling smile from the heart that tempted him to hope for more.

"What do I do? Well, old Charlie, my engineer, tends the engines—shifts fuel and water, maintenance, oil, generator, compressors—which he's been doing since he was my dad's engineer, and my stepfather's. My deckhand, Rick, humps lines. And I drive."

"What do you drive with? A joystick?"

"Joystick?" Ken laughed. "No, no, no. The old girl was built before you and I were born. She'd have been scrap years ago if she weren't so strong."

"How strong?"

"Six thousand horsepower."

"Six *thousand?*"

"She's got a couple of locomotive engines in her. Charlie and I pull them out of old trains."

"So how do you drive all those horses?"

Kate was leaning across the table, smart green eyes fastened brightly on his, like she really seemed to want to know how to drive a tugboat and it dawned on Ken that if he didn't spill the "inside scoop" on tugboats, she would persevere until he did. It further struck him that she possessed the inner strength to make persistence likeable.

"I have," he answered at length, "throttles, steering tillers for the rudders and flanking rudders and a fairly clear view from the wheelhouse. I'll meet a ship in the Upper Bay, put the pilot aboard and hook on—hipped up alongside, or with a hawser. The ship is doing everything she can to slow down, but with all that mass and momentum, she's still making eight knots. So for the next couple of miles, I'm basically the brakes."

She was wearing small earrings made of three shades of gold. They were quiet and suited her, like her pale summer dress which hugged her close on top and flowed easily from her waist to her sandals.

"When we finally get way off the ship, down to bare steerage, we help her through her turns, and work her alongside the pier. The pilot's calling down the orders. He's doing all the thinking. I'm just nudging—pushing, pulling, backing off, you know."

No surprise he hadn't noticed her earrings right off. She had beautiful ears—circled top and back by her short hair, and fronted by airy wisps. Poetic samurai swordsmen would have compared those ears to porcelain teacups, while chopping up rival suitors.

"How do you know how hard to nudge?"

"Good question. . . ."

Kate's breathing stopped as he lasered the middle distance with his impossibly blue eyes. He fastened onto a thought, and brought it back with a smile that told her that she had helped him to discover something new.

"I guess after a while you kind of feel the props through the deck. You know, right through your shoes. The tillers give your hand some sense of the water passing your rudders. You eyeball a hawser, watch how it's shrinking from the tension. You have to use that power—you can't be afraid of it—they're depending on you to hold the vessel against the tide and wind, so you have to use the power, but . . . how do I say it? . . . wisely. You know, keep it very, very light."

He touched her with one finger, so tenderly that Kate felt the downy hairs on her forearm bend slowly to her skin. Every other hair on her arm stood up and she thought, I cannot believe that no one ever touched me like this in my entire life.

"What happens . . ." Her mind had scattered. "What happens if you make a mistake?"

"Million bucks of crumpled steel if I'm lucky. Somebody gets hurt if I'm not."

"Is that how you lost your little finger?" She hadn't noticed it at first; he had a habit of cupping his hand to hide it.

Ken smiled into her eyes, enjoying her bravery. Few people—men or women—could even look where he'd been maimed. He uncupped his left hand.

"I had a friend once," Kate said. "Lost his arm in a genoa sheet. It happened so fast." She marveled. "The line just bent around it."

It was more than bravery, Ken thought. There was a hint of daring in her, as if she sometimes gravitated toward the edge of things.

"Boyfriend?"

"Not really."

They touched lightly on their failed marriages: Kate managing to compress hers to "different backgrounds, different goals"; Ken saying simply, "Both my wives wanted me to quit tugging. Get a job with normal hours. I tried construction, drove a cab, but it was too late to change."

"No kids, thank God," said Kate.

"I've got a grown daughter."

"You do?" Why not? she thought, remembering his age. But she hadn't considered him that way, just as she really didn't want to think about why he'd been divorced twice.

"Hell, she's almost your age," said Ken. Then, suspecting, belatedly, that he was beginning to sound old-geezerish, he hastened to explain. "I got married the first time when I was eighteen."

The subject of parents came up only briefly—well-heeled Newport yachties for Kate; sixth-generation tugboatmen for Ken. Many had owned their boat, and in the union days, even deckhands had earned solid livings. But none sailed yachts in Newport, or went to college.

The afternoon flew and suddenly it was time to either go their separate ways or think about dinner. Grown daughter or not—and discounting his first divorce to youth and his second to life—Kate knew she didn't want the day to end. She grabbed the check, pretended to read it, and said, "We hardly ate a thing. Are you hungry?"

Ken offered to cook linguine and pesto on his tug. Kate envisioned green flecks of basil stuck in her teeth on their first date—by now this was definitely a date—and said she'd rather eat out if he didn't mind.

They decided to walk down to Chinatown.

It was a beautiful June evening, the air crisp, the sun turning the buildings red. He kept stopping to exclaim at the light and point out a fiery brick wall or a sun-bronzed gargoyle perched atop a loft. "I love it down here where the buildings aren't as tall. When I was growing up, the buildings were lower everywhere, even in Midtown—there were skyscrapers, but not so many, not so dense, so you still got marine light. Any place in town you knew there was a river and bays and the ocean out there. You could smell it, hear the foghorns."

I am catapulting myself into geezer territory again, he thought as he described a once-bustling longshore rimming waterways carpeted with barges moving railroad trains and lighters tending ships. As if I'm seventy and she's twenty. Any second now, she's going to look at her watch and hail a cab.

Kate loved the sound of his voice, a rumbly rasp with inflections of an older New York—a fantasy town of smoky saloons, neon bar signs, cobblestones, sailors kissing girls in Times Square, factories in SoHo, and painters in Greenwich Village. She smiled, encouraging him to continue.

"Fact is, the port's come back bigtime. Five thousand ships a year, number one in petroleum, private ferries and dinner yachts, sailboats, motorboats, new tugs and barges. Coast Guard can hardly keep up. Weekends it's a zoo. And if the Mayor'll get off his tail to build the Brooklyn freight tunnel we'll be number one in containers, too."

Chinatown's narrow streets were packed with sailors on shore leave and there were lines everywhere. Ken knew a hole-in-the-wall Spanish-Chinese joint owned by the parents of New York Yes! TV reporter Jose Chin, whom he occasionally ferried around the harbor in search of stories.

Kate, who shunned tabloid journalists as she did cigar smokers, cellphone showoffs, and people who drove suburban assault vehicles, had never heard of Jose Chin. A flashy-looking hyperactive hustler, to judge by the photographs his proud parents had scotch-taped on their restaurant window, Jose Chin appeared to be in motion even in his headshot.

There were Fleet Week sailors lined up here, too, but the Chins welcomed Ken warmly and made room for them within splatter range of the hissing woks. Over dinner, Kate found herself talking honestly about her marriage.

"He was Jamaican," she said, "and it was long enough ago that I'm beginning to find it funny."

"Black Jamaican?"

"Brown, actually. He was a bright-work varnisher. You know, in a boatyard? A really top one. It was like a combination of ballet and brain surgery to watch him, his 'boys' flanked behind, swooping the sprayer hoses, slapping brushes into his hand."

"How did you meet?"

"I was in my boat-bum phase, having a wonderful time annoying my parents by dropping out of college to work on a yacht. Bill was so unbelievably handsome and he could charm a bird out of a tree. I had just broken off with a banker—the son of one of my parents' friends. 'One of us,' as Mother put it. And I was really wondering what I wanted in a guy."

" 'And along came Bill . . .' "

Kate smiled. "It's still a good song. I think I used Bill to stick it to my parents. Mother 'took to her bed.' My father threatened to 'pull strings' and have the marriage annulled—or, failing that, have Bill shot—which is not so hard to arrange in Jamaica. Things calmed down after a while, so I brought my beautiful brown husband home for a visit. Mother gave a party. I had to admire her. She really rose to the occasion. Guess what Bill did?"

"I don't know—a boat varnisher at a ritzy Newport party?"

"Oh, he was fine—in the high-end boat business you meet everybody, and Bill has wonderful dignity, really knew who he was. But by then he had figured out that his 'rich American wife' wasn't really rich; it's all Mother's money, and actually my grandmother's, and it surely wasn't coming my way in the near future, if ever. He saw that Mom was young and fairly healthy despite her drinking, and Gran was thinking of establishing a scholarship foundation. And poor Dad never had a penny, of course. So Bill put the moves on one of my truly rich friends from school."

"Ouch," said Ken.

"I thought I would die of jealousy. Then I wondered, was the money just an excuse? Was I too pushy? Did I drive him away? Did I demand too much? All that stuff. But it turned out to be the best thing that ever happened to me. Dumped Bill. Went back to college. Came to New York. Got a real job. And swore off men. For a while."

"Julia told me you stopped dating."

"I don't know any women who don't stop, at least now and then. We hit our thirties, and if we haven't met the right person, or settled for the wrong one just to have kids, we give up on guys and devote ourselves to career and friends and hobbies. . . . It's probably no lonelier than a nowhere marriage."

"Smartest thing I ever did was learn how to live alone."

"I find it hard."

Ken said, "This woman named Dorothy Parker wrote something about if you can stay out of trouble for the *evening,* you got a better chance of surviving the *night*. She was right. When you're alone in New York, five to seven are the killer hours."

"Are you close with your daughter?"

"I don't get to see her much. She married a Navy guy. They're stationed in San Diego."

I have got to ask, Kate thought, "Do you have, uh, grand-children?"

"Not yet."

"I guess you'll be a pretty young grandfather."

"Younger than lots of the graybeard fathers you see around."

They walked back uptown after dark, veering west, re-turning smiles from people who saw the couple they were becoming, drinking beers in bars, talking, still talking, walking the streets with a sense the night would last forever. Time and again Kate thought to herself, This is why I came to New York. Anything can happen.

Suddenly, around a corner reared the Empire State Build-ing, floodlit like white ice. Ken opened his arms, as if to hug it. "It's a beautiful ship that never sails away."

"Julia said you were a romantic."

"Julia's confused. She never met an optimist."

Kate lived in Chelsea, and they were drawing near,

bumping shoulders up Ninth Avenue. They turned into Kate's block. The traffic noise faded. Trees and grass perfumed the warm night, and a bell tower cut Gothic spikes from the sky.

Iron pineapples flanked Kate's front steps.

As she reached for her keys a razor-thin young man dressed head to toe in black leather burst out the front door. His Grim Reaper face brightened. "Hi, Kate."

"Hi, Peter."

Peter looked Ken over and said to Kate, "Well, didn't we get lucky? Gotta go. Late for work." He waved good-bye with a riding crop and vanished into the night.

"Neighbor," Kate explained.

Up two flights, keys dropped, heads bumped picking them up, and finally inside.

In Ken's experience, single women's apartments had shelves hung on brackets, bright colors, and sharp-edged furniture, with cats and throw pillows supplying the coziness. Kate's was all deep reds and soft greens and polished wood. "You got a lot of room," he said. "The rent must be a killer."

"My landlord claims that rent in Manhattan is like a cover charge for the entertainment—oh, hell!"

"What?"

It had become apparent to Kate, and to Ken, too, she hoped, that they were going to at least spend the night in the same room.

"I'm so sorry. I just remembered—my cleaning woman asked to come extra early tomorrow morning."

Ken took her hand. She had already noticed his habit of leaning close and gently rounding his broad shoulders into a sort of cordon, like a powerful bird protecting its young within the circle of its wings. He had done it when he said good-bye to tiny Mrs. Chin at the restaurant, and had once enveloped Kate herself when they were caught in a crush of sailors on a narrow street.

"Would you like to see my tugboat?" he asked. "I gave the crew the night off, there's tons of room, a nice shower, and plenty of clean sheets."

Kate had not gone to bed with a first date since her first round of college. But somehow, with Ken, it would have felt unnatural not to. Still, when she stepped into the bathroom to get her toothbrush, her heart was pounding and her ears blazed red in the mirror. She pawed through the medicine cabinet for her diaphragm, took it out of its pink plastic case, and held it up to the light, checking for holes; it felt like it had aged into an automobile tire. Quickly, she folded clean underwear into her leather backpack, and stuffed in jeans, a shirt, and a cotton sweater, knowing it would be cold on the river.

They walked back downtown toward Tribeca, holding hands now, sleepy voices echoing in deserted cobblestone streets. They kissed for the first time on the corner of Perry and Washington, an exploratory venture, a tasting of lips, tongues balanced precisely on the halfway tightrope between them, then rushing to feast. Kate loved his taste, loved how he caressed her cheeks with his fingertips, loved the way he was so sure, so soon, of what she wanted. She sighed in dismay as his soft mouth slowly drew apart from hers.

"We've drawn an audience of dog walkers," he whispered through her lips.

At Christopher, in the middle of the sidewalk, he circled her in his solid arms, looked into her eyes, and kissed her again; the inch or so he was taller made for a perfect fit. Kate felt safe and wild at the same time and she had a wonderful feeling that she had lived her life as a setup for this moment.

She pulled him into a doorway near Clarkson. Up to now, thought Ken, I've been kissing amateurs. At Houston Street they hailed a taxi.

*   *   *

When Charlie and Rick, Ken's engineer and deckhand, arrived at the pier Monday morning—old Charlie hung over, Rick starving—they found a note duct-taped to the stern line. They wandered off debating how long Ken meant by "Go away."

Kate had called in sick, and while Ken ran ashore for fresh orange juice, she had telephoned Julia to say, "Thank you, thank you, thank you. I can't believe you didn't grab him."

"I was nine months pregnant when I interviewed him for the *Voice* piece on offshore dumping. But I was tempted."

"Thank you, thank you, thank you. It's a hormone festival."

Julia had graduated summa in classics and comp lit, and triumphantly recited:

> *"Carpe diem*
> *when you see 'im*
> *looking at you*
> *with that gle-am."*

Ken returned with groceries and the gle-am.

They made love, napped, talked, cooked meals in the capacious galley, made love. But eventually, as the sun began to set over Jersey, Ken said, "I gotta go to work."

"Ohhh, I hoped this would never end."

"I got hired in to sail a new cruise ship from Pier Ninety. Just a few hours. Want to come?"

"Can I?"

"You can meet my crew."

"Would it be okay if I stayed up in the wheelhouse? I just don't feel like other people yet."

When Ken's crew came aboard, Charlie went directly to the engine room and Rick was busy down on deck. In the wheelhouse, Kate stayed out of Ken's way at the opposite end of the front windows as he made radio contact with the docking pilot and drove the tug up the river past the sparkling skyline. Fireboats were there ahead of them, waiting in midstream, pluming water through the beams of colored searchlights.

The cruise ship was the biggest Kate had ever seen. It stood taller than the aircraft carrier *John F. Kennedy,* which was docked at the next pier. Her ten-story superstructure was floodlit. Every porthole and window blazed light. A hundred-foot-long lighted sign on her top deck proclaimed "SOVEREIGN PRINCESS." Thousands lined her rails, waving to friends on the pier, whose number included four separate wedding parties.

Kate was impressed by how relaxed Ken was beneath the loom of the ship. With his boat stationed near the giant's stern, tugging a heavy rope hawser on commands radioed by the docking pilot, he still found time to explain some of what he was doing and flash her easy smiles. "This *Princess* is a hell of a lot easier to sail than a monster like the *Kennedy.* She's got so many side thrusters she could pretty much sail herself."

Slowly the ship backed into the middle of the river, and wheeled majestically until her bow was pointed downstream. When Ken was ordered to cast off, he and Kate stepped outside onto the abbreviated deck behind the wheelhouse, and watched arm in arm as the giant gathered way.

"Oh, look!" cried Kate. "They're on their honeymoon. They're kissing. Right under the P."

Ken found the kissing couple under the P in PRINCESS. "How do you know they're on their honeymoon?"

"She's still wearing her wedding cap. See her little hat? Like a pillbox? . . . She's unfastened her veil—it comes apart—but she left her cap on. That is so romantic. Look, she's still holding her bouquet."

Kate cupped her hands to yell "Congratulations!" in a

sailor's voice that carried. Ken circled her in his arms. The bride threw her bouquet. The wedding flowers danced on the updrafts buffeting the ship. Kate thought they would fall into the harbor, but they bounced on the hot exhaust jetting from the tugboat's smokestack. Ken batted them out of the sky and white rosebuds dropped into their arms.

The anchored Fleet Week visitors saluted the new cruise liner with their horns and searchlights. Scottish bagpipes shrilled from a Canadian frigate; a German brass band thumped "New York, New York"; and on China's *Zhaotong*, sailors of the People's Liberation Army perched on missile launchers and gun mounts, throwing firecrackers.

3

NEW YORK MAYOR Rudolph Mincarelli and his twenty-eight-year-old press secretary, Renata Bradley, were sharing a pizza on the mayor's desk at Gracie Mansion at two o'clock in the morning when word came in that the *Sovereign Princess* was on fire off Montauk Point.

"Get the helicopter," said the mayor. He hated helicopters. They absolutely terrified him, but they extended his reach. So when there was no better way to do the job, he toughed them out—stomach clenched, face a mask.

"No helicopter," said Renata, the youngest—and only woman—in a select inner circle which was permitted to say no to Mayor Mincarelli. "The doctor said lose the helicopter till you lose the cold."

She was a gangly, curly-haired brunette. And while her angular features and schoolgirlish galumphing gait would never stop traffic in a city teeming with striking models, beautiful actresses, and size-six socialites, she was not unattractive. Which was all the encouragement New York's tabloid media needed to debate, daily, nightly, and all week-end long, the mayor's fidelity to Mrs. Mincarelli—who had recently accepted the directorship of a prestigious environmental consulting firm in Seattle, and taken the children with her.

"That ship sailed from New York. The four thousand New Yorkers on it are my responsibility."

"Rudy, the doctor absolutely forbids you to fly." Addressing the mayor by his first name was a privilege enjoyed by fewer and fewer associates every year he'd held office.

"The New York media's going to be there. And if it's as bad as it sounds, so will the networks." His own voice echoed hollowly in his head. What had he become when he would automatically mine publicity out of tragedy? Was this the price of running for office? *No,* a sterner, angry voice shouted down the first. *Don't blame politics. You know better.*

Renata wavered. "We could lead the *Today* show."

Midway through his second fiery term, the mayor was determined to tilt at national office. All previous New York mayors who had tried it had failed, but Mincarelli's considerable talent for getting things done, and the credit he had received for destroying the city's felony class, had earned him a lion tamer's reputation. Already there was serious talk of a Vice Presidency for the man who had demonstrated how to govern a city of seven and a half million ambitious, iron-willed individuals.

"National coverage," Renata reconsidered, "is not worth permanent damage to your hearing."

Mincarelli was convinced he would make an even better president than he was a mayor. *But that is no excuse for diminishing your ethical standards,* noted one of several internal lawyerly voices that kept him on the straight and narrow. *Yet what was leadership,* asked another, *but the bold willingness to step in to fill the void?* And, *What honest leader wouldn't risk his hearing to do his duty?*

His narrow shoulders stiffened and he hunched into the familiar I-am-doing-this-now-my-way fire-hydrant stance. When she saw that, Renata knew she had better think fast.

"Hey, Rudy, it's Fleet Week, right? What do you say we drive down to the pier and send off the rescue ships?"

"What are you talking about?"

"Wave 'em good-bye and then you can come back here and sleep off the cold. Tomorrow, when they come back, you'll be standing on the pier to greet whoever got rescued."

He looked like he might buy it, so Renata quickly buzzed the NYPD security detail and ordered up the "Rudy Van"—the PR-friendly nickname that her assistant Larry Neale had coined for a six-ton black Chevy Suburban in order to blunt media attempts to compare His Honor's transport to a vehicle better suited to a suburban drug dealer.

She found her shoes, and put her suit jacket back on over the cotton shirtwaist and knee length straight skirt she had donned at six the morning before. The professional uniform was a pain. But the many, many pleasures of her job included power trips like beepering awake the entire mayoral media pool at two in the morning to announce a press conference—and the opportunity for photos and video of the mayor with ships in the background, bright lights and steam, and sailors hurrying back from shore leave.

Renata Bradley delivered. Along the piers, from Fifty-second down to Forty-sixth Street, warships were bellowing like bulls—horns and whistles chorusing an urgent refrain not heard in the city since World War II: "Shore leave canceled! We sail on the tide!"

As the mayor's vehicle drove down Twelfth Avenue, Renata hunted the best backdrop for Rudy. Pier 92, the superpier where the giant aircraft carrier *John F. Kennedy* was docked, was boxed in by the passenger terminal buildings, as was 90, where a big cruiser was casting off lines, and the empty slip at 88 from where the *Sovereign Princess* had sailed.

She found the images and camera angles she was looking for two blocks below the superpiers, at the foot of Forty-sixth Street. The broad plaza beside the *Intrepid* Sea-Air-Space Museum at Pier 86 offered excellent shots of several naval vessels getting underway. There was also a poignant, life-like statue of a sailor waving good-bye as if he were headed off to war. And—most importantly—room to accommodate the swelling crowd of the cruise ship passengers' frightened relatives.

When they grew noisy, pleading for information no officials had to give them, Rudy Mincarelli—whose mother and father and Jesuit teachers had raised him to fear a stern Creator—waded in like a family man from Brooklyn. Hugging, consoling, he projected the unassailable truth that deep in his heart the mayor of the greatest city in the world knew: *There but for the grace of God go I.*

Renata watched proudly as the cameras flashed their admiration. She had staged a triumph. When he went face-to-face with suffering, Rudy's warmth and compassion never failed to startle the cynical, nay-saying, gossip-mongering media.

A *Post* reporter observed Renata's shining face and told her rival from the *Daily News,* "There is no way that Hizzoner's not porkin' her."

"Don't look now, she's coming this way."

"Oh shit! She couldn'ta heard me."

Renata Bradley approached like the U.S. Army tank of the same name, raked both reporters with a look of thinly veiled contempt, smiled like a crocodile, and threw them a bone. "The mayor is conversing with a nice, young, very photogenic airman from the *Kennedy,* which, you have probably observed, has not sailed." The thousand-foot warship was too big for the rescue job, the Navy had explained when the reporters had asked earlier.

"The airman's name is Ensign Routh. Ensign Eldon

Routh. He belongs to the Dragonslayer Squadron. He's from Kansas or some place. You're welcome to take notes."

The reporters trooped dutifully after the press secretary—this was going to be really exciting—and came in on the conversation as Ensign Routh, who looked barely twenty-one and innocent as a wheat field, was telling the mayor, "Good thing I don't have to fly tonight, sir. We got hammered in Times Square. I had two beers in that bar next to the Disney Store."

"What do you fly, son?"

"Helos, Mr. Mayor. ASW."

The Mayor returned a look as blank as if the young Kansan were speaking hip-hop.

"Antisubmarine warfare, sir. Seahawk helicopters."

"Excellent." The mayor shook his hand. "Well, since your ship is staying, you can go back to the party. In New York City, the bars are open till four."

"No, sir. I'm hitting the sack. Going to the opera in the morning."

"Opera in the morning?" echoed the reporters, suddenly alert, curious who was running what scam on this child.

"This nice old lady invited us to the rehearsal in Central Park. The whole wing's going. We're going to have a picnic. And we get to see the whole opera outdoors. I'm real excited."

"What are you seeing?" asked the mayor, who was a great fan of the opera.

"Pilgrims, I think."

"Pilgrims?"

"Or Puritans. . . . sir."

"I Puritani!" cried the mayor. He broke into a pitch-perfect snatch of " *'Ah, per sempre io ti perdei. . . .'* Thomas Hampson is singing Riccardo. I envy you, young man. You are in for an unforgettable day."

*   *   *

Three hundred feet beneath the sea, sixty miles southeast of New York, Admiral Tang Li listened to the rescuers racing to the stricken *Sovereign Princess*.

"They roar like lions," whispered the submarine's captain—the officer in command of the boat that served as Tang's flagship.

"Dragons," countered Tang Li with a wink that drew smiles from the young men perspiring in the control room. What man, the admiral seemed to ask, would be anywhere but here with us tonight?

The Fleet Week celebration had swelled New York Harbor with warships from many nations. Tang's sonar and hydrophone operators identified their aural signatures as they growled and rumbled across the shallow waters of the continental shelf. His intelligence officer matched them to a sound library updated by satellite.

Admiral Tang himself possessed a highly developed submariner's eye—the ability to hold an ever-changing three-dimensional image in his mind. The wakes above were as clear to him as if he could see through his submarine's high-yield steel hull: the sharp V's of the fast U.S. and Canadian frigates, the deeper V of a big German destroyer; the flatter U of the British helicopter carrier; the trough plowed by the U.S. Navy hospital ship.

He hoped against hope to hear the thunderous passage of the aircraft carrier *John F. Kennedy*. But the smaller helicopter carrier doomed that hope. As he had feared, the U.S. Navy had judged the giant warship too ponderous for a rescue operation when nimbler ships were available and had left her in the port.

But though his ruse had failed to draw out the carrier, it had succeeded in distracting the naval air, Coast Guard, and Air Force bases along the East Coast: his electronic-warfare operators reported ceaseless radio traffic among the military aircraft circling the torpedoed liner; all eyes were pointed away from New York.

Tang could also hear the occasional pings of the rescue ships routinely scoping the sea bottom with sonar. Sonar radiated sound pulses, and listened for echoes bouncing back. His submarines were clad in sound-muffling paint and thick, anechoic tiles, which absorbed sonar. In the underwater world where the deaf were blind, returning no echoes made them invisible.

It was highly unlikely that the rescue ships were listening with towed hydrophone arrays, but the ten thousand men hiding on the ocean floor took no chances. They lay silent or, when they had to, moved with utmost caution amid the bundled wires, pipes, and valves that fringed the bulkheads and ceilings of their hulls.

They would have to surface soon. Tang had cut it close. With the exception of his flagship submarine, which had roved off earlier to torpedo the cruise liner, they had lain submerged here more than a day. The diesel boats were running low on air and battery power. And the assault troops, crammed in like African slaves, were suffering acutely.

An iodine smell pervaded the familiar odors of diesel, hot copper, and paint. Tang had ordered Cook to sprinkle shrimp over tonight's rice to celebrate their arrival after the nine-week secret voyage halfway round the world. As the men took their turns eating, he walked slowly through the narrow main passageway from bow to stern, pausing repeatedly to exchange a quiet word, showing his crew that submariners were brothers, regardless of rank, and that no commando wounded would be left behind.

"Long ago in the Pearl River," he reminded them in low tones, "a bold British fleet attacked China and seized Hong Kong from Emperor Daoguang. From that victory, foreigners enslaved Hong Kong for one hundred and fifty years. They still rule Taiwan. . . ." And then he promised, with a sly smile that made every man brave, "We are bolder. Our fleet is stronger. With New York as our hostage, we will take back what belonged to our emperor."

At last Tang gave the signal. Cued by a depths-penetrating, Extremely Low Frequency radio transmission, the vast, silent underwater armada began to stir. One hundred boats rose as uneventfully as turtles waking.

A testament to his highly trained crews, Tang thought. Proof of the admiral's legendary luck, thought his crews.

Now they pricked the surface with their periscopes, scanned the night-bound empty sea that Tang had promised—and radar confirmed in cautious bursts—and snorkeled fresh air into their fetid hulls. Global Positioning Satellite fixed each within ten feet on Tang's battle screen, and the armada set course for New York.

4

"YO, KEN. Captain Ken! Hey, buddy, wake up."

Jose Chin—loaded with camera, tripod, and umbrella satellite antenna—leaped from Jasbir Singh's taxicab before the yellow minivan stopped rolling. He climbed over a locked gate and sprinted onto Tribeca's Pier 25.

Dawn was still a vague promise, ashen slits of eastern sky barely distinguishable between the office and apartment towers looming over West Street. It was dark on the Jersey side, though he could see a misty, grayish light starting to ooze from the Hudson River.

"Yo, Ken!" he yelled at a beat-up red-and-black tugboat moored at the end of the long pier. It was called the *Chelsea Queen* and Jose foresaw the day when some bulked up iron-pumping gay, too raged on 'roids to care that Ken's great-grandfather had named it a gazillion years ago when people who lived in Chelsea worked on the docks, would punch Captain Ken in the face.

"Yo, Ken!"

Biggest disaster story since Flight 800 fell in the ocean and Captain Ken wasn't taking calls. Not radio, not beeper, not cellphone, not fax. Not even E-mail, which older guys sometimes forgot to check.

Jose Chin was young and wired. He had a beeper on his belt, a digital cellphone in his knockoff Armani jacket, and in his backpack a palmtop computer, CB radio, Pocketalk voice-message receiver, police scanner, spare batteries, and clean white T-shirts rolled in plastic. Among the tools he carried to stay mobile were insulated alligator clips for powering up his battery chargers from city light poles, and couplers to pirate television signals from cable TV lines.

His cellphone rang and he answered it still running: "Jose wants to know!"

"Know this, dickhead," said his news director, Arnie Moskowitz. "There's an ocean liner sinking off Long Island and you aren't on it. Why not?"

Jose Chin said, "I just hired a boat." True, the second he woke up Captain Ken.

You could overlook dissing like "dickhead" and "kid" when Arnie had rescued you from your first job at a nowhere station in Pennsylvania with a 145 ADI market rating and the motto: "If it's news, it's news to us." Arnie had brought Jose home to the number one market, where he belonged—for twenty-three thousand a year and no benefits—to be a full-time street reporter for New York Yes!, the city's twenty-four-hour all-news TV station.

"How long to get there?"

"Longer than it would take in the chopper for which New York Yes! says, 'No!' " Jose shot back.

"Choppers cost money, wise guy. Shoot the ship. I took you off the school-uniform protest, and the Clean Up Queens rally, and that Bronx roses thing at the Botanical Garden so you could shoot that goddamned ship before it sinks."

"Just don't let anybody touch my workfare story. I spent

a month getting the poor girl to trust me." For a report unlikely to advance Mayor Mincarelli's presidential ambitions, Jose Chin had been taping a seventeen-year-old mother of three with a mini-module as she shambled from city agency to city agency trying to find day care to watch her kids so she could sweep a subway platform to earn her welfare check. "If you blow her cover, I quit!"

"Shoot that ship. You want us to look like public television, always borrowing other stations' feeds?"

Jose hung up on his boss, and ran faster.

He was intimately familiar with Pier 25, a long, splintery dock sticking out into the river. Whenever he had to wait for Ken to pick him up, he would tape evergreen stories, which Arnie would bank until the station needed to air filler: a ten-second contrast shot of Battery Park City, squatting a few blocks down the Hudson like something trucked in from the suburbs; a human-interest on the nut who had erected the gigantic fiberglass iguana that crouched beside the pier entrance; a heart-warmer on the Wall-Streeters-versus-street-rat volleyball games fought on the pier's sand courts; and a tearjerker about the old ferryboat used as a teenage no-booze-no-drugs hangout.

Running harder, he got sniffed by a mangy German shepherd and stares from the guys fishing for PCB-marinated striped bass from their homemade houseboat anchored in the basin. Ducks and condoms and Styrofoam cups drifted on the tide. Ken's old tugboat looked right at home.

The end of the pier was coming up fast. The tide had stretched the tug's mooring lines, opening a wide gap between the pier and the boat. Jose Chin hugged his camera and flew.

"Tell him to go away." Kate had covered her breasts with the sheet at the first shout and now she poked her legs under the blanket and burrowed into Ken's chest.

Ken felt on the deck for his last memory of his jeans. "I can tell him, but he won't."

"What does he want?"

"A ride somewhere."

"Yo, Ken! Wake up!"

There was no door for Ken's cabin. He had only a curtain—as he had explained—because a door might jam when he wanted to get out quickly if the tug was sinking. A stubby camera poked through the curtain like an inquiring snout. Behind the camera was a slim, intense guy with straight, Chinese-jet hair and high, Spanish cheekbones that could cut glass.

Kate tugged the sheet higher. Dark eyes scoured the snug cabin in a glance. He wore a navy blazer over jeans and an immaculate white T-shirt emblazoned with the graffiti-gaudy New York Yes! TV logo familiar from bus-stop ads.

"Hey, Cap, Jose's gotta shoot the sinking." His eyes lit on the bouquet, which they had hung over the bed. "Good morning, sister, what's up? Jose Chin, New York Yes!"

Ken kept searching for his pants. "Jose, you want to meet me up in the wheelhouse while we get some clothes on— what sinking?"

"What sinking? Whaddaya talkin' what sinking? The cruise ship that sank last night. The *Sovereign Princess.*"

"You're kidding. We sailed her last night."

Kate said, "Ohmigod, Ken. That woman. The wedding couple . . ."

"The Fleet Week ships split to the rescue. I got on one but the Navy kicked me off. Biggest cruise ship in the whole world sank and you don't know? Buddy, we gotta roll."

"What about the passengers?"

"Drowning. Let's go, man. If it bleeds, it leads."

"Let me get some clothes on. Go up to the wheelhouse and I'll get on the horn and find out what's up. Go!"

Jose backed out of the cabin. Ken scrambled into his jeans

and running shoes and pulled a T-shirt over his muscled shoulders. Kate sat up to meet his lips as he bent to kiss her.

Forty-five miles from New York—a lily pad of a miniature satellite antenna popped out of the ocean.

The communication buoy that Admiral Tang had ordered his flagship to float for a final intelligence update exchanged electronic micro-bursts with a synchronously-orbiting PLA satellite, which used hardware and computer programs developed by U.S. defense contractors to maintain a rock-solid station 22,300 miles above the planet. The antenna sank beneath the waves as the submarine reeled it in. De-encrypted and decoded, the message beamed down was a last-minute bombshell.

The mayor of New York City would not be at City Hall when the attack commenced. Recovering from a head cold, Rudolph Mincarelli would work all day at Gracie Mansion, his residence on the East River. He had abruptly canceled his downtown appointments, including a long-scheduled luncheon for his party's national leaders which—Chinese intelligence officers posted to the Hong Kong Information Bureau on Fifth Avenue had promised Admiral Tang—had guaranteed the politically ambitious mayor's presence at City Hall.

Tang felt the first sharp timpani hint of drumming in his ear. Why hadn't Intelligence told him earlier that the mayor had a cold? His mission had fallen victim, once again, to the Chinese disease: it was easier to say yes than no; simpler to promise good things than warn of a problem; pleasanter to pretend everything was going swimmingly, instead of attacking the difficulty head-on while there was still time to do something about it.

But his battle plan was flexible. It had to be. Only in the last week—as his armada had circled a wide berth around the U.S. Navy's SOSUS underwater listening devices guarding the Panama Canal—had Admiral Tang learned which day the mayor would definitely be in New York.

Looking at the bright side, he could corner Mincarelli at the isolated riverside mansion more readily than in the labyrinth of lower Manhattan; and the lightly defended Gracie Mansion would be an easier target. But before he could attack the mayor's residence, he first had to sail a submarine to it, undetected, up the turbulent East River.

When Ken Hughes ran up the tight spiral stairs to the *Chelsea Queen's* wheelhouse, Jose Chin was already preparing a stand-up in front of his tripod-mounted camera.

"If you're gonna start taking waitresses home, you should at least keep the radios on."

"Her name is Kate. She's not a waitress. And if that smirk isn't history by the time she gets up here, you're going in the drink."

Ken switched on his VHF and radioed a cousin in Staten Island—a McAllister dispatcher at the towing company's operations office on a coffee barge in the Kill Van Kull.

"Bartender?"

"She's an editor."

From what Ken could see in the brightening dawn, the whole harbor had emptied out for the rescue. The *Lake Champlain* had put to sea. Gone, too, were *Cambeltown* and a Coast Guard cutter anchored farther up. How a man who sensed the tides in his sleep had missed all that activity said a lot about his second night with Kate Ross. The ship horns alone would have woken the dead.

Jose Chin took a remote control with a built-in microphone and monitor and did a white balance, aiming the camera at his own snowy T-shirt. "The editor looks a little young for you, Cap. First time with an old guy might be a novelty, but how long can you keep it up?"

"She makes me feel younger than you and a hell of a lot smarter—lose the smirk."

"This is not *my* smirk, it's *yours* reflected on my face. You're lighting up the whole wheelhouse, you look so . . . satisfied."

"Last warning." Of the visiting warships Ken had seen yesterday from his mooring, only the Chinese frigate *Zhaotong* remained, her long, slim lines spoiled by the ungainly surface-to-surface missile launchers that squatted fore and aft of her funnel.

Jose was focusing his face in the monitor. He zoomed out, and framed himself in a backdrop that included the tugboat's big brass compass and Battery Park City and the Statue of Liberty.

A big old wooden steering wheel with spokes would look cool in the picture. But the tugboat didn't have one; Ken steered with a couple of funny little tiller sticks. Maybe he could get the studio gearheads to matt a ship wheel into the picture to make it look more real.

Focused, framed, and white-balanced, Jose combed his hair and switched on the remote.

"Jose wants to know—what caused the biggest cruise-ship sinking ever?"

Ken always wondered where in that skinny little chest Jose produced his deep baritone-bass—an almost operatic voice that made people lean closer.

"New York Yes! continues live coverage from our own tugboat, which is speeding to the scene of the worst New York maritime catastrophe since the *Titanic*." Jose was, in fact, not live, but taping. He removed the tape and logged it. His cabbie pal, Jasbir, would deliver it to the station, where Arnie could roll it as an intro when Jose was finally beaming live shots back from the ocean.

Kate tiptoed quietly up the spiral stairs. Ken was talking on the radio and scanning the river. Jose Chin appeared to be interviewing himself.

Jose clicked off the remote control. "I hear you're a big gun editor."

Kate, who still worried that her boat-bum years had left her playing career catch-up, said, "Medium gun."

"*New York* Magazine? Naw, you're more the classy *New Yorker* type."

"Books."

"Books? I could write a dynamite book about me in TV news."

When Kate's only response was to glance at Ken, Jose said, "You're looking at the guy who's going to be the first Latino-Asian-American Peter Jennings."

"What about Connie Chung?" called Ken.

"She doesn't count. She's got no Spanish. I'm like a real ethnic New Yorker, man. I'm everything. Puerto Rican, Chinese, I even got a little Italian and some Irish."

"Isn't Peter Jennings a lot taller than you?"

"Yo, buddy, *everybody* looks tall behind the anchor desk," Jose shot back. "Nobody knows—you don't realize it yet, but this little camera, I'm like my own shooter. You see a soundman with a shotgun or a fish pole? You see a lard-ass union cameraman? 'Course you don't. I don't need a crew. You know what I'm saying?"

He thrust his camera at Kate.

"Get that out of my face!"

"What's the matter? I thought you wanted to see my camera."

"I don't want it in my face."

Ken looked over at Kate. "You okay?"

"Fine."

Jose was standing there looking hurt. He offered her the camera like a little kid trying to make up by sharing his favorite toy.

She was surprised how light it was; it was smaller than most tourist cameras—little more than a tubular lens attached to a flat body, the size and shape of a flashlight and a slim novel.

"DVC," said Jose. "Digital video camera. Totally legal; it shoots broadcast quality."

Kate cupped the viewfinder to her eye. The guys fishing on the houseboat appeared crisp as silver.

"Don't you get it?" Jose demanded. "It makes me just as slick as a print reporter. I'm like a writer. I am mobile. I can go anywhere, interview anybody, like a guy with a pencil. *Plus,* I get my own b-roll. I am the kit *and* the caboodle."

"But you're still shoving a camera in their faces," Kate retorted sharply. "You think you're a writer? You can't 'write' a word if you don't get the picture. So you swarm all over people like flies. And your swarm becomes the news."

"Yo, I don't do gang bangs. Everybody goes one way, I go the other." A sudden grin lit his face. "I *can't* do gang bangs—I'm not tall enough. Most cameramen are giants. I'm like a little mouse running around the dinosaur eggs. I get my own stories."

"I don't care how light your gear is, the people you're interviewing know they're on TV."

"Think so?" Jose put on glasses with thick black Elvis Costello frames. "Look in the monitor—the viewfinder."

Her own face was staring back at her, mouth popping open, eyes silly.

"What—how?"

Jose returned a smug grin. "Video modules. Mega-miniature. I can wear it like glasses-cam, with the tail in the band"—he showed her the antenna—"or necktie-cam, or belt-buckle-cam. Just shoot whatever I look at, tape or live, and no one knows but me and my audience."

"Ken, look at this!"

"Nostril-cam?" Ken asked without looking up from the radio.

Jose said, "You look good, Kate. Hey, I'll get a techie to

print you a still. Here's my card. Call me on the book idea. You got a card?"

Kate shoved Jose's New York Yes! card in her jeans. "I'll leave one with Ken."

"You on E-mail? I'm joseknows@nyy.com. Upper or lower, I'm not case-sensitive."

Jose Wants to Know? Who knew? Every mentor Kate had had in publishing could recite a list of the dumbest-sounding book ideas that they wished they hadn't rejected.

Ken signed off his VHF and phoned the Ear Inn, a dive on Spring Street where he stood a good chance of finding his crew sleeping on the tables.

"Where's it sinking?" asked Jose.

He showed Jose where he had penciled an X on the chart, thirty miles off eastern Long Island. Simultaneously, he spoke into the cellphone. "Charlie and Rick there? . . . Yeah? . . . You want to tell 'em we're going to work?"

Jose poked the X with his finger. He had, Ken knew, only the vaguest concept of distance outside the five boroughs.

"How long to get there?"

"Nine hours."

"Nine hours?"

"This is a tugboat, Jose. She does twelve knots."

"This is breaking news."

"Take a helicopter."

"Can't."

"Then drive out to the end of Long Island and hire a boat. A fast one." He copied a phone number from his book. "Here. Call this guy. He's an unemployed dope runner. His boat's a rocket."

"Thanks, bro'." Jose crammed his gear into his backpack, swung into it, and ran down the spiral stairs. He scrambled over the bulwark and onto the pier with his camera in one hand and his tripod over his shoulder. "*Jasbir!* The beach."

"What's Jasbir?" Kate asked Ken.

"Jasbir Singh is a six-and-a-half-foot-tall Indian taxi driver. He drives Jose around town, delivers his tapes to the studio, and makes sure Jose isn't blindsided."

"Blindsided?"

"Being a one-man band's a dangerous game. When Jose's got his face buried in a ten-thousand-dollar camera, he can't see the thief with a baseball bat. Listen, I gotta head out there. Too late to save lives, but there'll be work mopping up and plenty of ship handling in the investigation."

"Can I come?"

"What do you mean?" he asked. "On the boat?"

"I'd like to ride out with you."

"Don't you have to work? I'll be out for a couple of days at least."

"I can say I'm reading at home." Kate heard her own voice as if it were someone else's broadcasting a too-loud confidence at the next table in a restaurant. She was amazed: yesterday had been the first day she had taken off work in three years; she couldn't afford days off, competing with people who'd gone straight to work from college. Nor had she ever lied to anyone in her life, except literary agents. "Am I being pushy?" she asked. "I mean, all I'm really saying . . . I guess I'm really saying, 'What's next?' I *am* being pushy."

Ken took her hands in his as he had on their first night. "I don't know what's next. But it's obvious we've developed a strong tactile appreciation of each other, and we seem to get along. And to tell you the truth, I was interested in 'What's next?' about five minutes after we met. Want to give me a hand starting the engines?"

The submarines in Admiral Tang's armada were small by modern standards. Barely one-sixth the size of nuclear-powered attack boats, they measured their submersion time in days and hours instead of months, their warheads' explosives in pounds instead of kilotons.

But as a new Ford or Volkswagen offered the speed and handling that sixty years ago would have been available only in a Bentley, Tang's little boats were faster, quieter, and far, far deadlier than their World War II ancestors.

Like phantoms, they hunted in silence. Sound-muffling decouple coatings and noise-isolating machinery mounts developed for Cold War stealth let Tang's elite crews range the seas with a ghostly hush.

To seek targets and exchange information about their enemies, they employed search and communications innovations achieved over three decades by the competing navies of the United States and the Soviet Union. Satellite and ultra-low-frequency networks linked their admiral with every boat in his fleet, their support ships, their spies ashore, and—when he chose—the bosses back home. Refined echo ranging and listening sonar, and towed hydrophone arrays, sharpened the Chinese sailors' ears; radar and infrared, their eyes.

Their boats' machine guns and deck cannon would have surprised modern submariners. They were a strange throwback to World War I and II surface combat. The subs carried few torpedoes, freeing up more space for assault troops, weapons, and ammunition. And they were cruelly crowded, yet morale was high. Lifted out of rural poverty by Admiral Tang, trained to a standard as modern as any in the world—and proud to be the best in the Chinese fleet—the peasants' and fishermen's sons found the submarine's simple amenities luxurious compared to oil lamps and outhouses.

As Admiral Tang grappled with the problem of launching his attack so far up the East River at Gracie Mansion, his battle screen showed that the newer, air-independent fuel-cell German-built boats in East Wind's vanguard had forged ahead of the heavily laden troop boats with the main assault.

Even farther in the lead, making twenty knots—yet quieter than a whale—raced the highly automated, two-hundred-and-thirty-foot *Deng Xiaoping*—formerly H.M.S. *Unseen*, which the PLA had demanded as a pot sweetener in an aircraft deal when British defense cuts put the modern diesel electric boat on the auction block. After Tang's engineers had completed her upgrade, *Deng Xiaoping* was the boat that every skipper in the fleet longed to command. The admiral had given her to his younger brother, Tang Qui.

Thus Admiral Tang had no choice but to assign to his brother and his forty-man crew the unenviable job of attempting to smuggle her two-thousand-four-hundred-ton hull up the swift currents and busy, shallow channels of the treacherous East River. She needed thirty-six feet of water to run submerged. And over fifty feet to raise her periscope to navigate visually. The deepest the charts guaranteed was thirty-five at "mean lower low water," demanding of her young captain faith in the Port of New York's dredges, the accuracy of the charts, and a generous high tide surge hoisted by the full moon.

5

OVER IN BROOKLYN, Greg Walsh left his wife, Frances, dressing for work in front of the TV news, which was entirely about the sinking cruise ship, and headed out on his regular five-mile run to his office in midtown Manhattan. In the first mile, he passed through two hundred years of New York history, starting on his quiet, nineteenth-century Pineapple Street, drinking in the soaring density of Wall Street from the Brooklyn Heights Promenade, admiring the gray sweep of the East River from the Brooklyn Bridge, and then descending into remnants of the old downtown city, where the distinctive reddish-brown brick walls of One Police Plaza zapped him with his daily pang of regret.

Greg and Mayor Mincarelli had been best friends since they were altar boys in Bensonhurst; and with a solid twenty-eight years in the Department, Greg could have been police commissioner for the asking. He had already feasted on a taste of the job as acting commissioner, before Rudy was elected. And they had talked late into many long post-election nights about how to reorganize the hidebound Department and build a partnership of city agencies to clean the streets of crime and filth and fear. But as much as he wanted the job, Greg had known his string-jerking friend—and himself—too well to be Rudy's puppet.

So after twenty-eight years of carefully edging higher and higher in the NYPD, Greg Walsh had slipped sideways, effortlessly and remuneratively, into the private sector. He was suddenly rich, by every standard of a hardworking cop family; overnight, he earned more than both his daughters' hotshot husbands combined.

Rudy razzed him, mercilessly, teasing that Greg would lose his edge retiring young, laughing that Greg would find himself "gelded by golden handcuffs." Maybe he had been, or maybe he had taken the opportunity to grow. But one thing was sure. Greg Walsh had watched from the skybox as his best friend and several ill-treated commissioners made history.

Now he ran each morning through the city Rudy wrought—tamer, cleaner, easier to get around, and so safe in many neighborhoods that Rudy found himself in the peculiar position of being a law-and-order mayor of an impatient city where schools and infrastructure now loomed as much bigger problems than crime.

If Greg had missed out, at least their friendship had endured. Rudy still called regularly, plumbed him for ideas, and often acted on them. They'd still get together for a night of Diet Pepsi and the earnest debates they'd started in high school—Was Man evil? Was the price of order to be ordinary? Who will guard the guards?—Rudy always sure, Greg inclined to both sides. Prosecutor versus street cop, when they were young; "Il Duce" and "Plutocrat," today.

On the newsstands, the cruise-ship headlines had pushed Rudy's presidential toe-dipping off the front page. Greg wondered if Rudy would make it. His friend was the kind of character rarely seen anymore—a leader with a personality. People weren't allowed to sin anymore, drink, fuck, steal a little, make mistakes, or be self-righteous. They were whittled down as they advanced, their edges smoothed that might stand out.

Greg had seen it in the Marines, he'd seen it in the Department—hell, it had probably happened even to himself. When was the last time he'd stood up and yelled out loud? But somehow Rudy had stayed a character. And he still wasn't afraid to be self-righteous.

"Yo, Greg!"

Speaking of characters.

A police scooter putted alongside, driven by a handsome white-haired black police officer wearing a uniform that looked, as always, straight from the dry cleaner.

Harold Greene was the same age as Greg, had fought in the same Vietnam as Greg, had graduated the same year from the Academy. But Harold was still on patrol at City Hall while Greg rose through the ranks. Not rising into management didn't seem to bother Harold one bit. He had one child who was a doctor, another a career Marine, and his youngest—his "baby girl," who'd struggled since adolescence with a learning disability—was finally thriving as a rookie cop.

As Greg jogged through the old chaos of downtown, and Harold putted alongside, they traded news of their kids—Greg's youngest just accepted at the Academy, Harold's "baby" assigned to Gracie Mansion. Somebody they both knew was on the cruise ship—a hair bag from Records who wouldn't be the biggest loss.

They high-fived good-bye on Cleveland Street, in front of the former Police Headquarters—long since converted to a Beaux Arts luxury co-op—where both had trembled in their rookie years. Then they parted, Harold putt-putting back downtown to City Hall, Greg heading up through SoHo and the Village and finally cutting across scruffy Eighth Street to Sixth Avenue.

At Fourteenth Street, where early traffic was starting to thicken, a couple of radio motor-patrol cops sat up straight and returned salutes to Greg's nod. For a second, he felt like he was still a leader of the tribe. Then it struck him like a thunderbolt that Harold Greene putt-putted uptown with him every morning out of kindness. Not because Greg was the wealthy former commissioner, but because Harold pitied an old friend who wasn't a cop anymore; out of the action.

He continued up Sixth between the ornately columned, nineteenth-century Ladies Mile department stores, which had reblossomed as superstores moved into abandoned space; past cigarette-smoking, coffee-drinking working guys gathering early at the Apex Technical School; through the flower district, where immigrant guys were hustling lobby palm trees onto handcarts and unloading trucks while yawning florists wandered around the wholesalers, loading their station wagons and vans. Macy's was still shuttered, of course, but traffic was picking up in Herald Square as the city began moving firmly toward another day. As he did every morning, Greg marveled at the clean, precise Bryant Park behind the library where, before Rudy, three generations of Vice and Narcotics had always been able to make their quotas.

Across Forty-second, through a disconcertingly pristine Times Square. His knees were glad when the final stretch of Eighth Avenue led to the World Wide Building. They hadn't used to hurt and he wondered, as the air-conditioning iced his soaking shirt, how much longer before his knees wouldn't take the pounding anymore. Last year he'd been shocked that his hair was suddenly so thin that the sun burned his scalp. What next? Running indoors on a rubber track?

"Hold the elevator?"

Gill Bishop, an early-morning regular, hurried after him splashing coffee and gnawing a bagel. In his wrinkled shirt and scuffed shoes, Bishop looked more like a minimum-wage janitor than the owner of one of the richest hedge funds in town. He reminded Greg of the science geniuses in high school. Based on appearances—his rumpled clothes, his sprouting ear hair, his unibrow eyebrows—making money was Gill's grown-up equivalent of winning the science fair.

As usual, Gill pumped Greg for information, softening him up with a rumor that the cruise ship had suffered an "external explosion," which could only have been caused by a mine. Then Gill asked whether Greg's brokerage house was planning layoffs. It would be news to me, was Greg's reply, though he wondered whether the news ferret knew something about Aetolian that even he hadn't heard.

Gill asked if Greg had heard about a contract the NYPD was going to let for a new police radio, which would set a national standard. Greg had heard rumors, but of course he wasn't a cop anymore. Two could play this game—by the way, had Gill Bishop learned anything new about a potential Italian bond crisis? Mistake. The fund manager's eyes lighted up, and Greg could tell he was wondering if Aetolian was too deep in Roman treasuries.

Before Greg could repair the damage, Gill Bishop deftly changed the subject with a remark that Chinese investors were dumping New York City bonds this morning.

The *Chelsea Queen*'s crew arrived yawning, scratching, and belching. "Kate, Charlie, Rick." Ken introduced her. "She's got coffee in the galley. I got biscuits in the oven."

White-haired, potbellied Charlie O'Conner downed his coffee with shaking hands and thanked Kate cordially. He cocked an ear to the rumble of the diesels and the whine of their superchargers. "Ken, did you remember to blow the cylinders?"

"Yes, I blew the cylinders."

Charlie explained gravely to Kate, "I just don't trust kids around machinery."

"I was there," said Kate. "Ken opened all the . . . um—"

"Compression testers," Ken prompted.

"We cranked the engines to blow out water and fuel. Then we closed the compression testers and fired them up."

"Well, I'll just go down and have a look."

As Charlie stumped below, Kate said, "I can't tell if he's kidding or he doesn't trust you."

"Both. But mainly he's having a look at the vodka bottle he's got stashed behind the day tank."

Young Rick, overweight, baby-faced, and, Kate suspected, something of a lost soul, burned his mouth on Ken's hot biscuits. After he had cast off the heavy lines, he went down to the galley to watch television; the tugboat's mini-dish—a gift from Jose, who claimed it had fallen off an ABC live truck—was picking up CNN's helicopter coverage of the *Sovereign Princess*.

Kate was happy to be alone in the wheelhouse with Ken as he swung the old boat into the stream and headed for the sunrise.

"What was all that about," he asked, "when Jose was showing you his camera?"

"What do you mean?"

"You seemed a little upset."

She flashed him a grateful smile. "You notice everything, don't you? You always seem to know how I feel."

Ken reached gently for her with his free hand and touched her cheek.

Kate slipped into the crook of his arm. "Not just physically . . . yes, I was upset. I told you that my parents divorced when I was nine years old. What I didn't tell you was that the newspapers had a field day. They'd been a great-looking couple. They were both 'social.' And their drinking made for some horrendous scenes in public.

"Mom was totally freaked that Dad was spending her money on his girlfriends. Dad was fighting dirty not to end up broke. Every time I see a camera I remember the local reporters waiting outside school to jump me."

"Nine's a killer age. Just old enough to know what's going on, and too young do anything about it."

"But you're sure it's your fault."

"Tell me about it. My father died when I was ten. . . . Everyone tells me what a legendary character he was. He'd run down the East River dropping barges without stopping—and they'd float right into their piers."

"Is that possible?"

"All I know is my mom remarried in six months . . . married my uncle, if you can believe that."

"That's very biblical."

"At ten, I hadn't read the Bible yet. Look, there's a heron."

Kate watched the big bird pump its wings across the misty sky like a pterodactyl. It was quiet in the wheelhouse, the engines a distant presence. Down in the engine room, the sixteen-cylinder locomotive engines had thundered right through her ear protectors.

Ken spoke suddenly. "My dad was a drunk, too. So was my uncle/stepfather; worse than Charlie; falling down, breaking things; lost his pilot's license. I abandoned ship the day I turned seventeen—joined the Navy. Six months later I *had* to get married . . ." He sighed. "My father used to say to my mother, pointing at the door, 'The carpenter left a hole in the wall.' I sometimes wonder, was that my excuse for never totally committing? Two divorces. Never again."

"Never marry again?"

"No, never divorce again."

Kate felt another smile breaking out. That had to be the most romantic thing she had ever heard.

"What are you smiling at?" he asked.

Kate just shook her head. He wasn't "a" romantic, but he surely was romantic. She poured some more coffee from the steel thermos clamped to the dashboard pillar and touched it to her lips.

A Staten Island ferry loomed from the mist on a converging course. Ken, who'd been watching it on the radar, pulled the VHF radio microphone down from the wheelhouse ceiling, exchanged good-mornings with the captain, and offered to pass astern.

"Could I ask," said Kate, "how you happen to know the unemployed dope runner you recommended to Jose?"

"Deckhand, before Rick. Needed a job to get parole."

Ken swung the *Chelsea Queen* behind the orange-and-blue ferry, steadied up on his compass.

Kate asked, "Is there anyone in your life you don't take care of?"

Ken looked over with a grin that managed to look older and wiser, but not superior.

"Come on, Kate, you and I both know that children of drunks—who don't become drunks themselves—try to save people because we couldn't save our parents."

"I've always gone it alone. I've never saved anybody."

"You will."

"And I'm not somebody who needs to be saved, either."

"I know that."

"Can you deal with it?"

His blue eyes veered from hers and roved ahead of the tug. "Hope so."

6

SUBMARINERS LIVED by a maxim: ships sink slowly; subs sink instantly. No time to phone the conn to discuss a problem, no time for sentiment. Which was why every sailor on Admiral Tang's boats could perform every job. Why every man knew he would have to shut a watertight door in the face of a mate if that was what it took to save the boat.

East Wind 1, the admiral's flagship—an air-independent propulsion hydrogen-oxygen fuel-cell *Bundesmarine* Type 212—was the newest submarine in Tang's armada. At the pinnacle of German *unterseeboot* engineering, after eight decades and two world wars' worth of U-boat experience—and the finest quality control in the international arms trade—the 170-foot 1800-ton boat had performed flawlessly on the long round-the-world voyage from China.

At the remote fuel and maintenance rendezvous in southern stretches of the Pacific and Atlantic the mother-ship inspectors had passed her with flying colors. And had again at the meeting with the troop ships that had spared Tang's commandos the bulk of the voyage in the cramped submarines.

Thus, of all the crews of the hundred boats closing on New York—her sister AIP 212s, older diesel-electric 209s, the sturdy Russian-built *Kilos,* the Swedish AIP-battery extended *Gotlands* and the superb British *Upholder* class boats—*East Wind 1's* men were the least likely to hear their sub's near-silence suddenly shattered by flood alarms.

For a precious second, Tang Li couldn't believe his ears. Then the deck tilted like a dump truck.

His sailors were sprinting toward the bow, shoving the bewildered assault troops out of their way, shouting for their mates to shut the watertight hatches behind them. She was down at the head, sharply, steeply down, and accelerating.

The watertight door alarm shrilled.

Men scurried for their lives as steel hatches crashed shut. But she kept sinking. Her captain, Chen Liang, from Fujian Province, was watching the depth gauge and issuing quiet orders. Admiral Tang observed the chain of command, stifling the impulse to take charge of the other man's boat. In his mind's eye he saw the rapidly receding surface overhead, and the sea bottom rising swiftly toward them. The continental shelf had shallowed to two hundred feet, but at the speed they were falling, the mud and sand bottom might as well be granite when the bow hit.

Captain Chen said, "May I attempt to surface, Admiral?"

Tang pressed one hand to his ear, where the sudden air pressure tore through the drum like a siren. "No."

Chen touched knuckles to his forehead in salute. He had had to ask, for the sake of his crew, but he knew that the attack and the safety of the rest of the fleet depended on no boat being seen. He uttered an order. "Flood the stern ballast tanks and blow the bow."

Tang nodded his tacit agreement. Marginally better to try to crash flat than auger in with her entire mass concentrated on her nose.

The bow leveled off. The captain broadcast a shout to brace. Tang grabbed the nearest handhold and a second later she hit the bottom with a force to challenge every weld in her double hull.

The lights went out.

Men's voices echoed in the tight space, clattered on the intercoms. But Tang heard neither panic nor despair. Only exchanges of information tinged with healthy fear.

It was he who felt despair. What gods had intervened, what absurd fate had moved between him and the years of meticulous planning, cautious maneuvering, and bold action?

The attack would continue. All contingencies—even this curse of fortune, this bad joss to end all bad joss—had been considered and planned for. But with *East Wind 1* as severely stricken as his gut told him the boat was, he would not be part of it, much less lead it.

"Float a satellite buoy."

Their satellite communications system would store his order like voice mail until Commissar Wong Tsu checked in and heard the news that sweetened his dreams. With his boat down, Tang had to pass command to the Party political officer.

Tang's submariners would obey Wong. They had no choice. But Commissar Wong was capable only so long as complications remained few. His weakness lay in an utter lack of subtlety or flexibility or imagination—common failings in political officers who grew stupid on easy power.

Tang Li radioed his flagship's position and her situation. Then he spoke the death of his dream: "Commissar Wong Tsu, until I countermand this order, you are authorized to take command of the People's Submarine Expeditionary Force."

The future Emperor Tang was trapped in a stricken boat with a dwindling air supply, two hundred feet underwater, forty miles short of his goal.

7

THREE HOURS after they steamed under the Verrazano Bridge, the *Chelsea Queen* was thirty-six miles from New York, plowing her best twelve knots east. A warm, moderate southwest breeze was blowing pungent diesel smoke over the wheelhouse. Regular four-foot seas were sprinkled with whitecaps as the tops of waves dissolved in foam. Visibility had fallen to two miles as an early summer haze began to thicken.

"You ever get seasick?"

"Never," said Kate. "You?"

"It'll sneak up on me now and then. Not a nice roll like this. But in a certain kind of chop, when the tide's running against the wind, the guys know not to stand downwind of me."

They were alone in the wheelhouse. Ken's white-haired, red-nosed engineer was sleeping off his drunk in the engine room. On deck, the chubby deckhand was streaming a low-light underwater TV search camera behind the tug; Ken called it his "new toy." After Rick had the camera working, he went back to sunning himself on a ripped and corroded lounger he'd set up on the broad open towing deck in the back of the boat, oblivious to the thunder from the smoke-stack and the oily soot the wind looped down on him.

The VHF radio was alive with boat chatter, the sinking the main subject. Between it and News Radio 88, Kate and Ken learned that the *Sovereign Princess* had suffered a big explosion and an engine room fire, which was still burning out of control.

"Maiden voyages are always a mess," said Ken. "Nobody knows where anything is yet."

The cruise ship was dead in the water. Whether she was actually sinking depended on whom you talked to. The news station said she was sinking, but the captains Ken spoke to on the radio said that her pumps were holding their own.

Casualties were light so far, mostly some people killed in the initial explosion. It sounded like the English and Caribbean crew had done a good job of getting the passengers into the lifeboats, which were circling the ship, waiting for the rescue ships to pick them up.

"Not enough gore for Jose," said Ken.

"I hope our wedding couple is okay."

"Sounds like they'll get everybody out of the boats before dark. I gotta tell you, some of the foreign crews I see couldn't save themselves, much less the passengers—Jesus, you hear me?" He laughed. "I sound like my grandfather, bitching and moaning that deckhands aren't what they used to be."

Ken engaged the autopilot, freeing his hands to show Kate the Navy-surplus underwater TV scanner he had in-stalled in hopes of turning "the old broad" into a salvage vessel. "She's just an old-fashioned harbor tug, plenty strong, but not so nimble as the new ones with Z-drive. You know Z-drive?"

"My dad installed one on a twelve-meter. You could crank it up when you were racing, then crank it down to motor back."

"How'd it work?"

"Not very well. It cavitated when we flew the jib."

"They're dynamite on a tug. The new boats can shiphandle circles around me and burn a lot less fuel doing it. So anyhow, I got this idea to specialize in underwater searches."

"Have you done any yet?"

Ken nodded up at the heavy black iron derrick that crouched on the roof of the cabin behind the wheelhouse. "I just got that monster crane from the junkie; Charlie says it'll turn the boat over. Rick hooked me up with a guy who glommed onto the camera cheap after the Flight 800 search. It's previous generation now, but not by much. Look at that clarity, and we're doing twelve knots."

He fiddled knobs on the video monitor bolted to the dashboard. She couldn't take her eyes off his broad, scarred hands. I'm losing my mind, she thought—they're just nice, strong-looking hands, even missing a little finger. You could see hands like that on any sail-grinding gorilla. Perfectly ordinary, nice, strong-looking hands that were gnarled and scarred and callused. And felt like velvet.

He pointed at the monitor. "Isn't that amazing? It's like snorkeling in five feet of water."

Kate watched the sea bottom rolling behind them two hundred feet below the surface. There was a hypnotic sameness to the rippled sand, a sense of flying over desert dunes.

"What's that?"

Ken focused on a dark patch in the corner of the screen. "Looks like a monkey wrench. . . . Yeah, that's what it is. Some dummy dropped his wrench overboard. I tell you, deckhands aren't what they used to be."

The tool grew big on the black-and-white screen. Ken manipulated the camera to pan the area around it, but no more tools appeared as it faded behind them. "Guess he didn't go overboard after it."

"Look! Ohmigod, look at that!"

A swordfish was coming after the camera. Ken and Kate both flinched as its bill and a baleful eye suddenly filled the monitor. The picture shook and disappeared in a cloud of bubbles. When it cleared, the fish had gone.

"Guess the camera didn't taste too good," said Ken.

Kate said, "Once, on a transatlantic delivery, I pulled in the log. The metal was all scraped and gouged with teeth marks. After that, alone on watch at night, I'd imagine the 'things' swooping up under the boat. . . . It's so beautiful at night offshore. The stars are brilliant mid-ocean; that's the one thing that could draw me back to boat-bumming."

"I can't imagine you as a 'bum.' You seem too . . ."

"Driven? Pushy?"

"Not pushy. Just not that casual. You're the persevering type."

"The truth is, I was a complete failure as a boat bum. I'm so darned responsible—and Ms. Perfectionist—my last job I ended up captaining a two-million-dollar charter yacht. My crew were genuine boat bums. They were even needier than my needy clients."

Ken laughed. "We have deckhands in common. Listen, you can catch a ride from me anytime to see the stars. Somebody's got to take Herman to lun—"

"*What* is that?"

Ken throttled back the diesels and put the tug into a tight turn. "Wow."

"What is it?"

"Looks like an old wreck."

They studied the picture. Then Ken stepped out on the deck behind the wheelhouse and called down, "Rick, you gotta see this."

Rick groaned himself off the lounger and climbed the ladder to the wheelhouse. "What's happening, Captain?"

"You want to see a submarine?"

Rick looked at the video display. "Whoa! It's a god-damned submarine."

It looked, Kate thought, like a submarine in old movies, with a sinister conning tower and sharp edges and a long gun on the foredeck.

"Run down and wake up Charlie. Maybe he can tell us what kind it is." Rick took another long squint, then scrambled below to the engine room. "Charlie," Ken explained, "is a World War Two nut. It looks pretty old. Maybe he'll recognize the type."

Kate continued to examine the screen as the tug circled. "It's so clean. There're no barnacles on it, no seaweed."

"Some of these waters are really contaminated from years and years of dumping garbage and chemicals. Whole areas are dead. Maybe nothing grows here."

"I don't know. It's shiny, almost."

Ken studied the shifting image. "I haven't heard of any missing subs. Besides, it's a little guy. You ever see a nuke? They're big as freighters."

Kate had seen the colossal *Ohio* in the Sound once, while sailing past New London. Far more ship than boat.

Charlie came huffing and puffing up the spiral stairs, paused at the top to light a fresh cigarette from the butt in his lips, hitched up his overalls, which were patched with duct tape, and puffed closer for a look. A blast of vodka breath made Kate grateful for the secondhand smoke.

"Son of a bitch," said Charlie. "Excuse the language, Kate."

"What is it?"

"I don't believe it."

"What is it?"

"It's a goldarned submarine."

"No shit, Sherlock," Rick said.

The engineer ignored the deckhand and turned to Ken. "You know what that is? That's a Nazi submarine."

"Get outta here."

"That is a German, Nazi, World War Two submarine."

"How do you know?"

Charlie smeared the screen with a greasy finger. "See this? When's the last time you saw a deck gun on a sub? . . . You know what that thing's worth?"

"A lot, I guess."

"There's *one* in a museum in Chicago. There's maybe *two* in Germany. And nothing as late as this one."

"How do you know it's late?" Ken asked, excitement quickening.

"Look at the modern lines on that baby. Betcha it's a Type XXI—one of the 'Electro' super boats they were trying to launch when the war ended. They only built a few because the Allied bombing destroyed their canals and railroads before they could assemble the sections. But these babies could outsail Allied convoy escorts—underwater. Radical design. Influenced every boat since right up to the new Type 212."

Kate said, "Is that why it looks new?"

"Betcha it's filled with gold," said Charlie.

"Gold?"

"Nazi bigwigs making a run for it. Loaded their hottest boat with gold and headed for South America."

"They missed South America by a mile," said Rick.

"Obviously something went wrong. They sunk. Jesus, Ken. You got the chance of a lifetime here. We can all retire on this."

"I'm going to put a buoy on it."

"Absolutely, Ken. Absolutely."

"Rick, you want to launch the Zodiac?"

"What for?"

"I'm not diving off a tumble-home hull in five-foot seas when I can ease off a rubber inflatable. Launch the Zodiac!"

"Two hundred feet's a pretty deep dive," said Kate. She knew recreational divers bottomed out at around a hundred.

Ken fixed the sub's position on a handheld GPS and entered it in the *Chelsea Queen*'s log. "First we attach a buoy, put a claim on it. I'll get my gear. Charlie, we'll stream the Zodiac. Then you just let the *Queen* drift so we don't chop me up with the props. Kate, you can drive the Zodiac, can't you?"

"Sure."

"Okay, everybody. Let's do it."

Early June, and the Atlantic was still bitter cold. Kate helped Ken pull his wet suit over his muscles like a second skin.

"Tugman, lover, and now diver? Is there no end to your talents?"

"Underwater welder."

"That's a relief."

"Why?"

"I've heard that underwater welders have to be extremely competent divers. Not the type that drowns trying to get rich quick on a treasure hunt."

Ken stopped zipping zippers and jolted Kate with a frank and open smile. "Something tells me I already found my treasure."

Kate kissed his mouth, clung hard for a long moment, and then, a little stunned by the swiftness of everything, whispered, "Me, too. . . . Any other occupations I should know about?"

"Ran a bar once. . . ." He fell silent as he methodically checked his tanks and regulator; she enjoyed watching him. Julia had been wiser than she knew about the boat connection. Kate had grown up in a world where men owned tools and knew what to do with them; it bred a *do-it* attitude she missed in Manhattan guys.

Counting by the numbers, he really could be her father. But he listened. He remembered. He laughed. And he brought to bed a breathtaking marriage of refinement and animal desire. The elegance of his lovemaking had not surprised her—he was, for all his wharf-rat talk, a deeply civilized man—but nothing in his easygoing manner had foretold his passion.

Kate couldn't believe she had brought it out all by herself. But she found herself wondering what miracles he would perform outside of bed if she somehow found a way to help him tap such vitality.

Ken strapped on a diver's knife.

"I had the best dive instructors in the world: United States Navy SEALs—till I washed out." His eyes slid away from hers. "I couldn't hack the combat training."

Kate shrugged. "I gather it's like a triathlon with unpleasant people yelling at you."

To Kate's surprise, Ken felt obliged to explain—as if that thirty-years-ago failure was still a raw wound. "Physically, I had no problem. I could swim forty miles with a bayonet in my teeth, good as the next guy. *My* problem was when I hit the beach I just didn't feel like sticking anybody with it. Cops shoot guns, firemen put out fires. I learned I was a fireman . . . My loss. They're a great outfit."

"Big loss. My dad had a friend who'd been a SEAL. Fifty years old, he was still wired like a time bomb. And made his children call him Sir."

"But he earned his bragging rights."

"Zodiac's ready," called Rick.

Kate climbed over the thick, low bulwark that protected the open towing deck in the back of the tugboat and felt her way awkwardly into the Zodiac, a rubber inflatable runabout with a solid floor. The outboard was a small twenty-five horse attached to a six-gallon tank. She checked that the gas tank was full and yanked the starter cord. The motor was as old as everything else on Ken's boat, but it started on the third pull.

He threw a buoy and a three-hundred-foot coil of light line into the boat, flippers after them, and climbed over the bulwark. Rick poled them off. When Ken turned around, Kate had already engaged the outboard and was circling away from the tug.

"You look like a Viking," he said.

"Vikings had long hair."

"You look beautiful, Kate."

The compliment brought a big smile to her face. "Thank you."

"Like you were born on a wave."

"Conceived on a boat, according to my mother."

"Okay, let's circle till Charlie gets a little further away." He watched the tug, which loomed very tall over the bobbing inflatable, then directed Kate over the point he had marked on the GPS.

"Stop."

He touched his VHF radio to his lips. "Okay, Charlie. You want to stop there, take her out of gear? And do me a favor—don't engage again until I tell you to. Same for you," he said to Kate. "No props until I'm back in the boat."

"You got it," Charlie answered on the radio. Ken looked at Kate, all business.

"No props," said Kate.

He handed her the VHF, pulled on his flippers, secured the buoy to the boat, and, reaching to pull down his face mask, paused to smile at Kate.

Kate, shifting to balance the boat when he went over the side, reached out and ran her fingers down his cheek. "When I see your smile, I feel your embrace."

Ken kissed her fingertips. Then he pulled down the mask, bit his mouthpiece, and rolled over the rubber side, taking the line with him beneath the water.

Kate watched his bubbles. She was thrown back years by the smells of salt and gas and oil to after-school jobs she'd had on boats, in boatyards, bumming around the Caribbean and the offshore passages. Beautiful but oddly empty years in which, no matter how much of the world she saw, nothing changed, and no matter how far she sailed, she went nowhere. Until some Puritan streak she had picked up somewhere—certainly not from her mother or father—told her she had to leave that life to grow.

And now, her heart filling, she wondered if this beautiful man was to be her reward.

Ken had a powerful halogen lamp strapped to his wrist that he didn't need for the first sixty feet. Then, with startling suddenness, the sunlight percolating down from the surface was gone and he was descending into blackness.

His breathing sounded hollow, resonant, loud in his ears. He took thirty seconds to restore a sense of well-being, adjust to the blackness, and wrestle with images of sharks and hungry swordfish. Settled, he switched on the halogen, and swam down its hard white beam as if he were descending a shaft.

When his depth gauge read one hundred and fifty feet, the light bounced back from water that was roiled and murky. At one-eighty he spotted the angular line of a rakish bow. His heart started pounding. Though he'd seen the sub on the monitor, for the first time it seemed real.

Playing his buoy line off the coil, he descended to the boat's foredeck. It had a dome that he hadn't seen on the monitor. It looked like a big entry hatch or even a second forward conning tower. The main tower stood tall, a good twelve feet above the deck. Ken reversed his descent, got his feet under him, and landed softly.

Just as Kate had noticed on the video monitor, there was no sea grass or weed or algae, no barnacles. It looked like the submarine had sunk an hour ago. Funny. Where he'd have expected to see rivets, there were big Phillips-head machine screws.

Why that, of all the signals, tipped him, he would never know. But a moment later, when he saw a bubble rise from the bow, every nerve went to high alert.

Before a second bubble started a stream, Ken was streaking for the surface.

8

WHEN HE HAD risen fifty feet, rationality took hold. Racing straight up two hundred feet even from a brief dive was an excellent way to suffer a case of the bends with nitrogen bubbles crippling his joints. He stopped and looked down.

He couldn't see the submarine anymore, even when he poked the darkness with his light. It was as if the bottom muck had swallowed it up. Spooky, the bubbles. Weird. Or he was weird. Weirded out on too much imagination. Kate's fault, he thought with a smile. It was like she had opened every pore of his body, like she made him want to see everything in the whole world at once, touch it, embrace it, gulp it down, and reach for more.

He was still holding the buoy line. Still had to tie it to the wreck to mark his salvage claim. He pointed the light below him. Nothing. Spooky. Fuck it.

He started down again.

Twenty feet. Thirty. He paused, struck by an eerie sense that something large was moving nearby. He probed with the light at a fog of stirring sand and mud. His mind was galloping, fantasizing an image of a long, gray, slow-moving shape emerging from the murk.

Seduced despite his fear, Ken Hughes inched lower. In the murk-diffused beam of his halogen light he thought he saw a second submarine nosing alongside the first, a big gray shape like a gigantic shark nuzzling its injured mate.

Bubbles streamed into his face, dissolved the image. Sharks slaughtered their wounded, ate them. The bubbles tumbled past his light beam. There, from the sub's stern, her torpedo tubes were spouting scuba divers with lights, guns, and knives.

Ken switched off his own light and swam up as fast as he dared.

He might have stumbled across a U.S. Navy exercise, except as far as he knew, the Navy had no diesel subs. More likely, he'd interrupted the sort of drug smugglers he'd heard were using old subs in the Caribbean. No one he wanted to meet forty miles from land.

High overhead, the *Chelsea Queen*'s squat hull looked big and heavy and very reassuring with the seas breaking white and foamy against her sides. The Zodiac had been blown a hundred yards downwind; the inflatable floated like a seagull, a speck on the skylit surface.

He headed for the inflatable. Ten feet under it, he looked down and back and saw two divers heading for the tugboat. A third was coming after him. Ken shot to the surface, spit out his mouthpiece, and yelled to Kate.

"Start the motor!"

She took a long moment to scramble back to it and yank the starter cord. He swam hard, the flippers propelling him in long, swift surges through the water. The little motor caught with a whiny crackle. Kate threw it into gear and trundled the boat toward him.

He was ten feet away, close enough to see her horrified

expression when she screamed. Ken glimpsed a wet-suited diver surfacing behind him. A long black knife arced against the sky. He watched it in stupid disbelief. And suddenly it was descending on him. He tucked into a ball. Metal screeched hard on his tanks. He flung an elbow back and connected with a crunch that knocked the diver's face mask off and rolled his eyes back in his head.

Chinese, he thought. The guy's Chinese. It flashed in his mind that this could be a replay of the *Golden Venture*, the Chinese freighter that had grounded off Rockaway, drowning illegal immigrants. Unlawful aliens coming in by submarine? But this was a soldier, stubby rifle strapped to his back, an underwater commando recovering fast, striking out with fists as tight and small as a woman's. Ken punched him in the mouth.

Kate screamed. Two others exploded out of the water, wearing the same type of masks, the same stubby rifles. One came at him, one went for the Zodiac.

"Get away!" Ken yelled to Kate. "There's another sub. Get away."

Instead, she stood up and swung the boat hook.

She missed the diver's head but managed to tear a hose off his mask. Coolly, the guy treaded water, and reached back for his rifle. Like the first diver, he was a wiry little bastard. Ken broke free from the one he was struggling with, dove, and swam up behind the one Kate had hit, swarmed onto him and used his superior weight and strength to shove him underwater before he could level his weapon.

"Go," he cried as they came after him again. And when he saw she wouldn't, he yelled at her: "Get help. I saw another sub."

Kate raised the boat hook like a harpoon. But even as she tried to choose her target, the sea was suddenly alive with bobbing heads as black-suited diver after diver popped to the surface.

Gunfire clamored suddenly. They were climbing onto the *Chelsea Queen,* hauling themselves up her fat sides with ropes and grappling hooks. More shots. Glass flew from the tug's wheelhouse.

"Go!" Ken roared from a thrashing mass of heads and arms. "You can't help me. Get away!"

She circled warily, hefted the boat hook like a latter-day Queequeg. Suddenly two black-gloved hands lunged over the gunnel. She drove the boat hook at them, grabbed the outboard tiller, and twisted the throttle wide open.

The Zodiac started off heavily. The diver was holding on. Steering with one hand, Kate jabbed the boat hook at him with the other. He wrenched it away from her. She looked for another weapon. A rusty screwdriver was rolling around at her feet. But she was afraid it would pierce the rubber tube he was hanging onto. By the gas tank was a quart of motor oil. She scooped it up and threw it at the diver's mask. The container was made of plastic, and it simply bounced off his head.

He gave a kind of growl and dragged himself halfway into the boat. Kate went for the only solid object she had left, Ken's radio, and pounded it into his face mask. The diver grabbed her wrist. His wet glove slid on her skin like a reptile. She yanked free. He grabbed again, got the radio, and slipped with an angry yell into the sea.

The Zodiac leaped ahead, onto a plane and shot away, skimming the seas, crashing from crest to crest. Kate looked back. Divers in gleaming black wet suits were climbing onto the *Chelsea Queen.* One raced up the ladder to the top of the wheelhouse and pointed his weapon at her.

The water a foot from the boat was suddenly pocked like big raindrops. Something cracked past her face. She ducked, reflexively. The gunshots were muffled by distance. She was out of range. Where Ken had been she saw nothing.

She slowed the motor and tried to stand up in the bouncing boat to see better. A gray shape emerged beside the tug.

Had the submarine surfaced? Ken had yelled that there was another sub. Certainly something much bigger than the tug was lying alongside it now. She accelerated the motor again and fled. They'd have boats like this one aboard, only faster.

Her heart was racing with fear and adrenaline, and pounding with an intensity she had never felt in her life—part rage at the divers who'd attacked them, part crushing loss, part guilt. She could taste it poisoning her mouth, swelling her tongue. Ken had saved her life. She had to help him.

She had lost the VHF radio. But the gas tank was full. She had enough fuel to reach Long Island and she could steer a generally northerly course by keeping the haze-shrouded disk of the morning sun behind her and a little to the right.

She knew the exact location from when Ken had pinpointed the sunken sub's coordinates with the GPS. She knew that heavily armed divers had risen from the submarine. She knew the faces she had seen looked Chinese.

She opened the motor cowl and fiddled the fuel adjustments in a vain effort to coax more speed out of the little engine.

There was something else she knew and it gnawed at her deeper than the fear of pursuit: No one would believe her when she told them what had happened.

9

IT WAS ALREADY too late when it had occurred to Ken to draw the diving knife he wore strapped to his leg for prying metal, shaping wood, opening oysters. Though looking over his captors, he realized that maybe it was just as well he hadn't tried to fight them. These little guys—and they were really little, a hundred and twenty pounds tops—were armed to the teeth and moved with a killing-machine swagger of U.S. Navy SEALs.

He was lucky they hadn't killed him.

Lucky their boss had come up with them in the first wave and called them off before they carved him up like tuna steaks. The boss had immediately ordered the second sub to submerge to periscope depth. It lay a hundred yards off, watching the evacuation through a single eye. The divers climbed aboard the tug, where they now sprawled on the towing deck like a flock of seals sunning themselves in the Bronx Zoo.

Ken, closely guarded by a diver on either side, slumped

with his back against a steel knee and pretended to catch his breath while he tried to figure out what the hell was going on. Charlie and Rick were staring saucer-eyed. Neither looked like he felt lucky. Especially Rick, who had a bloody furrow across his forehead and a split lip swelling like a cantaloupe; the deckhand was scared to death. Old Charlie looked like he would trade his balls for a drink.

More and more men kept climbing aboard, either in diving gear or in a simpler evacuation outfit consisting of an air hood attached to a life preserver. Fifteen, then twenty-five. The later arrivals dropped their tanks and air hoods back into the sea, down lines they rigged to the sub lying on the bottom. At forty and counting, Ken realized that the entire crew were abandoning ship.

The boss pulled off his helmet. Chinese guy a little younger than Ken, early forties, with a streak of silver in his hair—the kind of cultured Asian face you saw pictured on the business page.

Even with a scar rimming his eye and a mashed ear, his was not a face that went with the weapons dangling from his belt. But there was a commanding stillness about him, a steely quiet. The other divers watched him like trained pit bulls, and snapped to when he finally spoke what sounded to Ken like the Cantonese of New York's Chinatown.

When they had boarded one hundred men, the *Chelsea Queen* was squatting deeper from their weight. The last aboard was carrying a length of pipe. He stripped off his headgear and Ken guessed by the broad build and the belligerent stance that he was the Chinese equivalent of any navy's bosun or chief petty officer—the enlisted man's noncom boss who got things done by teaching, guiding, and kicking ass.

The bosun stalked up to *his* boss and thrust the pipe into his hands. The boss bent his head over it. The angry bosun yelled. Finally, the boss turned to Ken and spoke in perfect, accentless English.

"Are you the tugboat captain?"

"It's my tug."

"What are you doing so far from New York?"

How did he know the *Chelsea Queen* was from New York? Written on her stern, stupid. "There's a cruise ship sinking off Montauk. You mind me asking what the hell is going on here?"

"Please examine this pipe."

"What?"

"Examine this pipe." No "please" the second time.

Ken took it. A chunk of three-inch pipe—lighter than it looked, some fancy alloy—broken at one end.

"Well?"

Ken glanced at the steaming bosun. *He* sure as hell knew what was wrong. And apparently understood English, too, because he nodded his walrus head in vigorous agreement when Ken answered, "I'd fire my welder."

"What do you mean?"

"I mean this braze is not exactly the quality I'd expect on a submarine. Just a matter of time or pressure till the joint popped. Is this what brought you down?"

The boss conferred in Chinese with his bosun and his second officer. Orders were shouted. The basking seals sprang to their feet and began trooping into the house, crowding the galley, the sleeping cabins, the storage lockers, and the engine room. The bosun led two men to the wheelhouse. Seconds later the *Queen* belched diesel smoke and commenced a long, heavy turn to the northwest.

"Where was that young woman headed in the rubber boat?"

Ken weighed the value of lies against Rick and Charlie's fate. If the guy had any idea where he'd surfaced, he probably already knew where Kate was going. But no way they could catch her in the tug. "Long Island."

"And how fast will that boat go?"

"Fifteen, twenty knots."

"Does she have fuel to reach land?"

Oh, shit, thought Ken. He's not alone. He can send the other sub after her. "She'll run out before she gets there," Ken lied, hoping Charlie and Rick wouldn't give it away with their faces.

Charlie didn't. Rick did.

The boss didn't seem to notice. "How well do you know the port?" he asked Ken.

"New York?" Ken asked casually. He had to hold this guy at bay until he figured out what was going on. They were okay so far, nobody hurt, Kate escaped. "Pretty well."

The boss gestured at Charlie and Rick. Five commandos grabbed Rick, five grabbed Charlie and dragged them to the stern.

"Hey!" Ken jumped up, clumsily, his feet encumbered by his long rubber fins. Two little guys hit him simultaneously in the back with the butts of their stubby guns. The pain knocked the breath out of him and he fell hard to the deck.

They dragged Rick and Charlie up onto the bulwark and heaved them into the wake. Charlie disappeared without a sound. Rick screamed.

Ken scrambled to throw him a line. The divers knocked him down again. He rolled the length of the towing deck, got his hands on a Styrofoam float, and hurled it over the side. They caught up and hit him again and this time he lost the will to stand.

"Pick them up!" he pleaded. "They won't hurt you. They're just guys."

The boss looked down at him. "I asked you, how well do you know the Port of New York?"

Far behind the tug, Rick was still screaming, but Ken could hardly hear him now over the roar of the stacks. He looked up at the boss. How the hell long could Rick hang onto the float? The cold would kill him in an hour. Slowly. Thanks for the help, Ken. Owe you one.

"I know the port like the back of my hand," he answered, deliberately. "I was born here. I've worked a tug since I was twelve."

"Excellent. What is your name?"

"Ken Hughes. My men—"

"I am Tang Li, Admiral of the People's Liberation Army Submarine Expeditionary Force."

It would have sounded like something out of a comic book if the guy hadn't just thrown Rick and Charlie to the sharks. But he *had* thrown Rick and Charlie to the sharks, and "Expeditionary Force" sounded to Ken like a lot more than the two submarines he'd seen so far.

"Please pick up my men."

He saw in Tang Li's aloof expression that they wouldn't. That Rick and Charlie were as unimportant as dust. And he saw in the contempt veiling the commandos' eyes that they didn't think Ken would try to stand again.

That bought him one second.

They didn't imagine he would go over the side forty miles from land, either. Which bought him another.

He rolled over the bulwark, sliced into the water, and, swimming hard with his rubber fins, followed the flat, smooth path of the tugboat's wake back toward Rick.

"Rick!" he yelled.

He couldn't see him yet. Warm in the wet suit, propelled by his rubber fins, he could probably swim as far as Long Island if he didn't get lost.

"Rick!"

But he was praying the Chinese would come for their private harbor pilot. Without a wet suit, Rick didn't have a chance. That bullets weren't immediately tearing him apart told Ken that maybe he'd guessed right. Maybe they needed him alive.

No one knew local waters like a tugboatman. There'd never been a Chinese tugboatman in New York City, and no

Chinese port captains, either, that he knew of. Without him, their "expedition" would be entirely dependent on charts and the *Atlantic Coast Pilot*, which was like visiting New York with a Fodor's instead of with a friend who lived there.

"Rick!"

Rick's answering howl came from just ahead. Treading water, Ken rose high on a wave. There was the deckhand, clinging to the float with one arm, thrashing the water with the other. A huge, crazy grin lit his face when he saw Ken cutting toward him like a shark.

Ken stopped just out of reach. A panicked Rick was big enough to drag him under. "You okay?"

"Freezing." Rick's expression changed to terror. "Oh, God, here they come."

Ken whirled around. The *Chelsea Queen* loomed in the mist, ramming the seas white around her massive bow. Her bulwarks were thick with commandos. On the monkey island—the roof atop her wheelhouse—two sharpshooters poised with rifles. Astride her bow was the admiral, guiding the helmsman straight at him and Rick.

10

FOUR HOURS AFTER she had wrapped up Mayor Mincarelli's rescue fleet press-capade and finally fallen into bed,
Renata Bradley was dreaming that Rudy was making love to
her on a blanket on a beach. At first, in the dream, she
thought it was a dream, then realized with blinding joy that
it was not a dream: his wife had died and his children were
in boarding school.

Then it got scary. Something crawled out of the ocean
and up the beach and started poking her shoulder with an insistent claw. She brushed at it in her sleep, felt its sharp
hardness, and suddenly awoke. She catapulted out of the
sheets, heart pounding, sleep-deprived brain screaming
Giant waterbug.

It wasn't a waterbug. It was something even scarier. A
long, skinny, snakelike thing had slithered from under the
bathroom door, across the carpet, around the four television
sets propped facing her bed, and up the box spring and mat-
tress. (Two years in her high-rise apartment and she had yet

to find time to peel off the mover's stickers from her furniture, much less buy the rest of the bed.)

Backed against the window, brain kicking into high gear, she observed with relief that the thing nipping at the sheets was not alive, but mechanical. A long, stiff wire. When she heard an electric tool whining somewhere through the thin walls, she stalked to the intercom and buzzed the lobby of the block-long, thirty-story white brick apartment building.

"Get up here! Now!"

Five minutes later the super, a doorman, the concierge, and the building's old, old, part-time black handyman—who introduced himself as "Captain Eddie, the stationary engineer"—were standing around her bedroom apologizing. Somehow, they explained, the electric plumber's snake that old "Captain Eddie" had used to clear her upstairs neighbor's clogged drain had traveled past the clogged trap, down through the pipes, and found its way out her bathtub drain, under the bathroom door, and into her bed.

On any other morning—say a morning when she had had six hours of interrupted sleep—it might have been funny. This morning, Renata Bradley was not laughing. The super shuffled his work boots, the doorman picked at his gloves and looked longingly out the window at the high-rise across the street, and the banker-suited concierge cringed, acutely aware that this particular tenant—encased to her chin in a flannel nightgown, hair a-tangle, eyes wintry—was by dint of her position in Mayor Mincarelli's administration one of the most powerful women in the city of New York. And, like the mayor, was known more for her temper than for her sense of humor.

"Miz," Captain Eddie wheezed, "it's my fault and I take allllll responsibility. Tell 'em to fire me if you want. I was snaking and snaking and snaking and snaking, but all the time I was snaking here, my *mind* was *mis*-snaking down to the Intrepid Museum, where I volunteer my spare time. You know where the *Intrepid* is docked, miz, on the Hudson, pier 86?"

"I was there four hours ago."

"Me, too! And that's the other reason I was mis-snakin' here, being so tired, up all night. But I wouldn'ta missed that fleet steamin' to the rescue. Reminded me of the war. You see, I was in convoys, and—"

Suddenly all four televisions flickered on at once—Renata's wake-up alarm—simultaneously blaring *This Morning, Today, Good Day New York,* and *Good Morning America*. She unmuted the sound on *Today,* which was rolling a clip of Rudy at the docks the night before.

"All right," she said. "Get out of here! All of you. And take that stupid thing with you."

She surfed the news over three coffees while they extracted their snake, then took a fast shower in a tub smeared with boot and finger prints, and telephoned Mayor Mincarelli for their morning exchange of tidbits. Rudy loved the snake story.

"Yeah, well, it wasn't in *your* bed."

"Work it into my road speech. It's New York. They'll love it out there. Whadd'ya think of last night?"

"Today was the best. *Good Morning America* wasted all your time on shots of those dammed ships."

"See the *Post?"* Rudy asked.

"What?"

"Front page with that Navy kid."

"You're kidding! Fantastic."

Rudy's cold sounded better and when he promised Renata he would catch a little more sleep until his eleven o'-clock, she knew it was a lie.

Still, she canceled her pickup, looped her necklace of plastic IDs and key cards around her neck, and walked to Gracie Mansion—ten stolen minutes of peaceful East Side streets, greenery oozing oxygen, old ladies walking dogs, smiling doormen, porters hosing the sidewalks, flower beds encircling the trees.

At nine-thirty in the morning, Gracie Square was so still she could hear birds singing in Carl Schurz Park. The private-school kids were all in class by now, the Wall Streeters car-serviced to their offices, lawyers downtown finishing breakfast meetings.

She passed a pair of lovers holding hands, and looked back enviously: they were dressed for work, probably late and not caring.

Gracie Mansion was ahead, across East End Avenue, a two-story clapboard house, draped with porches, that stood among lawns and gardens beside the East River. When the President of the United States had visited Rudy, he had called the mayor's official mayoral residence the greatest political perk in the nation. Rudy had told the President he liked *his* house, too.

Renata dodged a nurse wheeling an elderly patient into the sunshine outside Beth Israel Hospital North and quickened her pace. Verifying her morning schedule on her Palm Pilot while waiting to cross East End on the green light, she then headed for the iron gate, her shoulders tightening, her expression set, and her face seeming to gather years.

She glanced down, checking her outfit for lint and stray threads, and discovered in the bright sunlight that she had mismatched her suit, accidentally donning a navy jacket over a black skirt. Which meant that she would have to re-member to hide her lower half behind the podium today—a pain in the butt, as she preferred moving around the stage with a wireless mike while jousting with the media.

The cop at the gatehouse saluted. "Good morning, Ms. Bradley."

"Is Officer Greene on today?"

Rudy had discovered that the rookie patrol officer attached to Gracie Mansion's security detail was the daughter of a thirty-year veteran still walking patrol at City Hall.

"She's in the garden, ma'am."

Renata hurried through the gates and swung past the house into the gardens that cantilevered over the FDR Drive. There she spotted P.O. Harriet Greene, a tall, striking, black female cop with cheekbones the camera would love. Harriet appeared to be lecturing her partner, P.O. Hector Sanchez, a stubby, light-skinned Hispanic blinking up at her through his eyeglasses.

They weren't officially partners, as the NYPD teamed rookies with older cops to break them in. But the mayor's chief bodyguard and his head driver reasoned—or so they had told Renata—that the rookies couldn't do too much damage let loose, occasionally, in Gracie Mansion's garden.

"Officer Greene."

"Good morning, Ms. Bradley," replied the female rookie.

"*Live at Five* is doing a Father Day's profile on your dad and you. They'll shoot you here, Thursday morning. Get here by eight to see Monique."

"Yes, ma'am—who's Monique?"

"Makeup and hair."

"What about Officer Sanchez?"

"What about him?"

"Will they interview my partner, too?"

Renata looked at Hector Sanchez, who had a round, earnest face—a face made for radio.

"Sanchez, is your father on the force, too?"

Sanchez looked at his feet. "No, ma'am."

"Then you can't be on television."

"Hector goes to night school," Harriet Greene volunteered. "He's a prelaw student."

"Really? Thank you. That's very interesting. I will keep you in mind, Officer Sanchez. Thursday morning, Harriet."

She could see it already—crosscutting a bunch of hardworking young cops between the street and a night-school class heavy on ethnics—College Cops. Rudy would love it. Maybe Fox. Even *Nightline*.

Ten minutes after the markets opened, Phil Levy rushed into the Bishop & Levy trading room atop the World Wide Building, which offered orbiting-satellite views of the Hudson River to traders who rarely looked up from their twenty-inch split screens.

Gill Bishop, who spent every minute of his waking life on the telephone playing Mr. Inside Information to Phil Levy's Mr. Outside Investor-seducing Rainmaker, was holding two phones, and calling buy and sell orders to the hunched-over traders. He wore his usual smear of cream cheese where his bagel had collided with his cheek, and his shirt looked like he had slept in his office. (Neither Phil's four-thousand-dollar suit nor the four-hundred-dollar shirt beneath betrayed where the rainmaker had passed his night.)

Like all hedge-fund managers, Phil Levy and Gill Bishop restricted membership in their investment pool to ninety-nine, which exempted them from filing certain presumptuous paperwork with the Securities and Exchange Commission—exactly how their ninety-nine clients liked it. But if all hedge funds operated in the shadows, then Bishop & Levy's private partnership operated deep inside the belly of a crocodile, according to an *Economist* survey of the high-risk, high-profit derivatives trading business.

The Economist had gotten the crocodile idea from Phil complaining, off the record to their sympathetic reporter, that his cheapskate partner would prefer to maintain offices in a sewer—not just for the privacy, but also for the opportunity to invest the money they would save on furniture.

He and Gill were both "idea men," Phil had explained. But since it was his job to entice their wealthy clients into investing deep in the new funds he and Gill were constantly dreaming up, Phil regarded cash spent on decor as an investment in its own right: thus their trading floor fifty stories above midtown Manhattan; thus his baronial private office; thus the antiquities that hung in B&L's teak-and-nickel reception room—decorated with a blank check by Phil's wife.

Gill swiveled both phones from his mouth to whisper, "Say, I called your car phone. You weren't picking up."

Phil said there was something wrong with the battery.

"You planning on getting it fixed? In case your partner has to talk to you."

Phil thought he heard a certain testiness, or even suspicion, in Gill's tone and hastened to smooth things over. "I picked up a new one. That's why I'm late." He glanced over the shoulders of their busy traders at their screens. "What's up?"

Gill's job was to net caviar and lobster from the daily flood of information that could either drown or sustain them. Day and night his message board blinked like Times Square. (Phil had neglected to inform *The Economist* that Gill had a few select clients of his own who could meet the fund's merciless net-worth requirement with their pocket change, making Gill, for all intents and purposes, senior partner.)

Mr. Inside Information gave a yellow-toothed smile. "To quote my all-time favorite *New Yorker* cartoon, 'Every bubblehead with a buck is back in the market, thank God.' And what are they selling this morning, bless their predictable little hearts? Cruise lines. Less obvious is why certain Chinese generals are shorting New York City bonds."

Sometimes Gill would hit Phil with information so obscure, obtained by a gathering process so arcane, that Phil's feeling of self-worth plummeted as low as it had two years ago, when, in the men's room of the Pierre, a famous old Goldman partner had called across urinals to inform Phil, and everyone else listening, "Young man, you are playing

Salieri to Gill Bishop's Mozart." After Phil had looked up Salieri, he had decided it was time to change his life. (There were many ways to get respect in New York City, but a downtown girlfriend was turning out to be the most expensive.)

"How do you know?" Phil asked, meaning how could *anyone* know that certain Chinese generals—not all Chinese generals, not one particular Chinese general, but certain Chinese generals—were selling New York City bonds.

"I know," said Gill. "I just don't know why. Yet."

Phil tried to look sage. Everybody knew that the Communist Chinese military had a lot of capital invested outside China, both through People's Liberation Army businesses and in private accounts held by the highest-ranking officers who had skimmed millions. Generally speaking, he knew too well, investors who had stolen their fortunes preferred the safety of bonds.

"But they love bonds."

"Well, maybe they know something about *New York* bonds we don't."

11

KATE ROSS HUDDLED over the stuttering outboard like it was Mother, Father, and her only friend. The Zodiac slammed wave top to wave top as the shallower water caused the seas to fetch in a close chop. Despite her efforts to steer around the worst of it, the rigid bottom bounced hard, the side tubes flexed, the motor roar jumped in pitch every time the propeller churned too high in the water.

By her watch and an educated guess at her speed, she should see the coastline already. But all that lay ahead was empty haze at the edge of a diminishing visibility.

She was still as baffled, and frightened, as when Ken had first thrashed to the surface yelling for her to run. But the more details she replayed in her memory, the more convinced she was that the divers who had swarmed after him and those who had fired at her from the tug were military men rather than ordinary criminals—soldiers, not smugglers. Rick and old Charlie had been wrong about the submarine: it wasn't a Nazi U-boat; it wasn't a fifty-year-old tomb; its divers were very much alive and most certainly not German. And apparently not alone.

The haze was thickening, cloud smearing the sky, the sun shrinking to a dull white dot. If she lost sight of the sun completely, she'd have nothing to steer by except the waves, which the invisible coast was roiling too chaotically to be of use. She'd end up traveling in circles until she ran out of gas.

Memories of Ken laced between her fears, swelled, seized her mind. In bed they had come together freely and playfully.

A booming hollow groan blew her thoughts to pieces. Her stomach leaped—another submarine? She looked around. Nothing but gray. Then she raised her eyes up and up and saw, to her disbelief, a tall gray hull so wide it seemed to span the horizon.

She ripped the outboard around and the Zodiac started to turn. But before she could steer free of it, the boat bounced sideways, into the slow-moving hull.

She was thrown to the floor of the boat, picked herself up, and throttled back the madly screaming engine. High overhead, men were yelling down at her: "You nuts? Wake up!"

A ship. A gigantic, slow-moving freighter, gray as the water and the sky.

The freighter was an Atlantic Line's container ship inbound from Rotterdam, her captain a middle-aged American in a foul mood. First he'd been diverted to aid the sinking cruise ship, which had so much help that rescuers were bumping noses; then an oil pump had failed, and with it his power; then, just when he'd got the pump changed out and his ship moving again, he had to stop to pick up a crazy woman in a Zodiac.

"You don't believe me," she said.

"I don't have to believe you. Tell it to the Coast Guard."

He slapped a VHF radio into her hand and stalked out onto the bridge wing for a cigarette.

"He's pissed," explained the third mate, who looked young enough to be in high school. "We're way late."

The Coast Guard duty officer Kate raised on Channel 16 cut off her first babble of words with a brusque lecture on the misuse of emergency channels and told her to call back on 18. When Kate repeated her story, he told her to sit tight.

She waited, shivering as the air-conditioning blew on her wet clothes. Five long minutes passed. She wanted to find a blanket, but she feared that if she left the bridge the captain wouldn't let her back. Finally the Coast Guard radioed. An officer, this time, a woman, listened in silence as Kate again repeated her story.

"If you don't believe me," Kate finished, "try raising the *Chelsea Queen* on your VHF."

"We just did," the officer said gently. "Captain Hughes reports no submarine, no Chinese divers, and no missing Zodiac."

"He's alive? Oh, thank God." The relief swelled warm and solid in her chest, filled her throat, and squeezed tears from her eyes.

The woman said, gently again, "Would you put the ship's master back on the air, please, ma'am?"

He still existed. Even though Kate had abandoned him, even though she had run, they had been granted a second chance. His life was a gift.

The young mate reached for the handset and took it from her unresisting hand. Kate watched him carry it out to the captain on the bridge wing, watched them confer, heads bent, casting furtive glances toward her. That snapped her back to the grim reality that Ken was still in danger, still needed her help. But she could see in their faces that when the ship docked, Bellevue Hospital attendants would be waiting for her, serene in white.

She fished Jose Chin's card from her jeans. It was soaking wet and fell apart in her fingers. Frantically, she juggled the pieces into the reporter's telephone number. The juvenile third mate had come back in from the bridge wing. He was watching warily. Kate gathered her spirit, regained control of her face, and carefully manufactured what a cynical literary agent had once dubbed her Promises Smile.

"Do you have a cellphone on your ship?"

Out on eastern Long Island, eighty-five miles from New York City, Jose Chin was glaring at the monitor on his camera, which he had tuned to pick up CBS. Those Channel 2 bastards had two choppers circling the listing, smoke-shrouded cruise ship, while Jasbir's taxi was parked, ticking its meter, beside a littered stretch of sand beach next to the Peconic Bay. Jose had a view of the entrance to the Shinnecock Canal, which supposedly led to the ocean, but no sign of the doper boat Ken's buddy had promised would speed him to the sinking.

A soft, watery crackle of radio chatter filled the minivan. Two Radio Shack 1000 Channel Pro-2035 Hyperscans and a Realistic two-way were trolling the airwaves at once. Jasbir had wired the scanners to separate speakers. Cops murmured from the right; fire from the left; ambulances under the passenger seat.

Jasbir himself was pacing the potholed road, ear bent to Jose's backup cellphone, renegotiating his $226,000 Freshstart taxi loan. With recent interest-rate drops, he had explained, the money he had borrowed to buy the minivan and the city medallion should be costing him less than thirty-one hundred dollars a month.

Jose didn't care that his own financial life amounted to spending half his income to rent an East Village Roach Motel—because he was going to be a millionaire anchor one day. He turned to ABC, where Peter Jennings had a blimp with three cameras focused on the burning ship, a nautical-graybeard talking head in the studio explaining why the ship wouldn't sink, unless it did sink, and, on the monitor, a shaved-head, ex-Navy SEAL speculating whether the wreckage of a sailboat floating nearby indicated that terrorists had exploded a "suicide mine" against the ship.

Jose reached to dial the dope runner again, but before he could, the cellphone sang in his hand.

"Jose wants to know."

"Jose Chin?" asked a woman, a very frantic woman.

"You got him. What's the story?"

"I'm Kate Ross. We met this morning on Ken's tugboat?"

"The editor. What's happening? You want my book?"

"You're not going to believe this."

"Try me."

"We were heading to the cruise ship. Ken dove to attach a salvage buoy to a sunken submarine. Divers came up and tried to kill him and boarded the tug. Ken helped me get away."

"Jose does not believe you."

"Of course you don't. But will you please ask yourself why I am telling you this?"

"That's why I'm listening. Plus, I checked you out in the taxi. *Publishers Weekly* says you're going to be hot stuff someday. Tell me more."

"*More?* Are you listening to me! They attacked Ken."

"Ken alive?"

"I think so." She started to cry—the gift she didn't deserve, the sheer luck—then controlled herself to choke out the words. "He told me to run. He protected me."

"Who were they?"

"I don't know. They acted like a military unit."

"How do you know what a military unit acts like?"

"I mean they acted in concert. They wore identical gear.

They weren't a 'gang.' They were soldiers. The ones I saw were all Chinese and they communicated in Chinese. And there might have been a second submarine. Ken yelled something about it and I thought I saw one surface."

"Where are you now?"

"Ken helped me get away in the Zodiac. A freighter picked me up. It's heading for New York."

"They believe you?"

"No. Neither does the Coast Guard."

"Why don't you tell them to radio Ken's tug?"

"They did. They said Ken answered and is fine. They think I'm crazy."

"Why call me?"

"I'm worried sick about Ken. No one can help him."

"But why call me?"

" 'Jose Wants to Know.' Besides, you're supposed to be his friend."

"Give me a number where I can reach you."

"What are you going to do?"

"Give me your number."

He wrote down the number of her freighter's cellphone, hung up, and dialed Ken's cellphone. After four rings, the mellifluous James Earl Jones welcomed him to Bell Atlantic and then a recording informed him that the cellular customer he was calling was out of range or away from his phone.

Okay.

Jose dialed Ken's beeper and punched in his call-back number. Two minutes later Ken called back. PW's poster girl was hot stuff, maybe, but also a kook. Still, just in case Captain Ken was surrounded by Fu Manchu frogmen pointing spear guns at him, Jose played it cool.

"Jose wants to know, Cap. Is the editor nuts?"

"No." Curt as a 911 operator.

Oboy.

Picture this, Jose: Captain Ken held prisoner on his tug

by a bunch of scuba-diving commandos talking Chinese; they don't let him answer his phone. But when he's beeped, Ken thinks fast and tells them—if any speak English, that is—that other tugs will put out a May Day and come looking for him if he doesn't reply.

Or picture this: they're trying to assess what effect the woman escaping has on their plans; who has she told what? did they believe her?

Or picture this: they don't particularly give a damn, because whatever the hell they're in mind to do they're going to do before anyone can stop them. So the question is, when?

"Can you meet me at Pier Twenty-five in four hours?"

"Less than thr—" Ken's answer ended in what could have been a grunt of pain. Whatever, the phone went emphatically dead. And when Jose called back, James Earl Jones was covering.

His beeper nudged his side.

A GeekNet pager report quoted a Navy firefighter saying that the explosion on the cruise ship looked like it was external—as if the ship had struck a mine.

The GeekNet was an informal network of dedicated, volunteer disaster junkies who monitored every radio signal known to man and beeped out an unending flood of fires, accidents, explosions, and rescue efforts. While the GeekNet offered a reporter a constant heads up, it was raw stuff—a one-alarm fire in Nashville, Tennessee, got equal billing with a four-alarmer "not expected to hold" in Brooklyn.

Already this morning, GeekNet had reported the wrecked sailboat near the cruise ship—which was probably how Peter Jennings's billion-dollar network had nailed its scoop—along with speculation that Arabs had sailed a bomb in it; next had come a rumor that a fisherman had observed the U.S. Navy shoot the ship with a missile. If Krazy Kate hadn't called, Jose would have slotted this latest into the same wait-and-see file.

"Jasbir! Back to New York."

Jose telephoned Kate on the freighter and said, "Okay. Tell me—"

"Is he okay?"

"Sounded fine."

"Oh, thank God. Thank you, Jose. Thank God, thank God."

Then she started crying again, and this time she couldn't stop.

"Hey, hey, what are you doing? I told you, I talked to him, he's fine. Tell me exactly what happened."

"Just give me a second to—oh, God, I'm so relieved." She continued crying.

"Correct me if I'm wrong: you've known the guy two days?"

"You don't understand. He saved my life. But I left him—"

"Okay, okay. Give me the story. What the hell happened?"

He had his palmtop open on his lap and his hands-free headset on his ear and he typed down every word she said. When she was done he asked, "Where's your ship going?"

"Brooklyn. I'm going to try to get off on the pilot boat. I've got to help him."

"I want to shoot an interview with you as soon as we figure out what's happening—exclusive, okay?"

He telephoned Arnie. His news director had been doubling as Jose's producer since his regular producer had been axed by the station's new owners' cost-cutting, profit-inflating efforts to sell it again.

"Jose's got something big."

"Has Jose shot any bodies? CNN says the ship's almost evacuated."

"Not yet."

"What's wrong with you??"

"I haven't seen any yet."

"You still on *land?*"

"Without a chopper—"

"Before they invented choppers, good reporters still got the story—they're flying injured into Bayshore Hospital."

"I already stopped there on my way out. It's a gang bang. Eighty reporters getting zip from PR."

"Get over to the Suffolk County Morgue and shoot a line of ambulances."

"This thing is bigger than bodies."

Arnie stopped yelling. Washed up, burned out, dead meat the news director surely was, but he'd been big-time once— before the bankers gutted network news and threw the Arnies on the cable junk heap—and he had a nose for news. And maybe, Jose guessed, there weren't enough passengers drowned to give the sinking story legs.

"Whaddaya got, kid?"

"Chinese submarine attacks New York tugboat."

"Fuck you, wise guy." Arnie hung up.

Jose yelled at Jasbir. "Go faster."

"Your press plates do not make my taxicab invisible," Jasbir replied in English so precise he might have come from the country that invented it, instead of from a region in the north of India that sounded even worse than the Guang-dong village from which Jose's grandfather had escaped the Cultural Revolution, or from the long-ago-bulldozed San Juan slum the very mention of which would send his Puerto Rican grandmother straight to her rosary beads.

"I'll explain if they pull you over."

"This is not New York City," said Jasbir, his speedometer rock-steady on seventy-three miles per hour. A glance out the window confirmed that. Goddamned pine trees and pickup trucks.

"We gotta hit the Suffolk County Morgue."

"It's in Hauppauge," said Jasbir, who knew weird stuff.

Jose pondered where to shoot exciting pictures that he'd want his name attached to. "Jasbir, you want to hear something crazy?"

He told the taxi driver everything he knew so far, and concluded, "Who knows? Maybe Kate's nuts. Maybe Ken didn't mean anything. Maybe they had a fight and she jumped onto another boat."

"In the middle of the ocean, I doubt that is easily done," said Jasbir.

Pine trees gave way abruptly to strip malls. Jasbir found the morgue. But there was no line of ambulances, no flocks of choppers fluttering out of the sky. A sign directed all visitors to the front entrance.

"Back door," he told Jasbir.

He trudged in, camera on his shoulder, expecting zilch.

The attendants in dirty whites seemed happy to see him. Why the hell not? A genuine New York reporter was aiming a TV camera in their faces, which fell when Jose asked, "Jose wants to know, how many New York cruise-ship passengers perished in the explosion that ripped through the *Sovereign Princess* in the middle of the night on the Atlantic Ocean?"

The attendants shuffled their running shoes.

Jose looked sternly around the viewfinder and said, "Guys, I ask. You answer—" They were standing there like houseplants. "Hang on."

From his pack he fished out a fat microphone emblazoned with a big New York Yes! mike flag and shoved it into their hands. It wasn't wired to anything, but props always broke the ice.

"Ready? Three, two, one . . . Jose wants to know, how many New York cruise-ship passengers perished when the explosion ripped through the *Sovereign Princess?*"

"Two," the morgue rats chorused into the mike.

"Two?"

"A male and a female."

"Jesus Christ! What am I doing here?"

He turned off the camera.

"The male wasn't dead yet."

"What?" Jose turned the camera on again and the two attendants brightened. "Quickly," he urged. Any second now, their boss was going to walk in and kick him out.

"They brought him in thinking he was dead, but he was only a little dead."

"Where is he?"

"We got him in the back."

Jose flashed on an image of the passenger with his feet up, drinking coffee and chilling with the corpses. It reeked of Pulitzer. "Jose wants to meet him."

"He's dead."

"You said—"

"He, like, sat up a little, spoke, and fell over. We got the doctor in right away, but by then he was dead again. The doc pronounced him, for sure."

"Jose wants to know. You're telling New York Yes! they brought in a guy alive, thinking he was dead?"

"Happens all the time."

"Wait. You said he spoke? Wha'd he say?"

"He kept mumbling, 'Rita, Rita, Rita.' "

"Rita?"

"That's the name of the other one. It's his wife."

"She dead?"

"Oh, yeah."

This sounded more like a story. "Where they from?" Please God, say New York.

"Queens."

Bingo. Real people. "How old?"

"He's forty-one. She's thirty. Was."

Right down the middle, neither sadly old nor tragically young. "Any kids?"

"They were on their honeymoon."

Yes!

"What else did he say?"

"He was pretty out of it. Just mumbling."

"What did he mumble?"

The morgue rats looked at each other, slumped their shoulders, and went back to shuffling.

"What?" asked Jose.

"Joe heard one thing, I heard another."

Jose turned the camera on Joe. "Joe, wha'd you hear? Speak into the mike."

"Like, he was talking to his wife. Like, he goes, sort of like, 'Rita, go.' Like he's saying, 'Run!' "

Jose turned to the other guy. What was his name? Dave. "What did you hear, Dave? Joe, give Dave the mike."

"He didn't say, 'Rita, go.' "

"So what did he say?" asked Jose.

"He said, 'Torpedo.' "

12

"ARNIE, YOU GOTTA hear this—I got a morgue guy who says a dead guy on the ship told him it was a torpedo."

Arnie was silent.

"I mean before he died."

"Oh, yeah?"

"GeekNet says the explosion came from outside."

"Told you, I already heard that," said Arnie. "Maybe a Navy diver said it, maybe he didn't."

"I got a report of submarines attacking a tugboat. I got a report of a torpedo sinking the cruise ship."

"You got these 'reports' on tape?"

"I got the morgue guys on tape."

"What's the story?"

"What's the story? How about an invasion?"

"What do you mean, invasion?"

"Like a war?" Jose ventured.

There was a long silence. Then a flat, almost sad response, as if this time Jose had really hurt him. "Kid? Who drove all the way out to goddamned—Jesus, where the hell was it, Pennsylvania?"

"You did, Arnie." Even Pennsylvania was closer to New York than most TV reporters ever got in their life.

"Who gave you a three-pound broadcast-quality Panasonic DVC you could carry yourself without no union lard-ass humping your gear? Who got the station to pay for them little video modules to shoot the school guards' scam?"

"I'm grateful, Arnie," Jose answered sincerely.

"Jerking me around isn't grateful. Get your ass out on that ship. I'll cover any wars that come up."

Arnie hung up. Jasbir discovered a traffic jam in the middle of a six-lane highway in the middle of nowhere, and Jose—mystified by the weird stuff he'd heard, and powerless to do anything about it, much less shoot it—slid into a deep, uncharacteristic gloom.

Even the ceaseless fountains of chatter from the scanners had lost their usual blood-pumping appeal. But he was wasting time moping. And if there was one thing he couldn't stand, it was blowing the day sitting still. Do something! This wasn't the only story he was tracking.

His fingers flew, punching number after number from memory. He telephoned an NYPD detective for a mug shot for a follow-up story on a car jacking; touched base with another cop who had tipped him to an ATF gun bust maybe planned for the weekend, maybe not; sent a heads up to the New York Yes! traffic reporter about a Queens tractor-trailer collision he picked off the scanner; and returned a call from a limo driver who was feeding *him* tips about a big rap star's encounters with some DA's detectives.

Suddenly, Jose got an idea, a really wild idea that scared him. It scared him so much that instead of acting on it, he telephoned a heads up to a Fire Department public-information contact that he had the witness he needed to break an inspector-bribe story.

Hesitation was as uncharacteristic of Jose as gloom, but this was one weird day. Biggest disaster of the century and no coverage. No pictures. No bites. He had to stir the pot. Finally, he speed-dialed his personal contact in the mayor's office.

"Hey, Chin! What's up?"

Larry Neale was His Honor's press secretary's third assistant. He was usually stuck at Gracie Mansion, working the phones and puffing press releases while the mayor and Renata Bradley had all the fun taunting reporters downtown at City Hall. But today, the mayor was home with a cold.

"Jose's gotta talk to your boss."

"She's with the mayor and she won't talk to you anyhow. I will relay your question and get back to you in due course. All of which you know already, so why are you wasting our time asking the impossible?"

Jose took a deep breath. This was a lie that could get him banished permanently to some place that would make Pennsylvania seem exciting. "It's about that other thing."

"What other thing?"

"You know. What you said the other night."

Larry breathed noisily into the phone. "Hey, I just thought maybe you two would click."

"So . . ."

Another breathy pause. "What do you want me to do? You want me to ask Renata if she'll have a drink with you?"

"No! I'll ask her myself. I'll ask her for dinner."

This was complicated.

Larry—Jose's door into Gracie Mansion, and probably his best inside contact in the entire city—was a paternal kind of gay guy who worshipped his young boss. The two had met, fresh out of school, on some forgotten congressional campaign and stayed friends to the extent that Renata Bradley had time for friends.

Larry worried about Renata's long hours and resultant empty love life, and had taken it into his head that she might "click" with Jose.

Jose had laughed it off. Everybody knew she was hot for the mayor. But Larry—tanked on Jaegermeisters after a nineteen-hour day fielding queries about how His Honor's recycling crackdown had somehow led to the NYPD's strip searching a grandmotherly landlady—had insisted that as unlikely as a match might sound, he had an eye for these things. At worst, Gracie Mansion's Renata Bradley and New York Yes!'s Jose Chin might become friends; at best, they'd be turning out multimedia babies after a Page Six engagement and a *Vanity Fair* marriage.

"But she's hot for the mayor," Jose had protested.

Larry had gotten very cold. Funny how a fat man's face could turn so hard. "Don't believe everything you read."

They'd left it at that—a barroom confidence at the end of a night neither was obliged to remember.

Jose hesitated. This was his last chance not to throw his entire career down the toilet. But, Christ, if he was right, Renata and the mayor himself would owe him big-time forever. And Jose Chin would be smack in the middle of the biggest story in history.

Larry stopped in the men's room to tuck his shirt in over his gut and splash cold water on his face and comb his hair and ask the brutal mirror, What am I doing here?

All of his friends were buff. But since he'd taken this insane job, he'd stopped going to the gym and had gained forty pounds from desk lunches, pizza dinners, and midnight bar burgers with low-life news junkies like Jose Chin.

He found Renata at her desk outside the mayor's office.

"Can we talk?" asked Larry, when Renata hung up a phone. She had kicked her shoes off, usually a good sign she was approachable. He went on, albeit tentatively, "I've got Jose Chin on line one."

"*New York Yes?* I thought the Health Department shut them down." Her life had narrowed to the extent that even her jokes were the mayor's jokes. "What does the scum want?"

"To talk to you."

"Handle it."

"I can't. He's straight. I'm not straight."

She stopped in mid-grab at another phone. "Your sex life does not come as news, Larry. Though we did agree that you wouldn't flaunt it." She was learning manners from the mayor, too. "What are you saying?"

"He wants a date."

"With *me?* Jose Chin wants a date with me? Are you jerking me around? I'm busy."

"He's a really cute guy, Renata."

"I've seen him."

"And?"

"He's a really cute guy."

"With a killer smile. Go out with him. Have some fun."

"Go out with the jerk who did that story about Rudy mandating a dress code for tourists?"

"It was an April Fools joke," said Larry. "Remember jokes, before 'the Boss' became 'Il Duce'?" God, he was getting brave; next he'd ask for a promotion.

Renata's warning glance was heart-shriveling. Larry backpedaled. "He did it with affection and respect for the mayor. And not such a bad idea, when you see them wearing tank tops to the theater."

"That low-life scum excuse for a journalist would sell his sister for a ten-second spot on his bottom-feeding station."

"That is not true," said Larry. He knew for a fact that Jose's only sibling was his brother, Juan. "And don't forget, you liked his 'Paranoia Poll.' "

"Liked" was putting it strongly, but Jose Chin had shot a

New York Yes! opinion poll in bars and living rooms, health clubs and dance clubs, subways and taxicabs, in which a variety of photogenic New Yorkers agreed that their mayor probably wasn't that much more paranoid than many people they knew, worked with, or lived downstairs from.

"Get rid of him. I don't have time for that stuff."

Larry screwed up his courage again. "You mean you don't have the guts for that stuff."

"Go away, Larry."

"You're hiding in this job. You're hiding behind the mayor. You're hiding from life. You're hiding from love. You're hiding from sex."

"Larry, get out of here while you're still employed."

"You're twenty-eight and you're acting fifty-eight and soon you will be and you'll have nobody but yourself to blame when you're a dried-up old lady getting interviewed by graduate students writing term papers about the mayor's career."

"Put him on."

Larry punched up the line on her phone, said, "Here she is," to Jose and handed it to her with a whispered, "Be nice."

"He's dead meat if he says, 'Jose wants to know.' "

"He won't," Larry prayed.

"Hi," said Renata, shooing him away. "Larry says you want to ask me out. I gotta tell you I have a schedule like you wouldn't believe, but Larry says I'm going to end up a dried-up old lady and that you're the best thing on that skeezy station, which isn't saying much, but I'm willing to take a chance—seeing as how your 'Paranoia Profile' was a cool piece, considering—You got your calendar and a pencil? How are you end of July—make that early August—mid-August?"

"Promise me one thing," said Jose Chin.

"Promise? What promise? I don't even know you."

"Promise me you'll think about what I said after you hang up on me."

"Are you asking me out or not?"

"I'm going to tell you something. You're going to hang up on me. Ready?"

"Jose, I don't have time for this crap."

"A Chinese submarine sank that cruise ship. Another Chinese submarine's kidnapped a New York tugboat captain. That's two submarines, and I've got at least one source that's pretty sure there are more."

Amazingly, she hadn't hung up yet. More amazingly, she said, "Yeah?"

"I think they might be heading for the city."

Renata Bradley hung up on Jose, buzzed Larry, told him to clear out his desk.

"All he wanted was a date," Larry protested.

"He didn't want a date, you idiot. He was fishing."

"For what?"

Every piece of garbage she'd ever had to swallow from the press, every media insult heaped on Rudy, every word of gossip published about her, every time the so-called free press had blindsided her—all this had suddenly fused in the person of Jose Chin and she was too angry to think straight. "Don't you get it?" she roared at Larry. "It was a setup. He was trying to hustle me into confirming some joke rumor—and *you* let him. Goodbye."

"But we're friends."

"I don't have any friends." Renata Bradley banged down the phone, buzzed the mansion's NYPD security detail and told them to escort Larry and his belongings to the crosstown bus.

Larry didn't even want to think how he was going to pay his rent. All he knew, as his bus entered the Central Park Transverse, was that he had had more than enough of the straight world for one day.

Miserable, frightened and humiliated, he cellphoned Jon, the first friend he had made when he came to New York—Jon who used to say, "It's better to call yourself the 'younger man,' than me the older."

Larry told Jon he'd been fired. Jon said, "You're a good PR man, you'll get another job."

Easy for Jon to say. The owner of *Jon's Chelsea Couture* and *Jon's Luncheon Yacht* had gotten rich in the booming 1990s selling hipness to the unhip, fashion to the unfashionable, art to the inarticulate.

"My Rolodex was getting so hot," Larry moaned. "One more year in the mayor's office and I could have been a star."

"In the meantime," said Jon, "I'm short a waiter. If you can get down to the North Cove Marina in twenty minutes in a clean white shirt, we'll probably still be here. Peter's 'yacht' has a broken motor."

Larry sure as hell didn't feel like waiting tables, but he knew it was Jon's way of saying that he'd feel better hanging out with friends. He transferred to the downtown C train, got off at the World Trade Center, ran through the World Financial Center and out its glass-walled Winter Garden, which overlooked the river.

Anchored in the Hudson, off the North Cove, was the missile frigate *Zhaotong*—a long, battle-gray reminder of the job Larry had just lost. He had almost nailed a Mayor Rudy goodwill photo-op with the Chinese sailors when, all of a sudden, the PLA PR lady had stopped returning his calls.

Jon's Luncheon Yacht—a dinner-cruise boat leased for the afternoon—was still tied to the dock. Larry dodged a gang of Caterpillar Engine mechanics and panted aboard. A hundred pastel ladies were draining prelunch martinis and Manhattans in the main cabin as models paraded the latest Chelsea Couture on a runway that snaked among the tables.

Jon and skinny young Peter were watching from the kitchen door, quarreling as usual.

"Designer?" Peter led off. "Did you say designer?" Midday, Kate Ross's upstairs neighbor had exchanged most of his leather costume for linen. "You're not a designer. You're a decorator."

Larry thought that Jon looked a little too Prozac-ed today to put a sincere effort into the fight. But Peter, who had recently emerged blinking into the daylight from his core business servicing the upscale S&M market in the meat-packing district, appeared willing to help him out. "You slap a bow on a Geoffrey Beene silhouette and call it couture. Honey, that ain't design."

Jon said, "Hello, Larry; you've perspired all over your shirt. Would you like to know why Peter is trashing my designs?"

"No," said Larry, copping a roll from a passing busboy. He was glad already he had come. This was much more fun than getting fired. In the thin sliver of river visible from Jon's boat he noticed the *Zhaotong* emit a puff of blue from its smokestack, and sailors swarming on her decks.

"Peter feels *guilty* that this boat he rented won't work. I've got a hundred clients lapping up a six-thousand-dollar lunch Peter ordered from a 'caterer' friend and we're *still tied to the dock.*"

Oddly, thought Larry, the Chinese were lowering the American flag that port protocol required a visiting foreign ship to fly from its masthead.

"Where are you going with that?" Peter demanded of a distressed waiter who was hurrying a full plate *back* to the kitchen.

Larry snatched a wild mushroom.

"That rich old lady they call the Countess? The Holocaust survivor?"

"Now what?"

"She says she can't eat if her chicken is touching her vegetables."

"It's *game hen* and if she survived the Holocaust, she'll survive game hen touching carrots." Peter moved the offending chicken with the filter end of his cigarette, and resumed making excuses for the yacht's motor.

Jon said to Larry, with a significant nod at the kitchen door, "If you came to help . . ."

"Look at that," said Larry. "That ship is raising the Chinese flag."

"Perhaps they're Chinese," said Jon.

"They're not supposed to fly their own flag. I checked out the protocol when I was setting up Fleet Week visits for the mayor. You don't fly your own flag in someone else's port. Supposedly, it's an old custom to show that you're not an enemy attacking."

Jon said, "Rest assured, you're the only person in New York who knows that—ohmigod! Look at that."

Larry and Peter exchanged shrugs; nothing unusual about the coked-to-her-hairline model slouching toward the runway.

"Dear!" Jon growled. "Your eyelash is hanging from your earring."

She returned a doe-eyed sneer. "What are you, from the Upper West Side? That *is* my earring."

"Am I getting too old for this?" Jon asked Larry.

A seasoned political spinmeister should have been able to look Jon in the eye and suggest that despite a faithful intake of DHEA, melatonin, testosterone, and hGh to enhance his memory, Viagra to goose his sex drive, and botulism injections to paralyze his wrinkles, maybe it *was* time to open that cozy inn in Columbia County.

Instead, Larry pretended new interest in the harbor. The *Zhaotong* had steamed away.

*   *   *

The *Deng Xiaoping*'s deep wake trailed whirlpools on the harbor's surface where whirlpools weren't known to stir.

Undetected, the lead submarine penetrated the port entrance at Sandy Hook. She ran up the Ambrose and Anchorage channels, the Verrazano Narrows, and the Upper Bay. Then she turned between Governors Island and Manhattan Island's Battery and tried to enter the East River.

Her young captain, Tang Qui—Tang Two, as his sailors distinguished their skipper from the fleet admiral—was ignorant of the loss of his brother's flagship. Even if he had known, he was too busy dodging a three-hundred-foot Staten Island ferry to mourn.

The *United States Coast Pilot* (Chapter 11, "New York Harbor and Approaches")—a document read as reverently by the armada captains as their fathers had studied Mao's *Little Red Book*—warned of a dangerous current setting across the channel where the East River joined the Hudson River between the Battery and Governors Island. Native watermen called it "the Spider."

But the *Coast Pilot* was not written for submariners, so Captain Qui and his crew of boat handlers had been guessing ever since they had received their new orders how deeply the Spider might set. Did its tentacles merely riffle the surface or extend twenty feet down? Or did they scour the bottom of the forty-foot channel?

Tide and current reports from the Hong Kong Information Bureau, which had sponsored Dragon Boat races in the Hudson, threw little light on the forces beneath the surface. The armada captains had also studied the reports of the masters of Chinese merchant ships familiar with the Port of New York—contrary, independent seafarers who reveled in dire predictions.

The pessimists were suddenly proven right. Qui was concentrating on the *whirring* of the Staten Island ferry's Z-drive when all of a sudden *Deng Xiaoping*'s rudder man, her forward ballast man, and both her planesmen all shouted at once.

The boat lurched as if something much bigger than she had closed talons on her bow. In an instant, twenty-four-hundred tons of submarine were sheering sideways toward the shoals of Governors Island where Dimond Reef hooked into the river.

"Helm, full ahead, right full rudder."

It was nearly a thousand yards from the Battery's stone walls to Governors Island. But the deep-water channel that the submarine required was less than four hundred yards wide. And *Deng Xiaoping* was already close to Dimond Reef, as Qui had been forced to hug the Governors Island side of the channel to avoid the ferry churning from her dock.

"Planes, hold her bow down."

"We're almost on the bottom, sir."

"I don't care if you drill this city another tunnel. Keep her head down."

While he hadn't his brother's remarkable capacity to visualize a three-dimensional image of surface to bottom, he could imagine the moving water wall of the Spider as if it were a big wrestler herding an opponent from the ring with his bulk. Close to the bottom there might be some lessening of its force. But to go up—breaking surface in the busy strait in full sight of a million office workers, tourists, and visiting Fleet Week Navy veterans—would doom the entire invasion before it had started.

The boat began to come around, forcing her head into the crosscurrent. But Qui feared that his propeller wash was showing on the surface.

"Sonar, sir. I've got some sort of a hump across the bottom of the channel."

Tang Qui searched the chart, which he'd long ago memorized. Maybe the Brooklyn Battery Tunnel, though it wasn't shown? Maybe a gas line, maybe a steam pipe?

"We'll hit it if we don't come up ten feet, sir."

"Helm, ahead half." If he was going to scrape a tunnel top, he'd rather brush slowly across it than breach his outer hull or give the game away by collapsing an under-harbor crossing on top of a thousand cars and trucks.

He felt the current grab the *Deng Xiaoping* again.

"I can't hold her, sir."

"Ahead full."

In the open sea she'd be accelerating to twenty knots. But in the arms of the Spider, she was yawing and heaving and barely making five over the bottom. The current couldn't be that fast. The heaving increased, accompanied by an ominous roar from the stern. The propeller was cavitating, carving huge circles of air in the water.

"Reduce revolutions to one quarter. Straighten up your rudder."

The gods alone knew what their struggle looked like on the surface, or who was watching. If a warship was passing overhead, or even if a few Fleet Week visitors were riding on the ferry, they were dead. Experienced Navy men would instantly recognize the telltale thrashing of a submarine fighting for her life.

"Sir, there is a second ship approaching."

"Course?"

"Zero-nine-zero."

Coming up behind them, heading east. He could hear it now, inbound from the Upper Bay—the heavy, steady pounding of a single screw.

"Sonar, what is that ship?"

"I'm not sure, sir." There was too much ambient noise from the ferry and the swirling river currents. The sonar operator—who, like the rest of them, hadn't maneuvered in close harbor quarters for nearly two months—sounded close to panic. Tang spoke quietly. "What is her speed?"

"She's making five knots, sir."

"How many turns?"

"Twenty turns, sir."

As Tang Qui glanced at the acoustic analyzer to confirm that the approaching ship's propeller was turning at twenty revolutions per minute, the Spider shoved them back toward the shoals again.

"Tugboat approaching," Sonar called. "From the east, sir. From the East River."

The *Coast Pilot* had warned, "The channel between the Battery and Governors Island is very congested." A ferry, a ship, and a tug in the first thirty seconds. What next, a garbage scow?

"I think he's towing barges, sir. A long string, heavily laden."

Tang Qui tried to picture the three courses converging overhead, the ship from the west, the tug and barges from the east, the Staten Island ferry leaving its dock.

"A second ferryboat approaching, sir. Inbound."

The young captain couldn't hold the entire picture in his head while battling the Spider.

"Up periscope."

"Sir. They'll see it."

Better seen than rammed. *"Up scope!"*

At first, he saw salvation.

The strait between the skyscrapers leaping from the Battery and low, green Governors Island looked surprisingly wide. It was as if he had surfaced from a canyon up to a space where acres of free water beckoned. But the canyon in his mind was a truer representation of the space he had to navigate. Beneath the surface—where the Spider still mauled his submarine—the shoals squeezed the channel hard.

He saw the tug, dead ahead, pulling a tow of six barges, lashed side to side in pairs, on a short wire. Beyond them he saw two suspension bridges—Brooklyn Bridge, Manhattan Bridge—and a glimpse of a third, at an angle farther upriver, the Williamsburg.

He whirled the periscope through a blur of skyscrapers until he saw the ship behind him, a slab-sided freighter cutting right down the middle of the channel, seeking the deepest water. Another quarter turn revealed the second Staten Island ferry coming up on his starboard side. Spinning to port, he saw the outbound ferry.

"Down scope. Helm, come left. Half ahead."

"Captain, the ship is overtaking us."

He felt the boat refuse her rudder.

"I can't hold her, sir."

"Right rudder, reverse engine, astern one half."

That yanked her bow to port, into the Spider. But now she lay almost dead in the water and the East River current threatened to sluice her backward.

"Captain, the ship . . ."

"Sonar, where is he?"

"One hundred meters astern and fifty—forty—to port."

The ship rumbled alongside. They could hear the slow slashing of her propeller. Suddenly it picked up speed.

"He's seen us. He's ramming!" cried the planesman.

"He doesn't know we're at war. He has no reason to ram us," Tang Qui answered calmly. "He has no reason to ram us. He's fighting the Spider."

"It'll push him onto us."

"I am hoping that will not happen," said Tang Qui, seeing a threat transform into a godsend before his eyes. He was hoping the bulky ship would block the powerful current, while carving a path between the ferries.

"Helm, ahead one quarter. Good. Good. A little more. We'll pace him." With a little luck, the ship might provide a protective moving wall to cover the submarine's passage.

The submarine suddenly felt lighter. She answered her helm, and accelerated to a smooth five knots. "Come right. Give him room."

The Spider was pushing the ship sideways a little, but its deep-laden hull seemed to be shielding the *Deng Xiaoping* from the worst of it. Tang Qui watched the starboard sideband sonar display until the grasping claw of Dimond Reef fell behind them.

The men in the command room were staring at him. "Under different circumstances," he told them, "we would radio our thanks to that ship for providing an escort," and grins softened their frightened young faces.

The submarine forged ahead of the freighter, crossed its bow as the ship made for Brooklyn, and headed up the East River toward Gracie Mansion.

Jose Chin rapped his cellphone on his leg, banging out his frustration. Renata Bradley hadn't bought it. No one was going to buy it. No one was going to buy it until submarines started shooting at the Empire State Building. He felt like he was screaming in the wind.

He had destroyed his reputation with the station. And the mayor's staff. And destroyed his friend Larry. That left his family. At least he could save his mother and father. Send them home to Queens. Even if there were a thousand submarines, they would never attack Queens. Terrorists—whoever the hell they were—they'd hit Manhattan. Where the action was.

Most of his parents' restaurant's takeout customers were from the sweatshops and the tourist stores, so his mother answered the telephone in her pidgin Cantonese.

"Hi, Mom."

"Jose, Jose, you coming for lunch?"

"No, I'm stuck out on Long Island."

"Have you eaten?"

"Yeah, I ate."

"Cold food is not food." Somehow she'd picked up the habits of a *Chinese* mother, including a distrust of "cold" food, which included anything that wasn't hot off the fire. Like a bag of Fritos was going to give him cholera.

"Listen, Mom, I got to tell you something serious. Bring Pop to the phone. . . . Hi, Pop. Listen, you got to close the restaurant right now and go home."

"It's lunchtime."

"Listen to me, go home. Something terrible is going to happen in Manhattan."

"What are you talkin'?" said his mother.

"What's wrong with you?" said his father.

"Mom, Dad, I'm a reporter. I know things. I know that something terrible's going to happen. You don't want to be in Manhattan. Go home."

"We can't close the restaurant."

"Nobody's going to believe this until it happens. Go home. And tell Juan, too, okay?"

"We can't reach him. He's with that waitress."

Jose went reflexively to his brother's defense. "She's a really nice girl, Mom. She loves Juan a lot. Please promise me you'll go home."

"I don't have time for this," said his father.

"Mom, talk to him."

"You're tying up the order phone."

"Mom, nobody believes—"

"Do you want to be the boy who cried wolf, Jose?"

"Yes! When that wolf comes, they'd know who told them. Talk to Pop."

"I will," she promised and hung up. Jose had no choice but to hope. As for his brother, Juan was young and quick and, like Jose, had been born with the Luck of the Latin.

"Jasbir! New York."

Jose's phone chirped. Maybe Renata had reconsidered. He answered with a hopeful "Jose wants to know!"

"It's me."

Krazy Kate, again.

13

"DID YOU HEAR more from Ken?"

"Nope."

Kate was losing her mind on the slow-moving freighter. Three times she had begged for their cellphone to call Ken. Three times, no reply. The captain wouldn't let her use the radio.

Desperate, she had tried telephoning her father, thinking that the once-powerful Washington hostess whom he had taken up with could alert someone who was high enough up in the government to do something. But they were drunk before noon these days. "Indisposed" was the word the woman slurred, adult-speak, Kate thought bitterly, for "Daddy doesn't feel well."

Ever more frantic, she had suddenly gotten an idea about Jose Chin.

"Listen, I've been thinking," she told him. "You've got contacts. You could call the mayor's office."

"I *had* contacts. The mayor's press secretary just hung up on me."

"Let me call her. Maybe if she hears it again—what's her number?"

Jose laughed at her. "You think Renata Bradley will take *your* call? Sister, she wouldn't take God's call without an intro."

"What's her number? Don't worry, I won't tell where I got it."

"Tell what you want, I got nothing more to lose," said Jose, and gave her Renata Bradley's number at Gracie Mansion.

"Please," Kate said to the ship's officer. The captain was staring at her. "Just one more call."

When a staffer answered, "Renata Bradley's line," she said, "This is Kate Ross, calling for Harold Rosen."

Her boss, Harry Rosen, was a very public publisher, regularly quoted in the *Times* and *New York* Magazine on the state of the industry. The staff person sucked in her breath and said, "Just a moment, please." Kate waited, excitement mounting. This would work. She was sure it would work.

Renata Bradley was phoning around the word that she was seeking an assistant to replace her ex-friend Larry Neale, when the woman temporarily filling in for Larry hurried up to her desk mouthing, "Harold Rosen on line four."

Renata got rid of her call, sat up a little straighter, and punched line four. The hottest publisher in New York could be very helpful in the early phases of a presidential bid, pushing a new candidate's autobiography such as the one Renata was already ghost-writing from her files. "Renata Bradley. How are you, Mr. Rosen?"

Kate blurted, "Mr. Rosen wants you to know that Jose Chin is right."

"What? WHAT? Who is this?"

Kate cursed herself. She was so frightened for Ken that she had blown her opening. "My name is Kate Ross. I work with Harry. Jose Chin told you the truth. There are submarines—"

"You tell Jose Chin that City Hall is now off-limits to him. Gracie Mansion is off-limits to him. And if he pulls one more stunt like getting some bimbo to pester me, all of fucking Manhattan will be off-limits to him."

"Listen to me!"

Renata hung up. The nerve of some people. And now she was late for Rudy's lunch.

She hurried to the smaller of the mayor's wood-paneled, private dining rooms, where mullioned windows overlooked the garden and the river. The long, polished table had been set with eight places and Rudy was sitting down with some hostile union leaders.

Rudy had demanded "full and immediate compliance" with the recycling law, ordering police protection for sanitation workers who were being harassed by angry citizens ticketed for recycling offenses. The Patrolmen's Benevolent Association was decrying what the cop union called "garbage patrol." The Sanitation Police were demanding as loudly a trebling of their own force to escort the garbage trucks themselves.

Renata took her seat to the mayor's left.

"What's wrong?" he asked. He read her blazing red cheeks as the sort of pissed-off look that only the press could provoke.

"Not a thing," she snarled, and the mayor—whose soft spot for Renata allowed her the occasional hissy fit—bowed his head and led his guests in saying grace. He appended a codicil to the prayer, requesting that God smile upon the cruise-ship passengers.

At "Amen," the president of the Sanitationmen's Union picked up a fork, then froze when the mayor, who had not yet picked up his own utensil, looked at him like he was a rodent that had crawled out of one of his trucks.

Rudy waited until the fork was put back on the table. Then he turned to the business of this lunch, emphasizing it with a clenched fist that made the silver jump: "The law will remain paramount in New York City even if I have to put a police officer aboard every garbage truck in town."

The warring union heads exchanged uneasy glances. Mincarelli had established variations on that theme in every area of city life. The man believed in the rule of law. Cherished the law. Worshipped the law. The law was a god to him, a god who would make everything right. A god who demanded obedience, and destroyed the unruly. A god who would troll the uniformed-services union leadership for a human sacrifice.

Renata was shoving avocado slices to the back of her plate when it occurred to her that the New York Yes! rat-bastard Jose Chin had not asked a single question. He hadn't asked for a quote. He hadn't asked for an interview. And he sure as hell hadn't asked her out, which phony-date ploy, he had to know, would doom his own career as well as destroy his friend-slash-contact Larry.

She glanced out the window toward where the East River split into Hell Gate. The tide was racing up it. Waves and swirls glittered in the sun. Cheekbones Harriet and night-school Hector were patrolling the garden path that cantilevered over the riverbank.

Submarines? She'd had a high school boyfriend who'd been obsessed with a German war video called *Das Boot*. She hadn't gotten a lot out of it herself, but she knew subs attacked ships with torpedoes.

What if Jose Chin wasn't lying about submarines? Confusion about the cruise-ship disaster now included Internet-idiot rumors of an "external explosion," and a budding conspiracy theory that the ship had hit a terrorist mine. But why had Jose Chin called *her?*

And why'd he get that stupid woman to call her back? Actually, not so stupid. She certainly had known the one name to drop.

"Hold that thought." She cut the now thoroughly uncomfortable president of the Sanitationmen's Union off in midsentence, whispered, "Right back," in the mayor's ear, and hurried down to the kitchen, where a bunch of tall, photogenically handsome, and incredibly in-shape NYPD detectives were eating sandwiches and coffee while watching aerial shots of the listing cruise ship on the cook's TV.

"Hey, Renata."

Renata spent almost as much time with the mayor's bodyguards as she did with the mayor. They came as close to friends as her job had room for, which was why she had hired Judas-traitor Larry in hopes of having someone different to talk to.

"Bob, you want to bring the Rudy Van around front with some extra guys?"

Bob Thomas was growling orders into his radio before she reached the stairs, and when she glanced out at the driveway as she returned to the dining room, the long black Chevy Suburban was pulling into place. First-string driver Juan Rodriguez was at the wheel, with the gigantic Luther Washington riding shotgun.

"What's up?" asked the mayor when she sat down.

"We're ready to roll."

"I thought I was going to do a cruise-ship press conference in the garden."

"I'll keep you posted." She forced her gaze from the soft hairs that graced the back of his hand and picked up her salad fork.

The mayor resumed reaming out the head of the PBA, secure in the knowledge that Renata Bradley, come hell or high water, had things under control.

Out in the driveway, Bob Thomas parked behind the Rudy Van in a heavily sprung four-door, four-wheel-drive Chevy Blazer. With him in the escort vehicle were three huge plainclothes guys.

None of the escort squad thought anything peculiar about the order to beef up security. The mayor considered it his right, as well as his duty, to visit neighborhoods where the citizens were not shy about expressing their disappointments, and it fell, naturally, to the New York Police Department security detail to ensure that the Rudy Van didn't end up in a Dumpster.

The Fleet Week Press Kit—available to the invaders on the World Wide Web at www.nyfleetweek.org—included an updated detailed chart of New York Harbor locating the visiting United States, French, German, English, and Chinese warships. That gave acting-Admiral Commissar Wong Tsu a clear idea of what and where to order his boats to attack first.

When to attack was determined by the tide. With East Wind's boats requiring a depth of nearly forty feet to hide submerged, and over fifty to raise their periscopes, they needed every foot of tidewater that the Atlantic Ocean pushed twice daily into the port's dredged channels.

Today's tide tables predicted high tide for Sandy Hook, the harbor entrance, at 11:47 in the morning and, forty-one minutes later, at 12:38 at the Battery at the foot of Manhattan Island, times confirmed by the droning announcer on the VHF Marine Channel. And All-News Radio 88 confirmed that the mayor was still recuperating from his head cold at Gracie Mansion.

Political Commissar Wong had argued vehemently to attack at night, for the obvious advantages of concealment. But the reckless fleet admiral had insisted upon midday. Thousands of miles from Commissar Wong's powerful masters in Beijing, Tang Li had prevailed.

Just as he had prevailed a year ago in China when Commissar Wong had argued that a better target, two oceans closer to China, was San Francisco.

Tang had justified the longer voyage on the grounds that New York was a more important financial center than the smaller Pacific Coast city. He justified the daylight attack by claiming that in addition to seizing the mayor, a noon raid would strangle New York when its arteries were already snarled by traffic and would trap millions of commuters on Manhattan Island.

Tang Two's *Deng Xiaoping* ran submerged up the East River, under the Brooklyn and Manhattan bridges, guided by sonar around tugs, small ferries, and, once, the knifelike keel of a deep-draft sailing yacht. Two miles northeast of the Battery, they passed between the great piers of the Williamsburg Bridge.

"Up scope."

But Sonar interjected, "Something's blocking the channel."

"Stop." They waited. The sonar operator looked flummoxed. His eyes slid aside when Tang Two glanced his way.

"Put it on the intercom."

A chewing sound echoed through the boat. The young captain laughed softly. "Two days' Hong Kong leave to the sailor who IDs that noise."

Old Chen—at thirty-four, the boat's wise elder—whispered, "Harbor dredge."

The dredge was partially blocking the channel. Worse, it was near the point where Tang had to raise his periscope. As the first of the armada's captains to penetrate the East River, he had no choice but to risk it. At least the channel was deeper here—a full sixty feet. "Helm, come left to zero-zero-five . . . up scope!"

A quick periscope glance west revealed that the *Deng Xiaoping* was making better time than the automobile traffic on Manhattan Island's FDR Drive. He whirled east to scan the Brooklyn waterfront.

A Greek-flag freighter—rust-streaked and time-battered—was loading used taxicabs into her hold and a fleet of secondhand trucks onto her long foredeck.

At the next pier lay a tanker—brimful of diesel fuel—registered in Albany, New York. Self-propelled fuel lighters were nuzzling, tethered by cable and hose. To an onlooker, it would appear that they were transferring cargo, or fueling her for a long voyage. But in fact, the tanker was off-loading submarine fuel into the lighters.

Tang Two flickered a light-burst signal through the periscope. Both ship captains were on the ball: the tanker flashed back a coded confirmation that the lighters would refuel the invading submarines after dark; while the master of the Greek-flag vessel reported that five tons of high explosives hidden in her hold were ready to be delivered to the North Cove in lower Manhattan.

Commissar Wong had argued for the frigate *Zhaotong* to transport the dynamite, to avoid accidental discovery in a customs or random drug search. But Admiral Tang had ruled that the likelihood of the missile frigate being disabled in the initial attack made it necessary to deliver the explosives separately.

"Down scope."

Ahead, Roosevelt Island narrowed the channel by half. Heavy ships used the deeper main channel on the west side of the island. The *Deng Xiaoping* had no choice but to use it, too.

Tang Two switched on the intercom to address the crew. But the time for speeches had passed and he simply broadcast the words that every man on the boat had awaited for years. "Marines, prepare to attack. Deck Gunner, report to Conn."

The chief deck gunner squeezed into the tight control room. Like every sailor in Tang Li's armada, he was a Southerner, short and slightly built. Cantonese, Fukiens,

Shanghainese, all were small men—with the exception of a few burly bosuns. The gunner was Cantonese, a born waterman, heir to the centuries-old South China Coast seafaring tradition that had scattered so many millions so far from home.

"Ready, Comrade?"

"Ready, Captain."

"Are your men frightened?"

Ask a Beijinger and you'd get heels-clicking denials of fear—much less pre-attack jitters—and stalwart promises to serve the Party and the Chinese people to the death. But Admiral Tang had persuaded the PLA that big fat Northerners took up too much room on a submarine.

Things were different in the South, looser, more human. A white, gapped grin bumped the tension from the gunner's round face. "The men are no more frightened than they should be, Captain."

Tang Qui, too, was no more frightened than he should be. "Remind them," he said. "Admiral Tang Li orders we take the mayor alive."

14

KEN HUGHES STOLE a look at his radar when one of the commandos in the crowded wheelhouse moved aside. The twin towers of the World Trade Center were standing tall as the tug neared New York.

He was still shaking. Exhausted, he ached in the many places they had clubbed him with their gun butts. He was deeply relieved that Kate had found safety. But he was stunned with grief for Charlie.

Deckhands came and went. They got their master's tickets, they sat for their licenses, or they just stumbled ashore one night and never came back. But engineers settled in like hermit crabs.

Charlie O'Conner had tended the *Chelsea Queen*'s machinery for thirty-two years. He had known Ken's father, his mother, and his stepfather/uncle. Drunk, he had been a danger only to himself; sober, he had treated the old tug like his best friend.

Ken could only hope that when the Chinese had thrown

Charlie overboard, the ice-cold seawater had paralyzed his old man's heart and spared him the long death of drowning. Shoving Rick aboard—his own strength fading even as he dreamed of somehow saving Charlie's life—he had been forced to concede that no diver born could ever find Charlie sinking somewhere in a square mile of ocean.

The cold had nearly finished Rick, too. The deckhand had passed out on the towing deck. The commandos had slapped him awake, wrapped him in blankets, and locked him, half conscious, in the forward rope locker.

Then they had stripped off Ken's wet suit—giggling like children as he hopped bare-assed into his jeans—and marched him up to the wheelhouse, where Charlie's murderer warned him not to try to escape again or his men would shoot him dead.

Ken believed they would. Tang's troops were country boys, he realized, peasant kids who'd probably never seen a city before they joined the People's Navy. Like U.S. Navy SEALS, the kind of good kids who'd been raised to obey orders and give their all—an admiral's wet dream.

They got very excited as the twin towers of the World Trade Center hove through the haze while they were still miles at sea. Earlier—right after Jose had telephoned with the fantastic news that Kate had been rescued—they'd mistaken the Jones Beach water tower for that same landmark. Like dumb tourists, thought Ken. Heavily armed tourists.

Their admiral set a course straight for Ambrose Light. When they were close enough to read the white AMBROSE painted on the side of the unmanned navigational tower, Tang suddenly ordered the tug stopped. A commando tossed a hand grenade over the side. The explosion sent a narrow geyser of water into the sky. As Tang's bosun grunted orders, the commando threw another and another in quick succession. Long. Short. Short.

Ken watched the water, mourning Charlie, thanking God

Kate had made it back to civilization alive, wondering what next. Close call for Kate; God knew what they would have done to her. Her escape freed him up to take any chances that came his way.

A fourth geyser splashed spray on the windows.

A periscope broke water. Its cold glass eye surveyed the tug.

Tang Li looked around, confirmed on the radar monitor that they were still alone in the haze, and gave an imperious "come up" jerk of his thumb. Like a dolphin obeying its trainer, a fat black hull rose from the deep, streaming seawater. It lay low—nearly twice the length of the *Chelsea Queen,* with its conning tower amidships and a stubby black rudder breaking the waves astern.

Ken winced as the hulls touched, but instead of a screech of tortured steel, they rubbed in near silence. The Chinese submarine, he realized, was clad in rubbery anechoic tiles.

A hatch opened in the conning tower. Sailors climbed out, blinking like moles in the daylight, and quickly rigged a gangway between the two craft. Tang Li beckoned the skipper of the sunken sub. Then he said to Ken, "Bring the pipe."

They crossed the gangway. Tang gestured Ken through the narrow hatch and he descended a tight companionway into a cramped control room that stank of burned oil, diesel, and many unwashed bodies. It was lit a sickly green and white by video displays. Ken noted sonar screens by Krupp Atlas Elektronik, radars by Thomson-CSF. The sub was incongruously decorated here and there with blond wood paneling, like an RV home or a basement rec room. The builder's plaque showed that she'd been launched in Germany.

A high-ranking officer about Admiral Tang's age was eyeing him nervously and Ken quickly concluded there was no love between the two men. His uniform was crisp and formal, unlike the fatigues and overalls worn by the other submariners in the cramped and greasy space.

"Commissar Wong," Tang said. "We will speak English to spare your sailors unnecessary distress."

"Admiral," the well-dressed Wong responded with a slurry accent. His English came less easily than Admiral Tang's. "May I congratulate you on your . . ." He hesitated.

"Survival?" asked Tang. Snatching the pipe from Ken, Tang held it inches from Commissar Wong's nose. "Do you see this braze?"

Ken saw that Tang's habitual stillness served him well. When he did move, it was a commanding sight.

Wong flinched. "I don't understand."

"Even a political officer should see the problem, Commissar Wong." Tang mocked him. "Surely you can recognize the difference between a defective piping joint and a directive from the Party Congress."

Wong's face hardened. His retort in Chinese was hot with challenge.

"Speak English!" Tang fired back.

"Yes, Admiral. I said, it appears to be a faulty repair."

"This 'repair' was made during our fleet's final maintenance rendezvous in the South Atlantic. When it failed, my forward compartments flooded, four of my sailors drowned, and my submarine sank to the bottom. Four men dead and my best boat out of commission!"

"How did you—"

"Fortunately for me, the joint did not break while we were still in deep water."

"Fortunate for us all, Admiral. How did you—"

"How did I survive? This tugboat captain found us."

"It are miracle you survive, sir. Your lucky holds ever strong."

"My boat was sabotaged."

"Sabotaged? Who would sabotage the admiral's flagship—"

"Yes, who? And who demanded an indoctrination session for my officers while the repair crew boarded?"

Wong said, "It is the commissar's duty to inspire his officers."

"The commissar is a parasite."

"I serve the Party—"

"The Party apparatus breeds parasites. Bureaucrats, all of you!"

"I will report your disrespect for Party laws and regulations."

Admiral Tang turned to Ken like they were two guys in a bar: "In governing China, laws and regulations often take a backseat to personal relationships."

He snapped an order in Chinese.

The skipper of the sunken sub whipped out his pistol, held the barrel three inches from Wong's forehead. Tang said, "I overestimated you, Commissar Wong. I assumed that you had the intelligence to wait to betray me until *after* I had taken New York. You almost cost us our victory."

Tang's skipper pulled the trigger. The commissar fell backward against the bulkhead and sagged down it to the deck. The oddly wet-sounding cough of the gun echoed in the steel room.

Ken retreated into the chilly boat-handler part of his mind that measured time, mass, and velocity: little blood oozed from Commissar Wong's forehead; light-caliber ammunition and a small charge minimized ricochets inside a submarine.

He heard boots pound on steel. Commandos burst into the control room. When they sighted Wong lifeless on the deck, they jerked side arms from their belts. It's going to end right here, thought Ken. And I am dead.

Admiral Tang stared down the gun barrels.

He spoke softly and firmly. The commandos exchanged glances and Ken guessed that Tang was probably reminding them that they were thirteen thousand miles from home and that, with their boss sprawled dead at their feet, Admiral Tang Li was their only hope of ever seeing their wives again. Whatever, it worked. When Tang was done talking, the commandos lowered their weapons, and Ken took a cautious, grateful breath.

The Chinese admiral looked like a man who had won everything he ever wanted. It was pretty clear that by killing the commissar, he had made himself the unquestioned boss.

Tang addressed his skipper in English. "You're promoted. Take this boat. I'll stay on the tug." Then he switched to Cantonese and ordered, "Shoot the tugboat captain."

Ken Hughes did not react.

Tang said, in Cantonese, "I doubt he's that good an actor, so obviously he doesn't understand Chinese."

"May I suggest you kill him anyway," said the skipper.

"Why? He's got local knowledge."

"May I speak, sir?"

Tang nodded. "Quickly; you've got to get to the North Cove."

"There is a saying in the shipping business," said Loh, whose family had been sea captains since the days of sailing junks. "Better give a tugboat captain a ship than let a ship captain command a tugboat. They are quick and resourceful, and you should be wary."

"I stand warned. Now, Commissar Wong was to take the North Cove. Put the sappers ashore and clear a route from the cove to the World Trade Center."

Loh saluted and reached for the submarine's intercom.

In English, Tang said, "Let's go, Tugboat Captain."

Ken barely heard him. His eye had locked on the biggest video display, a twenty-inch screen which was winking like a Staten Island Christmas tree. If each blink indicated another submarine, there were one hundred submarines converging on New York.

He said, "Can I ask you something?"

"Quickly."

"Whatever you're doing, it looks pretty well planned. You don't really need me. Why didn't you toss me to the sharks with my guys?"

"I take all the help I can get," Admiral Tang said soberly. "Besides, you saved my life."

The thought had not escaped Ken that, in a weird but very real way, he was responsible for whatever death and destruction the Chinese admiral unleashed on his city.

"In Chinese," Tang reflected with a thin smile, "the fact that you saved my life means that you are forever *responsible* for my life. In 'American,' if I recall the street slang correctly, it means that I owe you big-time. Yes? All right, move it!"

The sub was already venting air as it admitted seawater to its diving tanks. The Chinese admiral quickly led the way up out of the conning tower back aboard the tugboat. Ken slowed on the *Chelsea Queen*'s wheelhouse ladder to watch the sub submerge.

A funny thought occurred to him: if these guys had come all the way from China, even if they'd refueled at that maintenance stop in the South Atlantic, that was seven thousand miles ago. No way they'd made another fuel stop off Atlantic City. They had to be running low on diesel, running on empty.

A commando shoved him to move faster. Ken stopped. Charlie's death was gnawing at his guts, and the numbness, the deliberate, self-protective calm—the cloak of detachment he had donned to survive—suddenly became fury.

The commando shoved harder. Ken exploded and kicked the bastard off the ladder.

They stomped his fingers from the rungs, threw him

down on the towing deck, and piled on, kicking. Twice Ken Hughes fought to his feet; twice they beat him down again.

Fifty stories above Eighth Avenue on the western edge of midtown Manhattan, Phil Levy was enthroned high in an antique English bootblack's chair, enjoying the river view over the heads of his hardworking traders. He was having his shoes shined before he took an elevator from Bishop & Levy's trading room to a limousine. The limo would drive him to the Thirtieth Street VIP heliport. From there he would be whisked to Westchester's Winged Foot—where he intended to lose a nail-biter round of golf, by two strokes, to a Spanish pension-fund manager.

Gill Bishop rushed from his private office.

"Here come the boss," said Roger, the shoe shine.

It made Phil crazy that the doddering fool seemed incapable of remembering that Phil was Gill's partner, not an employee.

"Mr. Bishop is my partner," he said evenly. Since he had acquired an English butler, he'd been learning not to shout and scream at underlings. Partners—Phil and Gill, Gill and Phil, Bishop and Levy—idea men. The four busy traders slaving over their split screens and punching computer phones were *employees*. The secretary was an *employee*.

"Boss Man's makin' tracks," muttered Roger. "Like a *Man In Black* chasin' a *Brother From Another Planet*."

Phil hadn't seen Gill move that fast since the last time Amazon tanked. He ran behind Phil and murmured softly in his ear, "There's a whole fleet of submarines about to attack New York."

Joke.

But one look at Gill's eyes—burning like a wolverine's on the scent of a crippled moose—and Phil thought, No joke. If Mr. Inside Information believed that submarines were attacking, then, crazy as it sounded, submarines were probably attacking, and if they were, there was big money—huge money—George Soros-Warren Buffett money—to be made out of knowing in advance that a disaster was about to destabilize New York City.

Investor fear of chaos would subtract value from everything whose price depended on stability in New York. Which was every bond and stock and index in the world.

No. Too crazy. He jumped down from the chair and whispered, "How do you know?"

"I know."

"We can't bet the store on 'I know.' Tell me how you know. I'll go with you, just let me in on your thinking."

"We don't have time for this shit!" Gill shouted, and their employees stared.

Gill lowered his voice and spoke very quickly: "I got a hundred twenty-four lights on my telephone board. I get a thousand calls an hour. I take a hundred, two hundred. I know which to take. I know which not to take. I will do you the courtesy of mentioning a *few* of the calls I took today. This morning I hear from a guy looped into the Pentagon. The NSA is sending over recordings of some weird transmissions emanating from New York waters; what does the Navy know about it? Then I get a call from a guy who says his guy says that cruise ship was sunk by an external explosion."

"I heard that on the radio."

"At ten. I heard at six. Then, like I told you this morning, I hear that some brokers who handle private accounts owned by Chinese military people are bailing out of New York City bonds. Dumping them. I make a couple of calls, I hear these same bond sellers are buying gold. Gold is for war. Then I get a call from a guy who sees a submarine from the jet he's landing at Kennedy."

"It's Fleet Week."

"It's a Kilo-class diesel sub."

"What the hell does that mean?"

"It means it's not the kind of sub that comes to Fleet Week. It's not American. It's Russian. And the Russians sell them to the Chinese. The same Chinese buying gold. He's flying his own jet, so he aborts landing, turns around, and goes back for another look. Sub's gone. The ocean's foggy as hell. But he thinks he sees a periscope."

"From a jet? Come on."

"He's a rich old WASP who flew Navy fighters as a kid. He spots another periscope and another."

"And he calls you?"

"He calls *everybody*. Five minutes ago. Soon—damned soon—someone will look into it. We're running out of time. You want to do this with me or you want to split?"

In the end, it was Gill's absolute willingness to go it alone that persuaded Phil. That and the wolverine shine in his eyes. The man believed that they could reap fortunes that would make their current fortunes look like peanuts.

What to sell? was the unspoken next question, and it took less than a second for the partners to chorus, "SPUs!"

Suddenly Phil felt that old "we're winners" surge he used to get when they'd been younger.

SPUs were S&P 500 Index futures. The most emotional, high-strung, stressed-out, weirded-up, fickle, wired, and sentiment-driven market in the financial industry. Float a rumor there was a tiger loose in Central Park, people would sell. Announce it had rabies, they'd buy. Total emotion.

Gill and Phil decided to sell futures contracts. When the entire world's banking center suddenly went down with New York City, S&P futures would drop like anvils. They would buy at post-submarine-attack, down-the-toilet prices to deliver at pre-submarine-attack high prices, their profit being the immense difference.

"To what level do I sell?" asked a trader, who knew that it would take about sixty seconds for the highly volatile, psychopathically incitable Chicago Mercantile Exchange pit locals to notice that someone was dumping.

"Whatever level," Gill told him. "Sell!"

Phil's weren't the only brows that rose at the drunken-sailor approach. Even old Roger looked like he was going to call *his* broker to say, Buy. This was a hedge fund, for crissake, the whole idea being to hedge your bets and cover your butt. Did they want to go the schmuck route of the Greenwich Nobel idiots at Long Term Capital?

"When do I stop?" asked another trader.

"When the phones stop working."

Gill pitched in with the traders, telephoning brokers to sell hundred-contract lots at prices that would be calamitous if the market kept going up, but which would make him and Phil unbelievably rich if prices crashed.

Phil retreated to the windows. Five men selling futures contracts worth almost $275,000 per contract in lots of one hundred were risking millions on every punch of their speed-dials. He gazed down at the Hudson River and prayed for submarines.

15

WHEN KEN HUGHES woke up aching in the rope locker, he felt around in the dark for a stubby little one-ton jack to force the hatch open.

"They break any bones?" whispered Rick.

"How long I been out?"

Rick guessed an hour.

An hour while the tug steamed God-knew-where. He was afraid he had a concussion. His body had stiffened up like cement and he hurt in muscles he hadn't known existed. He found the jack.

"What are you doing?" whispered Rick.

"Pop this hatch."

"Hold on, man. Don't piss 'em off again."

"I'm not waiting around while they change their minds and decide to kill us. We're outta here."

But just as he started to wedge the jack against a steel knee, the hatch banged open, driving bright lights into his aching eyeballs. The commandos who had beaten him up gestured him out and marched him up to the wheelhouse, shoving, prodding. His head ached where one of them had cracked him with a gun barrel, a painful reminder that he would have to keep his mouth shut if he was going to come out of this alive. And his hands to himself.

Admiral Tang was waiting in the wheelhouse. His bosun was driving, steering a course that was about to take the *Chelsea Queen* under the Verrazano Narrows Bridge. They had carried the television up from the galley, set it on the chart table, and tuned in ABC's aerial shots of the *Sovereign Princess*. The seas around the smoldering cruise liner were carpeted with lifeboats and warships.

Tang told Ken that a submarine was trailing the tug underwater, moving a hundred feet behind them as they crossed the Upper Bay. He wanted Captain Ken's opinion of the chart's depths in the area off Weehawken. The sonar was sounding the bottom, but like any prudent master, Tang wasn't going to rely only on it and the charts. Not when he had a local skipper aboard.

"You've already shown you're brave," Admiral Tang warned him. "Don't be stupid. I ask for the last time. Is there enough water there for my submarine?"

Ken knew he was at a crossroads. Help these bastards or they would kill him like they'd killed Charlie. Turn traitor or die.

He felt the Chinese admiral's eyes hard on his face. Tang probably knew what he was thinking. Knew he was wondering if he should play along, get in the admiral's good graces, bide his time, watch for the moment to strike back, watch for a chance to bring the whole attack to a screeching halt. But who knew if he could, if he'd ever get the chance, if he'd ever have the guts.

Ken Hughes led Admiral Tang Li to the chart. "You've got plenty of water here." Then he tapped the paper with a forefinger sticky with blood from touching a cut over his eye and volunteered to say, "It's not on the chart, but there's been some shoaling up here last couple of weeks. Beyond here, I wouldn't trust it."

16

AT AMBROSE LIGHT, a megawattage Promises Smile and a stomach-wrenching rope-ladder climb down the side of the moving freighter got Kate Ross a ride on the Sandy Hook Pilots' launch. But any hope of persuading the launch skipper who was racing to Staten Island's Stapleton Pier to pick up another pilot, to believe, much less report, what had happened to Ken was dashed by the freighter captain, who had radioed ahead that Kate was a nutcase.

A suit waiting on the pier flashed a badge as Kate jumped off the launch. "INS. This way, Ms."

"Why?"

"You've got to go through Immigration and Quarantine,"

"I'm not an immigrant. I live in Chelsea."

He reached to take her arm. Kate bolted, dodged around him, and ran the mile flat out to the ferry terminal at St. George, where she made the next boat with seconds to spare.

The city looked normal, dense ranks of skyscrapers

drowsing in the midday sun. As the ferry skimmed the miles, details materialized. The peaceful towers grew large and distinct, features sharp and ever more lively, until millions and millions of windows shone like eager faces.

Into her vision steamed a red-and-black tugboat. Her heart jumped. Like Ken's *Chelsea Queen,* it was painted in traditional colors. And it had a net-draped shaggy nose. But that was hardly unusual. Then the angle changed from the speeding ferry, and she thought she recognized the silhouette of the oversized salvage derrick Ken had installed behind the stack.

She blinked the wind-tears from her eyes and tried to read the name on the wheelhouse.

Her decks were deserted. Sunlight reflected off the wheelhouse windows, so she couldn't see through the glass.

The tugboat steamed like a ghost across the ferry's track. Kate had the weirdest feeling that the whole thing—the days since Sunday—had been a dream: the blind date; two nights in heaven; Ken pulling on the wet suit to dive from the Zodiac; the submarine; the Chinese soldiers; Ken grappling with them, shouting for her to escape; a deep, unshakable sense that she had abandoned the best man she would meet in a very long time.

She had thought the ferry would catch up with the tug, but their paths were diverging, the distance between them spreading rapidly as the ferry held its course for the Battery and Ken's tug veered toward Jersey.

Quickly she scanned the deck where people were coming out to be first off when the ferry docked. At midday, they were mostly tourists. But there was a tall African-American teenager hunched inside his sweatshirt hood. She saw he had a beeper on his belt. Feeling guilty for automatically thinking, Drug dealer, Kate screwed up her courage to ask, "Do you have a cellphone?"

"Say what?"

"Could I make a call on your cellphone?"

He stared down at her, trying to figure her scam. No white woman had ever stepped close enough to ask him for anything in his entire life—not even the time of day.

"It's a local call."

No one answered on the tug. She had left her own phone in her backpack in Ken's cabin. Maybe he would hear it. Maybe they'd locked him in there. But all she got was her own the-cellphone-is-off message. She left a message for him, which he would probably never get, and gave the kid his phone back.

Ken's tug and the ferry had veered half a mile apart. She glanced around frantically. So much had happened. It was only six hours since they had sailed out of the harbor and now Ken's boat was disappearing.

The ferry! She was riding a ferry!

This morning Ken had exchanged greetings with a Staten Island ferry captain. She ran up to the main deck, searching for the stairs to the wheelhouse, jumped over a NO PAS-SENGERS BEYOND THIS POINT sign hanging from a chain and bolted up the stairs. Startled, the ferry captain and a mate, both in civilian work clothes, whirled from the windows toward the intrusion. The mate stepped forward to block her way. Kate tried to appear feminine and nonthreatening.

"I'm sorry," she said, smiling.

"You gotta go below, miss."

"I know. Would you do me a favor?" She pointed at the VHF mike dangling like Ken's from the ceiling. "Could you radio that tugboat? The *Chelsea Queen.* It's Ken Hughes's."

"You a friend of his?"

"Sort of. I mean we . . . I . . . he's sort of my boyfriend."

The mate and the captain exchanged looks.

"Sort of?" The captain grinned.

Kate smiled back. "I'm not sure how official we are yet. Could I say hi?"

The mate got a big smirk on his face. "What's it worth to you?"

"Whatever Ken says it's worth."

"She's got you there," said the captain. He hauled down the mike, thumbed it. "*Chelsea Queen. Chelsea Queen.* This is the *Governor Lehman* on Channel Twenty-one, just crossing your wake."

Kate thrilled to Ken's voice. She could hear his rumbly rasp of Old New York even in cool captain mode. "This is *Chelsea Queen.* Go ahead, Cap."

The ferry captain winked at Kate. "Hey, Ken, I've got a passenger aboard requests verification of official status."

"Say again?'

"Here, I'll let her explain." With another wink, he said, "Keep it clean," and handed over the radio.

In the wheelhouse of the *Chelsea Queen,* Admiral Tang looked up from the television, where he was surfing news channels with the sound muted. "What is that about?"

This was the fourth routine VHF exchange between the tug and the passing traffic, and another reason, Ken realized, that Tang had brought him up to the wheelhouse.

Ken shook his head. "Beats me. Somebody hacking around on the radio."

In the ferry's wheelhouse, Kate paused with her thumb on Transmit. What could she say? How could she help him? Assume the worst. Assume they would hurt him. Assume they could cut him off at the first hint of a threat.

"*Go ahead,* Lehman," came Ken's voice.

Fortunately, the grinning ferry captain had set it up for her. She pressed Transmit and said, "*Chelsea Queen,* this is your dispatcher. We have a request for you to hip up at Pier 60." Sixty was at the end of Twentieth Street, the closest to her apartment.

"*Uhhh, sorry, Dispatch. I'm afraid I'm out of commission for the rest of the day.*"

"Did that old boat break down again?"

"*I've got a customer.*"

Admiral Tang gestured for Ken to wait. The admiral looked, Ken thought, like he regretted not having taken the time to kill both of them at the outset. Tang cocked his own radio astern where the sub was trailing underwater. "If your 'dispatcher' on that ferryboat causes me one ounce of difficulty, I will order that submarine to sink that ferry. Get rid of her."

"Did you read me, Cap?" Kate asked. "In case things change, come directly to Sixty. She'll be looking for you."

"*Tell her to go home and lock the door.*"

17

P.O. HARRIET GREENE and P.O. Hector Sanchez walked their Gracie Mansion beat beside the tide-roiled East River, rehashing an argument they had started their first day at the Police Academy: whether Mayor Rudolph Mincarelli was an anti-African-American bigoted white male—in Harriet's unyielding view; or a heroic exemplar of the majesty of the law—in Hector's.

Hector idolized the former prosecutor; Harriet said he beat up on blacks to make white voters feel safe. Not that law and order weren't vital—she was a policeman's daughter, after all. But security came at a terrible price when ordinary folks were terrorized by a new gang on the street that happened to be wearing blue.

As her father was fond of saying, "Who'll po-lice the police?"

"Do you remember," Hector said, "when the mayor addressed the Academy? That was the clearest statement anyone had ever heard on the power of the law: a densely populated, high-rise city is an inherently dangerous place and only law—fire codes, elevator codes . . ."

He trailed off, distracted by a strange movement in the river. Harriet, brisk as a mother wiping a kid's face, stopped to adjust his gun belt for him, tightening it up a notch to raise his rig higher around his waist. She chided, "You want the power of the law, you gotta take space; you gotta *look* like you own the street."

". . . building codes, traffic regulations—and vigorous enforcement—can make it safe. You see what the mayor's saying, Harriet? If taxi drivers don't run red lights, pedestrians are safe— Hey, what's wrong with the river?"

"I missed Hizzoner's speech," Harriet interrupted. The unarmed combat team had been granted dispensation in order to kick New Jersey State Police Academy butt at a meet in Hoboken.

"There's something under the water," said Hector.

Harriet reached to unbuckle her gun belt. "You think a car went in?"

It happened. Once a year or so, a car crashed through the FDR guardrail and fell in the river. They hadn't seen a crash, but the current was swift and the car could have gone off five or ten blocks uptown and been swept down in seconds. The driver might still be alive.

"Call Emergency Services. I'm going in."

"Hey, hey, hey, whaddaya, crazy?" asked Hector. "I don't see any car."

Harriet said, "There's something under the water. I'm gonna—oh, my God."

Fifty feet from the shore, a long black hull humped up out of the water. "Jesus Christ, it's a submarine."

"It's Fleet Week," said Hector.

"I didn't know they were coming up here."

Steel hatches clanged open and soldiers came pouring up on deck. Most had assault weapons strapped to their backs.

Those who didn't hurried to a long cannon mounted in front of the conning tower and aimed it at Gracie Mansion.

Harriet thumbed her radio. "Central, I think we've got a problem here. A submarine full of armed men—Hector, tell 'em to get outta here."

The big black boat was approaching the shore now. Cars screeched brakes and blew horns on the FDR Drive, which ran under the garden at the edge of the riverbank. The sub shoved its front against the rocks.

Hector yelled down, "Police! Get outta here! Restricted area."

"*ID yourself, Officer,*" intoned Harriet's radio.

"Police Officer Harriet Greene, Gracie Mansion security detail. I'm in the garden by the East River with Police Officer Hector Sanchez. These guys are armed like commandos. Request you eighty-five us, forthwith, with backup." No way she was going to get all rookie-panicky, screaming a ten-thirteen that would bring every cop in the city charging to their rescue. Not yet. This was some kind of screwup with an explanation.

"*P.O. Greene,*" said Central, "*God save you if you're playing games.*"

Harriet reached out suddenly, grabbed Hector's shoulder, and pulled her partner down with her as an automatic weapon *burrrred* and bullets clattered on the low stone wall.

"They're shooting!" she yelled into her radio. "Ten-thirteen. Ten-thirteen. Shots fired. Shots fired. Hector, you okay?"

Hector Sanchez straightened his glasses. "Yeah, I think so—where you going?"

Harriet was crawling along the wall as fast as she could. Fifteen feet from where she'd been, she popped up, pistol in hand, and emptied the fifteen-shot automatic at the figures crowding onto the bow of the submarine.

"What's wrong with you?" yelled Hector.

"Shoot at them!" she yelled back as she dropped down and hastily loaded in a fresh clip. She ran back toward Hector and popped up again.

Before they started shooting at her, she saw the submarine's bow was shoved firmly against the stone bank and that the commandos were twirling grappling hooks to sling ropes over the garden wall. She braced her pistol on her forearm and began firing at the leaders.

Hector hit her hard with his shoulder and knocked her down and landed on top of her. "Wha'd you do that—"

A tremendous explosion sent rocks flying from the wall.

"I think we should get out of here," said Hector. He was white as a ghost and looked fourteen years old and his teeth were chattering, but he kept a firm grip on Harriet's arm as she tried to rise.

"Who are they?"

"They have a cannon," said Hector in a voice flat with shock. "I think you should stop pissing them off."

A second shell blew a hole in the wall and sent rocks whizzing overhead. They ran to the dubious shelter of the mayor's house.

The NYPD Chevy Blazer that escorted the Rudy Van had an arsenal locked under the rear floor hatch. Bob Thomas and Mike Collins were tearing it open while two more of the security detail came running out the front door with the mayor and Renata Bradley.

"Go!"

Bob got them into the Rudy Van, slammed the door, and yelled for Juan to hit the gas. The tires screeched. Luther Washington slapped the mayor and Renata to the floor with one huge paw while drawing his pistol with the other. "Look out, Bob," he thundered. "Here they come."

Bob whirled back to the escort Blazer. "Oh, shit."

Ten men in black battle gear rounded the corner of the mansion.

"We're outta here!" He leaped in, and stomped the accelerator the instant two of the guys swung in the side doors, yelling, "Go, go, go!" and Mike Collins, who had piled into the open back, started laying down shotgun fire. Five *booms* as fast as he could pump the weapon sent the soldiers diving for cover.

The Rudy Van roared at the gate, which a fast-moving officer yanked open, and brushed a police car out of its path. But just before the escort Blazer reached the gate, the police booth beside it exploded in glass and splinters.

Bob looked back. They were firing rocket grenades. Down on one knee, taking aim. He thought he could see the next one coming, slow enough to see, way too fast to dodge. It flew through the open hatchback, where Mike was frantically pawing another shotgun out of the arsenal, and erupted in fire.

Greg Walsh was sinking his teeth into as fine a piece of lobster as he'd ever eaten and reflecting upon the rewards of public service. Beat cop, detective, organized crime strike force, chief of detectives, deputy commissioner, acting commissioner, retired at forty-fucking-five to head of security for an international brokerage house. And while you're at it, Mr. Walsh, sir—since your management experience includes managing thirty-five thousand police—why not take over Personnel as well? For which we better double your salary, which is already triple your best year at the Department.

Big bucks and big respect.

The Navy comes to town, Greg Walsh gets invited to the party. It was like he had a sign over his head that said, "This guy, maybe one day he can do you a favor." Not a bad life. And plenty of reunions with the old crowd at events like this one.

Except, he couldn't help but notice, that no one ever looked up from a low-toned serious talk to signal Greg Walsh to join in. If it was on the QT, guys who had worked for him—guys he had *taught*, for crissake—clammed up like he was wired.

The captain of the *John F. Kennedy*, a crinkly-eyed, scar-faced smoothie who had so many Vietnam battle ribbons on his chest that it seemed a miracle he was alive, had given a crisp welcome-and-thank-you-for-a-safe-and-happy-Fleet-Week speech. Now he was going from table to table, greeting the frontline guys who'd been invited, along with the top brass who usually got comped to these affairs. It was generous of the Navy, but the donkeys looked very nervous stuck aboard an aircraft carrier tied to Pier 92 while God knew what was happening to the thousands of innocent sailors wandering the streets.

Not that New York didn't love visiting sailors. The town had always had a soft spot for the kids on leave, buying them beers, standing them dinner, taking them to bed. Still, the donkeys knew exactly who would be blamed when certain elements took advantage.

"Range," whispered the commander of East Wind Boat Number 38. The whisper was hardly necessary under the noisy Hudson River, but the habits of stealth ran deep. Or perhaps, he thought, the majesty of the awesome target demanded respect.

He was about to torpedo the largest warship attacked by a submarine since the American *Archerfish* sank the Japanese *Shinano* in the last year of World War Two. As monumental as the Manhattan skyscrapers behind her, the aircraft carrier was a thousand-foot cask of steel, wider than a city block, and twenty stories tall.

"Four hundred yards."

"Bearing."

"Zero-nine-two."

The *John F. Kennedy* lay motionless, tethered to her pier by wire hawsers.

"Open forward torpedo doors."

"Torpedo doors open, sir."

"Arm torpedoes."

"Torpedoes armed, sir."

"Open stern torpedo doors." The instant he fired the forward torpedoes, he intended to swing the boat around and launch two more from his stern tubes.

Sonar interrupted. "Tug and barges coming upriver."

The captain spun the periscope away from the big square stern of the docked aircraft carrier. The tug towing two barges would cross right between his boat and the *John F. Kennedy*.

"Down scope."

The commander listened to the workboat's twin screws plod upstream. He turned to his second officer, perspiring in the hot, crowded conning tower. "At least the target isn't going anywhere."

The captain stopped at Greg Walsh's table. Said the right things to everyone and gave Greg a particularly warm "Welcome aboard." Who knew when *he*'d be tuning up his second career? He even lingered politely to compliment a DEA guy on the high-speed doper chase boat in which he'd rumbled to the luncheon. "I had to discipline some of my sailors who winched her aboard when you turned your back."

The DEA guy—what the hell was his name? Rossi— joined proudly in the laugh—all the other cops had arrived in cars. Then Rossi asked the captain about a show on The History Channel that said that diesel submarines were making a comeback because they were a hell of a lot cheaper to build and operate than nuclear subs.

The captain's crinkles deepened into the kind of smile you gave an informant who was telling you something you'd heard last week. "Diesel boats are probably adequate for some little country like Italy that's got narrow, shallow straits to patrol and no particular enemies anyway. But they lack the strategic mobility of a nuclear boat and I don't see them as a significant arm of American sea power."

Rossi, who any idiot could tell was Italian, didn't look happy with the swipe at Italy. But before he could invite the captain of the *John F. Kennedy* out to the parking lot, every lunch guest in the dining room reached for his beeper.

Eight seconds later Greg Walsh was hunched over his cellphone in disbelief. "Say again?"

"I said, sir, there's a submarine attacking Gracie Mansion."

Greg Walsh tried to revert from brokerage-house grandee to New York cop and found it slower going than he'd have thought. "Where's the mayor?"

"He was at Gracie Mansion."

"Did they get him?"

"I don't know, sir. Datawise, it's total chaos. D.L. wants to know if you agree we should send the employees home early."

Just then, the richly carpeted deck shook hard.

The dining room fell silent.

A second explosion shuddered upward from the depths of the eighty-thousand-ton ship. By then her crinkly-eyed captain was bounding for the navigation bridge. The killer expression searing his face told Greg Walsh he had earned those medals the hard way.

"Well?" Phil Levy asked his partner.

Gill Bishop gazed serenely at the harbor far below their

hedge fund's trading room. Miniature naval vessels were docked in the superpiers along Twelfth Avenue. A broad swath of the Hudson River was flecked with white wakes. The partners stood so high above the city that everything seemed frozen, the tugs and ferries, a freighter steaming down the river, another steaming up, all appeared as motionless as the hands of a clock.

"Well?"

Gill finally turned to him. "You remember back in the eighties we used to call ourselves Big Swinging Dicks?"

"What?"

"These days everybody's so corporate, they call themselves BSDs. We're getting old, Phil. I don't like a world of BSDs. I'd rather be a big swinging dick."

"Are you out of your fucking mind?" Phil shouted. "We just sold—"

Gill Bishop interrupted. "You ever think what you're going to do when you retire?"

Phil Levy looked at his partner in disbelief. Standing at the window with the remains of his lunch coating his shirt, Gill was babbling small talk. While the thousands of contracts they had promised to buy had gone higher, not lower. They were looking at a lava flow of losses.

"If we don't cover," ventured Phil, "if we don't *buy back right now*, we're looking at losing more money than we've made in ten years. Shit, what am I saying? It's too late already."

Gone in a flash, his house in Greenwich, the Park Avenue place, the butler, the kids' schools, his wife's subsidized landscape-design career, the Mercedes, the Jag, the Range Rover, the sixteen-hundred-square-foot loft he'd bought his girlfriend in Tribeca.

A trader looked over his shoulder for instructions.

"Keep selling," said Gill.

"More?" blatted Phil. "We could buy back. Take our

losses. Longer we wait the more we lose. We can get out now."

"When I retire," mused Gill, "I want to get a job as an IRS collection agent."

All gone, like ice cream in hell. "*What* did you say?"

"Those government collection guys have a neat time, shut a business down three o'clock on a Friday afternoon; if the owner's Jewish, wish him 'Good Shabbas.' Say, look at that!"

Smoke was rising from the aircraft carrier docked at the foot of Fifty-second Street. A thin dark line that thickened quickly to a black, oily billow. Suddenly, tiny tin-soldier sailors, their duties marked by the color of their shirts, were running around the flight deck.

"What did I tell you? It's starting," said Gill.

"What are you talking? It could be anything. A fire in the kitchen."

"Is *that* a fire in the kitchen?" asked Gill, pointing at some barges downriver. A whole bunch of them, floating off the Chelsea Piers. Where, before they were rich, Phil and Gill used to practice their golf swings at the driving range. Where they'd be teeing off again, after today.

"That's a tugboat between two barges. And so is that! And so is that!"

"Is not."

"Is so."

Phil scowled at the barges. Mr. Inside Information's knowing ten minutes ahead of everybody that McDonald's was flipping top management added value. But to bet everything on a geriatric jet pilot squinting through Coke-bottle eyeglasses—

"And look at that," said Gill, still sounding so certain that Phil wanted to kill him. Zelda, Phil's girlfriend, had made her tastes and standards clear from the start: bucks made the BSD.

"We don't have time for this crap," stormed Phil.

Gill merely pointed at another barge-and-tug combo out in the middle of the river behind the aircraft carrier. Phil peered at it sourly. Maybe it wasn't a barge. It was long like a barge, but narrower. Then something weird on the deck flashed.

The next second they heard an explosion, loud through the thick glass. Fire and burning pieces flew from a windowless building two blocks away on Tenth Avenue.

"Telephone switching center," Gill said matter-of-factly. "I guess they're taking out communications."

"Who?"

"Probably the ones who were buying gold this morning."

Thank God, thought Phil. *We are saved.*

Gill's cellphone chirped on his belt. "Hey, there. . . . Thanks. . . . Yeah, and here they hit the aircraft carrier and the phone building. Say, look at that. They're coming ashore at Fifty-seventh Street."

Phil had missed that. A black submarine was jammed against the Sanitation pier. Soldiers were swarming like ants across the West Side Highway. Cars were fleeing up side streets, running onto the sidewalks.

A second explosion shook their own building.

The shock wave knocked both men to the carpet. Phil gaped at the crazed glass, which was frosted by a million tiny cracks.

Then the window began to dissolve, pouring to the carpet with a faint hiss and tinkle, and then there was nothing but air where a glass wall had stood between them and the sky five hundred feet above Manhattan.

People were screaming in the stairwells.

Captain Eddie, the retired merchant marine machinist's mate and part-time handyman who had awakened the mayor's press secretary with his plumber's snake, felt his heart jump with terrible memories when torpedoes slammed into the *Kennedy*.

He had been directing the younger Intrepid Sea-Air-Space Museum volunteers cutting "tourist doors" through watertight bulkheads in the boiler room of the decommissioned Vietnam War destroyer *Edward Rollins*. Four blocks downriver, they felt the concussion thump right through the *Rollins*'s hull.

We're next, screamed the awful thought.

Five times around the world in World War Two, deep in the bowels of slow-moving merchant ships, Eddie had seen the ocean only twice—on D-Day, dog-paddling away from what a Nazi E-boat had left of the old *Susy Q;* and six months later, rousted into the South Pacific by a Jap torpedo. The English Channel had been thick with bunker oil; the Pacific, thicker with sharks.

His eye fell on a barrel of brooms kept ready to test for invisible superheated steam leaks that would cut a man in half. You crept through the narrow spaces waving the broom ahead of you until the leak chopped it. He saw cobwebs on the brooms. The *Rollins* was moored in the museum. Her furnaces cold, her boiler room silent as a tomb.

A second shock wave hammered the hull.

"Construction accident?" ventured Jake, the crippled ironworker.

"Big one," said Al, a subway motorman.

So Eddie and the boys snuffled and wheezed up on deck for a look. The old merchant sailors' lungs were hopelessly clogged with decades of bunker smoke and the climb from the engine room took a while. But up on deck, it didn't take them long to see there was a war on, with black-clad commandos shooting up Twelfth Avenue.

Eddie wouldn't have believed it if he hadn't seen it. Tourists were running and screaming, cops shooting, grenades exploding, trucks and taxis, cars and buses jumping sidewalks to get away. *"Look!"* The river was alive with submarines speeding on the surface. The volunteers concluded quickly that they were already aboard the best cover around, and snuffled back down to the boiler room.

Old Eddie watched his buddies, huddled, bewildered, and frightened, wondering about their kids at work and their grandkids in school, as they listened to the gunfire and waited for God knew what. He didn't have any kids, no grandkids, no wife—never married—didn't have anyone. Most everyone he had known in his long life had died, except these buddies and the super at work, and young Captain Ken and old Charlie.

"Maybe," he said, "we oughta light off one of her boilers."

Everyone looked at Eddie. On any other naval vessel in the museum, that would be a lame joke. But the *Rollins* was different.

The destroyer had come in under her own power—with a nudge from Ken Hughes's *Chelsea Queen*. Ordinarily, decommissioned ships were towed in as disabled hulks, the Navy having clamped seizing gear onto her shafts, or burned them up running them dry, or cannibalized vital parts for another ship. The volunteers had debated why the Navy hadn't disabled this particular destroyer: laziness, a bureaucratic screwup, or simply to save money on a tow. (Eddie was of the opinion that the decommissioning officer had served aboard her during Vietnam and had a soft spot for the old tigress.) Whatever, a couple of her high-pressure boilers still worked and there'd been plenty of quiet chuckles about one night hooking up a turbine and taking her for a ride—all four hundred and eighteen feet of her—when no one was looking.

Navy Airman Ensign Eldon Routh had telephoned home to tell his parents not to worry, he was getting along fine in

New York City. He'd already met the mayor. And a nice old lady, Mrs. Nussbaum, had invited the Dragonslayer Squadron to see the opera.

Lily Nussbaum was mother to four sons by two husbands—Moe Weintraub, killed late in World War Two taking Tinian Island back from the Japanese when Lily was nineteen; and Al Nussbaum, died at his desk typing headlines for the *Daily News*. Every Fleet Week, Lily blossomed as ambassadress of the opera and Jewish mother to sailors far from home.

She had synopsized *I Puritani* over a bagels-and-lox brunch on borrowed card tables in her tiny apartment, then loaded the young men with picnic baskets she'd been packing for days and shepherded them into Central Park to hear the Metropolitan Opera rehearse that night's special outdoor performance.

Blankets waited under a shade tree with a clear view of the stage—a coveted site staked out by Lily's mah-jongg companions, formidable as rhinoceroses and attended by reluctant granddaughters, whose sulkiness evaporated when the naval airmen turned out to be, not the dorks they'd dreaded, but frank and open, clear-eyed young men who looked more mysterious and much hotter than schoolboys in elephant pants.

Lily narrated the libretto while they gnawed on cold chicken, sipped white wine, and sized up the granddaughters. They had been politely attentive, even muffling their snickers when soldiers, played by the American Guild of Musical Artists' union chorus, plodded to Riccardo's rescue as dispiritedly as husbands sent to pick up the dry cleaning.

But when the five-foot-tall tenor, who was round as a beach ball, waved his sword like a steak knife at the six-foot-six baritone, the sailors collapsed in laughter. All but Ensign Routh, who was so enraptured by his first opera that he noticed neither his laughing companions nor the bevy of granddaughters clustered on his blanket like King David's concubines.

A distant explosion, muffled by buildings, brought the Dragonslayers' heads up sharply. It had sounded from the East Side. Minutes later a second explosion boomed from the West Side.

Then the music ruled again—sixty voices and a hundred instruments soaring over the sun-drenched park—suddenly shattered by a new noise, sharp and distinct.

Routh looked at his buddy Nichols. The helo pilots jumped to their feet.

"What the fu—"

Two miles away, muffled by six wide blocks of city buildings, it was the once-heard-never-forgotten roar of their ship's twenty-millimeter Vulcan-Phalanx six-barreled rotary cannons. Two of them, mounted aft, port and starboard, firing three thousand rounds per minute of spent-uranium, armor-piercing shells.

At what?

"Thank you, ma'am, for the music!"

The naval airmen bolted across the Sheep Meadow, west toward the walls of apartment buildings and the unfamiliar streets to their ship. Nichols sprinted ahead, he and Routh far in the lead, gaining with every long stride.

Police Officers Greene and Sanchez ran down East End Avenue, shouting at civilians to get off the street. Wild fire spattered cars, trees, and windows. They sheltered behind the stone wall of Beth Israel Hospital North.

"Those poor guys," Hector Sanchez kept mumbling. "Those poor guys."

Harriet Greene's ears were still ringing from the cannon fire by the river wall. "Inside!" she yelled at a hospital security guard poking a curious head out a window.

They had run through the house and piled out the front door in time to see the Rudy Van's escort Blazer dissolve in a pillar of smoke and flame. Before they could try to pull the guys out, the gas tank blew up and knocked her and Hector off their feet, and if the guys hadn't been dead already, they were now.

Only this morning, Harriet Greene had decided that if Bob Thomas kidded one more time about asking her out, she was going to surprise both of them by asking *him* out. Even if he was white and old and lived in Queens.

The morning felt like eighty years ago. Cars were burning. The black-clad troops were fanning into the streets. Police cars were scattered at crazy angles, bullet-riddled or on fire.

"Where'd the mayor go?"

"I don't know. But he got away."

"Now what do we do?"

Harriet felt weirdly, wildly, alive. Sure, she was crying and sure, her hands were shaking. But her brain was racing. And everything she locked eyes on seemed to move in slow motion. Like she could see motion almost before it happened.

"We better find him," she said.

"What?"

"Hector! Everyone here's dead. The mayor's gone. And you and me, we're attached to his security detail."

"But I don't think we should leave the house."

"They *own* the house. We're outta here."

"Where?"

"Downtown. Emergency Management or One-PP. He'll be down there somewhere."

Before they had run a block, Harriet spotted soldiers flitting through the trees in Carl Schurz Park, pulling ahead of them.

"They're flanking us along the river," she said, sprinting for the next cross street to burrow deeper into the island.

*   *   *

"Look!" gasped Peter.

"At what?" Jon fired back. Thick ropes still tied *Jon's Luncheon Yacht* firmly to the North Cove dock. "My clients have better views from their own apartments."

That appeared to have silenced the riding-crop queen, and indeed, Peter's bony face had frozen like a skull.

This prompted Larry Neale to interject, "Peter, have you ever considered hosting a Spanish Inquisition Night?"

"Look," whispered Peter. This time he pointed.

Larry Neale turned around and said, "Oh, my God."

A big black submarine was racing into the cove, its front crowded with soldiers.

"It's Fleet Week," said Jon.

"It's going to hit us."

Larry gripped the doorframe and steadied Jon by his elbow. A second later the submarine smashed the back of the yacht. The impact slammed him into the kitchen door and knocked Jon and Peter to the floor. The dining room was suddenly shrill as a birdhouse with screaming ladies, breaking glass, and cursing models.

Larry hauled his friends to their feet. "We better get these women out of here."

The yacht's bearded captain ran out the back door, shouting and waving his fist. The soldiers pointed guns at him. And to Larry's shock and utter disbelief, jagged red holes erupted in the captain's white uniform. The man pinwheeled backward, crashed against the windows, and slid down them, smearing the glass with his blood.

"Oh, my God," said Peter. "They killed him." But the killing had only begun. The soldiers sprayed the moorings, the steps, and the esplanade with their machine guns. Lunchtime strollers and hundreds in the outdoor cafes ran screaming. The submarine rammed past *Jon's Luncheon*

Yacht, shoved its blunt nose against a dock, dropped a gang-plank, and disembarked its soldiers, who, shooting and yelling, cleared a wide open corridor from the yacht harbor and across the plaza to Liberty Street.

Then, in only seconds, it seemed to Larry, a strange silence descended. Jon and Peter's clients had stopped screaming. The pedestrians and outdoor cafe customers had vanished from the plaza, except for bodies on the paving stones. Even the black-clad soldiers were quiet, some patrolling the corridor to Liberty Street, others streaming into the Winter Garden, while a second and third submarine steamed up to disembark more soldiers. Thirty or forty of the second wave looked like a Con Ed repair crew, laden with toolboxes and jackhammers.

"What are they doing?" whispered Larry as the new arrivals ran their heavy loads up the corridor guarded by the first landing.

Jon knew this corporate-suburbanized downtown district better than most New Yorkers. "They must be heading for the World Trade Center."

"Oh, no." Larry hunted his personal cellphone out of the shopping bag he had taken from his Gracie Mansion desk. No answer at Gracie Mansion. He called Renata's cellphone. Busy. Either she was juggling both lines or something awful had happened to her.

"Who are you calling?" murmured Jon.

"Renata. I've got to warn her not to come to the Emergency Control Center."

18

"MR. MAYOR, I told you to put on your fucking seat belt, sir," said Luther Washington. "You, too, Renata."

Both mayor and press secretary were hunched over their cellphones in the back of the Rudy Van with their hands cupping their ears to block out the shrieking sirens, whoopers, and air horns that Juan Rodriguez had screaming at full blast to bull through the traffic on Second Avenue. Six miles of midday traffic stood between them and the World Trade Center complex, where the mayor's Emergency Control Center had secure phones and power source, and food and water to support nearly a hundred emergency coordinators.

Twice they'd picked up impromptu radio motor-patrol escorts; twice they'd lost them. Juan Rodriguez wasn't waiting for anything. Twice the Suburban's double-size bumpers had shoved taxis out of the way, and a third time, at Fifty-sixth Street, some Jersey yuppie in a Range Rover, with a crunch that drew cheers from pedestrians.

Mayor Mincarelli automatically waved back.

The city was so big and dense that, less than forty blocks from Gracie Mansion, nobody on the street had a clue what had happened.

"I've got to get these people off the street. Renata, get me a voice patch into News 88, 1010 WINS, Bloomberg and CNBC and New York Yes!"

Renata was talking into two phones at once. "I'm putting it together now."

"Gotta get over to Lex," muttered Juan, leaning the monster into a hairpin turn that set taxis blaring and threw his precious cargo in a heap against the door.

"Seat belts," Luther roared again, pointing the gun he had yet to holster vaguely in their direction. This time they obeyed.

Mincarelli was too busy trying to figure out what was happening to think about danger, until he heard a sobering note of fear in Luther's voice. Luther had been the bravest cop on the strike force—point man on the ram—first through the door, first to discover that the maniac inside was better-armed and more vicious than informants had led them to believe.

But rocket grenades fired by elite assault troops were not supposed to go with the job. Poor Bob and the guys behind them hadn't had a chance, which had to be preying on Luther's mind as he sat there, powerless to act while Juan drove.

"Luther, poll the precincts ahead and find out if there's any route we shouldn't take."

Renata's cellphone beeped Call Waiting in her ear. "What?"

"It's Larry," yelled a hysterical-sounding Larry Neale. "You okay?"

"Yes, get off the phone."

"Don't go anywhere near the Emergency Control Center."

"What?"

"I'm downtown. Submarines are bombarding it."

Renata felt hope slide out of her. The control center had been their only chance.

Larry sounded terrified. "There's broken glass all over, cars blowing up, people are going crazy—oh, shit, more soldiers—I gotta go—don't come here!"

He cut off and Renata turned to her boss. "Rudy! They're shelling the streets around the control center."

All in the speeding SUV fell silent.

The blastproof Emergency Control Center in the World Trade complex had been built at a cost of fifteen million dollars to coordinate government disaster response. It was supposed to be safe inside, if they could reach it.

"Luther, what do you say?"

"This ain't no tank, Mr. Mayor. Shrapnel'll come in one side, through us, and out the other."

"So we go in underground, through the subway."

Luther shook his head. "I got to tell you, Mr. Mayor, even if you get through that mess, that building wasn't built to survive sustained shelling. Hell, that sub they sent after us had a regular *cannon* on the front. Who knows what else they got?"

"If they're shelling the control center," said Renata, "they've done their homework."

" 'Fraid so," said Luther. "They keep us out of there, there won't be any emergency management."

"Mr. Mayor?" Juan snapped over his shoulder. "You want me to head for One-PP instead?"

The mayor thought hard. One Police Plaza looked like a fortress, but it wasn't one. Only years after it was built had it dawned on anyone that the public parking garage underneath might prove attractive to terrorist bombers—revealing an old-fashioned urban-police preoccupation with mobs instead of guerrilla fighters, much less invading armies. Just as his Office of Emergency Management was geared to respond to normal disasters like blackouts, train wrecks, and storms.

He had just spoken to Greg Walsh, who had confirmed that the city was under a broad military attack: moments after the *John F. Kennedy* had been torpedoed at Pier 92, the ship that the Chinese had sent to Fleet Week starting firing rockets, which had already set ablaze a phone building supposedly built to protect vital switching equipment in the event of nuclear attack. He'd be a sitting duck confined within One Police Plaza's thin walls.

"Where are we now?" He looked out; they were just approaching Grand Central Station. A heavy explosion *whoomped* in the distance, the direction impossible to tell. He thought about the subway, but if the attackers knocked out the power, he'd be trapped on a dark train in the middle of nowhere.

Renata touched his shoulder. "They've come ashore in Chelsea."

"Luther!" barked Rudy. "Call the Tenth." The Tenth Precinct was between Seventh and Eighth avenues, four long blocks in from the Hudson River. "Just keep heading downtown," he told Juan.

In the front seat, Luther had holstered his pistol to work the radios with both hands. "The Tenth says they're responding to reports of gunfire on Eleventh Avenue—sir, I got the Seventeenth on the air—reports of soldiers at the Con Ed plant."

East Thirty-fourth Street.

Jesus, how many were there? He'd be caught in the squeeze if they were landing from the East River, too. "Renata, see if you can get me the White House."

But even as he spoke, the cellphone in his right hand rang and when he answered a White House operator said, "Mayor Mincarelli, the President of the United States will speak to you." The President, accustomed to instantaneous communication, started speaking immediately.

"Rudy, hear tell you're having a bad day up there."

Mincarelli was in no mood for a calculatedly folksy manner even if it was intended to put him at ease. "We've been invaded, Mr. President. They've landed submarines on both sides of Manhattan Island. And a Red Chinese warship is firing at our buildings."

"We are taking action. But while we sort out how big a war we've got going, I want you to get yourself to a secure military position without delay."

Mayor Mincarelli stifled the impulse to hang up on the jerk. Even if a secure military position existed, he would be a virtual prisoner of the military—like Charles DeGaulle stuck in London, begging favors while the Germans trounced France.

"Mr. President, I've got eight million people in very close quarters here. A military response could lead to major bloodshed."

"Get away now," ordered the president. "You've a duty to your people not to be captured as a prisoner of war—and you're sure as hell not going to make my job any easier if you're a hostage. Report to me when you're someplace safe."

The president hung up, leaving Rudy Mincarelli to ponder the chilling echo of, "We are taking action."

His worst nightmare had always been a plane crash in Manhattan. Back when he was in law school, a helicopter had crashed on the since-banned heliport atop the old Pan Am Building. In that relatively minor accident, flying debris had destroyed entire offices for a ten-block radius. But the thing that had never left his mind was that a broken rotor blade had sailed north from Forty-fourth and Park, skimming building tops, until it fell to the corner of Fiftieth and Madison, where it chopped a woman in half.

A military counterattack would kill tens of thousands. He

imagined the maimed and dying trapped on high floors with no elevators, no water to bathe wounds, and mountain descents to mobbed hospitals. Thank God his children were in Seattle.

Guilt immediately obliterated his relief, shame for thinking his family was safe when the millions who depended upon him faced unspeakable suffering.

"Renata, get me Marty Greenberg."

Renata was miles ahead of him. She passed him one of her phones and took his. "Marty Greenberg. He's just heading into the Oval Office."

The mayor and the president's chief counsel had fought their first battles editing the Fordham Law Review. They'd served as assistant U.S. Attorneys together and when Rudy had been appointed the Southern District's U.S. Attorney, Marty had stayed on to run his Criminal Division and had been a charter member of the strike force. Even while getting very rich in private practice, he'd done dollar-a-year consulting for the mayor. When Marty was finally persuaded to move to Washington, the President of the United States had told *Newsweek* that Marty Greenberg was almost as intelligent as Mayor Mincarelli and "a whole heck of a lot easier to get along with."

"Marty, we're under attack by Chinese submarines."

"We're talking to the Navy now, Rudy. What do you know?"

"They tried to snatch me from Gracie Mansion. They're landing on both sides of Manhattan. They torpedoed the *John F. Kennedy.* They're firing rockets at the phone buildings. And I just learned that they're shelling my Emergency Control Center."

"Mr. Mayor," called Luther. "They sealed off the Queens-Midtown Tunnel."

"What? On the Manhattan side?"

"Manhattan side. No reports from Queens yet."

"They've just hit the Midtown Tunnel, Marty. What do *you* know?"

Marty Greenberg said, "Just what's coming down from New York. CNN's reporting an explosion on the *John F. Kennedy*. And a fire on the East Side. I've got unconfirmed reports they've sunk some of the Fleet Week ships. Somebody saw a British frigate on its side."

"What other cities are they attacking?"

"None."

"None?"

"None so far. Just New York."

"No other cities are under attack? There's a war going on here, for crissake, Marty."

"Maybe some kind of terrorist thing?"

"There's way too many of them. These are troops, for crissake. And a Chinese warship. What did the Chinese tell you?"

"We're in the process of making contact."

"Get the lead out, Marty! I've got submarines shelling my city. Soldiers are shooting up the streets."

"Don't worry, we'll sink the subs and destroy their soldiers."

"No!" shouted the mayor. "I've got eight million people here. Marty, you have to convince the President, this is a city. It's not a war zone."

Marty turned formal. "I will inform the President of your concern," he answered coolly.

Two blunt reminders in as many minutes that the inequality of the mayor of New York to the President of the United States rendered him impotent further inflamed the mayor. "Inform him right now, dammit! No counterattack!"

"Gotta go. The Man just beeped me."

"Make it crystal clear to that wimp that the blood of New York City will be on his head if he sends in the military."

"Talk to you, Rudy."

"Marty, goddammit—" But the phone was silent.

Renata had never seen him this wired. Veins were popping from his temple, his shoulders were locked tight as compressed steel, his face was white, his lips like stone. She reached to touch him.

"Get me Greg Walsh, again! Marty doesn't know any more than we do. Luther, how we doing?"

"We better stay in the middle," said Luther. "They're all over the edges."

"You still want One-PP?" Juan asked again.

If they were attacking the phones and electricity and Con Ed and the tunnels and the Control Center, they surely knew to attack One Police Plaza.

"How about City Hall, Mr. Mayor?"

But City Hall was only slightly deeper within the island, a stone's throw from One Police Plaza. Manhattan was much narrower so far downtown. They'd surely attack it, too. City Hall was completely indefensible.

Renata handed him a phone. "Greg Walsh."

"Greg, you still on that ship?"

"What's left of it. The whole ass end's on fire."

"Do they have any helicopters?"

"First thing the bastards shot up. Six of 'em lined up for Fleet Week. Sitting ducks."

"That's a break. Give us time to defuse this before it turns into a full-blown war."

"I hear they're loading the last two with antisubmarine rockets."

"We can't allow that kind of a shoot-out."

"I don't see how we can stop them. These Navy guys are really pissed, putting it mildly."

"I'm appointing you my emissary to Washington."

"Thanks, Rudy. But I'm not in Washington."

"Get there."

Greg did not ask how he was supposed to accomplish the journey. Only, "What do you want?"

"I need you to hold Marty Greenberg's dick for him. Make Marty convince the President that we absolutely cannot allow a war to be fought in this city. No counterattack. Make it clear to Marty that whoever they are, they've got to be stopped some other way—outside the city."

Greg did not believe that Marty was Rudy's best route to the President. It was true that Marty had always needed someone to stiffen his backbone. But the mayor didn't understand that since Marty had become the President's lawyer he no longer regarded Rudy as his boss.

"Rudy, we've got two senators—"

"Pat's visiting Ireland. The Kid's in Israel. Call me when you get to the White House. "

"Union Square coming up, sir," Juan called over his shoulder. "I gotta commit."

Mincarelli listened to the siren shriek, watched the sidewalks, where people were starting to understand that something was wrong. There was a lot of head craning and looking around. Over the sound of the siren he was feeling heavy thumps of distant explosions. People were clustering at street corners to look east and west on the cross streets.

"Renata, where's that radio patch?"

"Coming."

"Now, dammit!" He was growing frantic. Every police report revealed the attackers squeezing the island; every phone call another precinct under attack. The lawyerly voices in his brain had been stunned into silence, so he retreated into himself for a moment and prayed to God. Almost immediately, a calm fell over him; he knew where to go.

"Juan! Head for the Old Place."

"Yes, sir," said Juan, and Luther nodded emphatically. Good move.

Only move, thought Renata Bradley. Her shoulder bag bulged like a shoplifter's; as they'd run from Gracie Mansion she had grabbed every cellphone she could. She'd had a premonition they'd end up there instead of at the control center.

It was in Rudy's nature.

Despite the occasional rumor, the reporters had never caught wind of the Old Place, thank God. They'd been too busy beating up on Rudy's Emergency Control Center, which they had misnamed—with a viciousness that made Renata hate every so-called journalist in New York—The Bunker.

The beautiful irony was that Rudy didn't need a bunker. He already had one, known to a select handful of his team from his days with the Mafia strike force. He hadn't used the Old Place in years—since long before he was mayor—but it lay quiet and empty deep beneath the streets. And ever-present in his mind, as comforting as a daydream.

The Old Place was hidden. It was fortified. It had secure phone lines because they had feared the Mafia was using corrupt phone-company workers to tap lines into the strike force. It even had escape tunnels.

The hideout was—a fact grasped by almost no one in his inner circle—a sort of model for the mayor's mental state. He might or might not be paranoid, but in the event things turned against him, he had a secret place to retreat to while he figured out who was after him and how to destroy them.

Mayor Mincarelli looked at Renata and took strength from the fact that they so often thought with one mind. Which made the gossip about them so outrageous; leave it to the out-of-control "free press" to impugn such deep and intimate understanding between a man and a woman as mere sex. He knew why: they hated that he was incorruptible.

"Radio patch." She handed him a cellphone with a direct line to every all-news station in the city.

"My city is under attack," the mayor began in the tones of sober outrage that New Yorkers had come to expect from him.

Renata nudged him lightly.

"*Our* city is under attack," he amended smoothly. "The attack is both unbelievable and real. Believe me, it is real. And it is deadly.

"Heavily armed soldiers have landed, apparently by submarine. Who they are and why they've attacked us, I cannot tell you yet. We have alerted the President of the United States. I hereby order all civilians to get inside and stay inside, indoors, in your offices and homes and off the streets. I order all building managers who still have air-raid or civil-defense shelters in their basements to open them to the public."

Renata nudged him and mouthed, "Water."

"Water. Fill bathtubs and sinks and buckets with drinking water, in case we lose electricity. Remember, if your building is taller than six stories, it requires electricity to pump water up to your tank. And I repeat, stay clear of the attackers, do not provoke them. I have seen them kill.

"I order all police and firefighters to report to their precincts and station houses, all doctors and nurses and ambulance drivers to their hospitals, all corrections officers to their prisons, all sanitation workers to their garages. I am ordering the Transit Authority to empty all subway trains at the nearest station, rather than risk being stranded in the tunnels if the MTA's power plants are disabled. Those passengers should remain in the stations where their trains have stopped."

Renata Bradley touched his knee. "Enough," she whispered.

"Finally, I want to encourage everyone in our city to stay calm and stand together until we find out who's behind this and how to stop them."

"The guy talks like a lawyer," said Harriet Greene.

"He *is* a lawyer," Hector reminded her.

The two rookie cops had ducked, just in time to catch the last lines of the mayor's broadcast, into Cirillo's Pizza on Third Avenue. A crowd had gathered around the owner's radio.

Five lanes of gridlocked cabs and trucks jammed the northbound avenue. If there was any weapons fire, it was drowned out by the horns.

"Those guys aren't street hoods," said Harriet. "We need a general, not a lawyer."

"You don't even like him, so why are you so hot to find him?"

"Because it's our job, Counselor-on-the-come. He's our assignment."

"Officer," someone asked, "what's going on?"

"Yeah, what's happening?"

"Who's attacking us?"

"What's the mayor saying?"

Harriet said, "The mayor's saying, keep your head down and go home. If you're not from the neighborhood, hang here with Mr. Cirillo. Mr. Cirillo, we're sorry for any inconvenience, but Officer Sanchez and I are commandeering your bicycles."

She wrote slowly, in a careful hand, "Two delivery bikes from Cirillo's Pizza at 1 p.m. Tuesday," on the back of a summons, dated and signed it. Despite every effort, she had reversed the *e* and *s* in "Tuesday," but there wasn't time to fix it. "Here's your receipt. Hector, let's roll."

19

THE STATEN ISLAND FERRY passengers huddled around radios heard the mayor's broadcast—underscored by the Rudy Van's siren and whoopers. They immediately started screaming at the hapless deckhands slouching by the mooring ramps to turn the boat around and go back to Staten Island.

Kate Ross was appalled—the ferry was so close to Manhattan she could practically touch the plain, strong lines of the terminal. But the passengers were pleading with the scruffy crew, pleas which turned to curses.

She spotted a life-raft canister, but reckoned slim chances of making it over the side. It was a long way down and the hull projected an enormous overhang. Even if she could launch the raft and climb in, then what? Drift around in the crazy currents and pray somebody would pick her up?

Frightened passengers were storming the stairs to the upper deck. Others were gaping at a ship turned over in the Hudson. Its shining bottom and gleaming propellers looked oddly toylike. Another ship was pillaring dark smoke into the blue sky. A submarine was racing on the surface, cutting a tremendous white-bow wave and belching black diesel exhaust, pursuing something obscured by the broad shoulder of Battery Park City.

More smoke was rising from Manhattan's Hudson shore. And yet the financial district, the Battery basking in the midday sun, and the ferry docks looked almost normal, except for the people running toward the terminal. Hundreds of them, thousands.

Kate bounded up the stairs to the upper deck and saw people fighting to get up the stairs to the forward wheelhouse, from which she had just radioed Ken. A crewman in blue overalls was sprawled on the deck, bleeding from his nose. Two others were trying to protect the stairs, kicking and punching at the mob determined to storm the wheelhouse.

The black kid with the cellphone was standing beside her, shaking his head. "Staten Island? These folks are crazy."

Kate said, "I don't want to go back, either."

Their gazes fell simultaneously on a fire station.

"You got it, sister."

She showed him how to uncoil the flat canvas fire hose. Then she took the nozzle while he threw his skinny weight against the valve. The fabric filled hard as a pipe. She twisted the long brass nozzle open and tried to train the icy spray on the mob on the stairs. The pressure was enormous, bucking the hose out of her hands. He lunged to help and they directed it at the tightest knot of the mob for a moment longer before they slipped and lost their footing on the wet deck. The nozzle flew from their hands and thrashed around the ferry cabin like a demented cobra, soaking people in every direction and knocking them down.

The mob scattered.

Another grouped.

Loudspeakers roared:

"Please be calm, ladies and gentlemen. Please be calm. This is your ferry captain. This boat is not turning back. We are not turning around. Repeat, not turning around. If we ran for Staten Island they'd sink us miles from shore. Anybody don't believe me, look over the left side."

Another ship was sinking, a tidy little Fleet Week visitor with twin square funnels aft and a pint-sized cannon on its bow. Already the water had risen up to its main deck. Some brave soul managed to fire a single shot from the cannon, while another defiantly raised the French flag above her superstructure.

The mob fell silent, mesmerized by her struggle, and when she managed to fire a second shot, several passengers cheered. A cheer that died when suddenly, with a flash of light and a muffled thud felt through the ferry's decks, she exploded. The back of the little ship appeared to break off and it collapsed in on itself as if giants romping in a mud puddle had stomped it to the bottom.

The passengers were still gaping in stunned silence when the ferry reversed its propeller and came to a screeching rubbing crunching stop inside its wood-lined berth at the foot of Manhattan.

Kate tried to run ashore. But another mob trying to leave Manhattan flattened the steel scissor gates and shoved her back aboard, even as the loudspeakers doomed any hope of escape: *"This ferry is not leaving the dock. Repeat, not leaving the dock. There is no service to Staten Island. No service leaving Manhattan."*

A chain link fence, topped with razor wire, stood between Jose Chin and a pier that jutted into the East River on the wrong side of the biggest news story in the history of the world. Instead of satellite-beaming battle scenes from Manhattan Island to the entire planet, he was stuck at Hunters

Point, where Newtown Creek divided Brooklyn from Queens, watching CNN like a couch potato.

Smoke drifted among the skyscrapers.

Directly across the half-mile-wide river was Thirty-fourth Street, Manhattan. He was probably standing on top of the goddamned Queens Midtown Tunnel, which was blocked by cars and trucks and—screamed panicked taxi drivers on Jasbir Singh's two-way radio—Chinese commandos on the Manhattan side.

"So?" asked Jasbir Singh, who was thrusting Jose's umbrella dish skyward like a high-tech Bengal Lancer to downlink the satellite feed from CNN.

Jose had tapped into a light pole to top up his batteries and power the TV in the camera. The electricity still worked, but not the phone lines. Even when he tried New York Yes! on his cellphone, he got zilch.

The GeekNet was beeper-casting a swiftly rolling eight-line kaleidoscope of fires, blocked ambulances and fire trucks, with looters running amok. Jasbir's fellow Sikh cabdrivers were reporting gridlock chaos. While, flickering in miniature, CNN was pretending to cover what the hell was going on.

"This is truly the most astonishing news event of our time," said anchorman Bernie, reporting magisterially from the great perspective that Atlanta, Georgia, gave on the city of New York. "And every correspondent filing the story is as shocked and baffled as I. The invaders, who numerous observers claim are Chinese nationals, appear to be blocking Manhattan's tunnels and bridges. If that is true, more than two million residents and commuters will be trapped on Manhattan Island.

"CNN news choppers have been grounded by the U.S. Air Force, but look at this live sky-cam view of what the people of New York are enduring."

"Oh, give me a break," yelled Jose when he saw they were scanning the smoking island with a thousand-millimeter lens which might have been platformed in Philadelphia for all the detail it revealed. "That's not the street. That's Sony Playstation. Goddammit, goddammit, goddammit!"

"Do you suppose we might enjoy better luck at the Fifty-ninth Street Bridge?" Jasbir asked dubiously.

"Do you?" Jose shot back.

"I fear not."

"Oh, shit, look at that."

On the screen was a tight shot of a dozen black-clad commandos sprinting west on East Thirty-fourth Street. It took Jose a moment to figure out the source. Somehow, those suburban CNN bastards had clipped into one of the Port Authority's remote traffic cameras. The Authority had a thousand of them scattered around the bridges, tunnels, and airports. This one was probably right across the river at the Queens-Midtown Tunnel. It was an amazing shot—he could actually see the lead soldier spreading his men with hand signals—and it turned Jose's blood cold to see what a bunch of geek engineers could cobble together while a real reporter was stuck on the wrong side of the river.

In a hot, small conference room on the sixty-fourth floor of the World Trade Center, a lone technician with sweaty palms was switching cameras from around the city. Vinnie Musto wasn't a director, but he was the only man left in the Port Authority's monitoring center and he was doing his damnedest to feed live video of the incredible attack to the outside world.

Up at CNN across from the Garden was a guy from the neighborhood named Richie Vetere. Richie had telephoned right after the attack started and they'd quick-slapped together a feed. The big question was how long before the bastards blew up Con Ed. Vinnie had backup generators making juice on the roof, but that would power only the studio, not his thousand cameras. Some of them had battery backup. Most did not. Any second now he expected to see a lot of screens go black.

He heard a commotion in the hall. Thank God, somebody else to help. "Yo! In here," he called. "C'mere."

The door was locked. "Hang on, I'll get it."

He ripped off his headset and sprinted to the door. As he reached for the knob, it seemed to explode in his hand. He fell backward, too shocked to feel pain, astonished by the gaping hole where the knob had been, and by the knob itself protruding from his stomach. Black-clad soldiers kicked the door open, raised their weapons, and riddled the monitors with automatic fire.

Jose's screen went dark. He checked his connections to the light pole. He still had juice. Then Bernie was back, reporting "We've lost our signal from Manhattan."

"Jasbir, I gotta get over there."

"Maybe a subway."

"Forget the subway."

The mayor kept warning that he had shut them down, afraid of trapping people underground. He'd been broadcasting audio intermittently for the last hour, fading at times as radio stations went down, coming back in fits and starts. Jose suspected he was patching cellphone calls into out-of-town transmitters.

WNYC, the public radio station, had lost it early. Jose could see the stump of their AM tower down the shore a ways, where the fallen steel spire now lay draped over several piers like a strand of linguine.

Mayor Mincarelli had sounded like he didn't know a lot more than Bernie in Atlanta. "Wonder where he's hiding," Jose mused.

"Look!" said Jasbir, pointing at the little screen.

"Hey, that's us!"

CNN was broadcasting a live feed with the New York Yes! logo in the chicklet in the lower right of the screen. Jumpy shots of the Upper East Side, burning police cars, traffic-jammed streets, deserted sidewalks. The camera tilted up and panned white faces staring from the windows. "*Who* is shooting that shit?"

"A brave man," said Jasbir. "Or a fool."

"His camera work sucks."

Suddenly, audio. A voice Jose knew too well: "This is Arnold Moskowitz of New York Yes! reporting live from Second Avenue and Seventy-fourth Street on New York's Upper East Side, where Chinese soldiers have invaded the city."

"Arnie? What the fuck is Arnie doing in the street?"

As if in answer, Arnie Moskowitz panned back down to the sidewalk, blurring the focus as he commenced a long, slow circle of the sidewalk, the street blocked with empty cars and yellow cabs, and the opposite sidewalk, on which stood a New York Yes! live truck, with its microwave antenna telescoped to its full height. Suddenly the moving camera locked on the corner of Second Avenue.

Black-clad soldiers entered the frame. The picture wiggled, as if Arnie and the live-truck guys had started running. But instead of a moving crazy quilt of pavement, car doors, and pounding feet, the camera firmed up rock-steady and fixed on the troops.

"No, no, no," breathed Jose.

The soldiers dropped to one knee and trained their assault rifles at the camera.

"Look out—Arnie, get outta there!"

Arnie's voice was trembling. "This is Arnold Moskowitz of New York Yes! bringing you—"

The screen went black.

Jose fiddled the monitor, trying to bring him back.

"Maybe he's all right," ventured Jasbir. "Maybe they just broke the camera. Maybe they just told him to shut it off."

But when CNN's Bernard Shaw finally came back on from Atlanta, he said, gravely, "We have a cellphone report from a New York Yes! employee that their cameraman has been shot. That was Arnold Moskowitz of New York Yes! reporting the invasion of New York live from Manhattan's Upper East Side."

Jose switched off the camera. He felt shocked by an unexpected sense of loss. "What the hell did he go out in the street for? He hadn't been a shooter since his shoulder gave out. He was a goddamned news director. Should have stayed at the desk."

Jasbir studied the reporter carefully. Jose seemed deeply shaken, though all he ever did was complain about the news director. For once he had stopped jumping around like a busy monkey. He was just staring across the river. His jaw was set. Only his eyelids moved, blinking rapidly.

"I am very sorry, my friend," said Jasbir.

"I got to get over there."

Jasbir shook his head. "I would suggest that the people trying to leave have the better idea."

"Arnie warned me all the time, 'The narrative of history is told by players. You're either a player or you scavenge scraps.' I got to get over there."

There were twenty-two tunnels and eight bridges in and out of New York. Jose ran the East River crossings through his head once more. "Willis Avenue Bridge?"

"No," said Jasbir. He had been polling his fellow Sikh cabbies on his illegally boosted high-gain two-way radio. No to the Triborough. No, the Brooklyn Bridge, the Williamsburg. The upper-river crossings had not been blocked by the invaders, but by drivers attempting to flee, jumping the medians and packing the inbound as well as the outbound lanes.

Jose looked downriver. The Manhattan Bridge was only a mile to the south. Worth checking out. He unplugged from the pole and jumped into Jasbir's taxi for a closer look. The minivan rumbled on narrow cobbled streets between rows and rows of ancient factories. They were mostly deserted, as was usual this close to the East River, though there were sudden bursts of activity at the occasional corner where Queens citizens had gathered tentatively to watch the action.

Several blocks short of the bridge, Jose had to admit it wouldn't get him to Manhattan. Not a car on it was moving, and when he squinted through the zoom lens he could see many car doors open, as if the drivers had abandoned their vehicles and hotfooted it back to Brooklyn. That was a pretty good gauge of how scared people were. It wasn't easy to remove a Brooklyn guy from his car.

"There's got to be a way in. Hey! The Sixty-third Street subway tunnel."

"The subways are blocked," said Jasbir.

"No, no—yeah, yeah—but there's another subway tunnel under the Sixty-third Street subway."

"A subway under the subway?"

"Not a subway. It's the Long Island Railroad. Runs to Second Avenue."

"I am not aware of any Long Island Railroad station at Second Avenue and Sixty-third Street," said Jasbir, proud to put the lie to complaints that the average New York cabbie was more at home in Calcutta.

"I know there's no station, for crissake. They stopped digging the tunnel there. It just stops. It's supposed to tie up with Grand Central. It stops. It's empty—no tracks or anything. They never finished it. Don't you remember 'Tunnel Vision,' my feature on that graffiti gang living in it?"

Jasbir, who did not watch as much New York Yes! as Jose supposed, turned his yellow minivan around and retraced their route north, past Hunters Point, and then onto Vernon

Boulevard. Jose kept craning for glimpses of Manhattan, but the East River was mostly blocked by brick factories and warehouses and crumbling piers. A glimpse of the wedge roof of the Citicorp tower on East Fifty-third looked normal. Like any normal midtown business day, except for the smoke, which was getting thicker.

They drove under the steel-girdered Fifty-ninth Street Bridge and stopped at the end of a park within rock-throwing range of a very tough housing project whose residents were watching from their roof. Roosevelt Island sat in the middle of the river, blocking Jose's view of the Manhattan shore.

"There's an entrance shaft somewhere over there," he said.

"Is there room for my taxi?" asked Jasbir.

"No."

Jasbir cast a glance at the smoke-darkened sky.

"Jasbir, we're looking at a career-making video half a mile across that fucking river—help me, and you can name your price."

"Like your boss Arnie's career?"

"Arnie was a newshound. When the fucking suits bought up the networks and fired everybody to save bucks, what does he do? He goes to cable. Takes a cut from two hundred thousand to forty just to do news. He taught me a ton. Now's my chance to use it. I got to get over there."

Jasbir Singh looked regretfully at his spotless taxi. Ten long years after he had stripped off his Indian Army uniform and fled the Hindu-Sikh religious wars in the Punjab, he had finally saved up the down payment for his own taxi. He had been so excited when he bought the minivan that he had followed the flatbed that took it from the dealer to the body shop so that he could watch them paint it yellow.

He was paying it and the city medallion off by driving

fourteen hours a day. In a few more years he would have enough equity to borrow against the medallion for the down payment to buy a house in Floral Park. It was a very good time to be alive.

But Jose was a good guy. Always paid on time, even if the money came from his own pocket while he waited for the station to reimburse him. Always picked up lunch. Always asked about Jasbir's children.

Jasbir's wife claimed he enjoyed the torrent of information that poured in through Jose's radios. Truly, as they cruised the city, they knew more than other taxis, sometimes more than the police. Sometimes, when fires and shootings and robberies gushed from the scanners, he felt as if they were invincible. But not bulletproof.

"We'll start with triple overtime now, of course. Combat pay. Please, Jasbir. I really need you."

"Okay," he said finally. "But first I'll call my wife and tell her I'm all right."

"You still got that police bar I gave you? We gotta jimmy the door."

His "Tunnel Vision" story had been one of those rare occasions when journalism produced a measurable effect. Thanks to his report, the Long Island Railroad had gone to a lot of trouble to barricade graffiti artists out of their empty tunnel. Getting in proved a safecracker job, which would have been next to impossible without Jose's tool kit and Jasbir's superhuman strength applied to a heavy steel pry bar of the type the police used to peel open car wrecks.

They tore through a fence, a gate, and a steel door, and when the door was finally sagging on one hinge Jasbir was breathing hard. "I better bring my two-way radio."

"And your flashlight," said Jose, shining his own Mag penlight down a deep shaft studded with cement stairs.

Jasbir returned with his flashlight in one hand and his two-way radio tucked under his arm. Jose led the way down into the cool, damp dark, feeling the weight of his camera pack, his batteries, and his antenna, and thinking that the two of them were like every other immigrant who'd ever headed to New York carrying stuff they thought they'd need in a place they'd never seen.

20

KATE FOUGHT TO escape the mobs storming the ferry terminal. At five-five, she couldn't see over heads and shoulders and had to crouch to wedge a path between chests and bellies. She thought that if only she could reach the open Battery Park City she could work her way along the river, but frightened people barricaded it like a living, ever-moving wall, and she was forced instead into the canyons between the tall buildings of the financial district.

Knocked down twice, nearly trampled, she tried to catch her breath in a tiny granite niche where a building overlapped its neighbor. She had to somehow get free of all these people, somehow get uptown, home, then find Ken. The concept of finding Ken seemed to elevate her above mere survival and it gave her new strength. *How* she would find him was not the question yet. First she had to get home, alive.

The office buildings blocked all views of the battle in the harbor, but it was clear that something was terribly wrong. Kate was reminded of a line storm that had hit her off the

Carolina coast: in the minutes before it had torn the mast off the boat, the air had gone dead still, the temperature had shot up twenty degrees, and boiling storm waves had approached implacably from a black sky.

The city was thick with that same palpable sense of all hell about to break loose any second: the crush of people pouring out of the buildings onto the choked sidewalks, the people already on the sidewalks, spilling into the clogged streets; drivers blowing horns in fear and futile rage, blocked by cars already abandoned.

Explosions rang on the river, echoed up the stone-and-steel ravines. Glass broke. People shoved and pushed toward subway stations, where other people were shoving and pushing and screaming up the stairs onto the streets. She had to get clear of the mobs. Tracing their ebb and flow, Kate shouldered her way through a sudden opening and raced toward Broadway, battled across the jam-packed thoroughfare, and struggled through a side street. The invisible river beckoned and she worked toward it, first fighting the flood pressing inland, then suddenly being swept along as thousands came simultaneously to the same decision that they were safer in the open.

At West Street, the highway had ground to a dead stop and many cars were empty. She saw that some people had locked themselves in their cars and were watching in horror; others were huddled down on their seats as if they could make themselves invisible. Not a vehicle was moving, and as she settled into a steady pace past Rector Street, Carlisle, Albany, she began to hope against hope that she might be able to run all the way to Fourteenth Street where Tenth Avenue angled off West, six short blocks from home.

Gunfire sounded ahead, the sharp, rapid crack of an automatic weapon, and suddenly people were running toward her, slamming doors, jumping out of cars, screaming, "They're coming, they're coming!"

A big man in a car-service-driver's black suit ran straight at her and slammed her to the pavement and kept going. Stunned, Kate sensed motion coming at her and rolled against a car as his passengers streamed after him, heedless of the young woman lying in the road.

She crawled under the running board of an SUV, huddled there, head spinning, then darted for profounder shelter under a huge truck. There she tried to get her bearings. Directly ahead was Liberty Street, which ran from the water past the World Trade Center. Suddenly she saw cars moving in the intersection.

Gasping for breath, trying to clear her head, trying to get her bearings, she saw soldiers with machine guns. Four black-clad commandos—exactly like those who'd come boiling out of the sea swarming over Ken's tug—were waving their guns, forcing drivers to move their cars. When a cabbie moved too slowly, the guns clattered loudly, a body was hauled from the driver's seat, and the car behind was directed to push the cab.

In moments the intersection was cleared. A Mercedes ahead of the truck Kate hid under was the first in the line of northbound vehicles and marked the edge of the cleared area. A soldier walked up to it and shot the driver. The car next to it was empty. A woman pleaded, "Don't shoot, please don't," from the third lane. A single shot silenced her.

Kate lay still as stone. Only her eyes moved as she looked for an escape route. The attackers appeared to have done the same thing in the downtown lanes, cleared the intersection and sealed it with the lead cars. When she took a chance and raised her head, she saw that Liberty Street was clear of all vehicles from the Hudson River, and inland along the south boundary of the World Trade Center plaza.

The soldiers ran briskly across the wide-open Liberty Street, deeper into the island, toward Broadway, leaving two of their number to guard the intersection.

*   *   *

The harborscape that Ken Hughes had known his whole life—the wide water flats crenelated by skyscrapers, chimneys, bridges, and piers—was slashed by smoke columns and scissored with wakes. From where his tug stood off the Jersey side—three hundred yards below Weehawken Cove, directly across the river from the red, white, and blue Chelsea Piers that occupied the Manhattan shore from Twenty-third Street to Seventeenth—he could count five sinking ships and several more burning at dockside, while blank-walled phone buildings from midtown to the Battery spouted flames.

He had a clear view of the battle from the *Chelsea Queen*'s wheelhouse—high in a catbird seat, for all the good it did him. He could see, but he couldn't touch. It was like watching a movie.

Yet there was one way he could do some good—he and he alone knew the exact location of Admiral Tang's "flagship." The admiral himself was standing directly overhead on the monkey island—the *Chelsea Queen*'s wheelhouse roof— completely exposed except for a flak jacket as he observed the battle through binoculars and issued orders into radio handsets. Ken could hear him through the open windows.

Kate had left her cellphone in his cabin. If the bastards hadn't found it yet, and if he could somehow get down there alone for a moment, he could telephone the vital information that the invading Chinese admiral had commandeered the *Chelsea Queen*.

Where in the smoke and fire and thunder was Kate?

Kate's ferry had landed all the way downtown at the Battery—if the bastards hadn't sunk it—four long miles from her apartment; the subways had probably stopped running. Two or three million people? All trying to get off the island or home or simply hide. He told himself that Kate was an unusually capable woman. But still, how long before the crazies came out?

At least it was daytime, he told himself. And most people were decent. If she were smart she would run alongside the river where there were other people out in the open. He could see thousands from Battery Park City all the way up to the Village, rippling bright dots in frantic motion. People running. People on bikes. People on roller-blades. Kate was strong and fit. She had told him she ran five miles on the days that she didn't swim two. Ken had benefited from her remarkable stamina—his memory-laden smile faded.

"Make you sad?" asked the Chinese bosun, who was running the tug.

"How the hell would you feel?" Ken shot back.

"Lousy," said the bosun.

He was younger than Ken had thought at first, early thirties at most. A weathered face, obviously not acquired on submarines, made him look older, as did a white scar that split the skin of his forehead. But he moved like a man still young and quick.

Ken's own body felt like one vast ache, a reminder that he needed to make friends, get the bosun to lower his guard.

"Where'd you get that?" Ken asked, indicating the bosun's scar.

"Rope break."

"That'll do you." Ken raised his hand to show his missing finger, and said, "Courtesy of a parting wire." He was thinking he'd have to choose carefully whom to call and then be ready to jump overboard when they sent a helicopter gunship to take out Tang.

The bosun opened his left hand. He'd lost the tip of his ring finger. "Steel hatch." He smiled. "Rolling sea."

"You speak good English."

"Not so good."

"A lot better than my Chinese. Where'd you learn English?"

"Apprentice boy Royal Navy dockyard Hong Kong."

"Hong Kong? I read the Communists don't trust people who worked for the British."

"Admiral Tang Li trust all good men," the bosun answered flatly. "He no follow book."

"What a guy," said Ken, wincing as a bulky sub running on the surface shelled the railroad yards that fed Pennsylvania Station. The sons of bitches were concentrating on infrastructure, tearing up the rails in case anybody was considering leaving town by train.

"Good guy." The bosun nodded, revealing that his English skills did not include an ear for sarcasm. "Man of people."

Man of the people? Ken thought. Tang Li, despite his scarred temple and cauliflower ear, looked more like a stockbroker with a house in Westchester. "Why'd the 'man of people' throw my crew to the sharks?"

"War," said the bosun. He gave Ken a flat look. Ken did not nod, but he did return the look, signaling his understanding that he and the Chinese bosun were two of a kind— working guys who had learned how to keep their heads down without surrendering more than was necessary.

"War? How long before my side figures out your side is using my tug for a command post and blows us out of the water?"

The bosun returned his gaze to the chaos. Ships, subs, smoke, and oddly empty skies. "Your side can't find ass with both hands."

"And fuck you, too," Ken shot back. The armed sailor guarding him stirred ominously. But the bosun grunted an order, and the sailor left the wheelhouse.

The bosun had a point. No one seemed to be fighting back. Ken had thought that by now the sky would be full of helicopter gunships. Damned good thing it wasn't. All New York needed was air raids, or the Navy steaming in to blast the city into small pieces. All the more reason to bring a strike in on the tug and finish it early.

"Beside," asked the bosun, "who think Chinese commander on American tugboat?"

"They'll have a pretty clear idea when the *Chelsea Queen*'s the last thing afloat."

Suddenly a powerful U.S. Coast Guard endurance cutter raced into the river view, boat-show white, bright red chevron a diagonal slash on her bow. Last Ken had seen her, she'd been tied up to Pier 82 at the foot of Forty-second Street. Somehow the Coasties had gotten a crew aboard and steam up and had given the Chinese assault troops the slip.

She charged a pair of slow-moving submarines like a Doberman hunting boxers. When they saw her coming, the subs separated, peeling off right and left. The Coasties fired their two-inch bow gun, twice. Two sharp, nasty barks in quick succession. Water geysered beside one sub. Burning steel exploded from the second's conning tower.

"They just found your ass," Ken crowed at the bosun, who was blinking in astonishment. That was remarkable shooting for any navy, much less Coasties trained in rescue and drug searches. Both Chinese boats stopped dead in the water.

Two more shots, disabling one sub's deck gun and hitting the other's stern. But now Tang Li's bosun was smiling. He passed Ken the binoculars.

Periscopes were aligned across the Hudson like fence posts.

The first torpedo crumpled the cutter's bow, the second heeled her over with force of the explosion, and the third detonated a *boom* that broke her apart.

Admiral Tang hurried down the monkey island ladder, took a swig of bottled water, picked up the remote control, and surfed the television, flicking through the networks and the cable stations. Some were blank, some broadcasting studio interviews, others transmitting from what appeared to be remote cameras in Manhattan.

Suddenly an NBC picture from a camera focused on Lexington Avenue. The shot was in the vicinity of the old red-brick armory on Sixty-seventh Street, and it caught Tang's attention. He spoke into his radio lapel mike.

Ken could only guess how Tang's orders translated into gunfire on the ground. But one thing was certain: television was providing Admiral Tang with accurate, up-to-the-minute intelligence about his own invasion.

"This is crazy," argued Hector. "We don't even know where the mayor is."

"He's downtown," said Harriet.

Hector squinted downtown. Lexington Avenue was blocked by endless lines of abandoned cars and trucks and buses, curb to curb, all the way to midtown, where the Chrysler Building jutted from the smoke. "Downtown" was a long way farther than that.

He and Harriet were two blocks north of the glass-enclosed bridges that crossed Lex to connect buildings of Hunter College. The red-brick armory marked Sixty-seventh Street, home of the East Side's Nineteenth Precinct, where he wanted to be right now more than any place in the world.

"He's downtown," repeated Harriet.

"No way! You heard Dispatch. They took out the Emergency Control Center." The police radio had been operating intermittently; half an hour ago was the last they'd heard it. "He could be anywhere: Queens, the Bronx, Brooklyn, Staten Island. He could have run to Jersey."

"He's downtown, 'cause that's where he has his hide-out."

Hector looked at Harriet. His ball-busting, superwoman

partner was flipping out. "Hideout? The mayor has a hide-out?"

"It's from the strike force."

"Says who?"

"My father told me. He's worked the First for fifteen years."

"So?" It didn't take a degree in police administration to know that if you had a fifty-year-old white-haired African-American police officer who still wore his uniform creased like a decorated Marine, you stationed that tall, handsome minority representative at the First Precinct so the public and the TV cameras would see him guarding City Hall.

Hector had met him once, and thought Harriet was pretty lucky to have a father like that. His own had split the week he was born, complaining about the noise.

So P.O. Greene was at City Hall for the same reason they'd assigned his tall black daughter to Gracie Mansion. How he—a short Puerto Rican in eyeglasses—had ended up on the tit, too, was a mystery to Hector; being first in his class at the Academy would have helped, but ordinarily you had to have a union hook or your old man and a bunch of un-cles on the force. "So?"

"So my father told me he heard the mayor has a hideout. Downtown somewhere."

"That's like alligators in the sewer. Everyone's heard of 'em, no one's ever seen 'em."

"Not true. They pulled out a six-footer once."

"Seventy years ago. Look, we're five blocks from the Nineteenth. I say we go to the Nineteenth, report in, get our orders."

"What makes you think there still is a Nineteenth?" Thick smoke was blowing east on the wind.

"If there's no Nineteenth, we'll keep going. Okay?"

When he put it that way, she had no choice. "Okay, Hector. We'll check out the Nineteenth—*look out! Back, back, back!*"

Three soldiers with assault rifles at port arms had suddenly filled the corner of her eye. Three of them coming east across Seventy-second from Third Avenue, moving in a fast crouch, nearly halfway to Lex and Third.

"Back, back, back!"

She and Hector eased their commandeered bicycles behind a stalled bus and, shielded by it, started pedaling down Lexington Avenue between the columns of cars. At each intersection Harriet charged ahead to check the corner, then slowed to let Hector catch up. With the heavily armed commandos behind them, both were praying hard that the solid brick-and-stone precinct house was still in the hands of the NYPD.

Three sharp whistles pierced the air.

Harriet stood on her pedals, skidded to a stop. In her father's time, three short blasts had meant distress.

"Heads up!" crackled her radio. "Heads up," and then a voice overhead. "Wait up!"

A sergeant from the Nineteenth was shouting down from the second glass bridge over the avenue. "Draw your weapons and get your asses under cover. They're right behind you."

Harriet drew her nine-millimeter automatic. "Subway entrance," she told Hector.

Hector drew his. Harriet had dragged him up to the Rodman range for some weekend target practice, but the gun still filled his hand like a brick. "No, they'll corner us down there and shoot up the civilians."

Frantically he looked around. There was cover in the recessed doorways of the brick armory. But a long, long block away. Harriet was already moving toward the subway. It was a death trap. "There!" The first floor of Hunter College was recessed. He pointed at the stone pilings which held the overhanging second story.

From the bridge above their heads, they heard the heavy boom of a sharpshooter's rifle. The sergeant had braced the sniper gun on the windowsill when he spotted the commandos on Seventy-second Street. Hector couldn't see much through the abandoned cars; it looked like he might have dropped one of them.

But in the next second the bridge exploded end to end in breaking glass. Unseen, a commando had slipped a full block closer and was hosing the span with rapid fire.

The soldier jumped up, caught movement even higher overhead, and sprayed the fifth-floor bridge. Hector pointed his pistol and pulled the trigger.

The commando sank slowly to the avenue.

"I hit him," said Hector, standing forward for a closer look. "*Madre de Dios*. I hit him."

"Get down, you idiot."

Hector ducked behind Harriet.

"Nice shot, Counselor."

"I didn't even aim. It just happened."

"You aimed. Like you're supposed to. It didn't just happen. Nice shot, Hector."

"Where's the other one?"

While they looked for the third commando, the one Hector had shot sat up, gave a violent shake of his head, and emptied his gun in their direction.

The noise was mind-shattering, the assault rifle's reports echoing from the buildings that hunched over the narrow avenue, the bullets smashing car windows, piercing steel, ricocheting from the pavement, bursting against stone. Hector and Harriet threw themselves behind the pillar, pressed their faces to the pavement, and prayed: Hector to a forgiving Catholic Mary; Harriet to a Methodist God whose promises to black people were rarely kept on Earth.

Rifle booms broke the eerie quiet, and high-powered bullets cracked the air as they whipped past the tall stalks of the streetlights. Harriet looked up and spotted the police snipers high atop the armory, shooting from the shelter of the red-brick crenellation around the turret.

"Let's do it, Hector."

For some reason which neither could explain—and without needing to consult—they both kept the bikes they'd dragged into the shelter with them. They surged to their feet and ran low, wheeling them, crouched across the sidewalk and among the cars. Harriet felt her back prickling, and expected to hear the crackling burp of the assault rifle.

Ten blocks down Lex, the glass towers at Fifty-seventh sparkled peacefully in the smoke-shrouded sun. They looked a million miles away.

"Head for the armory," said Hector.

"No, no, no."

"They got guns."

"So does the Nineteenth."

She ran around the corner. Hector decided he'd rather be with her than alone and caught up where she was slumped against the granite walls of the Kennedy Child Study Center.

"You okay?"

Harriet nodded, gasping for breath.

The curb was lined with radio motor patrols, camouflaged National Guard trucks, scooters, and unmarked cars. The Nineteenth was the next building along the block toward Third Avenue. Hector had always thought it looked less station house than old museum, but now it looked big, beautiful, and sturdy—four solid stone stories and a cupola on top—filled with cops and guns.

The police snipers on the armory roof had stopped shooting. A cop cautiously exiting the front door of the precinct spotted her and Hector and waved them in. Before they could move, Hector said, "Oh, no."

From Third Avenue a squad of eight commandos rounded

the corner at a fast trot, spotted the American flags hanging from the firehouse next door to the Nineteenth, and broke into a dead run. Hector and Harriet had one second to decide and again they thought alike, dropping the bikes on the sidewalk and shouldering each other behind a patrol car.

The commandos sprinted up the opposite sidewalk, crouched by the locked gates of the white-brick embassy apartment building across the street, and dropped to their kneeling positions to fire grenades into the precinct. The police inside tried to drive them back with pistols and shotguns.

The Chinese fighters held their ground, braved the blizzard of bullets and shot, and returned fire with their heavier weapons. A grenade bounced off the stone front and exploded on the entrance walk, fragments caroming off the railing. A second grenade pierced a window in the massive front doors and exploded in the foyer.

The double doors fell open, sagging on their hinges. A wounded uniformed patrol officer staggered out, clutching her face and screaming, her voice rising and rising until an assault rifle cut her down with an angry *snap-snap-snap*.

"Jesus," breathed Hector. "Right through her vest."

Harriet touched her own bulletproof vest under her summer blouse. Velcroed tight from neck to groin, it had never made her feel all that safe; she'd been five when her father came home wearing the Department's first bulky version of the garment. She remembered when her mother's happy smile had been flooded by tears of relief, and Momma sniffling an explanation. "It's okay, baby. Happy tears. Momma's glad. They can't stick your daddy no more, can't shoot him in the back." Which had made it clear to Harriet that before he'd gotten the vest, it had been a lie that Daddy would always be "safe in the arms of the Lord."

A Chinese commando darted into the street with a grenade in his hand. Stiff-armed, he wound up to throw. A police sniper atop the armory half a block away knocked him down. The hand grenade rolled under a car. The explosion flipped the vehicle on its side and set the chassis on fire. The commando's assault rifle clattered along the street and came to rest beside a motor scooter.

Hector's disbelieving "What's wrong with you?" was hardly out of his mouth before Harriet dove for the weapon and darted back across the sidewalk with it cradled triumphantly in her arms.

"Are you nuts?"

"You see any more ammo?"

She was peering over the cars, trying to see if the fallen commando had spare magazines among his gear. Hector had already noticed the soldiers carried the curved banana clips in a long pocket down their right thighs. When he told her, Harriet said, "Get it. I'll cover you."

"But—"

"I know how it works. We did it at Peekskill with the Feds."

Harriet darted behind a car and popped up to fire six shots at the commandos huddled by the embassy gates. "Go, Hector!"

Harriet's nostrils were flaring like a lioness's. Of all the partners! he thought. He tumbled into the street, rolled on top of the dead commando, and tried to turn the body over while simultaneously using it as shelter. The guy was tiny, shorter than Hector and forty pounds lighter. His ammunition pocket was empty.

"He's all out," Hector yelled.

"Get his hand grenades—get down, get down, get down!"

Harriet fired over his head. Hector ducked, then scrambled back among the cars, empty-handed, terrified, and sure that Harriet was thinking, Wimp.

Hector saw a second squad of commandos come around the corner behind them. Heavy weapons in their hands—

more rocket grenades, like they'd had at Gracie Mansion. He and Harriet were trapped between the two units. He considered a run for the blasted precinct door, but those rocket grenades told him there was no way the Nineteenth was going to hold out.

"Third Avenue," he said, running his bike along the sidewalk, leaning on it as he ducked low behind the cars, praying the commandos were all still across Sixty-seventh Street. Harriet was close behind him, catching up, overtaking. They ran their bikes past the precinct house, past the pink sandstone fire station, past the Byzantine, tiled Jewish synagogue. Ahead gleamed the white-brick apartment buildings of Third Avenue. Behind, the roar of concentrated gunfire.

Three miles downtown, on East Fifth Street on the Lower East Side, a somewhat scruffier station house, the Ninth, was under similar attack from a pair of four-man Chinese assault squads. Converging from both ends of the block, they repeated the gambit of blasting the doors open from the inside with a rocket grenade and mowing down the lightly armed police who staggered from the smoking building.

Then, as their counterparts did uptown, they entered the precinct house, shooting everyone they encountered, until they reached the holding pen in the basement, where the recently arrested were awaiting transport to Central Booking downtown. Three of the prisoners were local thugs whom the police had interrupted mugging a drunken sailor. The fourth was a motorcycle gangbanger named Gorgeous George.

George had had a Gothic *G* tattooed in black ink on his right biceps while serving eight-to-ten for manslaughter at Attica, and a *G* branded with a coat hanger on his left arm while doing eight-to-fifteen at Garner Correctional for rape and battery—overturned after his Avenue C Hell's Angels chapter persuaded his victim to recant her testimony.

This morning he had been arrested for assault, unlawful imprisonment, and attempted rape, and had spent speed-wired hours alternately threatening the lives of his cellmates and entertaining them with tales of his exploits. At eleven o'clock he had finally fallen asleep, to the relief of the muggers and of the police stenographer in the next room.

Awakened suddenly by the shooting, George groggily fantasized that his friends had come to bust him out. And indeed, the black-clad shooters had blown apart the cell lock. A ricochet whined past George's ear and hit one of the muggers, who fell down, yelling.

George stepped over him and eyed the broken lock hungrily. A gook motioned with his assault rifle, and spoke a funny kind of singsong. "You go. Be bad."

The muggers exchanged uneasy glances, but George was not waiting around for the dude to change his mind. He slid past him and started up the stairs. Dead and wounded cops everywhere. What the fuck was going on?

A cop had dropped a pump-action twelve-gauge. George snatched up the shotgun, grabbed a box of shells, and, when no one tried to stop him, blasted the door off the prisoners' property locker, from which he collected his cellphone and beeper. Still groggily amazed at his good fortune, he shot open the evidence locker. Jackpot! Like a candy store. He swallowed a handful of pills and strode through the shattered doors of the station house into a street where one look confirmed that all the rules had changed.

21

KATE HAD RETREATED down the lines of stalled cars. When finally out of sight of the soldiers guarding Liberty Street, she fled inland. Then she worked her way north again up Broadway, pushing uptown through crowds of frightened office workers.

Rumors goaded them: a man with a high, loud voice screamed that the black-clad soldiers had massacred people in a Canal Street subway station; another, wearing a Walkman radio, yelled, over and over like a demented town crier, that submarines were shelling midtown; and everyone's head whipped skyward at a shout that commandos had planted dynamite in the World Trade Center, whose twin towers loomed close enough to fall on them.

Crossing Liberty Street, passing the east side of the World Trade Center, Kate was sucked into a vortex of thousands streaming from its lobbies. She saw no more soldiers. But the streets were thick with broken glass blasted from the shorter buildings. A new rumor rippled through the slow-moving mob and set heads craning: the mayor's SUV had been seen circling City Hall.

The people frightened her. The men in particular; those not tight-faced with fear were staring at women as if to say, When it all falls apart, when it breaks down, I know what I'm going to take. She snatched up a fallen baseball cap, stuffed her short hair under it. Breasts? Forget it. She was wearing the same damp sweatshirt she'd donned to drive the Zodiac, when her only concern had been protection from the chilly ocean breeze.

At the corner of Chambers and Broadway, Kate was suddenly enveloped by a mob herding toward City Hall Park, and dragged backward. There were too many people, too ready to burst into a panicked stampede. She couldn't decide whether to continue up the narrow, clogged streets of the interior of Manhattan, or to risk again the wildfire and ricochets from the harbor battle that had swept the riverbank at the Battery. Glass shattered. Store windows burst and she saw men in suits reaching in, snatching things. The sudden shift from flight toward loot opened a narrow path. She pushed away from the throng and struggled north up Broadway.

The Old Place smelled of rust, damp stone and rat droppings, though the rats fled as the mayor's party descended a vertical labyrinth of ladders, stairs and vaults and unlocked the last steel door. The security detail entered first, guns drawn, flashlights probing the long space that curved away into a dark infinity. Renata shivered; it felt twenty degrees cooler than the warm June streets they had escaped.

"Stinks."

"Hit the lights."

Bare bulbs in the vaulted ceiling made spiderwebs gleam. Rivet-studded girders, entwined in snake nests of cable, seemed to be holding up the earth. She stole a glance at

Rudy. He was standing taller, his shoulders opening up. In this cold and dirty and remote place, she could see that he felt safe.

Someone had had the foresight to drape the desks and chairs with plastic drop cloths, which were thick with dust. Renata took charge. "Don't just yank them," she told Luther. "You'll scatter dust everywhere. Fold them up."

"Yes'm."

She helped Juan undrape the stack of televisions and switched them on. They were clunky old Motorolas and it occurred to her, fleetingly, that when Rudy had last watched them, she had been in high school.

Pictures flickered and sighed to life. The cable feed was still working, and Luther assured her they were also connected to a backup antenna for VHF.

"I want Greg Walsh, Marty Greenberg and the President," said the mayor as Renata emptied her sack of cellphones on the desk.

"Mr. Mayor," Luther interrupted. "I recommend you go easy on the cell phoning. They could track our signals."

"Thank you, Luther. Renata, see if you have any luck with the land lines, first."

Renata reported back, "All dead." She was kicking herself for not having scooped up any extra battery chargers. Polling Juan, Luther, and Rudy, she amassed a total of ten phones and three chargers.

A bell sounded, startling in the deep silence of the bunker. Luther hurried to the security station next to the steel door and switched on a multi-screen TV. Unlike the old Motorolas, Renata noticed, the screen powered up instantly, displaying six remote cameras. Surprised, she realized that Rudy had kept the vital systems of the long-disused hideout up-to-date.

"I got some people outside, Mr. Mayor. Rod Brown and Samantha Cummings."

"Let 'em in."

"Who are they?" asked Renata.

"Strike force. Samantha was an assistant prosecutor. Rod was FBI."

"What are they doing here? How did they know to come?"

"We spent a lot of nights in this hole."

Renata bristled the instant she saw Samantha Cummings. Leggy as a shore bird, the former prosecutor wore a tailored suit that screamed, "Retired to private practice and shopping at Bendel's." She planted a kiss on the mayor's cheek, close to his mouth, that lasted longer than it had to.

"Rudy, ya look terrific—oh, I marked you. Anybody got a handkerchief?" She looked around, and when her eye fell on Renata's mismatched suit, she exclaimed, "You must be the 'infamous' Renata. Great job you're doing for Rudy. Listen, Renata, there's a coffeemaker in the john and about ten cans of Bustello in my old desk. Where'd they put my old desk?"

Renata, who'd become accustomed to the deferential kid-gloves treatment accorded the mayor of New York City's gatekeeper and confidante, was too shocked to resist when Samantha Cummings took her elbow and steered her away from Rudy, saying, "Love your 'are-they-or-aren't-they-doing-it' ploy. It is a ploy, isn't it? Has to be. Rudy never plays around."

Samantha's sidekick, Rod, looked like he hadn't fared as well in the ten years since they had busted the Mafia. His suit was shiny at the elbows, his shirt straining buttons over a sagging belly. He smelled like he had been dipped in nicotine.

Rudy took Rod's hand in both of his. Juan high-fived the former FBI agent. Luther lifted him clear off the concrete floor in a bear hug.

Rod said, "I've never been so scared in my life. We just came up from Wall Street. The control center? The whole damn building is glass in the street."

"Unbelievable," Samantha called from the coffeemaker. "I was talking to a hedge-fund guy in the World Wide on Eighth Avenue. Four blocks in from the river, they lost their windows on the fiftieth floor—hey, here come the judge. The *federal* judge."

In walked the eloquent Danny Wong, the first Asian-American federal judge in America, and much-touted candidate for a Supreme Court nomination. Sometimes it seemed like everyone in the world had once worked for Rudy.

Danny Wong was holding a blood-soaked handkerchief to his cheek. A big man, he towered over all but Luther Washington. He said he had sent his clerks home when the shooting started and was leaving the courthouse when stray fire sent glass cascading from the Municipal Building.

"News conference," Renata interrupted. "CNN from Beijing."

On TV, a Chinese suit was addressing a thicket of microphones. A woman in a PLA uniform translated.

"The Chinese government is aware of the news reports of fighting in New York City. These reports are thus far sketchy and unconfirmed and it is the policy of China not to comment on unconfirmed reports."

"That translator's reading from a script," said the mayor. "Hey, Danny, is she translating what he's saying?"

Wong, who even as a federal judge would still occasionally find himself addressed on a Brooklyn street as "Chink Boy," answered, "Sorry, Rod, I was so busy at Harvard with glee club and boxing I did not have time to study Chinese."

On-screen, sixty reporters yelled at once, milling and shoving under the watchful gaze of the People's Liberation Army soldiers, who lined the walls of the auditorium. A tall Australian with a huge beaked nose and bright red cheeks yelled the loudest.

"Have you received any threats from the United States

warning of nuclear retaliation for the attack on New York City?"

The spokesman looked perplexed. He bobbed his head and smiled. The translator spoke over his reply.

"China cannot imagine any responsible government making such a threat. Nuclear war—all civilized nations agree—is simply not an alternative. Remember, contamination from a single, partial nuclear explosion at Chernobyl in Ukraine meant people couldn't eat the sheep in Scotland."

More shouts from the reporters.

The Chinese official ignored them. "And, of course, recent missile tests—doubtlessly observed by United States spy satellites—and the launching of two new nuclear submarines, suggest that China now has ample, accurate, long-range intercontinental nuclear-strike capability herself."

"Are those the submarines that attacked New York?" a voice shrilled from the pack.

The Chinese official chuckled. "I am informed by PLA naval officers that the enormous undersea ships you refer to would not be used in such a raid. Rather, they would stand—hidden beneath the waves—a thousand miles off an enemy shore, poised to retaliate with nuclear missiles if China were provoked."

"Stalemate," said Judge Wong.

"Greg Walsh, Mr. Mayor."

Mayor Mincarelli plugged one ear with his finger and hunched over the phone Renata handed him. It was an hour and fifty minutes since he had ordered Greg to Washington.

"Admiral Tang is man of experience," his bosun told Ken Hughes as they watched the battle from the *Chelsea Queen*'s wheelhouse. "Study in America—English, history, war."

Ken turned a stony gaze from the oil slick still burning

where the Coast Guard cutter had blown apart. Admiral Tang must have passed his courses with flying A's. Cute move, drawing the cutter out with the surfaced subs. A classic feint. And executed with the same cold calculation as the torpedoing of the cruise ship last night. No doubt now about the source of that explosion. Tang had probably dreamed it up while studying at the Naval War College in Rhode Island.

"Admiral Tang, Son of Revolution. Grandfather Tang Cheung on Long March. Eat from same rice bowl with Mao and Deng. Grandfather high commissar. Father rich man. Admiral Tang studies tactics of German tankers Guderian and Rommel."

Ken's mind leaped to a larger threat: was this attack on New York only a feint, too? Was Tang making the United States look one way while he prepared to attack from another? Washington? California?

"Tang Li," the heavyset sailor rumbled, "he say Rommel and Guderian are cavalry officers. Ride with soldiers. Like Israel officers, lead from front."

His hero was doing that, all right—up on the monkey island—the kind of flashy leadership that inspired reckless courage in his troops, if it didn't get him killed.

"Tang believe in unexpected," the bosun went on earnestly, parroting his commander's theories that sudden, unexpected, decisive military acts changed history. "Party say, Hong Kong humiliating loss. Tang Li say, English do as they please in south Asia hundred fifty years."

Ken looked at the bosun—who had taken about sixty seconds to master the *Queen*'s cranky old steering tillers—and reminded himself that broken English didn't mean the guy was dumb. Tang Li, he had claimed, was part of the Chinese Communist elite—like a Rockefeller of the Revolution. Granddad's war stories over the teapot had impressed his grandson with the values of perseverance and suffering.

Tang's father, by contrast, had studied technology in the Soviet Union, graduating from the Voroshilov Naval Academy, and come home an accomplished bureaucrat.

"A dull father," said the bosun with a knowing smile, "to a boy raised by revolutionary grandfather."

Tang's father had survived the Cultural Revolution—eventually flourished—and emerged a confirmed cynic. "Father believe in nothing but money," said the bosun. But instead of exploiting his formidable connections to make money, as did the cosmopolitan elite, Tang Li had parlayed his education and his foreign studies and his family's contacts into a fast-track career in the People's Liberation Army.

"Tang's father lots of girlfriends. Boy Tang comfort mother."

His father's philandering and his mother's pain had marked the boy with a puritanical streak.

Ken's heart sank. Just what New York needed: a puritanical zealot out to avenge his wronged mom. But of course nothing was ever that simple. "But why attack New York City?"

"He love China like his grandfather. But he know her better."

"So what's he doing here?"

"Explosions make stars. And destroy stars," the bosun answered darkly.

"What explosions?"

"Every thirty, forty years China explodes like the stars."

"You're losing me," said Ken.

"Crazy time. War. Death. Famine."

The last "crazy time," he explained, had been the Cultural Revolution in the 1960s. China was long overdue.

"But why attack New York?"

The bosun's huge hands floated easily on the tillers to hold the *Chelsea Queen* against the current.

"Tang Li great leader," he said simply. "Mighty helmsman. He steer Chinese people around themselves."

*   *   *

"Rudy? I'm in Marty Greenberg's office."

Mayor Mincarelli didn't ask how New York's former acting police commissioner had gotten from the burning aircraft carrier to the White House so fast. Greg Walsh did not volunteer that he had commandeered the chase boat that DEA Agent Rossi had driven to the Navy lunch, nor that the uniformed beat cops he'd drafted to help him had to draw weapons to convince the DEA driver to dodge submarines across the Hudson and race through the Kill Van Kull to a private airport at Port Elizabeth, where they'd employed similar tactics to commandeer an Exxon corporate jet.

"Does anyone down there know what's going on?"

"They're as clueless as we are, Rudy, other than that the Chinese are pissed about Taiwan. Everybody I've met says the same stupid thing, quote, 'In a nation of one billion people, anything can happen.' Marty says Beijing is stonewalling."

"Do you have the President's word not to launch a counterattack?" asked the mayor.

"He's promised to see me for ten minutes."

"Ten minutes?"

"It's a little chaotic here, Rudy. The President's worrying about the rest of the country."

"Who else has been attacked?"

"No one yet, but he's afraid this raid on New York is only a feint."

"A feint? Hold on—what, Renata?"

Renata was pointing at the TV. "The press is asking about the Chinese commander."

The red-faced Australian yelled the loudest again. "I said, we have reports that People's Liberation Army generals say that the admiral leading the attack against New York City is a renegade naval officer."

The official shook his head and denied, again, knowing an attack had been launched at New York.

But when a German reporter's question was translated, the official lighted with recognition, as if hearing the name of an old acquaintance for the first time in many years.

"Admiral Tang Li?" the translator said. "Admiral Tang Li is a competent young officer. One cannot imagine whether he has done as alleged."

"Alleged?" Mayor Mincarelli yelled at the televisions. "My city is burning. Submarines are marauding the harbor. Assault troops are shooting people in the street."

Greg Walsh filled the mayor's phone ear—solid, clear, and dependable. "Marty's got a statement from some private Chinese channel. Quote, 'We are in the process of establishing contact with Admiral Tang.' Looks like the Chinese are taking the rumor seriously."

"You mean they can't even find the bastard?"

"It's a huge country, Rudy. Lots of factions. Maybe he *is* a renegade."

Renata was steering her boss's attention to the TV tuned to a sober-looking Peter Jennings shucking off a windbreaker embroidered with his network's logo.

"Jennings says they interviewed China's UN ambassador."

A technician hovered, fitting the anchorman's ear with an IFB as Jennings slipped into the anchor chair.

Renata said, "It looks like that studio over in Jersey City they never got off the ground." The network had thought to cut costs across the river, until Jennings announced he would rather work for Public Television than commute to New Jersey.

Jennings raised grave eyes to the camera. "As this unbelievable story exploded, this correspondent escaped from New York City thanks to the sacrifice of many brave studio employees left behind to face the madness alone.

"To recap the little we know of these astonishing events so far: an enormous fleet of submarines has attacked New York City. They have sunk ships in New York Harbor and landed an estimated several thousand troops in Manhattan. This shocking footage, which cost the life of cameraman Albert Moskowitz of a local all-news station, shows assault troops shooting up the city streets. . . . Elsewhere, they are blocking bridges and tunnels and attacking communications facilities, among them this network's studios, and shelling railroad yards with high explosives. In a word, war has befallen New York. Many panicked witnesses report the soldiers appear to be Chinese, though we have no confirmation that they come from the People's Republic of China."

"Cut the crap," Renata yelled at the screen. "You promoed a UN interview."

"We have conflicting reports," Jennings continued, "that New York's Mayor Rudolph Mincarelli was captured by the invaders at Gracie Mansion; other reports suggest he escaped. In this footage from a traffic camera downtown, we see that the city's much-vaunted—and hotly debated—Emergency Control Center has been reduced to rubble, though there is no word that Mayor Mincarelli was in it. In either event, the mayor of New York City has disappeared, after broadcasting repeated warnings for New Yorkers to stay off the streets, and his whereabouts are currently unknown."

"Renata, get me that idiot."

In seconds she passed him a telephone. Everyone in the bunker cheered as Jennings inclined to his earpiece and then announced, "Apparently we have a telephone audio feed from Rudolph Mincarelli, the mayor of New York City. Hello, Mr. Mayor. Sir, can you hear me?"

"Peter, this is Mayor Rudolph Mincarelli. I want to tell New Yorkers that I'm still in the city and still in control. My administration has taken up emergency headquarters. And

again I repeat to all New Yorkers, difficult as it may be, this
is a time to keep our heads down while we figure out what's
going on. As such, I am invoking my emergency powers and
ordering all New Yorkers off the street. Violators will be arrested and prosecuted to the full extent—"

"Excuse me, Mr. Mayor, can you—"

"Not now, Peter. I want the people of New York to know
that my personal delegate is meeting with the President of
the United States right now and that I have full faith that
he'll help me defuse this situation with a minimum of bloodshed and destruction."

"Have you asked the President to repel the invaders, Mr.
Mayor?"

"Are you listening to me?" the mayor shot back. "New
York is a law-abiding city of eight million innocent citizens.
A military counterstrike would cause untold bloodshed, and
I will not allow it."

Suddenly every light in the bunker went out, the TV images collapsed into pinpricks, and darkness reigned.

22

KATE SAW A GUY eyeing her from a doorway as she crossed Canal on Broadway. She didn't like the look of him and she slowed to a walk, aware, suddenly, that the crowds had melted from the streets and sidewalks. She saw a few people drop from sight as they descended into a subway station, and frightened faces peering from storefronts on Canal, but no one to turn to for help. At least in the mobs, there had been safety in numbers.

She debated turning back, wondering if she could outrun him. Suddenly he turned inside and slammed the door shut. She heard locks snicking. Then, behind her, boot steps.

Commandos. They moved in a loose, fast pack across Canal, sweeping their guns up and down Broadway. Kate darted onto Grand and ran east. In two or three heart-pounding blocks, blocks eerily empty of a living soul, she saw the loom of the old Police Headquarters, which Ken had shown her on their walk home from Chinatown.

She kept looking back for soldiers.

Water was rushing in the gutters; she was dying of thirst, had run for miles and hadn't drunk a drop since the Evian they'd given her on the freighter. Rounding a corner, she saw its source. A broken fire hydrant, smashed by a runaway car, was pluming a four-story geyser. She worked her way close to the rock-hard stream and tried to divert mouthfuls with her hands.

It was icy cold, the most delicious drink she had had in her life, and she lingered there, lifting her face to the cooling spray until, gradually, she became aware of a new sound. A concerted roar, it grew louder, louder than the geyser. For an instant too long, she mistook it for distant gunfire.

When she realized her mistake, raw fear surged adrenaline through her legs. She spun on her heel and ran. But by then the motorcycles had rounded the corner—chopped Harley Davidsons, thundering after her.

Peter Jennings reported that electric power had been lost in much of Manhattan and that the entire Northeast grid was buckling under the sudden strain of power plants knocked off-line by the attackers. He promised his viewers that he would reestablish contact with the mayor, and introduced his in-house Pentagon expert. Major General Winfield Edwards, Retired, wore a golf shirt and a bright tan and appeared to have been dragged unexpectedly from lunchtime martinis in a Short Hills clubhouse bar.

"General Edwards, sir, what do we make of this incredible attack on New York City?"

"What I saw across the river was a full-blown marine landing supported by surfaced submarines firing cannon, rockets, and torpedoes."

"And what are our forces doing to repel the invaders?"

"Mayor Mincarelli just hit the nail on the head. This is essentially a hostage situation. There is some disparity between what U.S. forces *can* do and *will* do when the invaders hold eight million hostages."

"Have we no defenses?"

"I'd expect active-duty boys from McGuire are airborne as we speak. Brunswick ought to be getting their A-6s up any minute now. And you can bet reservists are burning up the highways up and down the East Coast."

"We've seen many cities reduced to rubble by modern firepower," Jennings said in a grave voice that conjured images of gutted apartment buildings and windowless towers. "Beirut, Sarajevo."

General Edwards adopted Jennings's sober demeanor. "The President and his advisors are faced with awful decisions, strategizing how and when to hit back. Collateral damage from an air response will reduce the city to ruins, and kill hundreds of thousands."

"Who will confront the invading soldiers on the ground?"

"Until we muster actual on-the-ground troops, the New York Police Department will bear the brunt as the raiders roll up station houses. Assembling troops could take many hours when you factor in distance, and particularly the chaos that surrounds any sneak attack—initial disbelief and confusion mean command and communication delays. Nature of the beast."

"And our first troops would be?"

"Marines, most likely. Rapid-response units from down South. Preceded by Special Ops scoping out the situation."

"Hand-to-hand street fighting?"

"Backed up by helicopter gunships. But let us hope it doesn't come to that, Peter. In such cramped space as Manhattan, civilian casualties will be horrific."

"General, when was the last time the continental United States was attacked by an enemy force?"

Winfield Edwards considered the question for a moment. "Well, Peter, our 'Star-Spangled Banner' was composed by the light of British Royal Navy 'bombs bursting in air.' Making the War of 1812—in which British troops burned Washington, D.C.—the last time. That is, if we discount some Japanese shells lobbed onto the California coast in World War Two, and Mexican border raids over disputed territory in what is now the state of Texas."

"But how could this happen, General? How could an entire fleet of submarines penetrate our defenses?"

"Good question, Peter. Until we learn a lot more cold facts, I'll have to give you an educated guess. Our defense establishment is long on technology and short on humans. We can see and hear a lot wherever we focus our extraordinary sound, heat, and electromagnetic sensors, but there's more information coming in than we can process. If we are looking the other way at last month's Iranian missile tests, for instance, or Pakistan's plutonium laboratories, or the island of Taiwan—where right now we've got both the *Nimitz* and the *Kitty Hawk* battle groups showing the flag—or the Balkans, then who's minding the store on the Atlantic coast? Who is watching for deep wakes, listening for submarine motors, intercepting electronic traffic and—"

"Good fucking question," Luther Washington roared at Rod Brown's flickering Watchman, which was casting a thin blue light about the dark bunker. "Who the hell's responsible?"

Mayor Mincarelli and Renata shared long glances, both aware what the other was thinking—an already weak incumbent President of the United States had just lost his last shred of credibility. If the mayor of New York managed to somehow protect his city, Rudy would transform himself, overnight, into an unstoppable candidate.

Of course, first he and the city had to come out of this alive, but the possibilities were electrifying and her heart soared. Yet when Rudy reached for her in the flickering dark, Renata felt it was more like a handshake to mark their political understanding than a display of affection.

"Excuse me, General," said Peter Jennings, "but isn't it the United States Navy's job to protect our coasts? Are you telling me the Navy doesn't listen for enemy submarines anymore?"

"Well, let's just say that our Sound Surveillance System passive sonar arrays weren't listening for fifty-year-old technology. Diesel electric boats are not considered strategic weapons."

"It would appear," Jennings remarked dryly, "that someone forgot to tell that to the Chinese. But how did these old-fashioned diesel submarines come from so far?"

"They've pulled off a logistical coup of which no analysts would have credited the Chinese Navy capable. Such an amazing feat would require a chain of mother ships to repeatedly refuel and replenish the boats and carry the assault most of the way. One would compare it to the remarkable British Vulcan bombing of the Falkland Islands' Port Stanley airfield writ large, when the Argentineans—"

"But why didn't United States forces see those 'mother ships' on the surface?"

"It's a big world, Peter. And a very big ocean. I would presume they disguised them as freighters—much as the Nazis did to resupply their U-boats sixty years ago—and rendezvoused in remote waters. Who knows what we might have 'seen' if we had enough humans to process the data? Not to mention that the Chinese have successfully had our entire military and intelligence establishment staring twenty-twenty at Taiwan for the past six weeks. Viewers over forty will recall how General Giap's Khesan siege distracted us while he prepared his Tet Offensive—" Suddenly, the general looked hard into the camera, and in that instance the amiable golfer and the affable historian stood aside for a veteran. "This is *basic* stuff—guts and guile win wars."

"You mentioned earlier that the Chinese have been buying acoustic technology for years. And upgrading their satel-

lite communications. As well as purchasing surplus submarines, according to a classified State Department internal
memo obtained by this network an hour ago."

"Clearly, no one in the United States defense establishment put all the intelligence data together and said, 'Uh-oh,
this means something.'"

"Would you call this a situation in which heads should
roll?" Jennings asked sternly.

General Winfield Edwards cast rheumy eyes back over
long years of institutional survival and answered placidly,
"No doubt we'll torment a sacrificial goat or two."

Jennings touched his earpiece. "Excuse me, General. We
have live video coming in from a remote security camera
downtown, where a motorcycle gang is attempting to storm
a luxury apartment building. I am advised to warn those
with children viewing, this is a situation turning very
ugly. . . . The building is apparently—yes, it is, I recognize
it—the old Police Headquarters at Cleveland and Broome,
between the neighborhoods of SoHo and Little Italy—a
Beaux Arts architectural gem converted to luxury co-op
apartments after the NYPD command moved to One Police
Plaza."

Kate had run for blocks never looking back, run blindly
from the motorcycles, soldiers forgotten. Sheltering in the
narrow alleyways between stalled cars and trucks, she had
found herself back at Broome Street with a horrifyingly
clear view of a dozen motorcyclists racing their bikes up and
down Cleveland Street. The building staff had driven several
cars up on the sidewalk and parked them against the front
gates as a barricade.

Suddenly a motorcycle charged forward with a ban-
danna-wearing, leather-vested gangbanger standing on the
backseat. Balancing with one hand on the driver's shoul-

der and swinging a heavy chain with the other, he jumped onto the roof of one of the cars and whipped a path through the doormen and porters. As they fell back, the rest of the bikers mobbed through the doors, swinging chains and fists.

They poured into the now defenseless building, and when a window broke on the second floor and a woman screamed, Kate turned and ran west across SoHo, the woman's "Nooo!" shrilling over and over in her head. She ran until the sight of commandos loping down Varick Street drove her into the dark hole of the Seventh Avenue subway station, sobbing with fear and exhaustion.

In the mayor's hideout, they had lighted the candles which Samantha Cummings had cached with the coffee in her desk. Then an NYPD Technical Assistance Resource Unit officer from the old days located the emergency generator and powered up the TVs just in time for Peter Jennings's live-looting video.

They watched, mesmerized, until one of the bikers looked up and spotted the security camera. Shielding his face with his spread hand, he jumped from the car, ran to his Harley, and yanked a sawed-off shotgun from a scabbard. He aimed it at the camera and the picture disappeared.

"Well, that's that," said Peter Jennings, shaking his head, then losing his famous cool. "The enormity of what we've just seen . . ." He looked down at his desk for a full ten seconds—an eternity in television—and when he looked up again, composed but for a trembling of his lips, he said, "And while we leave the hapless residents of the old Police Headquarters to their fate in a suddenly lawless city, we turn to Jeff Rice at the Pentagon. . . ."

Renata wished that the logistics officer had been a little slower. Rudy was devastated. "This is wrong," he'd kept saying as the motorcyclists overwhelmed the co-op's defenders. "This is wrong . . ." his voice trailing off.

The cops in the room, she noticed, watched with interest, but didn't seem as shaken. Rudy, she realized, as a prosecutor, had experienced crime only secondhand in the courtroom.

"This is a city of law," he whispered. And then, louder, "We can't lose control."

Renata felt Samantha Cummings's eyes on her. The lawyer sidled closer. "Has he been like this long?"

"What do you mean?"

"He's thrown. He's loopy."

"He's fine."

Samantha gave Renata a probing look. Finally, she said, "Sweetheart, I truly hope you're not rubbing up against the wrong tree."

"What?"

"Hon, I did the same thing you're doing. I loved the untouchable. I never got touched. I never got laid. I never even got kissed."

Renata crossed her arms under her breasts and squeezed as tightly as she could. "He is a good man. He works twenty-four and seven to make the city a decent place."

"You don't have to tell me. I used to get wet watching him prepare a RICO indictment."

Renata turned away, her face hot with anger. She felt invaded. No, she thought. I will not let this crude, horrible woman push me around. She thrust a Rudyesque finger in Samantha's face. "We do good," she said. "We have made the city better. If people don't like it, tough. Rudy has a vision."

"You might want to ask yourself why you chose to fall for a man who won't take you to bed."

"You can't talk to me this way."

"Sure I can. Maybe I'm still pissed about wasting so many years. But I'm an old friend of Rudy's. I don't need anything from the mayor's press secretary . . . and we'll all be dead by morning."

After Gorgeous George shot out the security camera, he ran to catch up with the guys who were already kicking open apartment doors deep inside the co-op.

He charged up a grand staircase and hurried down a richly carpeted hallway, past broken doors. Women were screaming. When he saw a door still locked, he raised his boot and smashed the heel on the doorknob.

Boom, it was open. People this rich didn't bother with Fox locks. Security was at the front door, not in your own apartment like on the Lower East Side. Their mistake.

He walked in, shotgun ready, just in case hubby was home and kept a rifle for shooting deer on his country estate. Huge living room, pale old rugs, paintings on the walls, books. One whole wall was glass shelves filled with little cups and vases. Go figure.

Jewelry in the bedroom. One door led to a dining room with a long table and chairs for twelve. The other led to a hall and, down it, bedrooms. As he headed toward it, he scooped a hassock off the floor and lobbed it underhand at the glass shelves.

Strike!

He poked head and shotgun into the bedrooms off the hall—kid posters and computers and TVs in each. The little bastards even had their own bathrooms.

A double door loomed at the end, closed, locked. He kicked it open without breaking stride and found himself in the master bedroom. Bed you could screw a cow on. Couch. TV. Paintings. Rug deep as snow.

Somewhere else in the building a woman was screaming like an ambulance.

This was the kind of place where Mr. and Ms. had their

own dressing rooms. He could see Mr.'s, through an open door, dark with suits. Ms.'s was through another. Mirrored closet doors, left open at angles, reflected six Georges, each of whom, when he flashed a grin, became more gorgeous than the other.

Jewelry box, wide-open; rings, bracelets, pins smiling up at the lights. George crammed a handful in his jeans pocket and was about to put down the shotgun to help himself with both hands when he saw her moving in the mirror.

He pretended he didn't, and watched her try to slip behind him. Must have been hiding in the bathroom.

Ten years old. Long blond hair. Face like Michelle Pfeiffer's. No tits yet. He turned, giving her a nice view of the sawed-off.

"Hey, kid. Your mommy home?"

He had run over a dog once; it had been chasing the bike and he touched the brakes and leaned just right. When he went back to see what he'd done, it was lying in the road with that same it's-all-over look in its wide, unblinking eyes.

His cellphone rang.

One eye on the little girl, he answered. Ricardo Cirillo, one of the big-balls new Mafia guys, straight from Sicily, smart, tough, and loyal. Ricardo had a specialty, and George had been half expecting to hear from him the minute the Chinks broke him out of the Ninth Precinct.

"Ricardo," he said. "What can I do for you?"

"Bring ten guys, meet me at the club."

The club was nearby in Little Italy.

"Your lucky day, kid," George told the little girl and hurried out, firing the shotgun at the walls to alert the guys to finish up quick. They had something much bigger to do.

Splashing through ankle-deep puddles that pocked the stone floor of the tunnel, Jose Chin and Jasbir Singh had walked under the East River. Where the tunnel ended at a scarred wall of Manhattan bedrock, one hundred and fifty feet under Second Avenue, they had climbed fifteen flights up steel ladders. Now Jasbir was struggling to pry open a door that blocked the exit.

"Jose, help," said Jasbir. Jose hurled his few pounds against the wrecking bar and Jasbir's muscles bulged. They sprang back and forth against the metal and at last popped the door with a screech.

They climbed a ladder in darkness punctured only by Jasbir's fading flashlight. The ladder topped out at last in a street vault, under a manhole cover. Jasbir put his shoulder to it. It thudded loudly. The street was silent.

"We're under something," Jasbir whispered. There was no traffic noise, no horns. But far off they could hear gunfire.

The good news was they could look around without being spotted. The bad news was they were trapped under a long, low city bus. They eased the cover off the hole, shoving the massive steel disk inch by inch across the asphalt.

"What the hell is this? Where is everybody?"

Jasbir ventured the reasonable guess that everyone was hiding in the subway tunnels, or staying indoors as the mayor had ordered.

A sudden racket sounded from uptown, pistol fire, crackling, then a heavy, staccato *burr* like a jackhammer.

"Is that a machine gun?"

"Yes," Jasbir said with the conviction of a man who had heard one before. "Against pistols."

"Cops versus soldiers? The Nineteenth Precinct up on Sixty-seventh. I gotta shoot that."

"And what do you think the soldiers will do when they see your satellite dish?"

"One problem at a time, Jasbir." He was mainly worried about how to beam a signal out from the tall buildings of midtown. A really hot live-truck engineer could reflect microwave signals off windows, bouncing them skyward like pool balls. But he wasn't likely to find one in the war zone.

"May I suggest, Jose, that with your cellphone you call a news station and describe what is happening, which they would relay to the people."

"The *New York Times* probably has fourteen reporters doing that right now. Words. We're doing pictures, Jasbir. Coverage. There is no television news without pictures. Pictures are real, pal. No pictures—no coverage—no TV. No TV, it didn't happen."

"And to whom will the satellite bounce your signal? All the towers are on the World Trade Center."

"No problem. NJN has a tower in Montclair." New Jersey's public television station had carried all the New York stations when their antennas were knocked out by the World Trade Center bomb.

Jose slithered out from under the bus. "Come on."

But the broad-shouldered Jasbir was trapped. All that Jose could see of Jasbir was the Sikh's disembodied face, chin barely clearing the manhole, turban pressed to the undercarriage.

"Stay there. I'll move the bus."

Jasbir looked like he wouldn't mind walking back to Queens. "There is no electricity. Who will watch TV?"

"Batteries. People will be sitting around Watchmans like campfires. Plus every viewer in the rest of the world. Crissake, Jasbir, we're talking a bigger audience than the Oscars."

"But New York Yes! is only on cable."

"Jasbir, I told you—every station has a microwave room where they pull in feeds. Through them, you and me can feed every station in the world. All we got to do is shoot the story and beam a signal up. Duck down when you hear the engine."

Jose slid out from under the bus again. Cars and trucks blanketed the street and sidewalks. Nobody in sight. But he felt eyes on him. He looked up. Hundreds of faces peered down from the apartment buildings.

Bullet holes in the windshield and glass on the seat explained why the bus driver had left his keys. Jose located Neutral and the starter. Compressed air shrieked. He put the engine in gear, eased forward until the bumper was touching the car ahead, and stomped the accelerator. The bus mashed the car into the next car. Again he hit the gas. Again the bus leaped. In the mirror, Jasbir climbed warily from the manhole and reached down for Jose's pack.

"Let's go, Jasbir."

"Soldiers!"

Silent as bats, they'd come out of nowhere, a block away at Sixty-fourth Street.

Jasbir crouched behind the bus. Jose eased his camera out of its bag and aimed it uptown. "Jesus, they're riding bicycles—hey, those aren't soldiers." He switched on his camera, stood, extended the shotgun mike, and waved the bikes toward him. "They're cops."

The cops rolled ghostlike between the lines of cars, a black woman in the lead with an evil-looking assault weapon slung over her shoulder, and a Puerto Rican guy in eyeglasses bringing up the rear.

"Officers! Yo, sister! Hey, amigo. Jose wants to know. Tell New York Yes! what the situation is two hours after New York City's been invaded by submarines."

"Get off the street, asshole."

"This is Jose Chin, New York Yes! with two of New York's finest who are traveling downtown through the war zone on bicycles. Can you tell us your mission, Officers?"

"Our mission is to clear the streets of civilians."

Jose edged around to fill the shot with a pillar of black smoke rising behind the two cops. "Have you seen any live trucks?"

"What?"

"TV-satellite trucks. So I can broadcast. This is only tape."

The woman glared contemptuously into the camera. "Get your sorry self indoors. These are killers. They just took the Nineteenth by killing everybody who got in their way."

"You're reporting that the Nineteenth Precinct fell to the invaders?"

"Twenty minutes ago. Get off the street."

"Hey, Jose," said the Latino cop. "I watch you all the time. I think you're great, but these guys are not exactly press-friendly."

Jose kept his tape rolling. "Where you coming from, amigo?"

"Gracie Mansion."

"Where's the mayor?"

"He got away."

"Where you going?"

"No comment." His partner cut off his response. "Come on, Hector. Let's roll."

"Good luck, Jose," Hector called over his shoulder as he wobbled after her. Jose taped them disappearing into the maze of abandoned vehicles.

"I think," said Jasbir, "they have spoken wisely."

Jose whipped out his cellphone.

"Who are you calling?" asked Jasbir.

"The mayor."

"How do you know where he is?"

"My buddy Larry might."

The call was picked up on the third ring, but not by Larry. Instead, Jose heard Renata Bradley's clenched teeth. "What?"

"Jose wants to know, is the mayor okay?"

"How'd you get this number?"

"It's Larry Neale's phone—is he okay?"

"He was fired before the attack."

"Is the mayor okay?"

"The mayor is okay and in charge."

"Where?"

"Good-bye."

"Hey, Renata?" Jose knew for a fact she was half Sicilian; there was no one more loyal than a Sicilian. "Who told you something was up?"

"I am grateful," she admitted after a stone-cold silence, and Jose could almost hear her molars grinding with the effort. "And so is the mayor."

"So give me a break."

"Where are you, Jose?"

"Second Avenue and Sixty-third."

"What do you see?"

"There are no traffic lights. The streets are blocked by abandoned cars. The only people I see are watching down from their apartments. I can hear the Fire Department trying to get through further uptown. Looks like something's burning up around Sixty-seventh. Couple of cops told me the invaders attacked the Nineteenth."

"You better get out of there before you get shot."

"I just got here."

"You see what happened to Arnie Moskowitz? Go home."

"I am home. Let me talk to the mayor."

"No."

"Give me a statement."

"He already gave it to Peter Jennings."

"What? Jennings interviewed the mayor? Already?"

"They're broadcasting from Jersey City."

"I was under the East River. What's the statement?"

" 'Mayor Rudolph Mincarelli continues to govern the city of New York from an undisclosed location within the five boroughs.' "

"Are you saying you're not in Manhattan?"

"Don't push it, Jose—"

"You safe?"

"We're in good hands," said Renata Bradley.

Jose made a connection deep in the disks of his mental database. He ventured a guess. "Old hands?"

Renata hung up on him.

Jose stared at the dead phone.

"What's up?" asked Jasbir.

"I heard a rumor once: back when the mayor ran the organized-crime strike force, he used to operate from a secret hideout."

"Why secret?"

"The story was that the Mafia had bribed telephone installers to tap the U.S. Attorney's phones. I heard another version that Mafia union guys miked the entire U.S. Attorney building during construction. So Mincarelli's strike force moved to a hideout."

"Where is it?"

"Somewhere around City Hall, supposedly. I checked it out. I looked everywhere. Zilch. Like alligators in the sewer."

Jasbir's luminous black eyes grew large. "There are alligators in the sewer?"

"I can't believe Peter Jennings already got the mayor's story. Shit!"

"Are there alligators in the sewer?"

"I could shoot soldiers for a week and never get tape like Arnie's. What he shot—and him getting shot—will be the war in New York for history. Like that kid jumping in front of the tank in Tiananmen Square."

Scooped by Arnie on the street. Scooped by remote cameras. Scooped by Jennings on the mayor—wait, wait, wait. What the hell did the Chinese want? What did they invade for? That was the story. Just like Arnie used to say. *The narrative of history is told by players.*

"We should move along," said Jasbir, "the Nineteenth Precinct is only four blocks uptown. The soldiers will surely attack the Seventeenth Precinct next. It's on Fifty-second Street."

Jose was kicking himself. If only he'd listened to his grandfather gassing on about Chinese history instead of pedaling after fire engines, maybe he'd know why they'd invaded New York.

Jasbir grew insistent, "We cannot stay here."

"Right. Down to Fifty-seventh."

Jose broke into a run and was far in the lead when two guys jumped him in the next block, bursting from a doorway, screaming, "Get the Chink. Get the Chink."

He caught a glimpse of their buddies up Sixty-first before a punch in the mouth knocked him to the pavement.

In the dull pools of daylight that seeped into the subway station from the vent bays, people huddled. A woman welcomed Kate into one of their circles and asked if she was all right.

"Just scared."

"Join the club."

"All I want to do is go home."

"Me, too. There's some kids are going to run up the tracks uptown. Are you going that way?"

"Chelsea."

"I'm in the Village. Want to try it?"

And Kate found herself transformed from a frightened woman running alone to a member of a group, mostly her age, sliding off the platform onto the tracks.

"Don't touch the third rail," someone warned, pointing at the wood-covered power rail.

"There's no electricity."

"You want to be touching it when they turn it back on?"

"Okay, everybody. Stick close."

After a block or two of shuffling and stumbling over ties

and pipes, someone screamed. A red-eyed rat crossed their path and stared. Then somebody laughed. And another voice said, "Fuck you, Rat," and then they were all laughing like this was a night walk at summer camp.

When they reached the Houston Street station, some dropped off and others joined them. A newcomer lighted a cigarette and the entire group stopped as complaints about the smoke turned into a shouting match. Finally the cigarette was snubbed out in the dark and they shuffled on, punctuated with remarks like, "Some people," and "Mind your own business," and "Up yours," and then, after an empty silence, "Sorry, I didn't mean that."

"Christopher Street!" Someone imitated a subway conductor as they neared the next station. "Fourteenth Street next. Change there for the Two and Three Express and the L."

The woman who had come to Kate's aid said good-bye. Kate plodded on, cocooned by twenty others, sticking close, talking quietly, smothering fear. She decided to get out at Fourteenth Street, where there would be more people on the street. Then a six-block run up Seventh Avenue, and home on Twentieth, two long blocks past the police station.

"Fuckin' Chinese."

Flat on his back, stunned, too angry to be scared, Jose yelled back, "I'm not Chinese. I'm Jose Chin, New York Yes!"

Stoned on something, too high to hear his story, they grabbed his camera. Jose hugged it closer and tried to stand. Then Jasbir caught up. The tall Sikh threw one of Jose's attackers over a parked car and backed down the other with a dangerous look.

When he helped Jose to his feet, they finally recognized him. "Hey, hey, it's Jose Chin. Look, Jose Chin, New York

Yes! Sorry, man. Thought you were the fucking invaders. What's up?"

Jose took the handkerchief Jasbir handed him and wiped his mouth. It came away blood-red, a shocking sight to a man who considered himself damage-proof. "Shit!"

"What's happening, Jose? Hey, man, it's Jose Chin."

"I need ice or I'll be too swollen to go on camera."

"Oh, man. I'm really sorry. So what's up?"

"Tune in tonight," said Jose, and just then the sound of breaking glass signaled the two that their buddies had scored a drugstore up the block.

Jose and Jasbir headed downtown, Jose wiping his mouth and wondering where the hell he was going to find ice.

They reached the corner of Fifty-seventh and Second without seeing any soldiers, and headed quickly west, trotting, walking, trotting again, Jose pausing for shots of people wandering aimlessly by broken store windows, and to pan up the office and apartment windows white with faces.

At the intersections, Jasbir climbed atop cars to see if troops were coming down the avenues. By the time they reached Park Avenue, all the people they saw were wearing Burberry raincoats, and when they reached Madison they could see the store itself ahead in the next block, where looters were jumping out of its broken windows—in raincoats, arms piled with suits, plastic-wrapped shirts, and colorful neckties. A mob was gathered several blocks up Madison, battering the gates of a leather-goods shop. Suddenly, a deep roar scattered them.

"What's that, motorcycles?"

Jasbir jumped onto the roof of a taxi and peered down Madison. "Hide!"

"What's wrong?"

"Hells Angels."

Jasbir jumped to the sidewalk, grabbed Jose, and hauled him into a doorway littered with broken glass. The bikes thundered closer. Jose stepped out of the doorway and counted ten of them. He was already rolling tape.

"Stay down," said Jasbir.

"Shhhh! I'm narrating: 'Up Madison like rolling thunder, ten Harley-Davidson motorcycles are piloted by bare-armed, leather-vested, long-haired bikers. Each carries a passenger wearing a dark Armani suit and a Halloween mask. Ronald Reagan, Al Gore, three Barbra Streisands, Princess Di, a Spice Girl, and Mayor Mincarelli hold shot-guns propped on their knees, barrels pointing high, like lances.'"

He swung the camera west across Fifty-seventh Street, and focused a tight shot on Tiffany's on the southeast corner of Fifth Avenue. "Jose wants to know! Are New York Yes! viewers about to witness a jewel robbery?"

He swung the camera back to Madison, focusing franti-cally, and caught the bikers swinging into Fifty-seventh Street. Yes!

The sharp, smacking exhaust of the revving, unmuffled engines set off a car alarm. In one corner of his shot of the rolling bikes, Jose held the blinking lights of a forlornly whooping Volkswagen, whose loyal driver had braved the extra moment to lock his car before running for his life.

"Let's go, Jasbir."

"What?"

"Come on, come on, come on." The instant the rear-guard bike completed its turn, Jose Chin bolted across Madison, weaved through the stopped cars, and darted up the north sidewalk. Two looters exiting Burberry's front window lunged for his camera. Jasbir Singh, trailing him like a locomotive, knocked both back through the shattered glass.

Jose kept running into the middle of Fifth Avenue, duck-ing low behind the cars, and braced his camera on the roof of a limousine. He had a clear view of the locked front doors of Tiffany & Co. The embossed nickel-steel gleamed quietly in the smoky sunlight.

A hundred feet away, the masked passengers climbed off the motorcycles with their shotguns and formed a cordon on the sidewalk. Their leader, a grinning Ronald Reagan, motioned the bikes farther down Fifth, where they clustered, snorting quietly, like patient horses.

Then Ronald Reagan ran to the front door with a roll of duct tape. A Spice Girl joined him with a stick of dynamite, which they fastened to the steel door with an X of tape.

Jasbir tapped Jose's shoulder. "Get down."

"Hang on, he's lighting the fuse."

Jasbir pulled Jose down beside him as the well-dressed robbers sauntered toward shelter.

It wasn't the loudest explosion Jose had heard that day, but it was the closest, and the first that sent debris screaming past his head. Ears ringing, he whispered into his mike, "The jewel thieves are emerging from shelter now—except for one who didn't get out of the way in time and is writhing on the sidewalk."

He got a tight shot of the robber's dynamite-severed leg, and panned up to the jewel thieves shouldering through the smoking hole where the front door had been. Jose's shotgun mike picked up the angry cursing. The sudden crackle of small arms fire from within the jewelry store sent the robbers reeling from the door. Two fell to the sidewalk.

The leader lit a second stick of dynamite and lobbed it in. The explosion was muffled within the foyer, and the surviving robbers piled in, shotguns blazing. Gunfire continued for a full minute and stopped abruptly. Two minutes later the robbers emerged with plump canvas bags.

Jose stood higher to shoot them loading the motorcycles.

"No," said Jasbir. But he was too late. One of the Hells Angels spotted Jose, gunned his engine, and charged through the tangled traffic.

Jose kept rolling tape until the biker filled his viewfinder. At the last second he opened his arms wide and yelled, "Press, press—*New York Yes!*"

The biker yanked a stubby sawed-off shotgun from a leather scabbard.

23

"PRESS! PRESS! DON'T SHOOT."

The biker, wearing a Barbra Streisand mask, had the initial *G* tattooed on one arm and branded on the other. Scarier than the brand, Jose concluded with a sinking heart, was the methed-up neon glow in the eye holes.

"You outta your fuckin' mind, man?"

Astonished not to be shot dead already, Jose yelled, "Jose Chin, New York Yes!"

"I know who you fuckin' are. You out of your fuckin' mind?"

Jose couldn't stop his leg from shaking. Gauging the connections between the biker's speed-fried brain and his trigger finger, he tried to smile, but his lips kept curling the wrong way. His voice squeaked up a full octave as he said, "Would I be doing this for a living if I weren't?"

"You outta your fuckin' mind?"

"This is an incredible story. You want to give me a quote?"

"Gimme that fuckin' tape."

"No way, man. I got incredible stuff on here."

"Give me that fuckin' tape or I'll blow your fuckin' head off."

"Give it to him," said Jasbir.

"Jasbir," said Jose, "stay out of this. Listen, there's nothing on this tape to hurt you. And the jackers are all wearing masks."

"You shot my fucking arms. What happens after we kick Chink ass? The cops'll come looking for Gorgeous George. Give me the fuckin' tape."

"What if I erased the part I had you on?"

"Jose, I'm giving you one more chance and only 'cause I seen you on TV. Give me the fucking tape or I'll kill you."

Jose hesitated. "You don't understand, man. This is my Pulitzer Prize."

"You too *stupid* to be afraid? Do it for your ragtop friend." He wheeled the sawed-off barrel at the beturbaned Sikh. "Say your Kali prayers—you're dead in two. One . . ."

"Here," said Jose, popping the camera's tape door. Gorgeous George threw the minicassette on the street and ground it to plastic splinters under the heel of his engineer boot. Then he turned the bike around to face Tiffany's again. "Power of fucking TV, Jose. Any normal dude pull that shit on me, he'd be dead."

A hard twist of the throttle yanked his front wheel off the pavement. But before the wheelie was complete, Gorgeous George threw his arms high, and crashed against a stalled taxi. The rest of the gang were suddenly dropping from their bikes, too.

Jose and Jasbir hugged the ground. They heard a shotgun blast and another, immediately drowned out by sustained machine-gun fire. In half a minute there was silence. Boots flashed by, two cars over. Cheek pressed to the pavement, Jose heard a single shot, then nothing.

He raised his head.

Slowly, stunned by the slaughter, he unlimbered the camera and rolled tape on the dead bikers, the dead Armani-suited jewel robbers, and dead George sprawled over his Harley like he'd passed out from too many beers.

Jose lowered the camera. Jasbir was staring up at him from the pavement. "You see what happened?" Jose asked.

"Chinese," said Jasbir. "Four men."

"Four men killed twenty?"

"They are soldiers, not street thugs. Why did you keep arguing with him?"

"George? I had to distract him so I could palm a blank tape out of my pocket."

"You kept the real tape?"

"Of course I kept the real tape."

"While he aimed a gun at my head?"

"I just shot a Pulitzer. What, are you out of your mind?"

"No, *you* are out of your mind." Jasbir stood up, brushing off his hands.

"Hey, where you going?"

"I am going home," said Jasbir.

"Hey, come on. With this footage, I'll get you a bonus big enough to go back to school and become an engineer."

"I have a son," said Jasbir.

"Girdup," said Jose, trying to charm the big Sikh into staying with him.

"If Girdup has a father to take care of him, *he* will become an engineer."

"Hey, you're with Jose. We got the Luck of the Latin."

And Jasbir, bless him, gave in. "Okay," he said. "Okay, Jose. But promise we will take no more crazy chances."

"Promise," said Jose.

They hurried three blocks uptown to Central Park, where they saw people peering from behind the stone walls. Heads whipped toward explosions from the river, whirled toward gunfire rattling downtown, flinched from a wild shell screaming overhead.

Entering, they discovered more and more people as they went deeper into the park. A hot-dog man was doing big business. Jose cruised the line, taping interviews—a legal secretary who'd fled her office on Fifty-seventh Street was worried that FedEx was not going to deliver a package they'd picked up a minute before the shooting started; a Bergdorf buyer kept saying, "This could not have happened at a worse time." Both women, who had just met, were comforting a third stranger, who was sobbing that she was worried about her mother in Brooklyn.

A public-relations man with a mouth full of dental apparatus made even better TV; a root canal procedure had come to a crashing halt when the windows were blown out of his dentist's Central Park West office. Jasbir helped him remove a molar clamp. "It doesn't hurt," the patient answered Jose's "Jose wants to know," but he was still cross-eyed on Novocain.

A white-coated hospital intern who'd been caught in the park on her lunch break had set up a first-aid station near the Sixth Avenue entrance, and a dental technician had pitched in to help with gunshot and falling-glass wounds. Jose videoed their bandaged patients, moaning in the shade of trees, and the Rollerbladers risking the streets to canvas drugstores for medical supplies.

No one Jose interviewed knew a thing about what was happening. Jasbir shoved a hot dog into his hand. "Eat."

"I'm not hungry."

"Eat while there's still food."

Jose wolfed it down, surprised to discover he was suddenly starving. A frightened guy in a suit hurried by, banging his cellphone on his hand. Jose realized he'd seen several people do that—batteries must be running down. He looked at his watch—a quarter to three. It had been going on for two and a half, maybe three hours.

Less than six more hours of decent light left. Even with a long June evening, before he knew it he'd be shooting in the dark.

Ken Hughes had never considered himself good at deception. He had never lied successfully to either of his wives, never fooled them—or any other woman, for that matter—and had long ago given up trying. But he had apparently fooled the Chinese bosun into thinking that he was a thoroughly cowed captive. When he asked permission to "hit the head," the bosun nodded consent.

"I'd also like to go to my cabin for a sec, if it's okay? Put on shoes and socks, if it's okay with you."

The bosun looked down at Ken's bare feet. They hadn't given him time to put shoes on when they took his wet suit. "Hurry."

He went first to his cabin, located Kate's multi-zippered backpack, found her cellphone on the fourth try, tied on running shoes, and stepped across the corridor into the head.

He knew he'd have time to make only one call, at the most, and he desperately wanted to call Kate. He remembered her home number from their playing phone tag while setting up their brunch. But even if the land lines were working—after the pasting the phone company was taking—and even if Kate was home, he did not trust her to do what she would have to do. Certainly, *he* would hesitate to sacrifice *her* if their roles were reversed. But someone had to get word to the military that Admiral Tang was still aboard the *Chelsea Queen*. Someone had to call in an air strike to blow the tug and Tang out of the water. Someone had to agree to let Ken Hughes fend for himself—risking his one life in order to save thousands. And that someone wasn't Kate.

His best bet was to call his cousin, the McAllister dispatcher. If their operations barge was still in business up the

Kill Van Kull, they'd have plenty of radios to alert the Navy, the Coast Guard, and whoever was cranking up to defend the city.

He turned Kate's phone on, its beep muffled by the idling engines' turbocharger whine and the gunfire in the harbor. The screen blinked a "V," indicating a voice-mail message, just like his own phone did. To get messages, he needed Kate's access code, which had come up in one of their many conversations: Five, for the five miles she ran one day, and two, for the two miles she swam next. That way, Kate had told him, if she ever slacked off, her guilty conscience would have to pay the next time she checked her messages. Ken punched #52.

The sound of her voice threatened to undo him. He had survived, until this moment, by deliberately uncoupling from his feelings—the boat handler, cold as a machine. Suddenly her voice was in his ear, reminding him that only hours ago he had been holding her in his arms.

Her thoughts seemed surprisingly well organized at first, boat handler to boat handler in rising seas: "Ken, I'm heading home on the Staten Island ferry. I borrowed a cellphone, hoping you were still alive and you'd hear my phone ring." This must have been before she radioed from the ferry, he thought. "I'll head for my apartment. And I will look for you from the Chelsea Piers. You saved my life, and I will help you. Now listen to me, I have to tell you, I've only known you two days. But if anything happens to either of us, you've got to know this: you made me feel more loved these two days than I've ever felt in my life."

His heart rose. Maybe she had made it home by now. But how much more time would the bosun give him? His hands were shaking and he had to call upon his last pretense of mechanical detachment to dial McAllister first.

If the dispatchers weren't still on their coffee barge, then they would have moved their radios to a safer location on

Staten Island or over in Jersey to try to keep track of their boats and help their captains run for cover.

The phone rang.

After this call, he was going to have to go back up to the wheelhouse and act like nothing had changed. Act like a normal prisoner of war—while cocking both ears for a helicopter gunship and praying the whole time that the Navy didn't send some faster-than-the-speed-of-sound missile or a Mach 2 jet fighter to destroy the Chinese admiral.

"McAllister," said a voice on the phone.

"It's Ken. I'm—"

The phone flew from his face. The bosun had reached through the curtain and plucked it from him.

Ken scrambled for an explanation for the bosun—"I'm trying to call my girlfriend, tell her we're standing off"—before the cellphone imploded.

"You wise guy?" asked the bosun. He opened his hand and spilled the remains of the phone on the deck. Blood was oozing from his palm where something glass or metal had pierced it, but this didn't seem to trouble him.

Ken felt his spirit crash. He had come so close to destroying Tang. But he had blown it, so now he was back to simply trying to stay alive. Bitterly, as if courting punishment for his failure, he said, "Apparently you're a Jack London fan."

"What you talk?"

"The Sea Wolf once did that to a potato."

"Next time I do it your head."

Kate sprinted out of the Fourteenth Street subway station, past some men gathered at the intersection. She ran six blocks up Seventh Avenue, turned into Twentieth. In the middle of the block, soldiers were shooting at the police station. Kate spun on her heel. Back down Seventh and across Sixteenth Street, she fled west.

Distant explosions echoed crazily, banging from everywhere at once. A man swung into Sixteenth and ran straight at her, black dresses streaming over his shoulders like Batman's cape. Kate shrank against a truck and he raced past, grinning like a crazy person. At Eighth Avenue she saw people running, weaving among the empty cars, arms hugging clothes.

They were throwing garbage cans through the Banana Republic windows and leaping after them, toppling the mannequins, grabbing pants and shirts. A drunk was waving a gun; a frightened old woman huddled against the subway entrance.

Kate raced past, through the intersection. The tall lofts and warehouses blocked the sun and it was strangely quiet in the narrow, traffic-tangled canyon between them. Ahead, one more long block past warehouse loading docks, trucks, and double-parked vans, lay Ninth Avenue and, soon after, home. But when she got to Ninth Avenue she could see, beyond the stopped cars and buses, that more looters were evident, staggering from the Chelsea Market with fruit and cakes, sides of beef, and clear plastic sacks of live lobsters.

Outside the housing project, even the winos had fled their benches. People were boarding up a bodega, hammering wood and looking fearfully over their shoulders. Up the block, looters were carrying beer cases from another bodega, while the Korean woman who ran the cash register stood by the door, tears streaming down her face.

The owner of the Calidad Restaurant was standing in front of it, arms crossed, his big cooks behind him. Parked right up on the sidewalk in a shiny Ford Expedition was a whole carload of men with shotguns.

Kate ran as fast as she could all the way to the corner of Twentieth Street. Only half a block from home, she heard a scream. She saw a girl running down Ninth Avenue, weaving like a figure skater through the cars. A gang of men, teenagers, galloped after her like vicious dogs. Suddenly blocked when one of her pursuers lunged from the side, she scrambled over the hood of a taxi.

They caught her at Twenty-first Street—a block from where Kate was about to sprint for the safety of her house— closed a circle around her so fast she just stopped, gasping for breath. Her frightened eyes searched their faces for one who would say, No, don't do this, she could be your sister.

Kate found her legs carrying her toward the girl.

The circle drew tighter. They slammed her legs from behind and she fell hard onto the sidewalk. One of the men threw himself on top of her, trying to kiss her face. She twisted her head frantically from side to side and screamed. He jammed his hand between her legs and ripped at her belt. She screamed again and again. A hand smacked tight over her mouth.

Ten feet away, Kate scooped up a heavy mesh litter basket and lofted it into the midst of the pack. It swished through the air and hit the boy on top of the girl with a loud thump. He arched backward clutching his nose. The wire garbage can bounced off another kid and rolled across the sidewalk. The others scrambled to their feet to see who had dared to attack them.

24

KATE HAD THROWN the litter basket without thinking. Now, as it rolled away, and the boy she had hit jumped up clutching his face and cursing through his hands, the others—Jesus Christ, seven of them—turned on her. What had possessed her? One second she was almost home—*almost home*—THE NEXT SHE HAD SCOOPED UP THE LITTER BASKET AND THROWN IT, DREAMING THAT SOMEHOW IT WOULD SCATTER THEM AND SHE WOULD TAKE THE GIRL'S HAND AND RUN—OR SOME STUPID THOUGHT LIKE THAT.

What in God's name had Ken done to her, opened her arms to everything in the world, opened her so wide she had gotten involved in something she had no chance of surviving?

Could she run? They were teenagers, long-legged as coyotes, and they would hunt her like a pack, like they'd run down the girl—a terrified high school kid, she realized now, fifteen or so. Kate looked around for help. There was no one, as if just a moment before, every decent person in the city had finally found a place to hide. She craned her neck back downtown, where they'd been boarding up the bodega; no one. Only empty streets, even where the restaurant owner and his posse had been.

Maybe she could outrun them. She was warm from the long flight uptown, loose and fast. They were still off balance, some looking at her, some looking at the girl. Maybe they wouldn't all come after her.

"Please," the girl cried from the pavement. "Stay. Please help me."

Kate's blood ran cold as one of the kids whipped out a box cutter. Was she really going to allow herself to be abused along with the girl? Would it make the horror of the girl's suffering any less horrible to suffer with her? What difference would it make? To the girl? To herself?

She had hesitated too long. They had circled around her. She kicked the closest one in his balls and, as he doubled over, jumped out of the circle. Desperate, she spotted a flash of blue halfway across Twenty-first. She filled her lungs as if she were calling boat to boat in a running sea: "Help! Police!"

The kids laughed. "Hey, lady, there ain't no cops."

"Don't do this," she said. The kid came at her with the box cutter. Kate's running shoe blurred from the sidewalk and he doubled over, holding his groin and shaking off the pain. His friends were laughing, egging him on, blocking Kate's retreat. He straightened up to slash at her.

Kate was breathing hard, sucking air, trying to burn off the adrenaline that was spiriting the strength from her arms and legs. Suddenly the box cutter flew out of his hand. He grunted in pain and there was a cop, backhanding him with another whack of his nightstick.

The kid threw his hands up to protect himself. The others backed away—slowly. Kate saw them counting eight of themselves and only two cops, a short Puerto Rican wearing eyeglasses and a tall black woman.

"Turn around," Harriet Greene ordered. "Hands on the wall."

"Spread 'em!" barked Hector Sanchez.

Like anyone was listening, Hector thought; like they couldn't look right through his uniform at the little guy in glasses. He was fully aware that he was no fighter, he had too busy a mind. Naturals, like Harriet, just did it.

But here he was thinking—thinking eight street scum against him and Harriet—thinking how they had just re-treated from the Tenth—thinking four precincts that they'd seen fall—thinking how this crazy war had sucked the fear right out of these guys. If Chinese soldiers were gunning down cops, it was Christmas in June. Go for it. No rules, no consequences, no fear.

Harriet plucked the assault rifle off her back and aimed it at the kids' faces. On any normal afternoon, that would have done the trick. Even if their uncles didn't own one, every-body had seen enough movies to know what to expect from an automatic rifle.

Hector sensed movement from a new direction. He looked and felt his guts shrivel. Harriet Greene wasn't the only New Yorker who had taken the opportunity to upgrade her weaponry.

The one holding his nose, the leader, got a big smile on his face. "Hey, look what Willie found."

All heads turned to the new arrival, who was holding a Chinese assault rifle just like Harriet's.

Hector read Willie for a group-home crack baby who'd arrived in his teens minus human feeling. An enormous, chubby child with a manatee smile and dead marble eyes and a finger on a trigger that would cut him and Harriet in half.

Hector lowered his nightstick and opened his other hand

to indicate he was ready to talk. The kid's eyes flicked toward the movement. Harriet shot him in the head.

*   *   *

Kate's house keys, like her phone and wallet, were still on Ken's tug. She banged on her landlord's window—reaching through the bars—until he opened the front door of the house.

With his spare keys, she let herself into her apartment and ran to her answering machine, which had battery backup. But Ken had left no message.

She drank two glasses of water as fast as she could swallow, quickly changed into dry clothes, drank more water, and ate two bananas. She knew that if she stopped moving for even one second, she would be paralyzed by memories of what she had seen in the streets. The fat kid with the gun had convulsed into a fetal naptime position when the black cop saved all of their lives by shooting him.

She found her old binoculars in her seabag in the back of her closet. Then she ran out of the house and down to the river.

"What about the Hong Kong Information Bureau?" Mayor Mincarelli snarled into the telephone.

"Stonewalling," answered Greg Walsh, who was still cooling his heels in Marty Greenberg's White House office. Twice they'd been told to be ready to go in; twice the word had never come.

"Goddamned spies," Rudy rasped in his ear.

"Yes, Mr. Mayor." It was the received wisdom of law enforcement that even before the Chinese Communists officially took Hong Kong back from the British, the Hong Kong Information Bureau had spied for Beijing.

Greg knew Marty's office by heart now: his military

baseball-cap collection, his well-stocked personal mini-buf-
fet—which explained why Marty had ballooned fifty pounds
since Greg had seen him last—his law books bound in
tooled leather, his photographs of famous people shaking his
hand, his TVs monitoring the newscasts and the security
cameras covering key White House rooms.

The camera that kept drawing Greg's eye was focused on
a situation room in the basement where officers and civilians
were bustling around setting up maps and monitors. Military
strategy, Marty had explained, would be formulated down
there, as would the counterstrike proposals offered to the
President.

Marty snatched up an extension. "It's Marty, Mr. Mayor.
I got to tell you the President's taking their missile threat seriously."

"Does that mean he won't counterattack?"

"I can't speculate when and how the President will retaliate or not retaliate, Rudy." He lowered his voice, conspira-
torially. "But obviously: we've lost the option to lob nukes
into Beijing."

"I want you to make it crystal-clear to him that military
intervention in New York is not an option, either."

Just then one of Marty's aides stuck his head into the office and beckoned. "The President's calling me now, Rudy.
Come on, Greg, you're on."

"Marty! Listen to me! A counterattack will slaughter
thousands of innocent people."

The mayor slammed down the telephone. His internal
lawyerly voices were shouting now, strident. *Looters are
roaming my streets. There is a complete breakdown of law
and order. I will not tolerate it! . . . What are you going to
do about it?*

His desperate eye lit on new faces arriving in the bunker:
Don Block had a bloodstained bandage on his left arm;
Mary Quilligan, another former assistant U.S. Attorney, had

fallen on her way there, tearing her pants, and scraping her knees.

"I want," said the mayor, "the Chinese delegate to the UN." Even as he spoke he wasn't sure what he would do with the man. But he had to do something.

"Here?"

"Right here. And that head guy at the Hong Kong Information Bureau."

"What if they don't want to come?"

"Bring them."

"Just so you understand, Mr. Mayor," cautioned Samantha. "These people have diplomatic immunity."

"Not from me they don't."

Two two-man teams of detectives donned bulletproof vests and slipped out of the hideaway on what they knew was a hopeless mission. Attention shifted to the televisions again, because CNN had nailed an interview with the Chinese ambassador in Washington, D.C.

The ambassador, smooth and businesslike, dripped concern and sympathy in perfect English. He acknowledged he had heard all the reports and had no doubt that "a terrible conflict is unfolding in New York even as we speak. But perhaps there is an explanation. Perhaps Admiral Tang Li perceived a threat to his forces and had to move quickly to defend them."

"Forces?" blurted the mayor. "What the hell are his forces doing here in the first place?"

The CNN reporter asked, "Are you referring to the Chinese missile frigate visiting New York's Fleet Week celebration?"

"No. There is no reason to believe that Admiral Tang is involved in any way with any part of the People's Fleet Week celebration."

"Why would Admiral Tang have Chinese naval forces in

the vicinity of New York City, Mr. Ambassador, thirteen thousand miles from China?"

"Ah. Perhaps he is confused. He is, after all, very young. And Tang Li gained deep affection for the United States when invited to join in special Chinese-American military exchange programs at Annapolis and Rhode Island, and while a student at Columbia University."

"Columbia?" echoed the mayor. "He went to Columbia? He's been here? He's lived here? In the city?"

Everyone he looked at shrugged and stared at the televisions.

"It is said that he wrote an outstanding thesis suggesting that China could defuse domestic upheaval by 'transporting' pernicious energies abroad."

The CNN interviewer asked, "Does China think that the United States would be justified to retaliate?"

The ambassador answered primly, "Beijing would express wonder, of course, that responsible governments would provoke widespread bloodletting and destruction in a city that houses a nation's central financial markets. It is my government's understanding that the stock market infrastructure has thus far been allowed to remain intact."

"He's threatening to attack Wall Street." The mayor stood up, red with rage. "Understand this," he told the televisions, and then everyone in the Old Place. "This was a city of law. And it will be again."

Nobody knew what to say. Even Renata looked away. But Rudy Mincarelli was neither embarrassed nor through talking. "I will never allow an army from a lawless totalitarian dictatorship to prevail in New York City."

Renata nudged him, Enough.

Mincarelli hesitated. *What the hell was he doing?* "Okay, everybody, back to work."

Work? Ben and Rocco—a pair of middle-aged NYPD gold-shield detectives with a combined fifty years' experience and sixty pounds of extra beef between them—exchanged the long-practiced silent glances they used to converse with while in the company of felons, witnesses, and prosecutors. *What work? We're sitting around watching TV.*

Rudy Mincarelli murmured to Renata, " 'Transporting pernicious energies abroad'? Bullshit. This Tang can't be on his own. They knew all along that this was coming. Get me Greg again."

Greg Walsh was still with the President.

He called back ten minutes later.

Rudy spoke first. "There's only one way out of this. The President's got to order a counterattack on China."

"I'm sorry, pal, he's not prepared to start an all-out war with China. Here's the deal, and it sucks. The President's on the fence. Congress is outraged, but of course it'll be days before they can agree to do anything, unless the President asks them to declare war, which Marty says he won't. At least not right now. But I've got to warn you, Rudy, no one is thinking that clearly. The Defense Department is catching hell because they didn't see this coming, and the Navy is taking it as a personal insult."

"In other words," said Rudy, "I can expect the worst from both of them. What is the President going to do?"

"He's dispatching rapid-response forces to the South China Sea. They'll probably base out of the Philippines—if they let us—and Taiwan. The Pentagon hopes to have them in place in a week. And, of course, we're moving aircraft carriers there."

Rudy Mincarelli braced to ask the question whose answer he most feared. "Is the Navy moving aircraft carriers here, too?"

"I'm afraid so, Rudy. And the Army, the Air Force, and the Marines, they're massing helicopter gunships. In case they're needed. . . ."

The mayor looked around the old hideout, seeking the faces of his comrades from the strike-force days. No one would meet his eye. Then his seeking gaze fell on a security monitor, which was focused on one of the street entrances. He was shocked to see it was still light outside. He looked at his watch. Only three-thirty.

He wanted more than anything to step out into the streets, whistle up an escort, take a long walk, talk to some people, get into a good argument, then maybe drive home with the sunroof open and stare at the building tops.

"This is the greatest city in the history of the world. This is an imperial city the likes of which history has never seen before."

"Beg pardon, Mr. Mayor?"

They were staring at him. The newspapers called him a control freak. *Well, you're looking at one control freak who isn't going to lose it. Ever.*

"I said, we are enduring a terrorist attack sponsored by a superpower—Renata, what's the population?"

"What?"

"The population! I've been saying eight million. Exactly how many people do we have?"

Renata, who believed that a command of statistics was one way to keep the press off balance, answered, "Seven million, six hundred and seventy-three thousand and change."

"It's a terrorist attack," he repeated aloud. "A terrorist attack sponsored by a superpower. And we're on our own."

In the back of the bunker, Federal Judge Danny Wong laid his big arms around Ben and Rocco. He spoke persuasively, at length, in a low rumble. When he was finished, Ben and Rocco stared at each other for a while. Then they signaled Rod Brown. Under Judge Wong's cool eye, the ex-FBI agent listened to the detectives. Then the three men quietly headed out.

25

IF THE GRUNTS' WAR he had fought in Vietnam had taught
Greg Walsh anything, it had taught him that a military force
in action was, by definition, out of control.

He paced a baffled circle around Marty Greenberg's
guest chair, stunned by the presidential dithering, racking
his brain for his next move.

"Jesus, Marty, you could have spoken up."

Marty walked heavily to his buffet, which a staffer had
replenished while they were in the meeting, plucked a slice
of smoked salmon with his fingers, threw back his head, and
slid it down his throat.

"You don't know him."

"I know the man needed somebody to shore up his backbone. You gotta go back in there."

"It doesn't work that way."

"Christ on a crutch, Marty, I've been attending pointless,
directionless, fruitless meetings since I made sergeant, but
that one took the cake."

"Trust me."

"To do what?" Greg demanded.

Marty lowered his voice. "Steer the President in a productive direction."

Greg snorted.

Marty got angry. "Who do you think persuaded him to keep a leash on the military so far? Jesus Christ, Greg, I got the President to recall a whole goddamned helicopter attack wing the Air Force had launched—unauthorized—from McGuire. Give me a little credit, okay?"

"You can't let up now. You have to force China to stop, *now*. Withdraw, or suffer the consequences. Rudy is right: we've got to take the fight to China. Don't fight in New York."

Marty fingered another slice of salmon. "I still don't understand how the Chinese could sneak a fleet of subs right into the harbor. How could the Navy let them penetrate their aural screens? You'd think SOSUS—"

Greg cut him off. "For crissake, the entire defense community missed an event that's just changed the course of history."

The main, though unspoken, agenda of the meeting from which they'd just come was to select which arm of the United States government was most blameworthy for the attack on New York. Sniffing the wind like a horny poodle, Marty had concluded it would be the Navy, conveniently ignoring the point that an embarrassed Navy catching all the blame was even more likely to fly off the handle.

Greg said, "It might have helped if the Navy had had any hint they were coming. The CIA had picked up enough anomalies—they should have raised a red flag."

"I thought that the CIA satellite guy made a damned good case for their shortage of analysts."

"He wasted ten minutes pitching the President for a budget increase." I'm getting dragged into this nonsense, too, thought Greg. "This is not helping the city. You can blame the Navy. You can just as easily blame the CIA's pre-conceived view of what the world should look like. Blame who the hell you want, later. First, go to the source—make the Chinese stop the attack, cease, desist, withdraw, immediately."

But talking to the President's chief counsel was like laying a linoleum floor. You pushed a bubble down here, another popped up there. "Intelligence is stretched thin," Marty countered vaguely. "Maybe Tang is a renegade. Jesus, I don't know. . . . You want a bagel? We get 'em straight from H & H. . . . Go home, Greg. Go back to New York. Tell Mayor Rudy we've been fucked the same way anyone who thinks they understand China always gets fucked."

Greg Walsh eyed his old friend severely. Did Marty have even the vaguest idea of what was happening on the streets of New York? Did he know what it was like to wonder what your wife was doing trapped in a school full of kids whose lives were in her hands? Trapped? Frances wouldn't leave her school if the Chinese Army sent a limo to take her home.

"*We* have been fucked. Not you Washington guys. Not your fucking CIA. Not the Navy. New York. New York's been fucked."

"Hey, I'm a New Yorker."

"Still?"

"I am the most powerful 'New Yorker' in the country."

Greg Walsh shot a disgusted glance at Marty's door to the Oval Office. "Then use your power. Get the President to muzzle the Navy and persuade China to get out of the harbor before they destroy us."

"I'm working on it."

Greg paced harder, thinking, There has to be a better route to the President than Marty. "Poor Rudy."

"Poor Rudy? What, are you kidding? Rudy's happiest hunkered down, back to the wall. That's when he shines." Marty glanced around his office, moved closer to Greg, and whispered, "And don't you think he doesn't recognize this opportunity to open his options—we got an incumbent in trouble. If Rudy comes out of this alive, he'll be the best-known, most-admired politician in the race."

Greg wasn't sure he'd heard right. "Marty, you work for this incumbent!"

"Hey!" Marty laughed, reaching to clap Greg on the back. "We're jumping way ahead. First we got to win this fight, and here"—Marty nodded at the TV monitor which was focused on the double doors of the situation room—"here comes the man to sink every submarine and kick every commando ass in New York."

Greg saw a grim-visaged admiral entering, flanked by his flag lieutenants. "Who's that?"

"Vice Admiral William Cox Titus," answered Marty with a phone-punching gesture: " 'Hello, Central Casting, get me Attila the Hun in navy blue.' Titus was a nuke-sub driver. Scuttlebutt has it he sank not one but *two* Akula-class Russian attack boats 'by accident,' playing chicken. Admiral Aggressive. He's got the rep. He talks the talk. And he's got the President's ear."

26

ADMIRAL TANG STOOD on the roof of the *Chelsea Queen*'s
WHEELHOUSE FLANKED BY TWO JUNIOR OFFICERS. ONE LIEU-
TENANT WATCHED THE HUDSON RIVER'S JERSEY BANK, WHICH
REMINDED TANG OF THE NEW PUDONG DEVELOPMENT OF
SHANGHAI WHERE HE HAD TRAINED HIS ASSAULT TROOPS, RUN-
NING THEM UP AND DOWN ENDLESS STAIRS IN THE DESERTED
SHELLS OF EMPTY OFFICE BUILDINGS.

Here, they were occupied; in Shanghai, you could see
straight through empty building after empty building—
thanks to the Communist bureaucracy forcing bankrupt
banks to underwrite pointless construction.

Another lieutenant scanned the Manhattan side of the
river where his commandos had established a beachhead at
Forty-second Street, four city blocks below the Intrepid museum, and another at Fifty-fourth Street two blocks above
the superpier where the *John F. Kennedy* was still fighting
back. Troops had streamed inland from both landings to take
police stations and telephone buildings; others had stayed to

ambush the aircraft carrier's sailors attempting to return to their ship.

Tang watched the river.

It was said the noise of a sea battle was unimaginable, and only in the thunder of guns and jet engines did an admiral learn whether he could fight. Perhaps. But he felt a powerful advantage positioned atop the tugboat. Separated from the battle, emotionally and physically, he could observe and act with a scientist's detachment.

As the pilot of the only helicopter to survive the strafing of the *Kennedy*'s flight deck—a Sikorski SH-60 Seahawk— Ensign Eldon Routh was the most heavily armed American in New York that afternoon.

Thanks to the ingenuity of the *Kennedy*'s armorers, who had ransacked the ship's magazine to jury-rig miracles, Routh and his co-pilot had at their fingertips the missiles to send a dozen submarines to the bottom of New York Harbor. The helo bristled like a lopsided porcupine. The cockpit was a spiderweb of last minute wiring. Everywhere Routh looked was a red Launch switch.

And if anyone tried to mess with him, he had a pair of totally insane Marine door gunners who had cut their teeth battling South American drug runners and had recently returned to active service in what they claimed was a Navy "work release program" from the Portsmouth Brig.

Thus armed and crewed, Routh feared nothing except the captain of the *John F. Kennedy*, whose battle-scarred face was suddenly looming into his cockpit, yelling over the turbine scream into a mouse which transmitted his voice to the headset in Routh's cranial helmet.

"I have one question to ask you, Ensign Routh, and I want it answered damned carefully, with due consideration of your place in the world and mine."

"Aye, sir."

Under ordinary circumstances, the young helo pilot knew that he had a better chance of having a conversation with God than with the captain of the carrier. But his own captain—the carrier air wing commander who bossed the ship's air crew—was miles away at a land base. So were the majority of the *Kennedy*'s aircraft—except for a sampling left aboard for Fleet Week visitors—beached until the ship put to sea again. His CAG might be hell on wings, but the captain of the ship was like a tiger that had missed its rabies shot.

"My vessel's sitting on the bottom, on fire, moored bow on. My catapults are aimed at a goddamned wall of buildings. And I have no wind over the deck. This helo is the only aircraft I can launch. Is there a man aboard this ship who can fly her better?"

"No, sir." Not since Bill Nichols, his buddy since flight school, had been cut in half by a burst from an assault rifle on the bloody dash back from Central Park. A Chinese patrol, dug into a warehouse loading bay, had ambushed them on Eleventh Avenue. Routh was in shock; he had never been to war and all that was keeping him going was his rigorous training and the ferocity emanating from the captain like a magnetic force field.

"Is your aircraft ready?"

"Aye, sir. Good to go." Ready as he could be, considering she was primarily designed to hunt submarines on the open ocean, and that even at sea he spent most of his flying hours hovering beside the carrier on rescue standby in case a plane went into the drink during launch or recovery. Instead, he was about to confront a bunch of submarines surfaced on a river, not to mention a well-manned Chinese frigate with a seemingly endless supply of missiles. With a visiting Coast Guard copilot he'd met an hour ago.

"What else do you need?"

"Shore leave," chorused Ensign Routh's door gunners, who were eavesdropping on the intercom. "And tell him to spike the Vulcans."

"Uh, sir? Could you tell the Vulcan crews to kind of look out for us, sir?"

Undaunted by the fires burning all around them, the carrier's six-barrel Vulcan-Phalanx rotary cannon were chewing up the harbor. Mounted in the stern for a rapid-fire, last-ditch defense against aerial attack, their fifty-round-a-second fire had put at least four subs out of commission, forced the Chinese missile frigate to run for cover, sunk several small ferries, destroyed two marinas on the Jersey side of the river, and started numerous fires on the Palisades.

The captain laughed, an awful sound. "Don't you worry. I've already told them, anybody who shoots you down by mistake has leave canceled. . . . Joke, son. Don't you worry. I've got three thousand sailors fighting to keep this ship operational so you can come back and reload."

"Aye, sir."

"Give my right ball to go in your place, son."

Slake, on the starboard door, growled that Routh should inform the commanding officer that he was welcome to relieve him right now.

"Good hunting."

At the captain's thumbs-up, the hanger deck's ballistic doors slid open and the elevator rose to the *Kennedy*'s smoke-roiled flight deck. The bang and rattle of rockets and machine guns and the roar of the Vulcan were deafening. Fire was creeping forward from the stern of the ship.

Routh spooled up his engines, and instructed his door gunners not to waste bullets on steel hulls: "You shoot the shooters, I'll shoot the subs."

"Been there, babe," said Stix.

"Done that," said Slake.

The copilot said, "Good to go!" and they were gone.

"Identify and take off," crackled an order in Routh's headset.

He had already launched his aircraft.

Half a minute after the carrier air traffic control center had deadpanned the routine order, he was screaming three hundred and fifty feet over the Hudson River with IRADS target-acquirers flashing hungrily on his screen.

It was set to target his many rocket pods and fifty-caliber nose guns on anything afloat. But the first thing the computer locked onto was a red-and-black New York Harbor tug. Routh's copilot eyeballed three idiot civilians standing out in the open on her wheelhouse and coolly overrode the IRADS system to find a real target.

It didn't take long. There were enemy submarines everywhere, glistening like sperm whales.

"Look at that mother go!" yelled Stix. "He's doing thirty knots."

One of the subs was racing north up the river, just beneath the surface. Routh, trained to pounce on movement like a cat, touched a switch on his cyclic stick. The helo bucked and the missile swooshed down on a tail of white exhaust. It disappeared like a harpoon into the foredeck of the dark, partly submerged hull.

A ten-foot circle peeled open with a red flash.

Stix and Slake roared their machine guns behind him, whooping and yelling their heads off. By then Routh was firing his second missile and trying to line up a third, hands and eyes flashing with the speed of youth and the precision of million-dollar training. The big Seahawk danced with him like a second skin and he could breathe fire.

He wanted the *Zhaotong*, which had been raking the *Kennedy* with her surface-to-surface missiles. The Chinese frigate had taken many hits, but was still in combat, and her defenders were all over the river. Every time he tried to close, tracer fire flashed by his windscreen. A picket line of subs across the stream was shooting heavy machine guns.

Stix and Slake fired back with their fifty-caliber door guns, scoring hits as if the helo were a stable platform instead of bouncing around the sky like a yo-yo. Jinking between the burning, listing carrier and the missile frigate, Ensign Routh lost count of how many times he crossed the Hudson River.

Then his copilot screamed.

There was a hole in the windshield—wind whistling through it—and when Routh glanced over, the man had slumped into the controls, his body twitching as if a huge animal were shaking him in its jaws. Stix leaped from his gun, yanked him off the stick, unbuckled the seat belts, and laid him onto the deck.

He touched Routh's shoulder. "You okay, kid?"

"Shoot the fuckers!"

An ESM alarm shrilled, warning that enemy radar was locking on. Somewhere below, a narrowing chute of electrons had focused enemy gun sights on his helicopter. He felt a fearless, crazy grin tug at his lips as he fired first, sending a rocket down the chute.

The submarine closest to the *Zhaotong* began running circles and black smoke poured from a crater in her afterdeck. Where the heck did they put sea-to-air missiles on that little sub? he wondered, lining up a clear shot at the missile frigate's superstructure.

The *Kennedy*'s air officer yelled into his headset.

"Break off, break off. They're painting you with lasers."

But Ensign Routh had his blood up and an eighteen-hundred-ton missile frigate in his sights. When the air officer ordered the helo pilot to disengage, Routh yelled back, "Get outta my face, you fucking sleeve!"

Stix and Slake cheered him on, "sleeve" being a SEAL insult of titanic proportion.

A new voice in his headset, throwing him again. "Ensign Routh, this is the captain. Break off and report."

"I read no illumination, sir."

"Break off—now." It was a voice accustomed to instant obedience from six thousand men and women.

"Aye, sir."

But even as he acknowledged the command he saw that it was too late. His IRADS screen showed a missile riding a thin beam of laser light like it was being reeled up to him on a wire. He banked at an angle that could shear his main rotor coupling, and jerked his pitch lever to drop toward the river like an anvil. The sea-to-air missile passed above him, cleared his tail rotor by twenty feet, and soared out of control toward Manhattan.

He traced its red tail with one eye—watching for it to turn around and take another shot at him—and hunted the *Zhaotong* with the other. He was practically on top of the little tugboat, blasting the idiot civilians with prop wash. Funny, he realized belatedly, the tug wasn't anchored like the others that huddled near the shore. Instead, it was maintaining position with its propellers, primed to move.

"There's gooks on that tug," yelled Slake.

"Illumination!" warned the *Kennedy*'s air officer.

Another sea-to-air missile, skimming the river surface. But this time Ensign Routh had nowhere to fall.

And, at a seven-hundred-foot-a-minute rate of climb, no way to ascend as fast as the Chinese rocket.

27

KEN HUGHES ROSE on his toes, pressed to the wheelhouse window, as if to somehow lift the Seahawk above the missile pursuing it. The big helo suddenly seemed small, less missile-studded warship than a crew of hapless men inside a fragile shell.

The pilot was damned good. It looked like he might fox the missile again. But it was chasing him three times as fast, halving the distance between them, halving it again. Four or five hundred feet above the river, it caught up, disappeared suddenly into the turbine exhaust port. A sharp explosion scattered burning pieces of the helicopter over many acres of water.

Admiral Tang shook his head in dismay.

The dead American helicopter crew would never know it. But by sheer chance, with their first rocket, they had sunk Boat 4, his most advanced electronic-warfare submarine. His early-warning eyes, designed to detect American air at-

tacks at long range. Tang had just dispatched it upriver to
take up station above the George Washington Bridge, moments before the Seahawk attacked. Now it was on the bottom, and if he was not now blind, his vision to the north was
severely blurred.

Kate Ross climbed an outside emergency stair and a service
ladder onto the sloping roof of the Chelsea Piers Sports Center, focused her binoculars on Ken's tug, and tried to convince herself that one of the shadowy figures in the
wheelhouse was Ken and that they hadn't killed him since
her radio exchange with him.

The men on top of the wheelhouse were surveying the
battle with binoculars. It did not escape her that she possessed special information that would be useful to the U.S.
military, that the Admiral Tang they were talking about on
the radio was likely on the tug. But so was Ken, she hoped,
and no force on earth would make her bring fire down on the
tug till Ken escaped. Others would soon realize what was
happening on the *Chelsea Queen*.

She had to get Ken off the tugboat.

Ken focused his binoculars hard on the Chelsea Piers. He
knew she was there like he knew his own name. He could
sense her.

He scanned each pier from south to north: 59, the marina,
which looked unscathed, the stacked tee-off cubicles from
which golf balls flew night and day, deserted; 60, the Sports
Center health club; 61, the ice skating Sky Rink and the
Spirit Cruises dinner yachts. Back again: the dinner yachts,
the skating rink, the health club; the walks at the head of the
slips; the five-story nets of the driving range, like a gigantic
birdcage, swaying in the freshening wind.

South of the Chelsea Piers marina, the ghostly stumps of what had been Pier 58 poked from the water. South of those pilings stood the institutional green Marine and Aviation Pier.

He traced the longshore North: a walkway beside the river, some park space, then the heliport, strewn with the smoldering shells of shot-up helicopters, and a blackened remains of the jet fuel tanks. Further north: the NYPD parking violations tow pound pier; the World Yacht's huge restaurant boats, burning beside Pier 81; then, at the foot of Forty-second Street, the long, lean Circle Liners, capsized; then the *Intrepid* Museum. The World War II carrier's island was studded with Chinese commandos using it as an observation post.

In the shadow of the carrier lay the destroyer *Edward Rollins*. Ken fine-focused on the old ship, puzzled. Oil smoke appeared to be rising from her stack. But she'd been decommissioned months ago. Probably on fire. Everything else seemed to be.

North of the *Rollins,* at Pier 92, the *Kennedy* lay burning at an angle that told Ken that she had settled onto the bottom; but a wide swath of empty river behind her demonstrated that the carrier was still fighting with her gatling guns, still capable of wreaking hellacious damage on any submarine that dared to cross her stern.

He felt Kate's pull again, and swept the glasses back to the Chelsea Piers. Sixty, she had said on the radio. "Hipped up" to Pier 60. The Sports Center. He could make out shadows in the windows. Who the hell was stupid enough to be standing by the glass with all the shooting going on?

He raised his binoculars and scanned the roof. A flicker of movement caught his attention. He focused on the top rungs of a ladder. Maybe somebody had just swung off the roof and down it. Maybe not. He couldn't see the rest of the ladder; an emergency stair blocked his view.

*　　*　　*

The *Intrepid* Museum volunteers trapped on the *Edward Rollins* had raised eight hundred pounds of pressure in her Number Two boiler when a joint suddenly opened somewhere in the maze of piping. They could hear the superheated steam roaring and they could feel the abrupt rise in heat and humidity, but they couldn't see the break that was spewing the invisible man-killing jet. The old men stood like statues, afraid to move an inch.

Then every white and balding head swiveled at old Captain Eddie, whose damned fool idea it had been to raise steam in the first place. He was only ten feet from the broom barrel, but every foot looked like a mile. If he just stood there, then after a long, long time the leak would bleed the pressure right out of her. Just then, under the roar of the leak and the oil fires shaking the furnaces, he felt an explosion *whump* out of the river as another poor bastard caught it.

When you gotta go, thought Eddie, you gotta go. And if you gotta go, you might as well go in style. He stepped boldly toward the brooms.

"Hold on!" yelled his young friend Al, a motorman two years short of retirement from the Transit Authority.

Eddie kept walking, standing tall. He made it alive, pulled out a broom, and started along a catwalk. He got two feet, felt a sharp tug that pulled the broom right out of his hands, and saw the straw evaporate before his eyes.

The boys came running and in seconds were plotting a shunt around the leak so they could fix the joint. Eddie's heart was pumping. Al yelled in his ear, "You don't look too good, partner."

"I need air."

Al helped him up on deck and once he had filled his leathery lungs with cool air, they ventured up to the bridge to check out the war. With the *Rollins*'s bow pointing at the river, the best view in town was from the destroyer's bridge, high above the long, graceful sweep of her main deck.

"Look at that," said Captain Eddie. "That's Ken Hughes's *Chelsea Queen*." To his amazement, an old harbor tug was sitting unscathed just south of Weehawken Cove.

"How do you know it's Ken?"

"See that cockamamie crane he stuck behind the wheelhouse? Looks like he sailed under a construction accident."

Al had been working his gig for the MTA and had missed the fun the day the *Rollins* had steamed in with the *Chelsea Queen* assisting.

"What in hell is Ken doing out there?"

Al thumbed his two-way marine radio and tried to hail the tug on Channel 16. The radio waves were going bananas and no one answered. He tried several times. Then, after they watched the poor bastards in the Seahawk helo get shot down two hundred yards off the *Rollins*'s bow, he said to the old man, "You know, Eddie, if you've caught your breath, might be time to go below before we get our heads blown off."

Ken's cellphone rang.

He and the bosun stared at it, cradled in the charger which was bolted near the steering tillers.

"Maybe I better get that," Ken ventured. Moments ago he had heard old Captain Eddie and Big Al at the *Intrepid* Museum trying to raise the tug on the VHF radio. Voices from another world. God knew what the old geezers wanted. He could only hope they weren't stuck at the museum, so close to the battling *Kennedy*.

The bosun had refused to let him answer the radio. Now he plucked the chirping cellphone from its charger and tossed it out the wheelhouse window into the river.

*   *   *

"Welcome to Bell Atlantic Mobile," James Earl Jones greeted Jose Chin, and a thinner corporate voice told him, "The cellular customer you—"

The reporter punched END.

Did James Earl Jones mean that Captain Ken wasn't answering? Or that cellphones weren't working in Manhattan? Even if the Manhattan boosters were all blown up, they had to be using relay towers in Jersey and Long Island.

Jose pondered his next move while standing in the middle of an abandoned traffic jam at the corner of Fifty-seventh and Sixth. He was definitely looking at a Pulitzer for the Tiffany tape, but that wasn't really the story. The story was the invasion. *Arnie, Arnie, Arnie, you stupid old man.*

"Hey, we haven't seen one single Chinese soldier since Tiffany's."

"If you will do the mathematics," said ex-hopeful-engineer, ex-soldier Jasbir, "you will conclude that even if Admiral Tang were to scatter his units in four-man squads per corner, two thousand corners from the Battery to Central Park alone equals eight thousand men. How many can there be? What does it cost to put a soldier on every corner, how many noncoms, what of communications? What happens when they are fired upon? If they go up to a roof, they've deserted their post and could be drawn into a trap."

Too thin on the ground to hold ground. Clearly, soldiers had passed through, shot up cars and windows, and kept going. But if they don't have enough troops to take the whole city, what the hell are they doing?

Jasbir ran from cab to cab, looking for one with keys so they could drive up onto the sidewalk. But even if he found wheels, Jose wasn't sure where to go. He could hear gunfire and explosions from the Hudson River. But the network cameras would be shooting that from the Jersey side with high-powered lenses offering extreme close-ups of impact, flames, and blackened steel.

Where was *his* story?

He surfed his Watchman.

Dan Rather, caught two thousand miles off base on an "America Loves Summer" shoot, was narrating a remote camera atop the Empire State Building. Jose was impressed by Rather's ability to imply that the drifting smoke was about to asphyxiate him in his Dallas studio.

More impressive was the ballsier way Tom Brokaw was reporting from high above the Palisades on a blimp equipped with amazing eye-in-the-sky cameras. The multi-millionaire anchor was actually aboard the blimp and doing a very good job of appearing unfazed that he made a great target for the Chinese rocket men. Unless, it suddenly occurred to Jose, Admiral Tang was watching TV to help coordinate his invasion.

He dialed the number Kate Ross had called from on the freighter. One ring. Two rings. Three. James Earl Jones. END.

He switched back to Peter Jennings, whose military geezer had been bumped to the outside chair by a foreign-policy think-tanker in a bow tie. A real pro. Jose could see him winding up to lob a softball as Jennings stated with righteous incredulity, "But anyone with a television set knows the Chinese are threatening to retake Taiwan by force."

"Our government has assumed all along that we could separate our common economic interests and our differences on the Taiwan issue. The Chinese, who are adept at telling us what we want to hear, led us to believe they would not do anything precipitous."

"I think we can safely call an attack on New York City precipitous."

The think-tanker lobbed Peter another. "All of us were lulled into thinking they would act rationally. We've always given the Chinese a big break. We overlook torturing dissidents and we give them anything they want, technology, missiles."

"This morning, it seems, they're giving it back."

"Yes, Peter. But keep in mind they have fooled us the same way they surprised everybody when they slaughtered the protesters in Tiananmen Square. As you no doubt recall those events of 1989, Peter, we had been expanding a dialogue with the Chinese since Nixon in '76—years of close contact, fact-finding tours, symposiums, conferences, private channels."

"And all of a sudden," interrupted General Winfield Edwards, with the bad-tempered expression of a talking head whose lunchtime martini had hardened into a headache, "in full view of the entire world without even an apology, Beijing took to the streets with battle tanks. Why were the experts fooled? Simple. The only Chinese talking to us were the Liberals. The Communist hard-liners actually running the country never talk to Westerners."

Jennings turned hopefully to his guest from the think tank. "Dr. Gordon, what can you tell us about this Admiral Tang Li?"

"Tang Li is either an obscure young officer or a player as discreet as he is powerful. Very little is known about him. He's of an elite family, grandfather on the Long March, high-ranking father. Wealthy, presumably, as the military often are. And I'm told he studied in America, as many of the elite's children do."

"It's been suggested he's a renegade."

General Edwards snorted.

"You had something to add, General?"

"There's one billion of them on a land mass almost as large as ours, ruled by a totalitarian government capable of fencing off entire provinces. They could tunnel right through the planet and the first way we'd know it would be a chop suey shortage in Iowa."

"Excuse me," Peter Jennings interrupted with undisguised relief. "We've got some exciting live coverage on Manhattan Island."

Jose leaned into his Watchman, wondering who the hell else was reporting on the scene.

No one, it turned out. Somehow they'd powered up a Shadow Traffic remote camera that normally covered the outbound approaches to the Lincoln Tunnel. It was way up high, probably atop the post office on Eleventh Avenue, tilting and panning the western fringes of Clinton and Chelsea, snooping up the jammed avenues and cross streets, homing in on the burning rail yards.

Panning the warehouses and lofts and the Javits Convention Center, it offered tantalizing glimpses of the fighting on the river: a ship on its side like a bathtub toy; damaged submarines drifting on the surface, smoke billowing from their conning towers. Another sub was half sunk with its bow in the air. On another, Jose could see the crew training hoses on a fire creeping forward from its stern.

A Chinese submarine raced across the screen firing rapidly from its cannon, but Jose's eyes locked on a familiar sight behind it.

"What the hell is Ken doing there?"

The swooping camera showed dozens of workboats pinned along the Jersey bank: anchored river tankers and oilers; tugs and their barges; freighters hiding from the fight. Some hadn't made it. A string of barges had sunk in shallow water off Weehawken, a drifting freighter smoldered, and an oil tanker was running slowly backward. But Ken's *Chelsea Queen* was sitting farther out, jaunty as a rubber duck.

A puff of dark smoke rolled from her stack.

Jose peered closely. The traffic-camera resolution was striking, revealing white water roiling around the tug. The camera swept on. Jose clutched his head with both hands, trying to figure out what his instincts were trying to tell him.

A couple of months ago, when the boat was in drydock, Ken had walked him under it and shown him the huge nozzles in which the propellers spun, the rudders behind, and the flanking rudders ahead which allowed him to hold the *Queen* in place or even walk her sideways.

Maybe that was what was happening now. Ken hadn't dropped his anchor like the other boats and ships! His propellers were holding the tug in place. Maybe the *Chelsea Queen* was primed to bolt, like a crack dealer with one eye on his lookouts.

Suddenly, "maybe" looked like a certainty. The backward-moving tanker bounced off the smoldering freighter and backed straight at the *Chelsea Queen,* which gave a puff of smoke and scooted out of the way.

"Jasbir! The piers!"

That was where the story was. On that tugboat.

"Jasbir!"

The Sikh waved from a yellow cab and, with a loud screech of metal, the taxi burst from the jammed rows of abandoned cars and scraped over the curb onto the sidewalk.

They got as far as Seventh Avenue and Fifty-sixth Street before they were hopelessly blocked. Jasbir pounded the steering wheel. The intersection was wedged building to building with cabs and vans.

"Bikes!" yelled Jose. A heap of them had been abandoned at the entrance to the subway station at Fifty-fifth. Underfoot, broken glass crunched—falling windows had driven the cyclists underground.

He heard an engine muttering, glanced around the corner, and saw a motorcycle messenger sitting on a Kawasaki 450. "Yo, buddy! Jose needs a ride to Chelsea."

The guy just stared at him through his helmet mask.

"Rent me your bike. I'll bring it back. Here, my station'll pay for it. Jose Chin, New York Yes!"

Jasbir tapped Jose on the shoulder. "He's dead."

"What?"

Jasbir directed Jose's attention to the messenger's back. A spear of glass had fallen from the windows above, and entered between the man's shoulder blades and plunged through his body. "Dead."

The bike was still running, idling in a quiet, rapid rumble. "Help me get him off. I'll drive. There's boats at the Chelsea Piers. We'll get a boat."

Jasbir started to protest.

"Don't you get it?" Jose interrupted, completely misinterpreting Jasbir's censorious look. "Ken's tugboat is back. Right? The Chinese must be using it. Betcha anything this Tang Li is on it."

"Why would Admiral Tang be on a tugboat?"

"Because no one will shoot at him on a New York tugboat. There's sinking subs all over the river. His whole attack would collapse if he got killed. Come on, help me move this guy."

Jasbir shouldered the reporter aside, eased the dead man off his motorcycle, and laid his body gently on the sidewalk. Jose vaulted onto the Kawasaki, kicked it into gear.

"Hop on. You know how to drive a boat, right?"

"I am going home," said Jasbir.

"Hey, we've been through all that."

"You should come home with me."

"No way, Jasbir. I got the story. Tang is the story of this war."

Jasbir knelt beside the dead motorcycle messenger. "No, my very good friend. *This* is war."

Jose knew with a grim certainty that he was on his own. "Okay. I got it. You're right. Go home. Thanks for all the help. You were great. Thank you."

"You're welcome."

"One favor?" Jose dug in his pockets.

"Of course."

Jose pressed the digital tapes he'd shot into Jasbir's hand.

"Here're my tapes. When you get to Queens, find a live truck or a college studio or whatever to beam them up."

"Remember to keep your head up, Jose. Watch your blind side."

"Yeah, yeah, yeah. And *you* remember you got my whole career on those tapes."

"I promise," said Jasbir, and the last Jose saw of the tall Sikh was his turban bobbing east on Fifty-sixth, heading for the hole in Second Avenue that led to the tunnel under the river. Jose revved the bike, kicked it into gear, and roared downtown.

Peter Jennings could have the mayor.

And poor old Arnie was welcome to a posthumous Emmy for his "War in Manhattan" story. Jose would even decline his Pulitzer for the Tiffany story so Arnie could win a Pulitzer, too. Least he deserved.

'Cause it's Jose who wants to know: who's the Chinese invader? What's his problem? Mano a mano, Jose Chin and Admiral Tang Li. Framed by burning skyscrapers. Ambient sound peppered with gunfire. The interview of the century.

28

AN NYPD HARBOR UNIT patrol boat cut toward the *Chelsea Queen*. Ken Hughes locked eyes on it, and for five seconds allowed himself to hope that it was actually manned by cops.

It rumbled alongside, dropped off three Chinese officers in battle dress, and moved quickly to the nearest of several grounded barges, where it sheltered under the overhang of its spoon bow. Down the ladder from the monkey island came Admiral Tang. But instead of descending past the back windows to greet his visitors on the main deck, he slipped into the wheelhouse, swigged from his water bottle, and surfed the television. Suddenly he turned on the sound. A Peter Jennings talking head was pointing at a photograph of a much younger Tang and explaining, "Admiral Tang Li's motives are obvious. He will do whatever it takes to capture Taiwan."

Tang muted the sound, started down the spiral stairs, calling over his shoulder to Ken, "The Party controls China's media; your press is free. Why do both always get it wrong?" The admiral was clearly not expecting an answer, and Ken was silent.

"You see," the bosun said. "I tell you. Great helmsman."

"I gotta hit the head."

The bosun said, "No phone."

"I'm all out."

"If you jump in river, we shoot."

"Understood."

He went down the spiral stairs. Tang and his visitors had gathered in the galley. The sailor they'd had tending the *Queen*'s engines was pouring them tea. Ken continued past to the head, stayed for a moment, and walked back toward the stairs. As he passed the open galley door, he got a better look at the new arrivals.

Radios clipped to their flak vests the way the transit cops wore theirs, pistols in holsters, cocky expressions, too pumped to sit. And indeed, only Admiral Tang took a seat at the yellow table, where he waited, still as sculpture. Ken leaned on the bulkhead. Immediately, he felt a brisk tap on his shoulder. The bosun had come below, remarkably silent for a man so big. He jerked a thick thumb up at the wheelhouse and shoved Ken toward the stairs.

"Topside, wise guy. You no speak Chinese."

Ken pointed at the hatch that sealed off the rope locker in the bow. "You mind if we see how my deckhand's doing?"

The bosun said, "I gave him water. Up!"

"Report!"

One by one, Tang Li's staff officers stepped forward to present his version of the battle situation.

Xiong Jinren was first—quick, alert, and remarkably cool. "Four submarines disabled by the American helicopter. Boat Thirty-one. Boat Forty-eight. Boat Four. Boat Thirteen. Thirteen may perhaps return to ready status."

"Can any make way?"

"Two, sir. Barely."

"Have them tow the two that can't to Sandy Hook and scuttle all four in the Ambrose Channel."

"How will we get out, sir?"

The admiral ignored Xiong's question and beckoned Zhang Quiang. "Report."

Marine Commander Zhang Quiang spread a map on the galley table. "The Expeditionary Force has moved inland from the super piers, the Chelsea Piers, Gracie Mansion, and the Consolidated Edison power plant at Thirty-third Street. They have captured police-station houses at East Sixty-seventh Street, East Fifty-second Street, West Fifty-fourth Street, West Twentieth Street, and East Fifth Street."

"What of the police stations uptown?"

"They've not fallen yet, but we have them pinned down."

"And Police Headquarters?"

Zhang looked uncomfortable. "The One Police Plaza building is proving more difficult than we had expected."

Tang turned to his third aide. "How many boats do we have in the East River, Lieutenant Hu?"

"Your brother's boat, at Gracie Mansion."

With the mayor escaped, that boat was wasted there, thought Tang. "Any more?"

"One at the Consolidated Edison electric plant. Two reserves bottomed off Queens."

"Order the reserve boats to shell One Police Plaza—Zhang, you should have told me sooner. Your marines are spread thin. This is no time for unit rivalry."

Zhang hung his head. "I'm sorry, Admiral. I acknowledge my shortcoming and—"

"Send the order!"

Hu Jiwei said, "I'm not certain that the One Police Plaza building lies within the submarines' field of fire, Admiral."

"Then divert some sappers from the World Trade Center."

Hu Jiwei spoke into his radio, and when he had passed the order to blow up One Police Plaza, Tang Li said, "Continue your report, Hu."

"The sleeper boats are in place, sir. But I regret to report we lost three boats in the Upper Bay."

"To what forces?"

"The French gunboat placed a lucky shot in Boat Eighty's conning tower. Boat Sixty-eight was rammed by a Staten Island ferry. She rolled over with her hatches open."

"Why in bloody hell were her hatches open during combat?"

"Battery explosion, sir. The crew was venting acid fumes when the ferry struck. They assumed it would flee for shore, but instead it attacked."

"Continue."

"Boat Seventy-four appears to have been struck by a torpedo that Eighty had launched at the French gunboat."

"Anything else?"

"The missile frigate has expended all her missiles."

"Yet that damned aircraft carrier is still firing back."

Tang Li had been weeks at sea before he'd learned of the *John F. Kennedy*'s last-minute change of posting. The spies had sworn the ship would join the Taiwan demonstration. By the time he learned she had been reassigned to the Fleet Week celebration, it was too late to turn back.

They'd been fortunate to destroy the Seahawk helicopters she'd had on deck; fortunate, too, that many of her crew were ashore. Unarmed, her sailors had been easily cut down as they tried to return to their ship; those who had survived the gauntlet were occupied fighting the fires set by the original torpedo hits. The surviving sailors who hadn't made it back, Zhang Quiang reported, were attempting resistance. With little more than knives and handguns begged from civilians, they were no match for Tang's commandos. But even that would change as Tang's troops tired and the American sailors caught ashore were given time to organize and collect more weapons.

The giant warship, though immobilized at the pier—where she had settled listing on the shallow bottom—was still dueling with his gunners, trading fire from twenty-millimeter Vulcan cannons. While better suited to air defense, the Vulcans and a blizzard of jury-rigged air-to-ground missiles were proving more than a match for his submarines' small-caliber deck cannon.

The Americans' Vulcans had a limited field of fire. And the *Kennedy*'s sailors wrestling aircraft missiles up from the magazine were more occupied with firing them at all than with firing them accurately. But Tang knew that he was in terrible danger of the carrier bogging him down in a protracted battle, which was the last thing a force so far from home could afford.

"Order Boat Sixty-two to put more torpedoes into her."

Then Tang asked the one question he was afraid to hear the answer to.

"What's our fuel situation, Lieutenant Xiong?"

"Critical, sir. Twelve boats report they are already running on electric. We hadn't expected so much maneuvering . . . the carrier, you see, sir."

Tang kept his expression hard and dark. Sludge in diesel tanks would clog fuel filters and stop the engines. No sub commander would empty his tanks to the bottom. But their batteries wouldn't last through the night. He had to refuel. But he couldn't risk tethering submarines to fuel lighters in the daylight. He touched his aching ear, glanced at the sun. Four long hours until dark.

Obsessed with China's inherent fragility—keenly aware that poverty-stricken hundreds of millions shambled on the rim of anarchy—Tang had always been struck by the slim margin between success and failure. A margin rendered even thinner by the unexpected.

Submarines that should have been supporting the landing parties and landing reinforcements were still engaged with the carrier. Marine troops that should be pressing the attack inland into the heart of midtown were instead fighting the marines and sailors who had straggled back to their carrier. And for all he knew, the American sailors would at any second brave another Seahawk up from the hanger deck, bristling with air-to-sea missiles.

"Break off action with the carrier. Order all boats not currently engaged to submerge. Bottom until nightfall."

"But the carrier will recover, sir, and—"

Tang interrupted. At that moment he suddenly saw the stricken carrier for the fortress it was, a fortress immobile as if it were sheathed in walls of stone. It was no longer a ship. "We'll go around her, when we land the second wave at twenty-two hundred." At ten o'clock tonight, the city streets would be black as coal mines.

He looked at the sky in sudden alarm. Erase the smoke and it was pure blue. Sometime in the course of the battle, the wind had veered from the south to the northwest. The predicted high pressure had arrived early. He recalled his New York days; the brutal humidity of hot summer would quickly evaporate when high pressure came down from Canada. Cool wind, clear skies, promised a battle by moonlight.

Victory went to the bold. Always to the lucky. Never to the unfortunate. He shivered. It was beginning to look like an excellent time to ask the gods for favors.

"It's time to get off this tug. Signal my brother to come around into the Hudson. I will make the *Deng Xiaoping* my flagship."

Hu raised his radio to his lips. At that second the *John F. Kennedy* cut loose with a long blast of the Vulcans. Tang and his officers, a mile downstream, just beyond the carrier's field of fire, could see a double hail of spent uranium shells converging on a thirty-foot square of apparently empty water.

"What are they shooting at?"

"Boat Sixty-two, I believe, sir. The fire control radar must have locked onto her periscope."

Frothed white and fleecy as meringue by the rapid-firing cannon, the water was suddenly parted by a submarine, which broke the surface, stern first, out of control. Tang fixed her in his binoculars. Her riddled conning tower looked like the Vulcan shells had penetrated the water with unabated force.

As he watched, the thunderous hail drilled jagged holes in the wallowing hull. Not a hatch opened, not a man escaped, as the boat rolled its belly to the withering fire and sank.

"Signal my brother to stand by. We will remain on the tug until dark."

29

KATE SPOTTED A two-person kayak drifting into the slip between the Chelsea Piers health club and the driving range
and scrambled down a greasy ladder to snare it. The receding tide was thick with battle debris: splintered teak decking,
a French flag torn to ribbons, ducks drenched in oil—black
but for the flicker of dying eyes—smashed boats. Charred
mooring line had tangled on the ladders that descended to
the water. In seconds she was light-headed from the over-
powering stench of spilled diesel fuel.

The kayak drifted closer, a godsend, exactly the quick, little, maneuverable boat she needed to slip through the chaos
unnoticed. It even had a paddle sticking out of the aft seat.

The flashy powerboats that belonged to the boat dealer at
the foot of the slip were gone, doubtlessly taken by people
making a high-speed run for it. When she climbed farther
down the ladder, Kate saw one that hadn't made it, flipped
over and wedged on its side between two pilings. A body
was hanging from it, head in the water. It wasn't hard to

imagine a frightened person mistakenly assuming that driving an overpowered speedboat was just like driving a car.

She stood on the bottom rung of the ladder, inches above the water, clung with one hand, and stretched out her foot. She got the kayak with her toe, first try, but hope dissolved at the sight of a two-foot hole in the bottom. It would sink like a stone when she stepped into it.

She swallowed despair—for a second she had come so close—gathered her spirit, hurried up the ladder, and screamed.

A Chinese man was waiting at the top with a big, scary grin. She was so startled she let go of the ladder. He caught her wrist in a wiry hand. "Jose wants to know. Where's Captain Ken?"

She's spacier than ever, thought Jose. He slowly repeated, in his deepest, most soothing voice, "Jose wants to know. Where is Captain Ken?"

"Where'd you come from?"

"Is Ken on his tug?"

"I think so."

"I called him. He's not picking up."

"I could almost see him in the wheelhouse."

"Where'd you get binoculars?"

"I went home."

Kate looked to right and left. They were not alone. Gym rats were staring down from the health club windows, which were crazy with bullet holes. A brood of rich old ladies in pearls and floral print pastels was peering anxiously from the banquet hall under the health club, whose glass walls were similarly riddled.

The troops had blasted the piers with automatic weapons with the same angry abandon they had raked modern hotels in Beijing during Tiananmen.

Kate scampered off the ladder and hurried past his motorcycle.

Jose ran after her. "Can we get a boat?"

"That one's sinking. There's a marina next pier down. If there's anything still floating."

"I'll help you."

"No way. They'll shoot at your camera."

"I got a phone. I got E-mail. I got—"

Kate rounded on him, color high in her cheeks. "Get lost. You want a story? Go interview those women stealing your motorcycle."

Two old ladies in pastel suits were edging toward his borrowed Kawasaki while their girlfriends watched from the bowling alley. Before he could stop them, the women jumped on. He had left the motor running. The driver seemed familiar with bikes; as her companion struggled onto the saddle behind her, she kicked it into gear and roared north toward Twenty-third Street.

"I'll get my own boat," said Jose.

Jose forged ahead. Kate followed close behind, through the pier building and out the south side to the marina. He stopped so abruptly that she bumped into him. "Look, I don't know a goddamned thing about boats. If you don't help me, I'll end up drowning myself."

Kate shoved past him, surveyed the marina. Five floating finger docks pointed south to a narrow channel that led west to the river. The channel which paralleled the pier was narrow, less than fifty feet wide, tightly bounded by a stump forest of black wooden pilings that had once supported a long-vanished pier. A pier which had burned, judging by the irregular height of the stumps it had left behind. South of the stumps was another narrow stretch of open water, a slip bounded by the rusty-green, four-story Marine and Aviation Pier that thrust into the river.

She cast her eye over the small craft. One long-ago teenage summer, her boyfriend had shown her how to hotwire an inboard boat engine. But it was too long ago for her to remember the fine points. And the outboard motors were padlocked in the uptilted position.

Moored to the floating docks were a half-dozen J-22s, quick and maneuverable little sloops that belonged to the sailing school. She found herself instinctively drawn to the sailboats. Sailboats she knew. She climbed down to the finger dock and stepped into the one nearest the channel.

"There's no motor in that one," said Jose.

"I don't need a motor." Crazy as it sounded, she thought she had a better chance under sail. There was something innocuous about a little sailboat. She ripped the sailcover off the boom, found a jib stowed under the forepeak, and hanked it onto the forestay.

She had a half-formed idea that she could sail right up to Ken's tugboat, through a clanking mass of submarines, unimpeded, if not unnoticed. She was aware that she wasn't thinking very far ahead, and equally aware that no action taken today would bear much thinking about. If she had once paused to ponder, she'd still be on the Zodiac, or on the bottom of the ocean with a knife in her chest.

"Hey, check this out!"

Jose had his camera pointed at a big river tanker. Twice as long as Ken's tugboat and vastly taller, the ship was backing ponderously into the marina slip. It was empty, riding high, showing its red bottom. Its propeller churned out of the river, half in the air. Blades as long as livery cabs thrashed the water.

"He's going to hit us if he keeps coming this way."

But Kate saw that there was no "he." The tanker's wheelhouse was bullet-riddled, empty. Its crew had abandoned ship while backing astern. As she watched in disbelief and dawning horror, the huge propeller sliced the bow off a motorboat moored at the outermost dock.

A forty-foot Swan sailboat was next, cut in half like a stalk of celery, then a Donzi racer and a Grand Banks luxury trawler and another sailboat—a Benateau that crumbled like sawdust. The runaway tanker backed deeper and deeper into the marina, its propeller chopping up the floating docks, motorboats, dinghies, and sailboats, its hull snapping pilings, crushing the wreckage, and shoving it toward West Street.

"We better get out of here," said Jose.

Kate had thought the pilings that anchored the floating docks would stop it, but the tanker kept coming, plowing over the pilings, snapping them, banging and crunching between the golf-driving-range pier to the north and the old stump pilings, chopping boats and docks into rubble and plugging the slip like a cork in a bottle.

"Hey! Get outta there." Jose jumped down on the finger dock and grabbed Kate's arm. "Wake up, sweetheart. You're next."

The ship loomed higher and higher, as tall against the sky as a floating warehouse.

Kate jerked free, grabbed the paddle in the bottom of the boat. "Quick. Untie us."

"Are you nuts?"

"You want to help? I need this boat. Untie that line."

Jose glanced fearfully over his shoulder at the ship chewing its way toward them like a hungry dinosaur. He fumbled the rope which was holding the stern.

"Shove off! Hard as you can."

The propeller cut into the next row of boats.

Kate straddled the bow with her feet brushing the water, leaned over the left side, and paddled with all her strength. She thought she saw a passage through the stump field if they could paddle and pull their way between the old pilings and sneak south of the marauding ship, which was veering north against the driving range.

"Shove off!" she yelled as they emerged from the finger dock.

Jose kicked at the dock, missed, and slid into the water up to his knees. The ship's shadow fell darkly on them. Jose kicked again and this time he managed to plant his foot for a solid push. The little boat surged into the channel. Kate plunged her paddle deep and, propelled by it and Jose's push, the sailboat glided across the open water toward the pilings.

The scything propeller plucked the mast off another sailboat and flung it after them like an aluminum spear. Kate thought it was going to plunge right through the bottom of their boat. But instead of sinking them, it smashed up the gunnel a foot from Jose's hand and tumbled into the water. Another desperate scoop of the paddle and they were inside the stump field. The burned-off pier pilings stood dense as swamp grass. Kate steered between them with the paddle, seeking passage, searching the murky, oil-smeared water for submerged timbers.

Behind them, the tanker had ground to a thrashing stop, wedged aground in the corner formed by the golf pier and West Street. The steel hull filled the space where their boat had been docked. Its propeller was still turning— chopping water, mud, and debris—and Kate knew they had to get through the stumps and out to the river before tide and propeller action wheeled the ship into motion again.

Almost through. Almost to the channel beside the old green pier.

"Stop!" said Jose.

"What?"

A submarine was rounding the pier. It was running on the surface, deck guns manned, lookouts on the conning tower.

Kate and Jose ducked flat to the floorboards and lay still as stone, praying that the lookouts could not distinguish their little boat caught in the piling stumps from the wreckage the oil tanker had strewn about the slip.

Jose counted ten seconds and risked a glance over the gunnel.

"Oh, shit."

Kate started to raise a wary head. Jose pushed her down. The submarine was turning into the slip.

30

"WE WILL NEED a fire at sunset. A smoky fire to obscure the moon."

Fleet Admiral Tang Li and Marine Commander Zhang Quiang knelt on the *Chelsea Queen*'s wheelhouse roof and unfurled the chart that covered Weehawken north to Fort Lee.

Tang Li traced the New Jersey riverbank between Edgewater and the George Washington Bridge. Zhang looked up the river and overhead at the bluing sky and across at Manhattan, where the fresh wind had cleared the air.

"May I suggest, Admiral?"

The marine commander pointed at Manhattan on the opposite side of the river, twelve blocks above midtown, where apartment buildings, so new that some were still abuilding, crowded the riverbank. Those still tended by construction cranes were draped with banners big as Party banners in Tiananmen Square. "TRUMP," proclaimed the banners.

"That will make smoke."

The Chinese looked up suddenly, ears cocked to an insect drone. A distant thudding.

"Helicopters!"

They whirled to the north, up the Hudson, knowing that the loss of Boat 4 to the Seahawk had left them nearly blind in that direction.

In the stump field, Kate Ross and Jose Chin lay on the floorboards of the J-22 frozen with terror as the Chinese submarine maneuvered silently alongside the green Marine and Aviation Pier.

"Keep your head down!"

But Jose could not resist looking over the gunnel. The big black boat was less than a hundred feet from where they were drifting among the pilings. Soldiers poured from hatches in front and back and from the conning tower and started climbing onto the pier. A lookout glanced toward the sailboat and before Jose could duck, their eyes locked.

"Spotted me," he muttered to Kate. "Stay low. He can't see you."

"What are you going to do?" Kate hissed back.

"Whatever they tell me to do. The guy's pointing a gun at me." He raised his hands. The lookout shouted. Thirty soldiers on the front deck dropped to one knee, aiming their weapons.

"Friend!" Jose shouted in Cantonese, one of five words he remembered from his grandmother. Whether the invaders understood his pronunciation or believed him, he would never know, for at that same instant they all leaped to their feet—weapons trained skyward—and the next second an explosion blew the soldiers and lookouts into the water.

Jose fell back into the bottom of the sailboat, landing on

Kate. Only then did Kate hear the thudding, whining roar of
the helicopter that swooped in low from the river, and the
earsplitting hail of steel on steel as it raked the stricken submarine with its heavy guns. She pressed harder to the bottom of the boat, huddled in a fetal tuck, and covered her ears
in a hopeless attempt to escape the noise, which clawed and
pounded at her body.

Renata Bradley felt guilty about Larry Neale, and was
deeply relieved when he answered on the first ring.

"Larry. Thank God you're okay."

"Are you okay?"

"So far. Where are you?"

"In my apartment. I have my next-door neighbor, Mrs.
Nussbaum, and her cats. And Mr. Simon, from upstairs.
There was shooting in the street. My apartment's in the
back." He lowered his voice. "The poor things are ancient.
Mrs. Nussbaum brought about eighteen picnic baskets of
food. I heard the mayor on my Watchman—presidential!
Note I'm not asking you where you are."

"Jose Chin saved our asses. Gave me a two-second
edge . . . Larry? . . . I'm really sorry I fired you."

"It's okay."

"He saved Rudy and me. He gave us a chance to escape.
And then you warned us away from the control center."

"Gratitude does not become Renata."

"I'm saying you can have your job back. For crissake."

"That's better. You sound yourself again. You had me
worried. How about a promotion?"

"Any job but mine."

"I couldn't hack the homework."

"Very funny . . . Larry?"

"What?"

"Tell me something honestly."

As she said this, she heard a heavy *whump* through the phone. Then Larry yelling, "It's okay. It's okay, Mrs. Nussbaum. I got the cat." Another explosion. Then crying. Then Larry, at last. "They're terrified—sorry, Renata, it's not a great time—what do you want me to tell you?"

"Remember what you told me about Rudy?"

"I remember you didn't listen."

"Say it again. Please, Larry. Things are so weird. Who knows what's going to happen? I don't know if we're going to live or die, and I'm thinking, At least I'm with Rudy. Am I crazy?"

"Listen to the wise queen. Rudy's got a hell of a deal. He gets to be a 'good boy' and a loyal hubby and have your love and loyalty, too. What do you get?"

"I gotta go," said Renata. A couple of the strike force detectives had come back and were reporting to Rudy.

Renata edged closer. Ben and Rocco noticed, and lowered their voices behind a barricade of fleshy backs and shoulders. Renata edged closer still, and Rudy opened the circle to admit her.

"This guy was Tang Li's professor when he was at Columbia," said Ben.

Renata followed Rocco's nod toward the shadows where an old man in a white suit was slumped exhausted in a desk chair. "We got him uptown."

Both men's snappy suits were grease-stained, and Ben's right sleeve appeared to be soaked with blood.

"Tang's professor?"

"Dr. Sydney Morton, professor of Chinese Studies, Columbia University."

Suddenly a heavy sound jarred the deep silence of the bunker. The mayor and Renata, Ben, and Rocco all looked instinctively up at the girders overhead, half expecting tons of concrete and steel to plummet from the ceiling.

"What the *hell* was that?"

"Big and close," said Rocco. They waited, but the sound did not reoccur. Finally, Ben broke the uneasy quiet.

"And just so you know, Mr. Mayor?" said Ben.

Mincarelli, anxious to interview this remarkable connection to the invader, nodded impatiently.

Ben picked up a metal tube he'd leaned against the mayor's desk and handed it to him. "We found this. It's a Stinger missile launcher."

"How'd you get it?"

"A Chinese stopped to puke his guts out, and we relieved him of it."

Which explained the blood on Ben's sleeve. "What were they sick from?" asked Rudy.

"They were carrying McDonald's bags. Maybe they hit a Mickey D's and aren't used to our food."

"They have McDonald's in China."

"For rich Chinese, not poor soldiers."

The mayor hefted the tube, painfully aware that, unlike his favorite cops, he had not served in the military. "Has it been fired?"

"No, no, no. Luther wouldn't let us bring it in loaded. He's got the warhead outside. See these Chinese characters, here, and here? So we think this is their own brand, not the CIA stuff we left in Afghanistan."

"In other words, they're making their own."

"New and improved."

"We saw a squad carrying them."

"Means they'll shoot back when the Air Force comes," said Ben.

"Means they won't miss," said Rocco.

Mayor Mincarelli felt his insides contract. A vision flashed before his eyes of helicopters and fighter jets pinwheeling into buildings.

"Mr. Mayor?" It was Luther Washington, hurrying

toward him with bad news edging his face. "Mr. Mayor. I'm sorry."

"What?"

"I just got a last transmission from Headquarters. They blew up One Police Plaza."

"*What?*"

"It's gone. Police Headquarters is gone."

"Where's the commissioner?"

"I'm sorry, sir," said Luther. "I'm really sorry. He's dead."

Rudy Mincarelli flinched. A blinding red haze gathered before his eyes. His most recent police commissioner, a fellow advocate of information management, had worked hard, been a good father to his children, maintained a low profile with the press, and taken orders without complaint. The cops had hated him.

Luther, like the rest, had wanted Greg. But Greg wouldn't serve. And so they blamed the mayor and took it out on his appointees. He looked at Luther, but the man couldn't hold his eye.

"Rudy, look!" Renata cried.

They surged around the televisions. A jumpy picture on the silent screens showed American helicopters swarming a submarine tied to a river pier.

"Gunships," said Rocco. "Jesus Christ, we're hitting back with gunships. Are they nuts?"

"That old green pier. That's Marine and Aviation, over in Chelsea."

"Camera guy must be treading water."

"Christ, they'll set the whole thing on fire and everything around it!"

Kate Ross tried to keep sane by leaving the battleground for a place in her mind. At the pond at her parents' house, which she knew with the intimacy of a childhood hiding place, the helicopters darted like dragonflies. The submarine lay still as a log. The soldiers hopped and crouched like frogs. Their dead floated like water lilies. And Jose Chin stalked as warily as a heron.

Any second they would shoot him. Bullets were flying, shrapnel ricocheting. He was not oblivious to the danger— he ducked fearfully when flying metal whizzed close, flinched when it chopped splinters from the pilings in which they had sheltered. But he wouldn't stop.

Kate had paddled the sailboat deeper into the pilings, closer to the stone-lined bank, where the pilings were thickest. There they were trapped; heavy cross timbers which remained from the floor of the razed pier blocked their mast. When Jose complained the boat was rocking so much he couldn't control his umbrella satellite dish, Kate snubbed the boat tight.

"It's still moving too much," said Jose, struggling to steady his dish with one hand while aiming the camera with the other. "I'm losing the uplink."

Waves were sluicing around them, stirred by the sub and the still-churning propeller of the rampaging tanker.

"You're making us a target."

"They're too busy shooting back at the helicopters to see me."

The Chinese soldiers had more pressing problems than two unarmed civilians in a twenty-two-foot sailboat.

For the moment.

Kate coiled the bitter end of the bowline and motioned Jose to hold his dish pole against a piling. She lashed it tight with several turns. The dish pointed firmly at the sky.

Another helicopter roared in from the river, strafed the submarine, and leaped skyward. Kate's gaze soared with it, celebrating the pilot's bravery. Suddenly the helicopter broke apart like a clay pigeon and rained burning pieces on the old green pier.

"What happened?" she cried. The helicopter had cleaved the sky like steel. It had risen with the power of immortality only to scatter in ashes.

Jose was already zooming in on the roof of a loft building on Fifteenth Street, where black-clad soldiers were raking the sky with shoulder-mounted missile launchers. Like statues, they lined the parapet, fifteen floors above West Street, still as death. Suddenly a thin popping noise, like firecrackers, sent them tumbling, one after another, down the front of the building to the sidewalk.

Jose swung the camera left and focused on the roof of the self-storage building on Sixteenth. As small-arms fire crackled, he narrated into his mike. "From the roof of the New York headquarters of the Drug Enforcement Agency, DEA agents are shooting pistols at the Chinese invaders firing missiles at American helicopters. Jose wants everybody to know, These guys got what it takes."

Jose swiveled the camera right again, taking in the Chinese missilemen who were hurling hand grenades across Fifteenth Street at the roof.

"The sub's backing out," Kate warned.

Listing, it began to slide slowly out of the slip, scooping its wounded from the water and the burning pier and pounding the DEA with cannon fire. Explosions puffed brick and glass from the face of the building, until the submarine wheeled around the end of the pier and disappeared from sight, trailing a deathly silence.

Jose Chin reloaded fresh tape with trembling hands. He had a tape in his own head replaying stuff he wished he hadn't seen. The day was beginning to close in on him, as if he had exceeded the limits of pretending to be blind while recording so much death and mayhem.

Kate was staring at him.

Jose tried to collect his spirits. "You still want to try for Ken's tug?"

Kate knew she was striking a deal with the devil. But if—in his desire to interview the Chinese commander—the resourceful Jose Chin could help her get even one foot closer to Ken, it was a deal worth the risk of partnership with someone she didn't trust.

Just then another submarine raced past the slip.

Reluctantly, she said, "We better wait for dark."

They paddled out of the pilings. Kate tied up along the stone wall at the foot of the slip, hoping the boat would still be there on their return. Then she led Jose cautiously toward her apartment.

"What the hell is Greg doing in Washington?" Mayor Mincarelli yelled at the suddenly black TVs. "Renata, get him on the phone. This city is not a goddamned free-fire zone."

Ben and Rocco went for the professor and gently walked him to the mayor's desk.

Dr. Sydney Morton wore a khaki summer suit smudged with subway grease. His cheeks were red, his hair thin and white. He looked hostile, the mayor thought, as any seventy-year-old suddenly dragged half the length of Manhattan underground by Ben and Rocco would.

"Professor Morton." The mayor rose to shake the older man's soft, pink hand. "I appreciate your coming."

"I didn't come voluntarily."

"I need your help regarding your former pupil who is leading this attack on New York City. What motivates Tang Li? What are his weaknesses? Do you know him well?"

"Very well. Tang Li was an extraordinary student—an extraordinary man. His grandfather was a leading revolutionary, yet the Tang clan is connected by business and marriage throughout Southeast Asia—Bangkok, Jakarta, Manila, Singapore. It is a remarkable commentary upon the

People's Republic's elite that Tang Li receives calligraphic company reports from his relatives in Southeast Asia's financial empires."

"How does that relate to this attack on my city?"

"Tang Li is an aristocrat of South China, with a Southerner's world view: the oceans beckon."

"Is he out of his mind?"

"Not when I knew him, Mr. Mayor."

"Are *they* out of their minds?"

"The Chinese are not out of their minds," Professor Morton answered bluntly. "The Chinese are out of options. They are afraid."

Rudy Mincarelli grew still, masking his thoughts from all but Renata. Years of practice in the law, years of attack and negotiation, had taught him the danger, as well as the value, of eliminating an opponent's options. When a person had nothing to lose, order was no longer more appealing than chaos.

"What do they fear?"

"Everything," said the professor. "Fear of a United States-European alliance. Fear of the United States Navy reestablishing bases in Singapore and the Philippines. Fear of Japan. Fear of Taiwan. But their greatest fear of all is the fear of internal explosion: civil war, chaos, millions slaughtered and starved. Fear that they will be fragmented into two Chinas—divided north and south along the Yangtze River—and torn to pieces by battling warlords."

"But what does Tang Li hope to accomplish by attacking my city?"

"Tang Li is a man of action. But he is also methodical. If he has indeed done this incredible act, you can be sure he has planned it well with very specific goals in mind."

"How do I stop him?"

"I don't know that you can, Mr. Mayor."

Mincarelli looked up, temporarily distracted. Luther was swinging open the steel doorway for Rod Brown, the ex-FBI agent. Where the hell had *he* gone?

"What are his weaknesses?"

"I've been considering that since your police broke into my apartment. I'm not all that certain that he has any weaknesses—at least none that might help you. He admires Ulysses S. Grant, you know—Grant the general, of course, not the president. Grant's precepts of fighting by moving; adapt by attacking; change tactics in midstream; don't wait for the enemy to recover the initiative."

"General Grant wasn't insane."

"Neither is Admiral Tang. He is acting upon his greatest fear: that another internal cataclysm like the Cultural Revolution, or the Taiping Rebellion, will destroy China. His 'excursion' abroad could act like a pressure valve—a release for all their millions' pent-up anger and disappointment."

"How does your theory—"

"*His* theory, in fact. Admiral Tang wrote it for my graduate seminar. By focusing Chinese thoughts on an overseas expedition, he hopes to prevent the inevitable internal explosion."

"He wrote this in your class?"

"Tang Li postulated what he called the 'release effect' of colonial venturing."

"He wrote about this and you didn't report it?"

"Report what? He was a student."

"You should be prosecuted for misprision of felony! You have a legal responsibility, as well as moral, to report a crime you know will occur."

"Nonsense. The whole point of a good education is to float 'foolish' ideas, play with them, challenge authority. Surely the Jesuits taught you to speculate."

"Within reason," said the mayor.

Renata, sensing that the professor had left much unsaid,

interrupted. "Excuse me, Professor. Was Tang Li happy in America?"

Professor Morton hesitated, his expression hardening. "At first."

"Then?"

"He was very busy. He traveled widely. He studied here, he studied through a summer exchange program at Annapolis, and he studied in Rhode Island."

"What does he want?" Rudy demanded desperately.

Renata wished that he hadn't cut in. Morton had been about to say something. Instead, he folded his bony arms and closed his mouth in a quivering line.

"What does Tang want?" Rudy repeated, more gently, as his lawyerly instincts told him he had blundered. He had failed to note the old man's anger.

"What does Tang Li want?" Dr. Morton parried. "For China? Or for himself?"

"Both, if you would please speculate, sir."

"Tang Li intends to restore the Middle Kingdom. The original Chinese empire."

"And what does he want for himself?" asked Rudy.

"He would be emperor."

"So would Donald Trump, if we let him."

Professor Sydney Morton sat up straight, raised his head high. Proudly, he formed his features into a set smile and said, "For this act today, I assure you, Mr. Mayor, the Chinese people will let him."

Exasperated, Mayor Mincarelli glanced around the bunker. Rod Brown and Danny Wong were standing shoulder to shoulder staring at him, and when Danny threw him a little nod, it was like all three were young again on the strike force.

"Got a minute, Rudy?"

Like old times.

"Excuse me, Professor."

Mincarelli joined Rod and Danny by a grimy pillar. "What's up?"

Danny Wong was watching him with a cool, steady gaze. Even as a kid assistant U.S. Attorney two days out of law school, Danny had had the poise of a judge. "Do you remember Tang Li?" asked Danny.

"What?"

"Don't you remember the name?" asked Rod.

The mayor looked at the retired FBI agent. Rod, too, bore the smudges of a run through the subway tunnels. He even had blood on his clothes, but unlike Rocco, it was his own. He had a dirty handkerchief wrapped around a cut finger. There was whiskey on his breath.

"Should I?"

"It looks that way," said Danny Wong.

And Rod added, "We've got a chicken come home to roost. In fact, we've got the whole goddamned flock."

Mayor Mincarelli listened with a sinking heart. Three times he interrupted to say, "This is insane." When Judge Wong and Rod Brown were done, he walked heavily back to his desk.

"So much for your theories, Dr. Morton. It's personal."

To which Tang Li's professor replied, "The Romans were the first to ask, 'Who will guard the guards?' You have lived by the police state, Mr. Mayor, and you will die by it. But don't flatter yourself. Tang Li has bigger fish to fry than you."

Rudy Mincarelli gestured for Luther. "See if you can get a couple of volunteers to escort the professor home."

"Too late," said Luther. "It's getting hairy uptown."

Mincarelli pressed forefingers to the bridge of his nose, closed his eyes, and tried to think. Not one of the horrors of the past eight hours could have been imagined the night before. But this latest piece of information that Judge Wong had given him was worse.

Renata ached for him. When stone seemed to spread from his eyes over his entire face—smoothing the whorls of early middle age, making him look touchingly younger—she knew that he was in deep distress.

31

"TUGBOAT CAPTAIN!"

Ken was staring at the Colgate clock in Jersey City, which was still visible in the fading light of the long June evening. It had stopped when the electricity went off over there at three-oh-five. Had Tang's commandos blown up electrical substations? Or had the river cities cautiously taken themselves off the grid? He checked his diving watch. A little after eight.

"Tugboat Captain!"

He had heard Tang the first time. Now the order was underlined by a shove from the bosun. Admiral Tang Li beckoned him to the chart table.

"Sleepy, Captain?"

"Long day."

"Almost night, Captain. We will proceed here."

Ken looked where the admiral was pointing on the chart. "Here" was a half mile south, off Castle Point, where a Minotaur maze of submerged pilings, concrete piers, and twisted steel girders and long-disused dolphins marked the ruins of an abandoned railroad pier. He swung his binoculars that way and saw that the foul ground had snagged a submarine.

"What the hell was he doing in there?" Ken asked.

"Engaging a helicopter," Tang replied tersely.

The boat lay at an angle that bespoke hard aground.

"Tide's coming in. It'll float him off."

"No," said Admiral Tang. "He's stuck in submerged pilings. You will haul him off."

Ken made a silent vow to do it very slowly.

With luck, helicopters would attack the instant someone noticed that the Chinese were using a New York tug to assist their stricken sub. With luck, they'd kill Tang. And he and Rick could swim for it.

"I'll need two men probing with long poles; we're dead in the water if I get anything tangled in my nozzles." He wanted the bosun out of his hair.

Tang fell for it.

"My bosun and engineer will watch your water."

"And I'll need my deckhand, Rick."

He was ready to argue that, but Tang surprised him. "I ordered that Rick be fed. He's finishing supper in the galley."

"I could use something to eat, too."

"Supper will be your reward for freeing my submarine."

It started badly and got worse.

Weaving through floating wreckage, Ken drove the half mile, sizing up the situation as he got nearer. If he could stall a half hour until it was darker, maybe—just maybe—he and Rick could go over the side, shelter among the pilings, and paddle quietly the four or five hundred feet to shore.

But as the tug drew closer, he could see that the sub's crew was swarming around on deck, rigging a towing bridle and a messenger line to receive the *Chelsea Queen*'s hawser. Worse, several of the Chinese sailors had suited up in frogman gear.

Rick came up to get his orders. His crusted cut lip was oozing blood again. The bruises on his face were turning blue and yellow. His eyes flickered fear.

"You okay?" Ken asked.

Rick said, "What are they going to do to us? Man, you look awful."

"We're going to work. They want *that* out of *there*. I'll back in. You bend their messenger onto our nylon hawser."

"You think it'll hold? He looks hard aground."

"Tang won't let us waste time hooking up the wire. He wants in and out fast before any helicopters spot us. And—listen to me—pay out the whole line, as much as we've got."

"What for?"

"Do as you're fucking told!"

Rick glanced over at the bosun, who was radioing the sub with a hand-held, and whispered, "We can swim for it."

Ken shook his head, emphatically. "No. They put divers on deck. They'll nail us in twenty yards."

"It's almost dark."

"Forget it. You can't outswim a man wearing fins."

"Look how close, Ken. Man, they'll kill us soon as they're done with the tug."

"Listen to me. If the helicopters attack, we jump. Otherwise, sit tight."

"Tugboat Captain!" Admiral Tang swung down the monkey island ladder. "All set?"

"Get down to the towing deck," Ken told Rick. He spun the *Queen* in a circle and backed in slowly, watching for signals from the bosun and the engineer, who were standing on the stern bulwark probing the murky water.

Ken backed the tug within fifty yards. The sub crew heaved their light messenger line. Ken shook his head in admiration; Tang's sailors were absolutely first-rate seamen.

The line sailed across the water right over the towing deck. Rick snared it on the first try—a miracle—and fumbled it through the eye of the hawser. Ken, walking the boat sideways to hold her in place against the incoming tide, was not surprised that the bosun checked Rick's knot before he signaled the sub crew to haul in the thick nylon hawser.

Ken kept watching the sky as they hauled the hawser slowly through the water, pulled it onto the sub's foredeck, and bent it onto the bridle. Any second, any second, he expected another helo wing thudding downriver. It had been a couple of hours since the last, and more were long overdue. He wondered why Tang was taking the personal risk.

"What's so special about this sub?" he asked.

Tang said, "Submariners are brothers."

Which reminded Ken of Tang's earlier statement. In the governing of China, laws and regulations often take a backseat to personal relationships. "Who's her captain?"

"My father's stepniece's second husband."

Ken still wasn't convinced. There was something special about this one boat. "You're taking quite a chance for your father's stepniece's second husband . . . what's under that blister on the foredeck? Looks like a radome. A lot of antennas on that boat. ECM?"

Tang ignored him. The submariners gave the go-ahead signal. Rick pumped his arm. The bosun guided him away from the hawser and Tang said, "Pull."

Ken edged the *Queen* ahead, slowly stretching the slack from the line. He was watching it extend when all of a sudden Rick climbed clumsily onto the stern bulwark, teetered for a moment, and belly-flopped into the river. Ken yanked the props out of gear.

Rick surfaced, swimming hard, heading for a shadowy thicket of pilings.

Admiral Tang spoke calmly into the walkie-talkie clipped to his chest, and from the sub, three frogmen dove like otters. Their shapes pierced the water, one after another, without a splash. They surfaced right behind Rick and caught him in seconds.

Ken could scarcely breathe. He should not have let the frightened deckhand down on the towing deck—should have done whatever it took to keep him from jumping.

A knife glittered in the air and plunged downward. All four men went under. After what seemed an eternity, the frogmen surfaced beside the sub and climbed up cargo net their mates had rigged for them.

"You're hooked up," said Tang. "Start pulling."

"He was just a dumb kid. Really stupid. You didn't have to kill him."

"Pull!" Tang said coldly.

Suddenly Ken saw something the admiral had missed. When he had disengaged the engines, the tension in the line had eased and the hawser had slacked over the side of the submarine. Draped into the river like a thick snake, it seemed to Ken as if it had formed a loop around the submarine's forward diving plane—a movable flap of steel that looked for all the world like a flipper. Maybe Rick hadn't died for nothing.

"Pull!" Tang yelled, dropping his hand to the butt of his side arm.

With pleasure, you son of a bitch! Ken threw both engines full ahead and the six-thousand-horsepower *Chelsea Queen* dug in her stern and pulled.

The sharp-eyed bosun leaped up on the bulwark and crossed his arms in an x shape, frantically signaling to stop.

"Stop!" barked Tang, but he was too late. "Back engines! Astern! Astern!"

"Astern," Ken repeated. He dutifully throttled down, taking her out of gear and attempting to engage reverse, knowing the process would take fifteen seconds. In the meantime, the heavy tugboat's momentum kept her plowing ahead. The hawser tightened around the submarine's diving plane and yanked the sub into deep water by its frail appendage.

The nylon hawser parted from the strain. One flailing broken end knocked the Chinese engineer to the towing deck. The other slammed three sub sailors into the river. Which was the least of Admiral Tang's worries.

"Goddamn you!" yelled Tang. "You bent her diving plane!"

"Hey, I just did what I'm told. You got a little damage on your sub, fuck you. You just killed my deckhand."

Tang moved as if to hit him, but instead whipped out his side arm, realizing that he shouldn't take on the angry tugboat captain without the bosun in the wheelhouse to back him up. Ken looked down the barrel of Tang's pistol for a moment, turned his back, and stalked to the aft window. He watched the bosun fish the hawser from the water where Rick had died. He caught Tang's reflection in the glass, shoving the pistol back into his holster.

The murdering bastard still needed him.

Ken's own refection showed a hard smile twisting his mouth. A little damage? How about two weeks in dry dock to repair that diving plane, before the admiral's father's niece's husband's submarine ever dove for cover again?

But his smile soon faded in the windowpane. He had disabled a single submarine. Maybe she was particularly important to Tang's battle plan—that ECM dome had the look of a late-model refit. But it was still only one boat. And for Charlie, for Rick, and for the city upon which he had visited this monster—Ken knew that he had to do better.

"Scuttlebutt has it," Marty Greenberg whispered gleefully to Greg Walsh, "that Admiral Titus was kicked up to the Joint Chiefs because he was too aggressive."

Admiral Titus was practically pawing the floor. The President was still closeted with DOD, State, and CIA, which were feeding him the latest on the diplomatic picture, security at other American ports, and the most recent intelligence from Taiwan. All this before Titus would be invited in to propose the Navy's war plan to counterattack New York.

"You know how aggressive you gotta be to be too aggressive on a nuke attack boat?" crowed Marty. "You gotta be more aggressive than a pit bull."

Marty Greenberg was so caught up in the military screw-the-consequences bravado that he could neither see the consequences nor sense that since the Air Force helicopter attacks had been fended off, the atmosphere was turning poisonous. And surreal: the war plan had a code name already, "Take Manhattan"—dreamed up, Greg presumed, by some wannabe in the DOD public-relations office.

Greg had seen this kind of reaction to crisis over and over in his years of police-and-strike-force strategy sessions: one of your people gets hurt; or a judge throws out a cherished indictment; or a leak's about to blow your cover. So everyone gets gung ho. Screw the facts. Kick it in. Tough shit, Reverend; got a permit for this Bible class?

"Marty, this is our last chance to moderate these guys before we lose control of the situation. Don't you get what's going on with Titus? If he leads a full-scale assault on New York, he'll be a hero. Next time there's a crisis, he won't have to stand out here with the peasants waiting to plead his case—he'll be sitting on the President's lap."

Before the President's lawyer could formulate an answer—if he even intended to—a lieutenant commander rushed in, saluted Admiral Titus, and commenced a long whisper in his ear. At the same moment, Marty cupped the beeper on his belt. "Gotta see the man."

Greg looked at him. "I need to come with you."

Marty smiled at the patent absurdity of Greg's presumption with a lofty "I think not."

Greg Walsh despaired. The President's staffers were polite, or at least correct. They weren't about to kick out the personal emissary of a New York mayor who could be a vote magnet VP candidate next election. But neither the staffers, nor the national security advisors, nor the military attachés gave a flying fuck whether Greg Walsh wandered out to the john and forgot to come back.

"Gentlemen," announced Admiral Titus. The situation room quieted. "I am free to relate, now, exactly what sparked this attack on New York. As the United States Navy suspected all along, PLA troops are moving in force on the South China Plain."

32

"**WHAT DOES THAT MEAN?**" barked an Air Force colonel who had been lobbying for a "full-blown, flat-out, balls-to-the-wall chopper assault and drown the sons of bitches in the river."

"Taiwan," said the admiral. "The Chinese invaders are holding New York hostage to divert our attention and prevent our interference while the People's Liberation Army attacks Taiwan."

"Are you saying that the entire attack on New York City is a feint?"

Vice Admiral William Titus looked through the Air Force colonel like a dirty window.

"PLA troops are boarding transport ships in Fujian Province, antiaircraft missile batteries are on high alert across Zhejiang, Fujian, and Guangdong provinces, and so many mobile SAM launchers are rolling they've got traffic jams.

"The Chinese Communist intent is clear. Whether they're

bluffing or not, they have been allowed to take up positions to establish a nuke stalemate."

With a look that accused civilian policy makers of falling for a Chinese bluff, Titus marched to a wall chart of the South China Sea and snatched a wand from a lieutenant.

"The Chinese know that the forward radar positions they've taken up here, and here, on Mischief Reef and Fire Cross in the Spratly Islands—to threaten our sea lanes—are vulnerable to our cruise missiles. So is their main naval base on Stonecutters Island, here in Hong Kong. And they also know that if we take these targets out, they'll be exposed to American carrier attacks on the South China Plain.

"So they damned sure as hell know that if they provoke the United States, then their richest cities—Shenchen and Hong Kong—and the entire Pearl River estuary can kiss their asses good-bye."

He touched each target with an obliterating tap.

"Unless . . . they hold New York hostage. American conventional retaliation is what this attack on New York was designed to prevent. They're trying to stalemate our conventional forces, too, by holding New York hostage."

He looked around the room, met every eye that dared to make contact. It was, Greg discovered, as pointless as trading stares with a shark.

"The United States Navy will not let that happen. I will inform the President that the United States Navy is prepared to counterattack New York City at midnight."

Greg Walsh felt hope wash out of him. Midnight—less than four hours away. The time it would take for him and Frances to walk to a neighborhood joint for steaks and a bottle of wine, then wander home holding hands to catch the news or read or maybe even take each other to bed.

Even if—he reflected in a fantasy so farfetched it was like a deep-sleep dream—he were to disarm one of the several Secret Service agents and used his weapon to shoot Admiral Titus, it wouldn't help New York one bit. There simply wasn't enough time.

Titus would be replaced in a flash with one of the uniforms crowding the situation room. The place was crawling with Navy; and the Marines, of course, who would catch the brunt of any counterattack landings; and worried Army and Air Force, afraid the Navy would cut them out of the action.

In despair, Greg kept scanning their faces, looking for a ranking officer with the brains to see a counterstrike for the bloodbath it would be. But all he saw were careerists with agendas.

Admiral Titus stopped pontificating abruptly, his attention seized by a new arrival. Greg followed his stare and saw a broad-shouldered, silver-haired officer standing subtly apart.

Genius Mayor Rudy! That's why you sent me down here.

"Major General Connelly," Admiral Titus called to the new arrival. "Are your boys ready?"

"Marines are always ready, Admiral."

Titus flashed a mean grin and told the room, "We sailors inform new recruits boarding ship that if they bump their heads three times, they qualify for service in the United States Marine Corps. Welcome aboard, General."

Marine Major General Patrick John Connelly returned a smothering silence, and the nervous laughter died stillborn. He had always been a powerful presence; age had magnified it. Not, Greg noticed, that Pat had aged much. His hair was silver, but thick as sheep's wool.

Greg strode across the situation room, squaring his own shoulders, his pulse pounding with anticipation.

"*Semper fi*, General."

Pat Connelly spun on his heel, gripped Greg's arms in both hands, and, ignoring the stares, boomed his name like a basic truth.

"Pat," Greg greeted him back.

"What are you doing here? Rudy send you?"

"Of course."

"I met him last month, told me he was still hoping you'd re-up with the cops."

That confirmed it. Drawing on his prodigious memory, the mayor had remembered that General Connelly was back in Washington, attached to the White House, and had remembered Connelly's deep bond with Greg. They moved quietly toward the coffee, where they could stand with their backs to the wall, and spoke in soft tones.

"It's a mess."

"It's going to be a slaughter."

Pat Connelly nodded toward Admiral Titus, who was surrounded by staff officers extending telephones. "Captain Hook will lend new meaning to the terms 'collateral damage' and 'friendly fire.' "

"What do you think the Chinese guy's up to?"

Pat paraphrased von Clausewitz. "The conquest of territory don't mean shit if you don't wipe out your enemy's army. I have to assume that our War College reminds visiting Chinese admirals what the Russians did to Napoleon and Hitler. I agree with Captain Hook that we've got a hostage situation."

"But that means he's betting his entire fleet and all his men that the United States military won't counterattack."

"That's what I don't understand. He's got to know that by now, every U.S. military satellite in space is scoping him out with night optics, infrared heat, and wake analysis. We've got AWACS airborne, radar-mapping enemy positions and recording every electron from his radios. Either this Admiral Tang is deeply confused or is stupidly optimistic. Or he's got one hell of an ace in the hole. He's got to have one—he's taking chances like a man who knows something we don't.

"I've got to stop the counterattack, Pat."

"I don't know that you can. The Navy's boiling mad. So's

the Air Force. They slipped six choppers down the Hudson. One made it back. Something crashed their computers. DI thinks the Chinese projected a software virus into the fire control systems."

Greg, whose professional concerns included keeping viruses out of his employer's worldwide computer network, said, "My people didn't think they could beat us to the punch."

"It seems they did. Wipe out a man's software, you might as well cut his balls off. There's no way the Services are going to take a Beijing virus lying down."

"I have got to stop them," Greg said again.

"They've already started."

"What?"

"Recon teams scoping out the terrain."

"But the President indicated he hadn't decided, he said he was still considering—"

"No one wants to go in blind. So even if MacDill," by which Pat meant Headquarters of the Special Operations Command, "hasn't posted Green Berets and SEALs *officially*, there's covert insertion—Green Berets sneaking down from West Point, Air Force cowboys busing in on Pave Low choppers."

Pat looked at him and as much as admitted that he himself had already "unofficially" inserted Marine Special operations units: "There is no way I'm sending *my* boys in without real intelligence."

Greg nodded, reluctantly. "Real" intelligence meant placing humans close enough to eyeball the enemy. "At least they won't be shooting."

"Recon's their first job. But you better believe that anything in that harbor is fair game."

The opening bell for slaughter.

"Pat, you have to help me stop this."

Their debts to each other ran deep as bone. After they

fought a year in the Mekong Delta at age eighteen, neither man's wife or sons or brothers had as deep a call on his loyalty. They'd met rarely in the thirty years since the war, by silent, mutual consent; that way, it was easier to forget what they'd done to keep each other alive.

"I don't know if I can, Greg. The President's mighty deep in the Navy's thrall. First question he asks when he's got trouble in the world is, 'Where's our nearest aircraft carrier?' Second is, 'Where are the Tomahawks?' It's a Navy world again. The British Empire ruled with gunboats, we've got supercarriers and cruise missiles. I'm still a grunt."

"Will you sit in on the meeting?"

"I'm coming aboard late. I was down in South Carolina. Means Titus'll run the show. And you can bet your boots he's already primed the President to regard me as a glorified crew boss contracting to drive my boys ashore. So you better believe that Admiral Titus has grabbed himself a corner on the clout."

A uniform appeared at Greg's elbow, one of the many soldiers who had quietly replaced the young White House staffers. "Telephone, Commissioner Walsh, sir. Mayor Mincarelli."

He took the phone, nodded to Pat he was welcome to stick close. "You okay, Rudy?"

"I'll make this quick. Luther's worried they might home in on the cellphone signals. I have something to ask, but I need to know if you're on a secure line."

"I'm in the White House. I think we can assume the military are listening, and the CIA. What's up?"

"It looks like I made a serious mistake about fifteen years ago."

Greg sat down on the nearest chair. It had been some years since his friend had admitted to mistakes. "Yeah, what?"

"You probably won't remember this, but when I was U.S. Attorney and Danny Wong was one of my assistants, he brought me a police brutality case. The civilian was demanding a civil rights investigation. I concluded that the Department was conducting its own investigation properly, and passed."

"What was the beef?"

"A Columbia student got into a brawl with a couple of uniforms."

"What did the Department rule?"

"The student was way out of line. But the cops overreacted. They were suspended for a couple of weeks, without pay, for excessive force, and the city settled twenty-five thousand dollars on the complainant, out of court. Case closed. Ring any bells?"

"It could be any one of ten cases a year. Especially back then. I assume the student was black?"

"Chinese."

Columbia, particularly the Columbia Business School, had hundreds of Chinese students. But it was suddenly clear where Rudy was going. Greg asked, "This relates?"

"Admiral Tang Li."

"Not possible."

"Rocco and Ben just brought me his professor. And Rod Brown found a woman who'd been Tang's girlfriend. She's a surgeon now, at St. Luke's-Roosevelt. She couldn't leave the hospital—they've got wounded in the halls—but she told Rod that Li got beat up bad."

"What's *your* connection? How did it get federal?"

"Tang went for a civil rights violation. Even before the Department ruled. As I understand it, he wanted the U.S. Attorney to apologize because, according to this son-of-a-bitch professor and the woman, Tang Li thought he deserved an apology from the top because he's from a top family back home. It's supposedly the Chinese way. It wasn't my way—never will be—when some arrogant kid gets out of line with cops who are risking their lives every day on the street."

"I presume you did not apologize."

"No apology was called for. Now he's attacked my city with a hundred submarines."

"That is ludicrous. There isn't any connection."

"Oh, yeah? How come they attacked *my* city, not another?"

"New York's a deep-water port."

"So is San Francisco. This son of a bitch is after *me*!"

"Hold on, Rudy. Let's just think this through."

"San Francisco is a lot closer to China. So is goddamned Seattle."

"Who gives a fuck about Seattle?" said Greg.

"Boeing and Microsoft, Starbucks and my goddamned wife. She couldn't wait. She couldn't goddamned wait—"

"Listen, listen, listen. Admiral Tang attacked New York to distract the United States from Taiwan. He chose the most valuable hostage he could—high-profile, in-your-face New York City."

"He's attacking *me*! West Coast cities are six thousand miles closer to China."

"No, New York was the logical target for this kind of attack. Lightly guarded—not guarded at all, for crissake—deep water, and the most important city in the world. And the Fleet Week invitation made it easy to sneak in his support units. When you look at it that way, Admiral Tang had no choice."

"You're telling me the police brutality thing is coincidence?"

"Rudy, think this through."

"Don't tell me I'm paranoid."

"I'll agree that if it came down to a choice between New York and San Francisco, maybe—just maybe—he chose New York because he blames you for something that happened fifteen years ago. But it's pretty clear he was coming anyway, Rudy. You're at most a pot sweetener."

"I'm going to get him."

"What?"

"I'm going to get the bastard who did this to me. I'm going to nail him to the wall."

"Rudy!"

"He will stand trial in this city for all the world to see."

"You're not a prosecutor anymore."

"Screw you, Greg."

"Like I'm not a cop anymore. We've moved on. We've got more important fights than 'getting' Admiral Tang."

"If not me, who? If I don't do it, who will?"

"Rudy, you've lived by the law your whole life. It *is* your life. What are you going to do, go out and punch the guy in the face?"

Rudy said, "That's a great idea, Greg. Thank you. You've put all my thoughts into words."

"Wait! Rudy!"

"Talk to you," said the mayor, and hung up.

"Luther!" called the mayor.

Luther Washington lumbered over. Livery-gray pouches had gathered under his weary eyes. "Yes, sir."

"Sit down, Luther."

Luther, who had overheard the mayor's conversation with the former commissioner, warily took the chair beside the desk. He had been a cop long enough to be cautious around people who took things so personally that they couldn't roll with the punches. Mincarelli motioned him closer. "Luther, fill me in again on this cellphone problem."

"They can track us here."

"How?"

"Two ways. First, every few seconds your phone transmits a little beep saying, 'I'm here.' That allows the system to track your phone, so wherever you move, the antenna you're closest to can relay your call. Now, there's a central switching station on Fourteenth Street that the Chinese haven't blown up yet. Why? We have to assume the worst—that they've taken it over for the purpose of tracking. That's the bad news. The good news is, all the antenna that receives your periodic pulse can tell them is whether you're nearby; it does not know in what direction. Follow me so far?"

"Yes. My cellphone tells the phone company which antenna I am closest to, but not whether I am downtown, uptown, east, or west of it."

"Actually, the three or four closest antennas. So if the Chinese are monitoring the central switching station, they can draw circles around each antenna your phone has beeped. Where those circles intersect, they find you."

"How accurate?"

"Not precise. Block, two blocks. But—" He held up a finger thicker than a Sabrett's hot sausage. "But if these Chinese bring radio direction finders and signal analyzers to the area, several RDF squads can home in, triangulating your signals. Like we used to trail the Sicilians' two-way radios. And, like with us, if the Chinese happen to know your phone number, then they're a lot closer still."

"But we're deep under the ground."

"That's why you had me install the cellphone antennas four, five years ago. Remember when you upgraded? Like the Port Authority wired the tunnels?"

"But what I'm thinking is, where do our signals emerge?"

"Some get through concrete, but most will broadcast out the end of this tunnel."

"So if the Chinese home in on our cellphone signals, they

would locate us not where we are, but at the far end of this tunnel?"

"Keep in mind, *we're* at the other end of this tunnel."

"Thank you, Luther." The mayor picked up a cellphone and called his wife in Seattle.

33

KATE LOCKED HER DOOR, closed all the blinds against the
fading daylight, and lit the candle on the mantelpiece. While
Jose nosed around her living room, she went directly to the
vodka bottle she kept in the freezer, unscrewed the cap with
trembling hands, and poured two inches into the first glass
she found on the drainboard.

Her whole body was shaking. The explosion kept replaying itself, a maniacal rewind, where the soldiers flew into
the slip as if a giant hand had slapped them off their submarine. Jose was staring at her.

"Would you like some?" she offered.

"No, I gotta write up my notes." He leaned his backpack
against the couch and took out his laptop. "Hey, listen,
thanks for stabilizing my uplink."

"It's okay."

"You took a chance. Why'd you help?"

"You looked like you needed it." In fact, Kate had no idea
why she'd helped. Jose had been a fool to risk his life to

broadcast the battle and she had been a bigger fool to help him.

Kate lit more candles. At least the high school girl she'd helped had been innocent. Jose was looking for trouble.

Jose said, "My mom told me that nine months after the big New York blackout, thousands of babies were born. Must have been the candles. It's like a classy restaurant in here."

"You can use my desk." She cleared her own work from the desk, and pointed him into the alcove.

Jose spotted her laptop, popped it open without asking her permission, took her battery to replace his, and started typing.

Kate poured another slug of vodka and was about to throw it back when it occurred to her she should check on her elderly neighbor. Lighting her way with a candle, she discovered that Mary Ahern had invited their landlord up from the basement, as well as young Peter and a middle-aged friend down from Peter's attic loft. They invited Kate to share a meal that Peter and Jon had brought in plastic bags—Mary was setting the table with her best china—but fear hung heavily in the room. Peter and Jon had seen the soldiers kill a party-boat captain. A heavy explosion from the river was greeted with silence and averted eyes, though Peter, whom Kate had always considered a self-absorbed airhead, made a gallant effort to comfort both poor, frightened Mary and his older friend.

Kate went back upstairs. The warmish yoghurts she found in the refrigerator smelled all right. Jose inhaled two and kept typing.

"GeekNet," he reported over his shoulder, "says they blew up One Police Plaza."

"The whole building?"

"Killed the police commissioner. Wonder where the mayor went. I thought he might be there. They knocked over every station house from Harlem down, Con Ed, and most of the phone buildings. So far they're leaving the hospitals alone, except they took over NYU Downtown for their own wounded. And Saint Vincent's got blasted by a stray shell that hit the tenth floor."

"God." Kate hugged herself, sipped at the vodka. Gunfire rattled somewhere over on Ninth or Eighth Avenue. Scared and lonely, she suddenly wanted to talk.

"What's GeekNet?"

"Breaking news from volunteers with six pens in their pocket protectors—my kind of people. I grew up chasing fires on my bicycle."

"Peter Jennings seems a very strange role model for you. You're not an anchor type, sitting around."

"I'll be Jennings when I'm old. When I'm thirty. You really think we can sail out to Ken after dark?"

"If he's still there." A big "if." A heart-shrinking "if."

Jose stopped typing, saved, and turned off his laptop. He stood up, stretched. "How do you know boats?"

"My parents had a boat and then I worked on yachts."

"What were you doing working on yachts if your parents owned a boat?"

"It was a way to be bad."

"Bad? Where I grew up, 'bad' was shooting back at the cops."

"Cut it out, Jose. Your parents own a restaurant."

"They had to pay off loansharks, and tuition for parochial school for two kids. Jackson Heights was the furthest from the Chinatown gangs they could afford to rent; we moved in just in time for crack."

As he talked his busy hands had been pawing through Kate's newspapers and magazines and mail. "Hey, what's this? You keep fortune-cookie fortunes?"

"Ken and I ate at your parents' restaurant."

His klieg-light eyes glittered in the candlelight. "Ken tell you the Chinese way to read these is to add the phrase 'in bed'?"

"Ken managed to restrain himself."

" 'You never hesitate to tackle the most difficult problems . . . in bed.' Hey, do I sound like I'm throwing a move on Ken's girl? You really only known Ken two days? Must have been a pretty heavy date if you're risking your neck for him."

"He *saved* my neck."

Jose nodded. "I guess you owe him."

"It's not just that."

"What is it?"

"He's a keeper."

"You know that in two days?"

"I knew in one. . . . Actually, I was pretty sure in an hour."
Jose yawned. "Jesus. A romantic."

"I'm not a romantic. I'm like Ken—I'm an optimist."

"Yeah, me, too." Jose yawned again. "What do we got, about an hour till dark?"

"Less."

"Man, I gotta crash. Bed in the other room?" He shambled off to her bedroom and, before she could stop him, threw himself—filthy clothes, shoes, and all—on her silk duvet, and instantly fell asleep.

When Kate went to pull off his running shoes and cover him with a blanket, she discovered that he was astonishingly thin. He had curled up like a couple of paper clips.

Exhausted, she set her travel alarm for forty-five minutes and went back to her living room to sleep on the couch. Moving Jose's pack out of the way, she was amazed how heavy it was.

An explosion that rattled the windows woke her up before the alarm.

*   *   *

When Marty Greenberg sent word that the President of the United States had summoned General Connelly and Admiral Titus up to the Oval Office, the two officers quick-marched shoulder to shoulder across the situation room.

Greg Walsh caught up with them at the elevator. "Excuse me, Admiral."

"Who the hell are you?"

Pat introduced him, wondering what Greg was up to. "Admiral, Greg Walsh was New York's Police Commissioner. He's here representing the mayor. We were in 'Nam together."

"Admiral," said Greg, "we have two million innocent people trapped on Manhattan Island. You and the President—"

"This is no longer a civilian issue, Commissioner. Let's go, General Connelly—the President's waiting."

Greg took his last shot. "Just a minute, Admiral." He stepped closer, cocking his elbow tight against his side, and envisioned a point six inches behind Titus's spine. Pat saw it coming and reached to stop him. Too late. Shielding the act with his and Pat's bulk, Greg drove a heavy-bag punch into the admiral's solar plexus.

Admiral Titus doubled over with a gasp heard across the situation room, and collapsed into the arms of General Connelly. Pat looked at Greg in disbelief.

"Back me up," Greg muttered in Pat's ear. "You've got about five minutes before he can speak to turn me in. See what you can do with the President."

He helped Connelly lower the gasping admiral to the carpet. "Go. Get up there!"

Pat Connelly was shaking his head. "You crazy Mick!"

"Remember the school we saw bombed in Long Xuyen?"

"Yes."

"My wife's in a school right now. She's trying to protect fifteen hundred kids. Get on the elevator."

Frantic aides rushed and loosened Titus's necktie and opened his collar. The expression on the stricken man's face mingled rage and utter disbelief.

Speechless, gasping Titus was using all his strength to stab an accusatory finger in Greg's direction.

General Connelly spoke at last. "The admiral is indicating he wants a glass of water." Then he turned on his heel and marched into the elevator.

Pat Connelly's private meeting with the President lasted five minutes. When he emerged, Greg Walsh was surrounded by confused Secret Service agents.

Ignoring the incredulous stares of every ranking military officer in the room, Pat Connelly addressed Greg Walsh over the heads of the agents. "Negative on a midnight attack. The President will wait until dawn. Sorry I couldn't do better."

Six hours. Greg looked over at Admiral Titus, propped up in a chair, and saw Marty Greenberg lean down to explain the President's decision to delay the attack. Titus went pale with rage.

Six hours, not a minute more.

Marty talked the Secret Service into releasing Greg in his custody. Greg telephoned the mayor. Rudy sounded much calmer than during their last conversation.

"Dawn. Well done, Greg. Well done. We should be able to wrap this up by dawn."

"What do you mean? What are you doing?"

"Talk to you later," said Rudy, and hung up.

Greg headed for the door. Marty grabbed his elbow. "You know, you and your Marine buddy are a couple of nutcases. Where you going?"

"Home."

*   *   *

Kate started to blow out the candle.

"Hang on," said Jose. Quickly, he fixed another lens to his camera with duct tape.

"Infrared module," he explained, coupling wires. "I use it for night surveillance. It sees heat. Gives you and me a leg up in the dark."

Kate checked the street through a crack in the venetian blind. "So strange, not seeing the Empire State Building lighted."

She heard Jose grunt into his pack.

They felt their way down the stairs, cautiously opened the front door, and peered out at the dark street. Seeing no one, they went down the front steps and slipped through the gate.

To the east, an orange moon was sliding up into the black sky. West, a red glow flickered near Tenth Avenue. As Kate and Jose drew near, the shadowy figures turned out to be spraying garden hoses on the scorched front of a town house.

Jose had the camera out and up fast, blinding Kate with the sudden blaze of his sun gun. "Don't do that on the boat," she said. "I won't see to steer."

Two blocks down Tenth Avenue, as Kate's night vision recovered, they saw a flicker of candlelight through a slit between curtains. "Hey, that's where my brother's girlfriend works."

Jose darted around the corner and knocked on the door of the neighborhood's French restaurant. Kate watched Tenth Avenue with her back to the building and her eyes everywhere. When she glanced around the corner, she saw Jose embrace a slim man with a smile even brighter than his. Jose ran back to Kate.

"My damn parents didn't listen. They stayed in Chinatown. Juan tried to get down there. Soldiers everywhere, and where there weren't, our fellow New Yorkers were beating up people who looked Chinese. So Juan's hiding out here with his girlfriend, and my parents are holed up in their restaurant. That's the last he heard, anyway, before the phones died."

They hurried across Tenth Avenue, wedging their way between stalled trucks, and moved west on Eighteenth Street under the abandoned railroad High Line that ran along lower Manhattan. The huge girders of the trestle loomed blacker than the sky.

"What's that noise?"

Kate and Jose froze, listening. The distant tramp of many feet quickly grew loud.

"*Soldiers!*" whispered Jose.

The double-time boot tread came from everywhere in the dark, ramming fear into Kate's throat. She was paralyzed, trapped by conflicting desires: to shove through a fence under the old railroad, to flee across Eighteenth Street, or to turn around and run for home. She broke into a run, toward the river, and even as she tried to slide into the night, the sound of the boots seemed to run with her, the Chinese commandos invisible yet everywhere.

Jose looked up, and realized the source of the sound. Soldiers were double-timing down the abandoned elevated freight tracks. They'd probably climbed onto it at Thirtieth Street. Hundreds of them, in tight formation, dead silent but for their boots. When he stepped back to tape the shadow force with the infrared module, he saw that each wore a small blue light. Low-power LEDs, he guessed, to identify their unit in the dark.

Kate had disappeared.

Jose ran into the dark toward the river. "Hey, wait up!"

He saw her clambering over the concrete lane divider. By the time Jose struggled over it with his gear, she had run into the nearest pier building. He caught up by the water's edge. She was hugging the wall, scoping out the slip where they had left the boat.

*   *   *

"Are you worried about your girlfriend?" Gill Bishop asked Phil Levy.

The moon spilled ghostly light onto the hedge-fund partners' trading floor.

"What girlfriend?" asked Levy.

They were standing shoulder to shoulder, staring at the black city through the empty space where the wall used to be. The traders, the secretary, the classy receptionist, and old Roger had all fled down the fifty flights to God alone knew what fate in the streets. The name partners had stayed, captains of their ship.

The wind was cold, with a mean edge. Phil Levy was shivering in his fine suit. Gill Bishop was wrapped snug and warm in a priceless eleventh-century unicorn tapestry he had liberated from a display cabinet in their reception room.

"Phil." Bishop sighed, an avuncular sigh that clearly articulated the question: when, if ever, was Phil going to grow up to be a mensch? "We've been partners ten years. We're trapped in a cold, dark building on the fiftieth floor with no electricity. The batteries in our cellphones are dead. We've got no computers, no E-mail, no Reuters, no Bloomberg, no screens at all. Chinese gunmen are roaming the city and that sucking sound you hear is every investor on the planet moving funds to other markets, thereby creating, I don't have to remind you, opportunities beyond fucking belief if we could only communicate with them. So I'd think you'd realize that on a night like this, I'm not going to rat you out to your wife. All I'm asking is, are you worried about Zelda?"

Jesus Christ, he even knew her name, "Yeah. She's all alone."

"Looks like they haven't hit Tribeca. At least no fires down there."

What they could see of midtown and downtown was dark. Far across the river, twenty miles inland, a few lights shone dimly in New Jersey. The buildings on the Hudson banks were dark, though the river itself reflected moonlight like a white, phosphorous flare. Upriver, near the George Washington Bridge, a fire was growing larger, smoke rolling heavily from it, swelling the sky with red shadows.

Phil tried to contain the uneasiness in his voice. "Could I ask how you know she lives in Tribeca?"

" 'Cause that's where you spent the million-five you diverted into your personal account," Bishop answered mildly. "Did you think I wouldn't notice?"

Phil scraped his jaw off his shoes and attempted an expression both innocent and defiant. Both failed, but it didn't matter in the dark.

Gill went on in the same mild voice. "I could tolerate your fucking around—even though the last thing we need is a divorce in the firm. I could even tolerate your blowing good money on tchotchkes. But this is different. . . ." Gill sighed again. "At least I learned something about partners. You gotta have similar goals. Our problem is, all I care about is making money. All you care about is spending money. . . . So we learn by our mistakes."

Phil, experiencing a rare flash of humility, suddenly realized that he'd never make the kind of money he needed by working alone. Contritely, he said, "Maybe you could see that I made a mistake."

"Mistake?"

"Maybe I could say I was wrong."

"Wrong? I *trusted* you, Phil."

"Well, very wrong," Phil admitted, flinching in anticipation of Gill's anger.

But instead of raging at him, his partner shook his head as if exasperated with a spoiled and not especially intelligent child.

"I couldn't decide how to handle it at first," said Gill. "I sue you, you sue me. Lawyers up the wazoo. Depositions, counter-depositions. Nor does the wise fund manager invite the scrutiny of Johnny Law. Because other stuff unrelated, but not necessarily purely innocent, begins to seep out and all of a sudden there's a United States Attorney sitting in as a Friend of the Court, and then some hotshot out to make his bones at the SEC. At which point you and me start to look like a couple of schmucks. And, Phil?"

"What?"

"*Nobody* invests their money with schmucks—say, look at that!" Gill leaned out the empty window, peering into the dark.

Phil Levy stretched to see, grateful Gill Bishop had been distracted. "What?"

"You know, Phil, you're going to be lost in the crowd."

"What crowd?"

"There's going to be a lot of dead bodies before this is over."

Phil felt Bishop's shoe brush the back of his leg. It was hardly a kick, but it buckled his knee, anyway. As he started to tip forward, he pinwheeled his arms to catch his balance and twist away from the deep, dark hole of the night.

"Why?" Phil cried, trying to claw his way back into the moonlit office.

Bishop watched him carve the air with his hands. Less than an arm's length separated the two men. But Gill had both feet planted firmly on the glass-strewn carpet, while Phil was flapping like a downy chick too young to fly.

"*Why?* You were robbin' me, you bastard. And you thought I wouldn't know?"

Phil's final plea rose to a shriek, then faded like a speeding siren. "Can't we can work something out?"

"At last I know why humans love war." Bishop addressed the body diminishing into the night. "We get to start all over."

*   *   *

"Admiral," reported Marine Commander Zhang Quiang, "our Stinger forces shot down twelve American helicopters."

Twice, American helicopters had taken them completely by surprise, sweeping down the Hudson River behind a scrim of electronic countermeasures which had rendered them virtually invisible. The attackers had destroyed twelve of his submarines before the shoulder-launched Stingers had routed them.

He had expected electronic surprises from the Americans—such was the experience of every enemy that had challenged them since the Korean War. And he had dealt back surprises of his own to their computers. But the actual phenomenon of being simultaneously blinded and targeted was daunting nonetheless.

Twelve helos for twelve subs.

But hardly a draw. Tang had no reserves so far from home, while the United States had thousands of helicopters. They would attack again—soon, and in force, he had learned from the final transmissions from his sleeper-picket boats offshore, just before the Americans sunk them with Harpoon missiles. The boats had observed helicopter carriers moving into position, and aviation fuel tankers converging, and a nuclear-powered supercarrier steaming from Virginia. Spies inland had confirmed the expected buildup at the nearest air bases.

By now—less than twelve hours since he'd commenced his main attack—the military was ringing New York City with troops, establishing staging centers in Connecticut, Westchester, and the north part of the Bronx. The Air Force would be arming bombers and attack helicopters at McGuire. And if Tang knew anything at all about the United States Navy, they were battling the Pentagon for the honor of leading the counterattack from the approaching supercarrier.

Soon they would close the circle.

He had obeyed the first rule of war: seize the initiative. The second rule was to never let it go.

The marine commander interrupted his thoughts. "May I suggest, Admiral—"

Tang motioned for silence.

Soon the moon would start drawing the tide back out of the harbor. He checked his watch. Dawn would conspire with low tide to reduce his choice of hiding places.

He had ordered the fuel lighters to leave their Brooklyn berth and take up positions. The first group of submarines was just now rendezvousing with them. Of his eighty boats still operational, most were so low on fuel they had switched to batteries while waiting their turn with the lighters, and he had reports that their captains had begun to hesitate, husbanding their power reserves.

Refueling was fraught with risk: the moonlight strong, the harbor bright despite the fires Zhang's commandos had set to make smoke. Tethered to the lighters by fueling hoses, the submarines would be vulnerable. So he had trained the crews to hold their submarines deep in the water while they refueled, decks awash, to reduce the danger of being seen by enemy radar.

Those of his shore troops who had endured the heaviest fighting taking the police stations were low on ammunition, as were the Stinger crews nearest the river.

Of equal consequence, his squad leaders and boat officers were getting tired. Tang himself had been awake for twenty hours; keyed up as he was, waves of exhaustion had begun to cloud his eyes. He had to goad himself to keep moving. Weariness was tightening its insidious grip. At the U.S. Naval War College, he had observed that all the money won and lost in the late-night poker games changed hands between two and four in the morning. But one could be the victim—or the beneficiary—of the human biological clock when weariness eclipsed instinct and blunted aggression.

"Commander Zhang," he ordered, "withdraw from all positions north of Houston Street."

Marine Commander Zhang was too tired to hide his disappointment. The land-forces commander stared unhappily at the Manhattan towers. Their windows were dark, their faces shone coldly in the light of the moon. The area north of Houston Street included Greenwich Village, Chelsea, and the great haunch of commercial midtown. How long would it take the enemy to reactivate their communications and electricity?

"Retreat, Admiral?"

Tang looked at the weary officer and rubbed his ear. It felt like it was on fire; the whole side of his head hurt. "Of course not," he said. "Attack! We will fly our flag from the New York Stock Exchange, the Federal Reserve Bank, Number One Police Plaza, the World Trade Center, and City Hall."

"There's not much left of Police Plaza, Admiral."

"Then we will place our flag on the rubble! Lieutenant?" He beckoned an aide. "Signal my brother's boat. We will rendezvous directly across from the World Trade Center—and tell my bosun we're done with this tug."

"Yes, sir."

"Commander Zhang?" Tang redirected his attention and the marine commander stepped closer.

"Do the cellular telephones still place Mayor Mincarelli near City Hall?"

"Within a quarter mile."

"They are to radio me—direct on Channel Eight—the instant they find him."

"Do you still want him alive, Admiral?"

In Tang Li's mind the question ignited memories of a

searing flurry of police clubs. The pain had nearly stopped his heart. The final explosion had crushed his ear.

The brutal beating had been his life-defining moment. Without it he might never have accomplished what he had today. In retrospect—from the vantage point of maturity and many victories—it was possible to speculate that perhaps the cops were justified in punishing his arrogance. But from no vantage would he ever forgive the humiliation he had endured begging his way through the "democratic" legal system, being forced to grovel for his due.

"Sir? Do you still want the mayor alive, Admiral?"

"More than ever."

34

KEN HUGHES COULD taste ash, sharp and oily on his tongue. The thick smoke obscured the stars, dimmed the moon. The wind stank.

Blacked out, illuminated only by shifting reflections, the familiar Manhattan skyline looked as remote and elusive as a faraway mountain range. Blue hollows formed where thin moonbeams strayed. Faint ruby shadows were cast by the flickering fires.

Fire, still burning on the *Kennedy*. Fire on the Upper West Side's Trump buildings. Fire on the New Jersey Palisades. Fire on the old piers of Union City and West New York. The fires had been heaving ash and soot into the sky since the sun had set.

A bleary-eyed staff lieutenant climbed down the ladder from the monkey island, opened the wheelhouse door, and shouted at the Chinese bosun.

Ken didn't have to understand Chinese to recognize new orders. The jumbled emotions rocking the bosun's broad face, and the sideways slide of his eyes, spoke volumes.

Tang and his staff were through with the *Chelsea Queen*. And through with her captain.

"What's up?"

"Orders." The bosun engaged both engines Ahead, and headed slowly down the dark river.

Not a submarine in sight. In fact the *Chelsea Queen* appeared to be the only boat sailing on the Hudson River. No wonder Tang was abandoning ship. It wouldn't be long before some high-flying reconnaissance Stealth fighter night-scoped a moving target.

P.O. Hector Sanchez didn't feel like a rookie anymore. Not with the stuff he and Harriet had seen go down today—the assault on the One-nine, even bloodier attacks on the One-seven and the One-oh, looters, gangs of drunks, the girl almost gang-raped in Chelsea, Chinese soldiers chasing them in the subway. And everywhere the bodies on the streets, the fires, and fear.

No rookie tonight, huddled beside Harriet under a truck in the middle of Centre Street, a block from City Hall. Not with an assault weapon in his arms and extra magazines bulging his pockets while they staked out St. Andrew's Square, watching for another sign of an entrance to the mayor's bunker.

They'd gotten their break, if one could call it that, right after they finally crossed Chambers at the end of their day-long odyssey from Gracie Mansion. Harriet had spotted a guy creeping past the Municipal Building whom she recognized as a detective. She had "Yo-ed," him, but he was already gone, disappearing suddenly as if the ground had swallowed him up.

"He hit on me at the Tribunes barbecue." The society of black police officers. "He was bragging he was strike force in the old days. Guess I should have believed him."

And from that slender evidence Harriet had deduced—
and Hector had been inclined to agree—that they just might
have gotten lucky and spotted a strike force veteran sneaking into the mayor's bunker.

Trouble was, they'd been watching the area for two
hours—the church, the doorways in the triangular plaza, the
Municipal Building, manholes in the street, and hatches in
the sidewalk—and no one had come or gone since.

"Yo, Harriet," he whispered.

"What?"

"You awake?"

"What do you want?"

"I've been wondering. How come when we graduated the
Academy we both got Gracie Mansion?"

"What are you talking?" she hissed back, in her I-don't-
want-to-talk-about-it voice. Somewhere out on the river another explosion boomed.

"I mean, you're there because you're a great-looking
black woman, right?"

"Yeah?"

"Well, you are."

"Thanks, Hector."

"I mean, that's why you're there. It's a high-visibility job.
You're in the public eye, right? Like your old man's as-
signed to City Hall, down here, because he looks like a U.S.
Marine. Why do you think you're starring in the Father's
Day Special? You're a PR dream."

"So?" She was worried sick about her father. She realized, now, that half the reason she'd insisted on coming
downtown was to check him out. But she hadn't seen hide
nor hair of him—or any other uniforms who hadn't been
killed. She was praying to God he hadn't retreated to One
Police Plaza, which had been blasted into a burning pile of
brick.

"Plus you're a minority."

"Puerto Ricans are a minority, too, in case you've forgotten."

"I may be a PR, but I'm no PR dream. I'm not beautiful and I don't look like anybody's idea of a Marine."

"I'll watch, Hector—why don't you catch some sleep?"

"I think you know. I think you had something to do with it. Don't lie to me. We've been through too much today. How did I get lucky? I'm just a guy who barely beats the height requirement and I end up on a tit job a lot of cops would give their left ball for."

Harriet sighed. "Hector, you're like a computer that they forgot to boot up the street-smarts floppy."

"Tell me."

"It was a trade. They said I had to go to Gracie Mansion. I wanted Narcotics in Bed-Stuy," she said, her eyes tracking a hint of movement at a point far uptown.

"Of course."

"They said tough. I bluffed, said I quit. They said give it six months. I knew that was the bottom line. Take it or quit the job even before I started. But I figured I had some juice left, so I said, Only if I partner with Hector Sanchez. So they said yes, and I got you as my partner."

"Wha'd you want me for?"

Harriet said nothing for a while. Hector waited, used to her pauses. Finally she sighed. "Let's just say I wanted to keep an eye on you—keep you from shooting yourself in the foot before you make lawyer?"

A minute ticked by, punctuated by distant gunfire. Finally Hector said, "Thanks. But I don't want to be a cop anymore."

"Me neither," said Harriet.

"You? Why not?"

"No way I could go back to jive-talkin' beat cop after this. I'm joining the Marines—*shhh*!"

Hector heard it a moment later, the muffled tread of another Chinese patrol sweeping across Reade Street. This one was the third they'd seen, commandos spread wide covering the roadway and both sidewalks, checking doorways, looking into cars and under trucks.

Mother Maria, bless Harriet for making him take the fat kid's assault rifle. He'd never fired one, but as Harriet had pointed out, forcefully, the world was full of illiterate teenagers who knew how, so it couldn't be that hard.

Harriet gave him a sharp look and pointedly jiggled her Safety. Hector switched his off.

"What's he carrying?" Harriet whispered.

Hector rolled carefully onto his shoulder. One of the soldiers had his weapon slung on his back and was holding in his hands something that glowed pale green on his face.

"Is he carrying a laptop?" Harriet whispered incredulously.

There wasn't much light, but in the long night without electricity, Hector's eyes had adjusted to a dimmer standard, and even by the smoky shadows of the moon, he thought he saw an antenna.

"What's he doing? Checking his E-mail?"

"Maybe it's a signal analyzer."

"Say what?"

"For tracking radio transmissions."

"Like walkie-talkies?"

"And beepers and cellphones."

Harriet's eyes flashed at Hector. "Like the mayor's?"

Hector nodded grimly.

Harriet clenched an exultant fist. "Excellent! They'll take us right to him."

And then, thought Hector, we will shoot it out with hundreds of trained commandos, and when we've shot them all, I'll be a lawyer and Harriet will join the Marines. He shook his head violently. *No, no, no.* Harriet was an awesome fighter, but sometimes she missed the point.

"They're coming this way!"

Harriet leaned in close. Her hot breath burned his ear. "Do this," she instructed. Then she laid her rifle across her belly, hooked her feet onto the undercarriage of the truck, reached up with her hands, and pulled herself off the street. "Do it!" She glared down at him like a hanging bat.

"I don't think I can." Hector hooked his feet, and dragged himself up to the greasy bottom of the truck. It was sort of like an upside-down push-up, and in seconds every muscle in his body was weeping for relief. His arms were aching, his legs were shaking, and his foot was starting to slip.

"Hang on," Harriet murmured. "Here they come."

Hector watched a flickering yellow flashlight beam poke at the asphalt two feet below. Harriet let go of one hand to trigger her rifle. He was barely hanging on with two.

The light licked the pavement under them.

Clinging for his life and watching Harriet's muscles strain as she did the same, he allowed a strange thought to enter his mind. Every morning in the security detail's locker room under Gracie Mansion, Detective Juan Rodriguez—the mayor's driver—had used to ride Hector about Harriet.

"Thighs on that woman, Sanchez, she'll squeeze your brains to mush."

Every morning Hector would turn red. Getting jerked around went with being a rookie, but for Harriet's sake, he would protest. "Hey, we're just friends." Later he'd see her joking around with Juan and Bob and Luther and the others and he'd realize she didn't need him to protect her at all.

Of course he fantasized about her thighs. But it only struck him now—tonight, hanging here under a truck, about to get killed—that Juan had fantasized about Harriet, too, and so had Bob and Luther and the rest of them. And that razzing him was just their way of dreaming.

The light slid closer, rose, brushed the sole of Hector's boot.

Suddenly the Chinese started yelling. But instead of machine gunning him and Harriet, they gathered in a bunch on the sidewalk. Hector lowered himself enough to see them clumped around their signal analyzer and pointing at the screen. Then one of them thumbed a radio.

"They got him," whispered Hector. "They got the mayor."

"You sure?" Harriet whispered back.

"They nailed his signal. They're radioing for backup."

"Damn!" Harriet dropped to the pavement. Four heavily armed men—one illuminated by the green screen, two watching the street, another raising the two-way radio to his lips.

They still didn't see her. Slow motion, again. She saw them all slow down—like Michael Jordan once described on ESPN how the ball and all the other players went slo-mo. But suddenly she knew that in spite of every horror she had seen today, to pull her trigger would reek of murder. For a crazy second she thought, What if I just shoot the radio?

Then they saw her. Their eyes widened in astonishment. Now they were bringing their guns to bear. Now the radio operator opened his mouth.

Harriet triggered her weapon. Under the truck, the noise was deafening. Ears ringing, blinded by muzzle flashes, she emptied half a clip before she released the trigger.

Hector dropped beside her to cover her back. Harriet was so still that he feared she had been shot.

"You okay?"

She didn't move.

"Harriet?"

"Yeah."

"We gotta get out of here."

Harriet didn't move. She stared at the dead men heaped over their weapons. It was too dark to see blood, or their expressions. "They look like sleeping puppies."

"What? . . . Yo, Harriet. Move it!"

"I don't think I can keep doing this."

"Hey, you okay?" he asked. It was frightening to see Harriet—the strongest person he knew—suddenly at a loss. As terrifying as the first time he'd seen his mother cry.

Harriet shook her head. "That was like murder."

Hector reached to pat her shoulder, then thought better of it. "Yeah, well, their buddies'll murder us if we don't get our asses out of here. Yo! Wake up. You saved the mayor's ass."

"There'll be more of them," said Harriet in a dead voice.

"Here they come now," said Hector. A flash of laptop-green light up Park Row indicated that the dead men were not the only Chinese squad that had been tracking the mayor's signals.

35

THE J-22 SLOOP that Kate had tied among the old pilings was still in the slip. She and Jose climbed down a slippery stone seawall into the sailboat. Jose followed Kate's orders as they shoved and paddled the boat into deeper water.

"Aren't we supposed to have wind?" whispered Jose.

"We're in the lee of the pier. We'll pick up a breeze in the river."

"Jesus, it's dark out there." Jose looked through his infrared module. "I see some crap floating, but I don't see Ken's tugboat."

Kate hauled the mainsail up the mast. "The pier head is probably blocking our view of him." But with no lights in Jersey to silhouette the *Chelsea Queen*, and with the eye-burning smoke blocking the moon, it would be tough for them to see on the dark river. If Jose couldn't pick up a clear image through the infrared, the best she'd be able to do was try to sail to the point she had last seen Ken, listening for the distinctive rumble and turbocharger whine of the *Queen*'s big engines.

The little sailboat grew lively as they reached the end of the pier and the wind Kate had promised filled the sail. "Hold this," she told Jose. She put his hand on the tiller, and hauled in the jib halyard to raise the forward sail. "Sit here." She took back the tiller. The wind was from the north, an easy run across the river. The tide, she had noted, was high, but the current indicated it had begun to ebb.

"How fast does this thing go?" asked Jose.

"Four or five knots."

"You're nuts! Ken's boat does twelve knots, he told me."

"He's sitting still."

"What if he starts moving?"

"Jose, duck down and look under the sail that way. Tell me if you see anything we're about to hit."

"See? Man, this is like we're inside a whale—shit! Look out!"

Kate ducked to see what Jose was pointing at. Whatever it was, it was big, rising from the water like the rib bones of a dinosaur. She threw the rudder over and cut around it, into the wind, then hauled it in to fill the sails. Looking back, she saw the burned-out, half-sunken hull of a Spirit Cruises dinner yacht, drifting on the tide.

"And what's that?" Jose pointed ahead.

Kate tried to puzzle out this new shape. The way the breeze would slow and rise again, the smoke was an ever-changing scrim, sometimes thick as canvas, sometimes so transparent that light from distant fires would penetrate.

Jose scoped it through his camera. "Looks like a couple boats plowed into each other—hey, hey, don't get too close."

Kate steered straight for it. The strange apparition, she realized, was made up of not two but three boats—a cabin cruiser, a big runabout, and a catamaran sailboat—nor had they "plowed" into each other. Rather, they had remained entangled with their floating dock, which had broken free when the runaway tanker had chopped up the Chelsea Piers marina, and had drifted off like three strangers trapped in an elevator.

"Hey, what are you doing?"

Neither the cabin cruiser nor the runabout would have keys in its ignition. But the little catamaran was a wind rocket, which in tonight's stiffening northwest breeze would leave the J-22, Ken's tugboat, and most of the Chinese submarines in the dust.

"You know," Ken said to the bosun driving the *Chelsea Queen*, "I better go down and shift some diesel into the day tank. She's been running since morning, must be getting low."

"Enough fuel," said the bosun, still avoiding Ken's eye.

"Okay, if you say so. Listen, if you don't mind, I'm going to go below and catch some sleep."

"Stay here," said the bosun.

The Chinese was a big man, twice the size of Tang's commandos. Twenty years younger than Ken. Two inches taller. Forty or fifty pounds heavier. Maybe a little muscle-bound? Maybe not. Physically run-down from nine weeks in a cramped submarine? Dream on. Ken would get one and only one shot before the bosun cleaned his clock.

Tang, the marine commander, and two aides were up on the wheelhouse roof. All wearing side arms. But at least the engineer, knocked cold by the parting towline, had been taken off.

He couldn't see any way he could survive on the tug. But swimming for it didn't offer odds much better. They'd never give him time to put on his wet suit, or even his flippers. It was going to jump without warning into the dark. Into a river peppered with battle debris and oil slicks. Hoping he didn't hit something, hoping he cleared the hull, hoping the

Queen's gigantic props didn't suck him under, hoping he could swim a half mile to Jersey, hoping he'd find a spot in the dark where he could climb out of the water before he died of hypothermia or sheer exhaustion.

The bosun opened the throttles wider. The *Queen* was pounding ten knots. Where the hell were they going? They'd be lucky if they didn't hit something. The bosun was leaning into the glass, peering uncertainly.

Ken moved closer. "Going a little faster than you can see, Cap."

"Radar," said the bosun, indicating the *Chelsea Queen*'s screen, which showed a virtually empty middle of the river.

"Yeah, well, I wouldn't trust it to show you everything half sunken."

"I can see," said the bosun.

"Yeah, well, you know that's fine when you're driving the People's Army's boat. But when you're driving mine, I'd rather you don't smack into anything."

"Be quiet." The bosun gave him an angry, pleading glance as if to say, I don't want to kill you, but it's not my call. Ken planted his running shoes solidly on the deck and waited for the man to look back at the river. He knew that he had to shift every ounce of strength he had left from his aching, weary arms and legs and torso into his left hand in order to launch the sucker punch to end all sucker punches.

Now.

His clenched fist struck the bosun's temple with the thunk of a butcher's cleaver. But he wasn't a fighter; his willingness to kill had failed him, and while he had put all his weight and muscle into the punch, his fist had involuntarily unclenched, very slightly at the last moment. The startled cry of pain was Ken's own, as a finger bone snapped from the impact.

The bosun pivoted and looked him full in the face. The radar glow revealed an expression of shock and the dark rage of betrayal. Slowly, he raised a big hand, fingers spread like a grappling hook. But the light was leaking from his eyes, his knees gave out, and he spilled slowly to the deck as if every bone and muscle in his body had turned to oil.

Ken grabbed the *Chelsea Queen*'s tillers with his right hand. With his left—shattered finger afire—he tried to tune the radar to fine-search the water's surface for something heavy and hard to run into. With luck, the impact would throw Tang and his officers from the roof.

Ahead, too far for him to eyeball in the murk, the radar showed a cluster of targets. On the monitor it looked like a small, single ship—maybe a big tug, maybe even the Chinese missile carrier—surrounded by a constellation of smaller targets. All were stationary, moving neither ahead nor in relation to each other. Right on the course the bosun had set.

Whatever they were, he would reach them in four minutes. If Tang and the rest would only stay up on the monkey island, they'd be in for the ride of their lives.

He knelt and patted the unconscious bosun's shirt and trousers for a gun. No gun. Wisely, the bosun had removed it for guard duty.

Suddenly the radar showed something big and fast moving up behind him. It painted a large target on the screen, but it was maneuvering much more quickly than a ship. Helicopter? No, it was on the river surface. He looked back, trying to see past his salvage crane. Nothing.

The radar didn't usually lie that way. It missed stuff, but it rarely made things up, aside from wave clutter—and there were no waves to speak of. This thing was moving, veering left, right, left again. Suddenly it faded.

Once more he examined the cluster target ahead. One longish shape, with what looked like a bunch of grapes surrounding it. It resembled an aerial shot of a pod of whales.

Submarines! They were clustered around a ship. A lighter. They were bunkering in the dark, taking on fuel.

The thing behind him was back. Swooping across his wake, it suddenly steadied up astern, matching his course, drawing closer. It was chasing him.

"Fuel lighter dead ahead, Admiral Tang. Eight—no, nine boats fueling."

Tang had drilled his men in this vital operation in the dark, night after night, on replicas of New York Harbor lighters. He watched with satisfaction, raised his night glasses, and scanned the water a half mile beyond the lighter where his brother's submarine, *Deng Xiaoping*, was supposed to rendezvous.

"Jump down and tell my bosun he's steering too close to the lighter." It was an odd lapse in judgment, allowing the tug's heavy wake to disrupt the refueling operation, but the bosun, like all of his men, was getting tired, and tired men made mistakes.

That night on Broadway he had been this tired—exhausted by the constant effort for months and months to play the chameleon while he observed and studied and crammed information into his head. Too tired to check an angry impulse when he saw the cops hassling a Shanghainese delivery boy. Too tired to explain diplomatically that the immigrant's bicycle was his own, not the restaurant's, and that if they confiscated it he would be destitute. Too tired to rein in his contempt for their stupidity. Too tired to stay focused on his purpose. Too tired—or too arrogant—not to laugh in their faces when the distraction he had created enabled the delivery boy to escape with his bike. Too tired to realize that in their sadistic minds, one helpless victim was as good as another.

He pressed his hand to his ear, but it was a reflexive gesture. It did not in fact pain him now. He was growing calm, easy in his mind.

Ken Hughes peered ahead. A slant of wind was shredding the smoke; moonlight fluttered on a two-hundred-foot fuel tanker. Ken recognized the house; it was an Albany boat, not often seen below Rocky Point. It was surrounded by the conning towers of ten partly submerged submarines. Chinese seamen appeared to be walking on water as they splashed around the slippery decks, humping hoses.

Suddenly he saw a fantastic opportunity to kill two birds with one stone: prevent the refueling of ten submarines and disable Admiral Tang and his top officers.

A voice called down sharply. Chinese, he guessed, for "Slow down!"

In a few more seconds it would be too late to stop him. Ahead, through the murk, he could see sailors on the subs' decks, looking up anxiously at the tug steaming straight at them.

He touched his tillers, and altered course toward the narrow alley of hose-strewn water between the subs and their fuel boat. Now the sailors were shouting and someone was scrambling down the ladder behind his wheelhouse. Ken stepped away from the tillers, searching for a weapon. The nearest fire axe was on the deck below. He ripped the heavy coffee thermos from its bracket.

Tang's lieutenant shoved through the back door and ran to the tillers. The radar glow fell on the pistol in his hand. In the instant before Ken was on top of him, he whipped around and pointed it at Ken's face.

For a fatal split second the lieutenant hesitated, as if trying to choose between stopping the tug or shooting the captain. Ken threw the coffee thermos with his aching left hand. The Chinese tried to block it with his gun. Ken body-punched his thin chest and kneed him as he doubled over and fell back through the door.

Frantically, Ken felt around the deck for the pistol the lieutenant had dropped, found it, and jerked the trigger at movement in the back windows.

The fuel lighter was a hundred feet ahead. Ken aimed the *Chelsea Queen* at the first submarine tethered to the lighter and ran full speed toward it. Shots exploded overhead, bullets drilling through the roof into the deck, one tugging at Ken's sleeve, another knocking him off his feet as it creased the sole of his running shoe. He pointed the pistol straight up and fired blindly through the roof.

The tugboat struck near the submarine's bow, caromed off, and careened, crashing and scraping along the side of the lighter.

The first submarine had heeled so far over that water was gushing in her hatches. The air was thick with the stink of spilled diesel as the charging *Queen* parted hose after spewing hose. But nothing had caught fire yet. Far worse, Tang and his officers on the wheelhouse roof had clearly had plenty of time to brace for the collision, and none of them had tumbled off the wheelhouse.

The *Queen* was plowing ahead, still leaving havoc in her wake. Hadn't knocked any fatal holes in her hull yet; hadn't fouled either propeller, by a miracle; hadn't snagged the Kort nozzles; hadn't even bent a rudder. Nor, with all the momentum of the weight of her steel hull, two sixteen-cylinder locomotive engines, and eighty thousand gallons of fuel, was she slowing much as she tore through another hose connection at ten knots, banged her fourth deep dent in a submarine snout, and plowed toward the last.

It was time to take his chances in the water. He slid a window down and prepared to squeeze through it. But one last glance at the radar drew his attention to a pair of bright targets flaring on the screen. The thing that had been moving behind the tug was still catching up. And ahead was a new target, one that was close enough to eyeball in the next wind shift.

He saw a submarine surfacing in front of him—moon-dappled water streaming from its sides. The flagship to which Tang would transfer his command. Sailors stormed out of the conning tower and made straight for their deck cannon.

Ken whirled to the light panel, closed one eye to protect his night vision, and swept his good hand up a row of switches. The tugboat's work lights blazed down on her fore and aft decks and, shining down from the masthead, illuminated the wheelhouse. He wanted the gunners to see their admiral on the roof and hesitate just long enough for the *Chelsea Queen* to sink them all.

Kate Ross and Jose Chin were tracking Ken's tugboat by the roar of its engines and sporadic glimpses through the smoke with Jose's infrared video module. The catamaran had proved worth the scramble from the J-22. Smaller, and rigged only with a sling between the widespread hulls, Kate found it as fast and maneuverable as any she had driven. But with the crazy wind shifts and the explosions from the shore, they kept losing the trail.

"Hey, what's that thing up there?" yelled Jose, pointing at the mast.

"Radar reflector, so you don't get run over in the fog."

"So people with radar can shoot at us?"

"I tried to lower it. The halyard's frozen."

Mid-river, she had felt a strange flatness in the water which could have been the *Chelsea Queen*'s broad wake. Then had come the crashing and yelling. When she skidded close by on the catamaran, she had seen the wreckage of a huge refueling operation, with submarines blundering about a lighter and sailors struggling to contain flailing hoses.

Smoke gusted over the moon. The way ahead turned as dark as a blacked-out theater, the water in front of the speeding boat a mystery. "Slow down!" yelled Jose. "You're going to hit something." But Kate stayed her course, and then, as suddenly and unexpectedly as a theatrical stagehand caught on stage in a swiftly moving follow spot, Ken's tugboat materialized before her eyes.

"There he is!" yelled Jose.

Lit up bright by her own work lights, the red-and-black *Chelsea Queen* was spewing diesel smoke and boiling an angry wake. In her path slid the ominous contour of a submarine maneuvering slowly on the surface.

The sub was a hundred feet longer, its conning tower as tall as Ken's wheelhouse. Kate heard the pop, pop of pistols. Men were milling around on Ken's roof, waving at the submarine and firing guns at their feet. On the submarine, shadow figures grouped around the silhouette of its deck cannon.

A mile away, at the end of the Intrepid Museum pier, old Captain Eddie squinted at the sudden splash of color in the middle of the coal-black Hudson, rubbed his eyes, and felt in the dark for binoculars. Ken Hughes's *Chelsea Queen* leaped big and bright in the lenses.

"Al," he whispered, "that's Ken's tug."

"Gimme them glasses!"

They were crouched on the bridge of the *Edward Rollins*. The Chinese had established an observation post high up on the flight deck of the *U.S.S. Intrepid*, less than a hundred yards south of the destroyer, and commandos were patrolling the pier with assault rifles. But with all eyes and ears inclined two piers uptown, where the *Kennedy* was still fighting back, none of the invading bastards had tipped to the fact that an ancient skeleton crew had already been aboard the *Edward Rollins* when the shooting started.

The rest of the boys were down in the engine room, thanking the Lord there was so much smoke in the sky the commandos hadn't noticed a little more puffing from the *Rollins*'s stack. And thanking Him, too, for no more broom walks tracing burst pipe joints.

Half an hour ago—when it finally looked like they could hold the pressure in the Number Two boiler—Eddie, being senior in years, and Al, who'd been a quartermaster in the Navy before he'd become a subway motorman, had taken command of the bridge.

Al had his VHF radio. They'd been afraid to use it in case the Chinese were monitoring the channels. But if that was Ken out there, it was worth risking another shot at raising him. Eddie puzzled over the buttons, pushed the right ones for Channel 16, and whispered, "*Chelsea Queen. Chelsea Queen.* Hey, Ken, that you? It's Captain Eddie."

Al, who was still young enough to watch TV with his naked eye, said, "Looks like he's playing tag with a sub."

"*Chelsea Queen. Chelsea Queen.* Hey, Ken, that you?"

"Sons of bitches probably tossed him to the sharks."

"So where they taking his tug?"

"Looks to me like it's heading to help that submarine."

Pat Connelly's U.S. Marines eyes-on-the-ground-intelligence forward recon team—who were paddling a rubber boat down the Hudson River from Alpine, New Jersey, gathering information about subs, fires, and floating wreckage, sketching charts, and whispering their observations into tape recorders—came to the same conclusion when they spotted the *Chelsea Queen*'s work lights: the Chinese raiders had commandeered a New York Harbor tug to tow damaged submarines.

Hugging the Jersey bank, the four men in night camouflage and blackface had already made it past two Chinese picket subs lurking under the George Washington Bridge, whose darkened span flickered red reflections from the fires on either side of the river. Detecting their periscopes with night-vision glasses, the Marines had marked the submarines' positions, but refrained from calling in missiles just yet, as their arrival would compromise the intelligence-gathering operation.

Suddenly, they saw the red-and-black harbor tug light up like a surprise party.

At last, something to shoot at; a target too far off to draw enemy fire back at them. With a laser range finder, they established the tug's distance and bearing, five miles to the southeast of their rubber boat, and calculated its position off their own GPS coordinates. The Special Operations lieutenant keyed his digitally scrambled radio and transmitted the target fix to the United States Navy cruiser *Lake Champlain* prowling off the coast.

Kate was caught wrong-footed on the opposite tack. The wind was bearing her catamaran away from Ken's tugboat, which was seconds from crashing into the Chinese submarine.

"Coming about—duck, Jose!"

Jose hugged his camera to shield it from the spray, and ducked. Earlier, she'd tried to have him help sail by holding a line; now she was controlling them all and the rudder, too, hands flying like a Ninth Avenue shell-game scammer.

Kate kicked the tiller.

The swinging boom brushed Jose's hair, wind banged into the sail, and the little catamaran nearly leaped from the water as if it were an extension of her mind and desire. Kate felt she had been born and trained for this moment, as if each and every one of the thousands and thousands of miles she had sailed was a crucial step from her first breath to her first true union with life.

"What are you doing?" yelled Jose.

The *Chelsea Queen,* which loomed like a tenement over the tiny catamaran, was roaring toward a collision with a submarine which looked even bigger. Kate was steering between them.

"I am taking Ken off that tugboat."

Jose raised his camera. Two Chinese sailors on Ken's wheelhouse were shooting holes in the roof. Another was waving frantic X's with his arms at the Chinese gunners on the submarine.

"Put that camera down," Kate said to Jose in the same firm voice. "I need your help."

No way. He liked Ken. Liked Krazy Kate, too. Wanted to help them both. But whatever she thought she was going to accomplish was going to get them both killed. And if Jose Chin was going to die, he was going to die shooting the moment, and a tugboat ramming a submarine in extreme close-up would make great TV. The tugboat's bright work lights were spilling onto the submarine, which gleamed wet and shiny as Broadway in the rain, and almost as beautiful. With Latin Luck, they'd find his tape before the water ruined it.

With less than a hundred feet separating the tug from the *Deng Xiaoping,* Admiral Tang raised his brother, Tang Qui, on the VHF radio.

"Hold your fire," he ordered coolly. "And close your hatches."

The submarine's gun crew still aimed at the charging tugboat. Then suddenly they gaped up at the conning tower as their captain began bellowing through a bullhorn: "Hold your fire! Hold your fire!"

Young Tang Qui, captain of the *Deng Xiaoping,* had surfaced cautiously with watertight doors all shut, and only his conning tower's top hatch open to exit the gun crew. He had blown his ballast tanks, assuming that the tugboat heading his way was his brother's commandeered flagship. When he realized, too late, that the tug was going to ram him, he had concluded that it was a different tug and had come within seconds of slaughtering the fleet admiral.

"Brace," he warned on the intercom. "Brace for collision." And, through the bullhorn: "Heads up on deck. Help the admiral. Jump, Brother. Jump!"

As the distance between the two vessels closed to yards and the yards to feet, Admiral Tang and his staff officers scrambled down the ladder from the monkey island. Tang was six feet above the main deck when the tug hit the submarine with a hollow boom and a screw-popping screech of ripping steel. Slammed painfully against the ladder, he knew instantly that the tugboat's shaggy bow fender had not absorbed the impact.

The workboat had hit steel on steel—obliterating the thin layer of anechoic tiles—where the submarine's hull bulged below the waterline. The submarine was built to resist enormous pressure evenly distributed. But the tug was overbuilt, her bow reinforced to withstand concentrated blows, and even as the Chinese admiral ran forward, climbed onto the bow fender, and jumped into the arms of the submarine's gun crew, he feared he had moved his command to a sinking ship.

36

KEN HUGHES WAS FLUNG against the windshield, starring the glass with his brow. Reeling, he made his way out the back door and down the ladder.

The tug was still moving, rubbing past the submarine, staggering like a dying horse.

From down on the towing deck he saw Admiral Tang climbing up the submarine's conning tower. The Chinese boat was listing but still making way, while her gun crew struggled to train her cannon on the *Chelsea Queen*.

"Ken!"

He whipped around. A deep baritone-bass shouting again. "Ken! Ken!" He must be hallucinating from the whack on his head. He knew he was for sure when a big white bird materialized out of the dark and floated into the strait of water between the tug and Tang's submarine.

Not a bird. But a creature that flew across the water just the same. Its giant wings were not of feather, but of gleaming dacron. A sailboat, nearly as wide as it was long—a catamaran with straining sails, tilting precariously on one hull. Jose Chin was clinging like a spider to the net floor between the two hulls, camera cranking, shouting Ken's name.

Kate Ross was driving—ropes in her hands, a line in her teeth, and one foot on the tiller—steering for the back of his tug.

A smile like a bonfire and I'm a goner. The woman was thoroughly nuts, risking her life to save his—brave and determined and focused and generous, everything he'd seen in that first smile. And if they ever got out of this alive, man, had she vaulted them over the pitfalls of a second date.

Kate spat out the line. "Get on!"

Ken was across the towing deck and perched on the bulwark when he felt something enormous pass close overhead. The sensation was trailed an instant later by a roar like the sound of a 747 landing. Then a brilliant explosion fireballed into the sky a half mile away, billowing from the exact place where the *Chelsea Queen* had left nine submarines floundering around the fuel lighter.

Ken heard a heavy thump. He felt the sharp smack of a shock wave, and then the heat of the fireball on his face. On Tang's submarine, the gun crew backed away from their cannon with expressions fearful in the firelight, and fled to their conning tower.

The shock wave knocked the catamaran off course and it slewed away from the tug before Ken could jump.

The exultant Marines Special Operations team that had called in the missile sobered rapidly as its rubber boat floated downriver into the *John F. Kennedy*'s field of fire. The stricken carrier still had teeth—her Vulcans snapping at every movement within their sweep, including, the Marines feared, four American commandos in a rubber boat.

Could they just swoosh past and hope the Vulcans' radar would overlook their minimal signature?

"Heads up!"

A mile to the southeast, something big was moving through the smoke, veering from the Intrepid pier below the *Kennedy*. Maybe another submarine. But it was longer than the Chinese subs, and it stood too tall.

"That's the *Zhaotong!*" The PLA frigate had wreaked havoc with its missiles.

"Thought the *Kennedy* got him."

"Wait—lost him! Where the hell did he go?"

"There he is!"

"It's not the *Zhaotong*, it's that goddamned tugboat again."

The lieutenant ended the debate with an order to zap the tug with the range finder. Reading in hand, he radioed a fire control officer on the *Lake Champlain*.

"I told you so," wheezed Captain Eddie. The smoke was killing him. Couldn't hold a breath. "I told you them engines would snap those mooring cables like string."

"Well, you were right and I was wrong," said Al. It had been twenty-five years since his last watch at the helm of a United States Navy destroyer, and he had his hands too full to argue nonsense with Captain Eddie.

At first there'd seemed to be no way to cast off lines without the Chinese patrols spotting. Wrong about that, Chink boys! Old Jake had swung down from his walker to crawl to the wire cables with a giant monkey wrench, and turn by painful turn had undone their turnbuckles. The manila lines, many weakened by silent strokes of knives and hacksaws, had parted like spiderwebs. She had steamed into the museum under her own power, and now she was steaming out.

Old Eddie was jumping up and down so hard he could hardly breathe.

Al had no illusions about their long-range chances. The old girl was flying but wouldn't for long—too much to go wrong in her thirty-year-old systems, too few hands to fix it.

But right now, the boys had steam up on two boilers, and the museum piece was churning into the harbor looking for trouble at a stately eight knots. Worried that any large, moving ship would draw fire from the *John F. Kennedy*'s gatling guns, Al had peeled away south.

"Yo, Ed. If you would kindly turn that searchlight on, we're going to find us a submarine."

Eddie had made a point of locating the power switch ahead of time. The *Rollins*'s twenty-thousand-candlepower searchlight blazed ahead like a white spear.

Lord, the destroyer was long. They'd never seemed this long when Al was a kid in the Navy. And back then, the quartermaster steering was never alone on the bridge. You had the Officer of the Deck yakking where to turn, fourteen sailors calling numbers from the radar, Loran, and Sat Nav. Not to mention the skipper glaring over your shoulder.

Al was getting lost already.

No lights on shore. Best thing was to steer toward the fire in the middle of the river. "Gimme them glasses. Hold the wheel."

Captain Eddie held the wooden ship's wheel as if Al had passed him a newborn baby. Al scanned the water ahead. *There* was a sub, creeping away from the fire, sneaking toward New Jersey. Al manipulated the searchlight and caught the bastard in the spear of light.

"Tell the fellows down there to hang on tight," he told Eddie. Eddie cranked the intercom, shouted down the order. Al circled into mid-river, south of the limping sub, and lined up his shot.

With luck he'd cut the sub in half and blast right through

the wreckage without tearing out the *Rollins*'s bottom. If he could, they might just get a second shot at another. Unless one of them heard him coming and blasted him with a torpedo.

"We're getting him, we're getting him," yelled Captain Eddie.

They braced for impact. But at the last moment, the Chinese submarine turned smartly to port and accelerated, and the *Rollins* lumbered past, roiling empty water. Al tried to turn her, but the sub was streaking away.

"You missed him, Al. You missed him."

Now the river appeared empty but for dancing reflections of firelight. And the old destroyer felt like she was losing speed.

Eddie thumbed the radio again. "We gotta find a target."

As Ken watched Kate circle to make another pass at the *Chelsea Queen*'s stern, and he poised to jump, his VHF radio suddenly squawked his name.

"Ken. Captain Ken Hughes! Hey, Ken, hey, Ken. Captain Ken Hughes."

"Who the hell?" Balanced precariously on the bulwark, Ken fumbled for the radio on his belt.

"Chelsea Queen. Chelsea Queen. Ken, you there?"

"This is the *Chelsea Queen* on eighteen. Come in."

"Ken. It's Captain Eddie."

"Who?"

"Captain Eddie. You know, from the museum? Ken, me and the boys are out here on the Rollins. *We're looking for the enemy."*

Ken tried to churn his exhausted brain into gear. Captain Eddie was eighty years old. The "boys" were scraping by on Social Security and union pensions. The *Rollins* was a decommissioned Vietnam-era destroyer. "Out where, Eddie?"

"We got steam up. Big Al's driving. We're making eight knots. Don't you see our searchlight?"

"You're under way?" Ken still couldn't believe it. But there in the firelight, a mile upriver, a long, lean greyhound of a ship was moving—

"Me and the boys almost got a sub—"

Two ships!

The dark second gliding out from the shore revealed the boxy silhouette of her missile launchers.

"Go back!" shouted Ken.

"You see any targets?"

"The *Zhaotong*'s coming at you. Run for it. Hug the shore."

Kate maneuvered flapping sails behind the *Chelsea Queen*. Ken jumped, just as something roared close overhead.

"Sounds like a 747," said old Eddie.

"It's not," Al said grimly. He was watching its red tail streak up the river. When it turned over Manhattan and looped back, he said, "Cruise missile."

"How'd they get a cruise missile on those little submarines?"

"It's one of ours."

"Friendly fire?"

"Not that friendly. Eddie, it's been good knowing you."

"They can't do this to us. We just got rolling."

Al threw an arm around the old man. "We almost did it, Eddie. Almost did."

"It's such a waste."

Al was philosophical. He had already rejected the idea of jumping off the destroyer, because he couldn't swim. And in a way he was glad, he couldn't imagine leaving the old guy to die alone.

"War is waste, Eddie. You seen it. I seen it. We always knew it was a fucking waste—what are you doing?"

"I'm praying, and if I was you I'd watch my language."

The Tomahawk cruised the length of Manhattan at six hundred miles an hour, swooped over the Upper Bay, turned back upriver. Programmed to search the harbor for a large, moving target, it found two.

Mistaking Al and Charlie's museum relic for the vanguard of an American counterattack, the brave and battered crew of the *Zhaotong* sallied forth from behind the parking violation tow pound piers. They had taken refuge to repair the many hits from the *John F. Kennedy* and the second helicopter attack. Missiles expended, torpedo launchers wrecked by rocket hits, listing to starboard, pumps falling behind a flood of underwater penetrations, she brought her one remaining 3.9-inch gun to bear on the *Rollins*.

Ken landed in the catamaran's net, knocking over Jose and his camera. The flat little boat lurched under his weight and one of the hulls went underwater.

A third roar of jet thunder passed overhead and a bright flash lit the Hudson River. The light of the explosion showed the *Zhaotong* sinking by the stern and the *Edward Rollins* moving slowly toward Chelsea.

Kate pushed her tiller and nursed a sheet, and they tipped slowly and heavily away from the tug.

"You," Ken told her, "are really something."

One look at him and Kate knew she'd been right. *I was right. I was right. It's not a dream.* "I am so glad you're alive."

But Ken was staring at the big submarine, which had started moving, creeping from behind the tug. It was listing and barely making way. Yet it commenced a wide turn to the east and straightened purposefully onto a course that would bear it into the North Cove Marina at the World Trade Center.

"Go back," Ken said. "Put me on the tug."

"No."

"Now!"

"No."

"If Tang dies, the war is over. Put me on the tug!"

"For bragging rights?"

"Call it what you want, but I've got the best chance in New York of stopping Tang."

"How?" asked Jose.

"I'm going to sink that bastard before he reaches shore. He's on his own, Kate, like a warlord. He's a one-man show. His bosun told me as much. If he succeeds, China celebrates and Tang's their hero. If he fails, they'll say he was a renegade, that he was crazy, that he was acting entirely on his own. If we take him out, it's over."

"Let's do it," Jose yelled. "Let's do it. Come on, Kate, Ken's right."

Kate screamed at him, "You are so fucking transparent, Jose. You just want pictures."

"Kate." Ken reached for her hand.

She jerked it away. She had felt deeply satisfied, convinced for a blissful moment that she had him back, and too utterly exhausted to care what happened next as long as she could keep him. "I want you. Alive."

"Put me back on, please. I gotta do this. I gotta stop him—*get out of our faces, Jose!*" He pushed the reporter away from Kate and reached for her again and this time she took his hand firmly in hers.

"Why won't you let yourself be saved?" she asked. "I want you. Let me save you."

"I want you, too. But take me back or I'll swim."

Kate believed he would. She caught the wind, filled the sail, and plowed toward the drifting tug. She said, "Take the bowline with you. We will tow this boat. Maybe if we're lucky we can get back onto it when yours sinks."

"No," he said. "Get away from the tug."

"I won't leave you," said Kate.

"You can't help me."

"Ken. Let me turn the boat around. We'll sail away."

"I can't."

"Then take the bowline," she said again. "And I'll be right behind you."

Ken hauled his aching body over the high side of the tug, secured the thin line to an enormous cleat, then raced up the ladders and doused the work lights so the *Chelsea Queen* would no longer appear the brightest moving object on the river.

A two-hundred-yard circle of burning oil where the fuel lighter and the submarines had been was painting miles of the river and the dark city bright orange.

He located Tang's submarine on his radar, then spotted it visually. It was still on course for the World Trade Center and picking up speed. Kate climbed up the wheelhouse ladder. Ken took the controls. Kate edged fearfully around the enormous supine body of the bosun at his feet.

"Is he going to get up?"

"I don't think so."

"Is he dead?"

"I hope not. Where's Jose?"

"Down on deck, picking up his gear."

Ken pushed the engines Ahead, and goosed the throttles. The *Chelsea Queen*'s old diesels shuddered to speed. She lumbered through a tight turn and took off after the submarine limping toward shore with Admiral Tang.

A minute ago Kate had thought Ken looked like a madman with burning eyes. But now she could see, by the glow of his radar screen and the firelight on the river, that he'd been hurt. His hand on the tillers was swollen, one finger ballooned like a fat sausage. His face was cut and bruised. The soft skin under his right eye was twitching from fatigue.

"What did they do to you?"

"Nothing like they did to Rick and Charlie. You okay?"

His whole body was coiled toward the fire-speckled darkness ahead. She tracked his restless gaze as it shuttled between the radar monitor and the windshield.

He was locked in a race to the riverbank. His tugboat was overtaking the submarine. She could see it now in the smoky murk: it was riding high in the water, leaning to the left. The tugboat was making twice its speed.

"Why doesn't it submerge?"

"I think I knocked a hole in him."

They were nearing the riverbank. Kate could see individual windows in the loom of the World Financial Center. The World Trade Towers reflected smoke-softened firelight.

"Ken, what are you going to do?"

"Ram the bastard, again. And this time I'm going to sink him."

The submarine was half again longer than Ken's tugboat. But he seemed oblivious to the likelihood he'd sink the *Chelsea Queen* in the bargain.

He kept saying, "Hang on," and now, as he overtook the submarine, he circled wide and aimed to strike it amidships.

Kate screamed, "Ken! Soldiers! Turn away!"

Ken tried to shift the tug from one lumbering turn to another.

"Get down, get down!"

The soldiers were high on the conning tower, training guns on the *Chelsea Queen*.

Kate and Ken pulled each other to the floor and as they struggled to protect each other with their bodies, the wheelhouse windows disintegrated in flying glass.

*   *   *

The tugboat lurched away, out of control. Tang Li slapped the gunner on his shoulder. "Well done—Brother, put me ashore!"

Captain Tang Qui shouted down to the *Deng Xiaoping*'s control room and his stricken boat moved heavily alongside the seawall that sheltered the shattered remains of the North Cove Marina. His boat was down at the head and listing sharply to port, her double hull breached, her pumps overwhelmed by the invading seawater.

Tang Li spoke into his radio, and fifty heavily armed marines materialized from the shadows of the World Financial Center buildings, double-timing it to the seawall. Each wore a red light, marking Tang's honor guard—the admiral's men. The wallowing submarine banged and screeched against stone. His brother's sailors wrestled a gangway into place and fought to keep it steady as Admiral Tang Li stepped foot on Manhattan Island for the first time in ten years.

The fleet admiral returned eager salutes from the bright-faced fresh reserves, and knew in that moment that he had regained the initiative by his lightning shift of tactics.

He glanced back to wave farewell to his brother. But young Qui was gripping the conning tower rails with both hands and shouting urgently down the hatch to shift ballast. In the seconds since the admiral had stepped off, her port list had steepened severely. The gangway detail were losing control of the rig, and dropped it as they themselves began to slip and slide down the slanting deck. Two sailors fell between the hull and the stone wall, their frightened screams cut off abruptly.

Suddenly the submarine straightened up. At first it seemed a miracle had shifted the water in her hull. But then she continued rotating, and careened the other way, toward the river. As Admiral Tang watched, powerless, his brother's boat leaned steeper and steeper, held an impossible angle for an impossible moment, and suddenly turned turtle.

Tang cried Qui's name when he saw her bottom glitter in the firelight. She righted partly, but water was pouring in her conning tower and she settled deep on her side.

Admiral Tang watched in disbelief. The best boat in his fleet was sinking like an anvil. And where his only brother had stood commanding her raced a whirlpool as the rampaging water sucked Qui and his crew into the depths of the foundering boat.

Tang lunged as if to help. His honor guard followed loyally, close at his side. But he stopped at the water's edge, seeing it was hopeless.

"Too late."

"But there may be air pockets, Admiral."

"Too late." Already the tide was tugging the submarine into the stream, dragging her to a grave in deeper water.

He watched her disappear. And his heart was a maelstrom of grief, loss, and self-recrimination as he turned his back on the river graves and led his soldiers into the smoke-shadowed city.

37

"THE SON OF A BITCH GOT OFF. There he goes."

The left lens of Ken's binoculars was smashed, but squinting through the right, he tracked Tang and a dense troop of commandos by the winking red lights the men wore on their shoulders. They trotted swiftly around the World Financial Center and onto Liberty Street.

The running tide had pulled the *Chelsea Queen* along Battery Park City, several hundred yards downriver from the sinking submarine. The machine guns had riddled his controls. Only his port engine would engage, and the steering tillers were useless.

"Ken, there's a ship!" yelled Kate.

She pointed south, downriver toward the Battery.

"Where?" He saw only dark smoke and looked automatically at the gaping hole that had been the radar monitor.

"It was heading right at us . . . wait! There!"

Ken saw a raked bow part the smoke. It was almost on top of them, a break-bulk freighter of six or eight thousand tons moving up the river at a good clip. Ken reached to blow a warning blast on the whistle. But it was veering away.

"Where the hell is he going?"

The freighter swung past the *Queen* and headed in to shore toward the North Cove. Jose tracked it through his infrared lens. "There's a bunch of box trucks on it."

Too big to enter the yacht cove, the ship maneuvered its bow to the esplanade. "They're lowering a ramp," reported Jose.

Kate passed Ken the binoculars and he could see by the light of the burning oil upstream that the ship's crew was winching down a gangplank. "What in hell are they doing with those trucks?"

A flock of at least a dozen straight-back box trucks, big ones, was lined up on the freighter's long foredeck.

Kate said, "I was down here a couple of hours after it started. The commandos cleared a corridor along Liberty Street. Cleared all the cars."

"For those trucks?" asked Jose.

"Maybe. What's in them?" asked Kate.

"Nothing's in them," said Jose. "They must be empty. They must be stealing gold—the Federal Reserve Bank is on Liberty Street. I did a story on it. Half the gold in the world is in there. They hold it in their vaults for safekeeping for other countries."

"No," said Ken. "They didn't have to bring their own trucks. The city's full of trucks. They're carrying something *in*, not out. Something too heavy to hump on their backs."

"Spare ammunition?" ventured Jose.

"Explosives."

Tons and tons of explosives. Way too much to bring in by sub. Too heavy, too risky, too likely lost if a sub were sunk in the attack.

"They already blew up Police Plaza," said Jose.

"The World Trade Center?" asked Ken. "It's right on Liberty."

"City Hall?" asked Kate.

"Or the Federal Reserve Bank?"

"Or all three," said Jose, camera cranking as the crew struggled with the gangplank.

"Twelve trucks? Twelve buildings," said Ken. Terrorist bombers had almost destroyed the World Trade Center with a single rented van. Each of the big box trucks on the freighter's foredeck could hold ten times the explosives carried in a van.

"They could blow up every building with a name on it." But if Ken was right—if he had guessed what Tang was going to do—he was helpless to stop him. He could barely steer the *Queen* toward shore, much less try to ram the much bigger freighter.

Eddie! Jesus, old Eddie on the *Rollins*. He whipped the radio to his lips. "Eddie! Captain Eddie. You still there?"

The airwaves were nuts again, people screaming and yelling and jamming them up. Then suddenly a weary-sounding, defeated Eddie radioing back. "We're running out of steam."

"Can you still move?"

"We barely got steerage. Al says we gotta beach her."

"Where are you?"

"Big Al, where are we—Al says we're right off the Holland Tunnel ventilators."

Half a mile. "You got your target at the World Trade Center. There's a freighter pulling into the North Cove. Tell Al to come right down the shore. Cut him in half."

The first truck was already easing down the gangplank, guided by the soldiers on the esplanade and the sailors on the ship.

"Come on, Eddie. Come on. Where are you? Jose, you got him on the infrared?"

"Not in this smoke."

"Is that Eddie?" asked Kate. "I think I see his bow."

Ken saw a vague bulk through the binoculars. And then the *Edward Rollins* swept slowly out of the dark and the smoke. He whipped the radio to his lips. "You're veering off, Eddie. Get in, get in."

Slowly, painfully, the old destroyer shifted course. Ken estimated that her speed had dropped to three or four knots; at that speed there was no way she would sink the much bigger freighter.

He radioed Eddie again. "Listen, Eddie. Tell Al to hit his bow. Hit him forward. You got to knock him loose, break his moorings."

On the freighter, Chinese soldiers saw the *Rollins* looming toward them and started firing rocket grenades, which exploded against the destroyer's bridge.

"Dead on," yelled Ken. "You're doing it."

The Chinese kept firing, joined by commandos on the shore. The range was long—the ship's bridge stood far aft of her bow. But suddenly a lucky hit pierced a window and flames began pouring from it.

"Eddie? . . . Al? . . . Steady as she goes."

Their radio was silent. Then the *Rollins* hacked into the freighter's port bow with a crash that staggered the bigger ship. Mooring lines parted with a bang, cutting like scythes through the men around the gangplank, and the ship started to drift. The truck on the gangway accelerated, fell hard to the esplanade, and roared away.

The next truck was already ramping up onto the bow and the soldiers urged it ashore. The driver floored the accelerator. Roaring, it half lurched, half flew off the ramp. The front wheels landed solidly on the esplanade. The rear tires bounced down on the edge of the seawall. For a brief moment they hung there. Then, slowly, the truck slid backward and tumbled into the river.

The gangplank splashed after it, marooning the ten trucks still on the foredeck.

"You did it, Eddie. You did it! . . . Eddie? You there?"

Locked in a sinking embrace, the freighter and the fiercely burning destroyer drifted into the dark.

"Where's Tang?"

Jose scoped out the riverbank through his infrared lens. "Gone."

Estimating the number of deliberate shadows by clumps of ten as he taped the commandos, he lost count at two hundred.

"Where's the truck that got off?"

"Gone."

Shifting the *Chelsea Queen*'s port engine forward and reverse, Ken worked the stricken tug shoreward. When he finally ground her against the seawall, Kate was ready on the foredeck to heave a hawser around a piling.

"Okay, let's get him."

Jose wasn't sure he'd heard right. "What?"

"Son of a bitch killed my crew and he's destroying the city."

"Ken, you don't even have a gun."

Ken patted down the unconscious bosun again, and found what he was looking for. "I have a knife."

Stone-faced, Renata Bradley handed Mayor Mincarelli a cellular telephone. "It's your wife."

He seized it eagerly and asked, "How are the kids taking this?"

"I'd hang up on him," Samantha Cummings muttered in Renata's ear. "Whatever happened to 'How are you, darling'?"

"He misses his children," said Renata and moved away. Rudy had been acting strangely, telephoning everyone he knew and leaving a long message for his wife. And now she was finally calling back.

Rudy flashed Renata a distracted smile as he hunched over the telephone and Renata smiled back, her heart lifting. She was sure it was really only his children he was worried about, and his smile confirmed it.

"Mr. Mayor?"

Big Luther Washington was back again, the second Rudy said good-bye to his wife, lowering over Rudy's desk like a bear. "Mr. Mayor, I got to tell you again, you are risking your safety and your liberty hanging on those cellphones."

"I *know*, Luther."

"They'll nail us here. Give 'em enough time and they'll triangulate those signals, just like we did the Sicilians'."

"I know, Luther. Now here's what I want you to do. It's time to round up everyone in here who's not armed, who's not a trained professional fighter, and get them out one of the back doors."

"Yes, sir."

"Volunteers only stay."

Luther jerked his thumb at Samantha and Renata. "You heard the man, ladies."

"I'm staying," insisted Renata.

Samantha Cummings surprised her with a sudden skinny-armed hug. "Good luck," she whispered. "Forget my big-mouth theories. In the end, we all get exactly what we want."

Renata hurried back to Rudy.

Luther Washington gave her a stern look. "Keep your head down, hon. I don't know exactly what the boss thinks he's up to, but it won't be face time and sound bites."

Ken lost sight of Admiral Tang when his troops bundled him into the South Tower of the World Trade Center. Jose Chin edged ahead with his camera. Ken shoved him back. "You want to get killed, get killed on your own."

"I'm just trying to—"

"Don't draw fire on me and Kate." He looked at Kate. Twice he had begged her not to come. Both times she demanded he stop following Tang. He wouldn't. "Then I'm coming," was all she said, and nothing could dissuade her.

Tang's troops were not difficult to follow. Uptown, Jose said, they had fanned along the streets in independent squads of four men. But down here they were bolder. Here they marched in formation up Liberty Street, in a regimental style. Like they own the place, he thought.

Some wore small green lights, others blue, others yellow, marking units, he supposed. But only those with Tang wore red.

But there was still a wildness to them, as if they were so pumped up they were about to explode. A block back on Albany Street, they had shot the windows out of a row of stores. Tumbled-open boxes spilled onto the sidewalk from a Rollerblade shop. A dead teenager was sprawled across the window display, a wheeled boot in each hand and a skateboard wedged under his back.

"You know what I think?" whispered Jose. "I think Admiral Tang's down here hunting the mayor."

"Maybe you can interview them together," said Kate.

"Look," whispered Jose. "Look, look, look." He had his camera taping and he narrated in a barely audible murmur, "Admiral Tang Li is emerging from the World Trade Center, accompanied by several hundred troops. Jose wants to know, what in hell is the Chinese invader up to now?"

When he pulled his eye out of the camera, he discovered he was alone. Kate Ross and Ken Hughes were crouching low, running east on Liberty Street, shadowing Admiral Tang's commandos as they marched purposefully across Church Street, then east on Dey.

*   *   *

Jose caught up at the corner of Liberty and Broadway. They were hiding behind a FedEx truck, warily eyeing another large detachment that had surrounded the Federal Reserve Bank of New York. Ken pointed up Broadway, where Tang's contingent was turning left off Dey and double-timing north.

"Heading toward City Hall," Ken whispered.

"The mayor can't be in City Hall."

"Maybe he's near it," said Kate. "Or under it."

Jose said, "Let's do it."

Ken caught his arm in a firm grip and hauled him back behind the truck. "We're stuck here. If we cross the street they'll see us."

Jose tried to squirm loose. Ken held him tighter.

Kate said, "Look!"

The Chinese flag was suddenly illuminated by fifty powerful flashlights. It was hanging from the pole over the front door of the Federal Reserve Bank. The soldiers saluted, cheering, clapping each other on the back and firing shots in the air.

Ken saw that it was the best chance they would get. "Go!"

Harriet Greene and Hector Sanchez were six blocks north of the Federal Reserve Bank, in the trees of City Hall Park. They'd shadowed another Chinese electronics squad, which had circled around the ruins of One Police Plaza, south down Gold Street, then west on Ann and into the park. It was there they'd heard the admiral's detachment double-timing up Broadway.

The electronics squad stopped abruptly, heads up like interrupted bloodhounds, when they heard the boot steps echo.

Harriet and Hector dove for cover behind the structure

that housed the elevator that took handicapped passengers
down to the subway station below the park. Hector's heart
stopped as a powerful hand closed over his mouth and jerked
his head up, exposing his neck to a gleaming blade.

38

HECTOR HAD NO CHANCE to utter a sound to warn Harriet, but her animal sense tipped her off and she spun like a top, her rifle muzzle whirling to bear on Hector's assailant.

A big, angry voice boomed, "What in blue blazes are you doing here?"

"Daddy!"

The elevator doors opened wider. Police Officer Harold Greene dragged Hector inside and beckoned Harriet to follow. "Watch your step. We're standing on top of the elevator cab."

Hector planted his feet on the girders of the cab, which had stalled between levels when the electricity went out. Officer Greene cranked the door shut and lit a match. Harriet threw her arms around her white-haired father and stunned Hector by bursting into tears.

"What the hell are you two doing down here? You're supposed to be watching the mayor's house."

"Me and Hector thought we should come looking for the mayor."

"Get in line." Harold Greene blew out his match, opened the door a crack, pointed toward Broadway, where hundreds of Chinese soldiers were trotting into the park. "Where'd you get the weapon?"

"I took it from one of the commandos who attacked the One-nine."

"Good girl."

"Daddy, they're tracking the mayor's signals with a radio direction finder. I think we can follow them to find the mayor."

"You, boy," Harriet's father demanded of Hector. "She been acting like this all day?"

"No, sir."

"I'll bet." He patted Harriet's cheek. "Would you believe when she was a little girl she always played the Lone Ranger?"

"Yes," said Hector.

"Young lady, if I had been a Chinese commando lying in wait in here, you'd be fish bait."

Harriet hung her head. "Yes, Daddy."

"You, too, boy, egging her on!" he said to Hector. "All right, both of you stick close, do what I say, maybe we'll come out of this alive. Pair of damned fools."

Hector had been through enough today, and he didn't feel like being called a damned fool by anybody, even Harriet's father. So instead of answering, "Yes, sir," as he would have done yesterday, he said, "Harold, are we the only cops down here?"

"Hell, no. Them that got out of HQ before they blew it up, and us from the First, we're stationed around, up in the buildings, over in J&R, up in the offices. My Lou's established his HQ in the hardware store on Park Row."

"What are we doing?"

"Biding our time, boy. Biding our time. Wait there while I sneak another look."

Hector glanced at Harriet and saw, to his surprise, more

tears bubbling out of her eyes. "Hey, what's wrong?" he whispered.

"He looks so old."

"He's just tired."

"He's too old for this. I never saw such lines in his face." Hector patted her shoulder.

Harriet shrugged him away. "The man should be at home. He already fought his war."

"Get down! Both of you, get down, down! They're coming this way."

Hector lowered himself through the roof hatch, feeling for the bottom with his feet. Harriet was right on top of him, and an instant later her father piled in, too, and swung the ceiling hatch closed. He touched his lips and held up a finger, signaling, *Wait.*

The ice-white light of a halogen bulb suddenly filled the shaft above the elevator. By the stripes it cast through the hatch rim, Hector saw that Harold Greene had prepared an escape route by prying open the interior cab doors. Leaning in the corner was a pump shotgun.

Hector suddenly viewed the entire insane situation differently. There had to be hundreds of survivors like P.O. Greene dug in around City Hall. Thousands, even, who'd survived the first onslaught and gone underground. The next vital step was to make the mental switch from paramilitary police to urban guerrilla. And one of the several survival skills he had learned so far today was that urban guerrillas kept moving.

The light overhead disappeared. Boot steps faded. In the distance, orders were barked.

"Harold," Hector whispered, "what's our next move?"

"Told you. Wait our chance."

"No," replied Hector. "We've got to trail those RDFs. We've got to protect the mayor."

Both Greenes were near-invisible shadows in the dark. Harold's bulky as a bear's, Harriet's lively as she started shifting her weight from foot to foot like a hungry panther. And it came as no surprise that it was the panther who said, "Hector's right. Our assignment is to protect the mayor."

"Well, first you got to find him."

"I know one place he isn't," said Hector. "That's here. Let's go, Harriet."

"Hold on," said Harold Greene.

"Cover us, Dad. Okay, Hector, let's do it."

39

HARRIET AND HECTOR got directions for Harold's escape route in whispers, climbed out the doors he had forced open, and followed the yellow beam of Hector's fading flashlight through a motor room and an electrical closet into a public section of the City Hall subway station.

Civilians huddled around a track worker's porta-light, pressed fearfully into the shadows as Harriet and Hector followed the signs to the exit on the east side of Park Row. Crouched on the steps, the rookies peered through the railing.

City Hall Park was crawling with Chinese soldiers. Their colored LEDs glowed like campfires miles away, but the invaders were all right there across Park Row, standing at parade rest, massed in the park like they owned the place. Hector saw none along Park Row, none on the sidewalk.

"Want to know the reason," said Harriet, "why I did it?"

"Did what?" Hector stuck his head up, hoping it wouldn't

get shot off. No commandos on the corners of Frankfort or Spruce or Beekman.

"Why I got you on the tit at Gracie Mansion. The reason is that I like being around somebody smart. I'm not that smart myself—"

"You are so!"

"I am not. I'm dyslexic. They didn't find out till it was way too late to help me with it."

"Whaddaya talkin', dyslexic—you went to City."

"Two years—remedial all the way—till I could apply to the Department. I'm not smart—Hector, I can hardly fucking read. Okay?"

"Okay."

"I'm not *stupid* stupid. I can think on my feet for both of us. But you can think ahead—like, you see further."

Suddenly, Hector knew that she was right. The things he had always hoped to learn all through high school and college had fallen together. He could finally see the big picture. It was like he had grown new eyes. Different eyes.

Like now he could see that the Chinese soldiers had changed tactics. They were acting like an army. Filling space like an army. Locking themselves in place like an army.

"Listen up. What do you see happening?" Hector pointed into the park. "They're massing. No more little hit-and-run squads—there's four, five hundred soldiers in there."

"Yeah?"

"Let's say your dad is right. Maybe there's a thousand cops hiding in these buildings. How do we get them to all start shooting at once? What is the one way to get all cops running your way?"

"Call ten-thirteen. Officer needs assistance. But Dispatch is down. Besides, everybody's radio is dead by now."

"We need megaphones," said Hector. "Ghetto blasters with mikes. Boom boxes. Can you get us into J&R Music?"

The city's biggest electronics discounter occupied most of Park Row. From what Harriet had seen, it hadn't been looted like the shops uptown. More cops than mutts down here. She removed her hat, before raising her head to scope out a route.

"Okay, Hector. Get your weapon in your hands. We go east on Frankfort, south on Gold, west on Ann, slip into J&R's loading dock. Ready?"

At the word "ready," she was already running. Hector pulled his rifle off his back and scrambled after her, east a block, down three, west one, to the J&R receiving bay. He found Harriet pressed against the wall. She rapped the door three times, hard. Then whistled, softly, through her teeth three times; and, miracle of miracles, the door opened wide enough to emit a double-barrel shotgun. "Greene and Sanchez, Gracie Mansion detail."

There were cops inside. A jowly, red-eyed sergeant who had opened the door, and thirty or forty lethargic-looking uniformed patrolmen of a type Hector and Harriet privately referred to as "jive-asses from the burbs"—white Long Islanders who had grown up watching cop TV, still lived at home, and thought "ethnic" was a fancy word for "felony."

"Hey, Sarge. What's everybody waiting for?" asked Hector.

The sergeant eyed the pumped-up Hector warily, as if Internal Affairs had sent him to rate his command skills. "Some direction," he said. "And some heavy artillery would be kind of nice, too."

"Any chance of boosting some ghetto blasters with microphones and batteries?"

"How'd you get all the way down here from Gracie Mansion?"

"With her," said Hector.

The sergeant studied Harriet, who was high in panther

mode, shifting her weight from foot to foot, juggling her assault rifle like a drum majorette's baton.

"Okay." He detailed some suburbanites, who shuffled off and returned with boxes. "Open them," ordered the sergeant. "Move it! You, you, and you, get batteries."

Hector turned on a ghetto blaster, and tapped the sing-along mike. His amplified fingertip echoed from the ceiling. He gave another to Harriet, who explained what they were going to do, and demanded volunteers.

By the time they led a dozen men and women out the front door and onto the moonlit sidewalk, the number of Chinese soldiers in City Hall Park had tripled, well over a thousand now, streaming in from uptown, forming up like a parade.

"We've got to get right next to them," said Harriet. "Hold your boom box and your weapon over your head and walk across Park Row toward those bastards like you're surrendering. Then duck behind the last row of cars and start yelling. Ready? Do it!"

The commandos spotted them before they had moved three feet from the door. The front ranks raised their weapons.

"Yell, 'Don't shoot,' " said Harriet. "Yell, 'surrender.' If you know Chinese, yell it in Chinese."

"I do," offered one of the volunteers, a skinny blond kid shaking from head to foot as he marched forward.

"Do it. Yell, 'We surrender.' In Chinese. Do it now."

They moved briskly among the stopped cars, toward the guns in the park.

Ken Hughes and Kate Ross and Jose Chin had worked their way north and east and were watching City Hall and the park from the corner of Chambers Street and Broadway when an amplified chorus boomed suddenly through the trees: *"Ten-thirteen! Ten-thirteen! Ten-thirteen!"*

" 'Officer needs immediate assistance,' " Jose translated. "In other words, save us now or we are toast."

The plea bounced off the buildings, echoed from Park Row to Broadway, rallied down to Vesey Street and up to Chambers. The response was almost immediate. Even before the commandos firing at the cars stuck on Park Row drowned out the Ten-thirteens, pistol fire began to crackle from surrounding windows and rooftops. Shotguns bellowed. Rifles boomed into the park.

Jose turned his camera on the muzzle flashes—they looked like a million fireflies on a hot summer night. The crackling thickened to a staccato boom and then a long-drawn-out, endless roar as hundreds upon hundreds of cops poured small-arms fire into the park. The Chinese commandos, coolly seeking cover behind trees, lamp posts and benches, fired back.

The troops started to shift downtown, raking the Park Row shops, the office windows overlooking Broadway, the churchyard on Vesey, and the storefronts on Fulton.

Kate saw a tightly formed squad running in the opposite direction. She tapped Ken's shoulder. "Look!"

Ken had to yell for Jose to hear. "Check it out. Red lights. Is that Tang?"

Searching with his infrared, Jose scoped a second squad running. "Here comes another RDF unit." Their radio tracking gear registered a hot spot on his scope.

The RDF unit merged with Tang and his elite guard heading uptown. They raced past City Hall, charged with sudden purpose past the Tweed Court House, crossed Chambers and disappeared up narrow Elk Street.

Ken, Kate, and Jose ran after them, hugging the building line on Chambers, and peered around the corner of Elk, a dark street too pinched for the moonlight to penetrate, where Tang's men were milling through the doorway of a gloomy old office building. Jose dropped to one knee and switched his eye from his infrared lens to the low-light optic.

"Tang's with them."

"They must have nailed the mayor's transmission. Jose, you better try calling your pal with the mayor."

Jose tried to focus with one hand while speed-dialing with the other.

Renata Bradley answered Larry's phone. "What?"

"Jose wants you to know! They're coming through a building on Elk. If you're in there, you better run."

Mayor Mincarelli and Renata Bradley had never seen eye to eye on the Tweed Court House, the three-story Victorian palace next door to City Hall.

Renata, whose grandfathers were quarrymen, could not help but admire the multiple uses, inside and out, that "Boss" Tweed's contractors had discovered for marble.

To the mayor it was an abomination—a monument to fraud, built by the corrupt to house the shameful. He had despised the nineteenth-century boondoggle even before Luther Washington had stumbled upon a Prohibition-era speakeasy in its subcellar.

Luther, accidentally demolishing a wall while installing the cellular antenna to update the mayor's bunker, had unearthed a three-hundred-foot tunnel. It had connected the disused subway station and the speakeasy, which had apparently been installed by Jazz age crook and adulterer Mayor Jimmy Walker.

Mincarelli hated every tile and mirror and every glazed brick in the speakeasy's vaulted ceiling, and was particularly offended by the ornate gas chandelier with its arms depicting acrobatic naked women. But the Chinese commandos were suddenly closing in on his bunker's Elk Street entrance. So it was into the old gaslit speakeasy that Rudy and his team retreated to set a trap for Admiral Tang.

The mayor had cleared the bunker of all but himself and Renata and Luther and six heavily armed detectives in bulletproof vests. Samantha Cummings and Danny Wong led the other civilians through the several escape doors to join the thousands hiding in the dark subway tunnels.

Luther stationed himself at the speakeasy end of the tunnel with the Stinger missile that Ben and Rocco had captured. The mayor and Renata lit the gaslights inside the speakeasy. The detectives sheltered behind the brick arches that supported the tunnel. The hope—in Luther's and the detectives' minds, a very slim one—was to turn the hostage game on its ear by snatching Tang.

40

IN THE LOBBY of the Elk Street office building, Ken peered dubiously into the stairwell down which Admiral Tang and his elite guard had disappeared.

"This is insane," said Kate.

"We're getting close," said Jose.

Suddenly, automatic gunfire, amplified by brick and stone and concrete, clattered and echoed up the stairwell. A thin sprinkling of pistol shots answered the fusillade. A brutal noise of heavy weapons sounded again. Then a dragon roared and an explosion rocked the floor. Deep silence followed, until the faraway sound of shooting on the other side of City Hall became audible once more.

"What happened?"

Jose plunged down the stairs, taking them by twos. Ken charged after him. Kate followed slowly, promising herself, *One last time*.

Three deep flights brought her to a dark subcellar where a massive door, wreathed in smoke, swung drunkenly on one hinge. Squeezing past, she saw a long, narrow, low-ceilinged tunnel.

To her right sprawled Chinese soldiers, dead and wounded in a tangled embrace. Others were staggering away, probing the dark with flashlights, leading blinded comrades. She'd lost sight of Ken and Jose ahead.

To the left she saw light. With a mantra of "light at the end of the tunnel" racketing in her mind, she headed for the source. Acrid smoke and the sickeningly sweet smell of blood hung in the air. Every few yards she came upon a grottolike indentation behind an arch, and in each slumped a silent figure. Americans, in torn, singed suits. The mayor's detectives, their bulletproof vests no match for heavy weapons.

Nearing the light, she heard voices, and when she stepped into the room her heart soared. Ken was on his feet.

Jose was alive, too, holding his camera. As was Mayor Mincarelli and his dark-haired press secretary. All four were staring, transfixed, at two commandos with stubby automatic rifles. Between them stood a slight, weary, distinguished-looking man in battle gear who could only be Admiral Tang.

One of the commandos whirled his gun at her; he'd been wounded and blood was oozing from his neck.

"Kate!" Ken grabbed her like lightning and pulled her to him. As he did this, the commando collapsed in a pool of blood, his gun clattering on the tile floor.

In that sudden improvement of the odds, Jose saw a split-second window to save them all. Leading with his camera, he lurched at Admiral Tang, barking, "Jose wants to know, Admiral Tang. What is your problem?"

He had moved too quickly. Neither Ken nor Kate nor the Mayor had taken advantage of the distraction, and Jose found himself hunched over alone with a gun in his face. *Estúpido.* Don't make news, shoot news.

Okay! Deal with it. He switched On. "Jose Chin. New

York Yes! Jose wants to know, Admiral Tang. What brings you to New York?"

He was deep into the viewfinder, framing the admiral, who seemed on the verge of answering, when Tang's remaining bodyguard smashed his rifle butt into Jose's skull.

The blow drove Jose to the floor. Funny, didn't hurt. Just made a big noise. Going to be some headache, though. What a day. Jose wants to know . . . now what?

Do it!

He turned over, tried to rise—found to his amazement that he could not. The camera was shaking like he was some old, burned-out union lard-ass.

He sank back, hoping, praying, dreaming that Jasbir Singh had uplinked his Pulitzer tape. He better have, because this Interview of the Century was running short. So what if the narrative of history was told by players? It was *videoed* by shooters, and Jose Chin would stake his rep on "Gorgeous George Does Tiffany's."

Kate knelt to help him. Ken pulled her back as Tang drew a pistol from his holster and said, in unaccented English, "Mr. Mayor, I will accept your unconditional surrender of New York City."

Rudy Mincarelli couldn't take his eyes off the kid shivering at their feet. "I'm not surrendering my city to you or anyone else."

"My troops control your streets and I hold you prisoner."

"No one controls New York's streets for very long," said Mincarelli.

"And I gotta tell you, Tang," said Ken Hughes, "this city could get by without a mayor for a while."

"Tugboat Captain, shut up! Mayor Mincarelli, I have your city, whether you are dead or alive. But if you care about your people, you will intervene to protect them both from me and from the United States military."

Tang gestured. His bodyguard aimed his rifle at the

mayor's head. Mincarelli tried not to flinch from the gun barrel. But of all the assaults on his essence and all the shocks to his soul this grimmest of days, this was the worst. Guarded by his security detail, cosseted by Renata, and yessed day and night by truckling staffers, here he was suddenly as helpless as an elderly tenement dweller cornered in a dark hall.

Renata stepped between them. "Please," she said to Admiral Tang, "these are matters we can negotiate."

Her heart was pounding with fear. She was intensely aware of Jose Chin growing stiller and stiller at their feet, and the woman named Kate sliding her arm around the husky tugboat captain. Protecting her man, as she herself was trying to protect Rudy?

Rudy said, in his obey-me-instantly voice, "Renata, get back."

To her shock, the Chinese admiral reached out and grazed her cheek with an insolent caress.

"Renata?" he said, locking eyes with Rudy, mocking him, daring him. "The mayor's concubine? Your revels have enlivened Beijing's newspapers."

He trailed his finger over her lips. Renata bit hard and deep.

Admiral Tang jerked his hand away, cocked his arm. Rudy pushed clumsily between them and shoved Tang with both hands.

Kate felt Ken coiling beside her.

Tang's bodyguard struck again, a lightning arc that smashed the mayor to the floor with the butt of his rifle and knocked Renata sideways with the barrel. Kate tried to stop Ken.

But he was already in motion, slamming the bodyguard down with his shoulder and slipping under the admiral's pistol to take him from behind, then clamping his left forearm across the admiral's throat, knocking the pistol from Tang's hand, and drawing the bosun's knife.

Bastard was wearing a thick Kevlar flak vest. No way he'd puncture that. And Tang was amazingly strong, strong and slippery as double-braided nylon, squirming loose.

The bodyguard sprang to his feet, rifle barrel cavernous.

Ken jammed the point of the knife into Tang's damaged ear. "Tell him to drop the gun or I'll shove this through your skull."

He felt Tang gather his strength. "Admiral, you don't have a chance. It'll come out your other ear before he stops me. *Tell him to drop that gun.*"

"Release me," Tang retorted fearlessly. "Or I will order him to kill everyone in this room, starting with your 'sweetheart.' "

"You won't get to see it happen."

"*I do not bluff,*" said Tang.

Freed by fear and anger and a crystalline sense that no options remained, the boat handler in Ken's mind gauged space and mass. Instinctively he shifted his grip on the knife; with the heel of his hand behind the hilt, he'd be able to push the blade deeper into Admiral Tang's head.

Tang Li felt the tugboat captain brace.

"No!" he cried. He shouted in Chinese. Shouted again, suddenly filled with fear. The bodyguard laid his weapon on the floor and backed away, eyeing it hungrily.

"Tell him to get down! Facedown, hands behind his head."

Tang spoke again. Slowly, the bodyguard obeyed.

"Kate," said Ken, "pick that up."

Kate let the breath slowly out of her lungs, and stooped to retrieve the assault rifle.

"See if you can release the clip."

Kate, who had seen more than a few guns in Jamaica, found the catch that released the banana clip. Then she picked up the pistol Tang had dropped.

"There's a safety on it?" asked Ken.

"The safety's off."

"Point it at him while I step back. Shoot the son of a bitch if he moves an inch." Ken loosened his left arm first, stepped away, and withdrew the knife from Admiral Tang's ear. He took the gun from Kate. She knelt to help Jose.

"Mr. Mayor," said Ken. "Mr. Mayor, you okay?"

Mayor Mincarelli was kneeling over Renata Bradley. He helped her stand as he climbed groggily to his own feet. He had an oozing cut over his ear. Renata pressed her palm against a broad, bloody furrow on her cheek.

"Mr. Mayor, you gotta deal with this guy."

"Are you all right?" the mayor asked Renata. She nodded. "Are you?"

Ken Hughes called to him again. "Mr. Mayor, we've got the head of the snake. Admiral Tang is a one-man show."

"Admiral Tang is a criminal," retorted Rudy Mincarelli, shaking with rage, glaring into the invader's smoke-reddened eyes. "Admiral Tang, you've declared war on New York. By law I could have you shot. Because you murdered men I've worked with for fifteen years, I could, if I played by your rules, kill you myself. But I am not an animal. Instead I appeal to you to stop this madness. Tell your gunmen to surrender."

"Surrender?" Tang laughed in his face. "My troops hold your Federal Reserve Bank and your New York Stock Exchange, your World Trade Center, your police headquarters, your power plants, and your Municipal Building. Most importantly, I hold the lives of two million of your citizens in the balance."

"Your gunmen cling temporarily to one corner of one district of this vast city. And since I hold you, they have no one to lead them."

"They will free me."

As if confirming this statement, gunfire echoed down the tunnel and nearby, overhead, an explosion shook the ground.

Ken Hughes said, "They're tired and hungry. And they

don't know their asses from a hole in the ground without the admiral to draw them a chart."

"Stay out of this!" snapped Mayor Mincarelli.

"Screw you, Mr. Mayor. You don't know what's going on here. I do."

Kate Ross looked up from Jose's body. "Mr. Mayor, Captain Hughes has seen Admiral Tang's troops with his own eyes. You have not. It is in your interest to listen to him."

"His subs are out of fuel," said Ken. "It's over. They just don't know it yet. Only you can tell them, Tang. You can save them, too, not just us. Your boys have had it. The Navy will sink every sub and drown every sailor."

Tang stood as still as ice. "It" was most certainly not over. He knew that his men were tired. He knew that his submarines were running dry. He knew that the American military would attack. But he had not lost—not as long as he had his fallback position, his "ace in the hole." The mayor was appalled by the destruction of his police headquarters? He had not yet known the meaning of destruction.

Mayor Mincarelli ransacked his mind. When was the last time he had negotiated for anything so precious? When was the last time he had negotiated at all? His prosecuting days were far behind him. Whatever give-and-take he had practiced during his brief stints of private lawyering was now a blurred memory.

He said, "It is not as if you have kidnapped a family's favorite daughter, Admiral. There are elements in America that would not be saddened to see New York City brought low." An unreasoning rage began pounding through Rudy Mincarelli's body. This monster, this criminal, would continue to destroy, street by street, house by house, life by life. *Greg,* he thought, *what would you do?*

The answer was impossible for him to accept; he had known it before he'd asked himself the question. Greg would apologize. Greg would say the words Tang wanted to hear. Greg would let this criminal ride roughshod. Greg would lie. Rudy hated lies.

He shot a glance at Renata. Her face was bleeding, her cheek cruelly ripped, her skin pale with shock and pain. But she met his glance and held it fiercely. No point in asking Renata what he should do; they thought too much alike.

He looked down at the kid reporter crumpled on the floor, staring back at him with sightless eyes. What was he, Spanish, Chinese? Jose Chin. Both. The best future of the races in New York; God bless his grieving parents.

He looked at the tugboat captain holding the gun on Admiral Tang, face beat to a pulp, eyes primed to act. Your basic outer-boroughs working guy, built like a fireplug, big arms, catcher's-mitt hands, about his own age, maybe older, Irish with some Scots, some German, some English, an arm around a woman not much older than Renata.

She was uncommonly sure of herself; he might have pegged her for a detective except for a touch of class you didn't usually find on the force. Good-looking woman. Manhattan. Chelsea or the Village—how did such a couple ever meet? How did anyone ever meet in New York? Sometimes you got lucky. Wasn't that the whole point of their magnificent city? A place to get lucky?

Greg, what would you do? Don't tell me, I already know.

"Admiral!" Mincarelli barked.

"Yes, Mr. Mayor."

"I believe that the city of New York owes you an apology for an incident that got out of hand some years ago."

Tang shook his head. "No, Mr. Mayor. The city of New York has already apologized to me. The 'city' paid me twenty-five thousand dollars. I spent a month parceling it out to the homeless."

The bastard was going to make him beg for it, make him lie to save the city. Angry voices raged in Mincarelli's head,

Give me a fucking break! There was nothing for a busy U.S. Attorney to investigate! An arrogant student challenged two peace officers and suffered the consequences. The cops might have been wrong, but the student surely wasn't right. Then one of his lawyer voices interrupted, a lawyer voice that spoke in the stately tones of Judge Danny Wong: *Mr. Mayor, who's looking out for your people?*

Rudy spoke aloud. "I, too, owe you an apology, Admiral. As the United States Attorney for the Southern District of New York, I was in a position at that time to investigate your complaint. I did not."

And if I had been mayor back then, the visiting Chinese lawbreaker would not have collected one thin dime.

"I regret I did not take up your cause," Rudy forced himself to continue. "New York is a very big city and sometimes injustice prevails. As, I'm sure, it sometimes prevails in your cities, too."

"Regret?"

"I am saying I am sorry," said the mayor. "I apologize."

Tang's cool reply sounded both defiant and modest. "I accept your apology, Mr. Mayor. But it alters nothing. My efforts are but a small part of a larger enterprise."

"Taiwan?" Mincarelli shot back scornfully. "I promise you, Admiral, the instant the Pentagon learns you are my prisoner, United States forces will savage your innocent cities as you have dared to savage mine. It's all over but the weeping, and as 'Captain Hughes' here says, you, and only you, can save thousands of lives. This is your last chance. Radio your men to surrender, or I will tell the President of the United States to unleash our armies."

Renata Bradley whipped out her cellphone. But when Rudy Mincarelli looked into the admiral's eyes, he saw only mirrors of death.

"Taiwan," Tang replied softly, "is not my goal."

Boots pounded down the corridor and a dozen of the admiral's elite guard burst into the domed room and leveled their weapons at Ken.

"If you think this is a Mexican standoff," Tang told the tugboat captain, "you are wrong." A word to his soldiers caused every rifle to be aimed at Kate Ross.

"I stand corrected," said Ken, and carefully laid his gun on the floor beside his dead friend.

41

GREG WALSH MADE IT as far as Kennedy Airport with the help of Pat Connelly's staff lieutenant, who had bundled him aboard a Marine transport. To get any closer to Brooklyn, he would have to walk. The Army had closed all roads. The Air Force had taken over the airport. But the chief of the Port Authority police was an old, old friend, and he took Greg up to the roof of the new control tower, which offered a panoramic three-sixty of Queens, Brooklyn, Staten Island, the edge of the South Bronx, Manhattan Island, and the Atlantic Ocean.

Out beyond the dark water, the sun began to stir.

Greg could see, in the predawn June light, that Kennedy's runways were already swarming with helicopter gunships. Giant transport planes were landing every sixty seconds. HumVees and armored personnel carriers roared down their ramps; infantry cut the age-old silhouette of laden men shouldering weapons. And for a moment so vivid he could taste the fear, he and Pat were eighteen again, double-timing across the apron at Tan Son Nhut.

Manhattan huddled in the west, the skyline a hint of black against the gray. East, over the Atlantic, where the coming dawn had suddenly lit the rim of the ocean, he could see miniature black silhouettes. Countless warships patrolling the approaches to Sandy Hook, sweeping the depths for submarines.

Though he couldn't see it, he sensed another presence farther out at sea, miles to the southeast. Puzzled, drawn to something as real as it was indefinable, he kept staring in that direction. There was no precise demarcation between absence and presence, but gradually a delicate form took shape—a flat perched gracefully on a tapered pedestal.

Soon a vertical line appeared on the edge of the horizontal, and Greg recognized, with a sinking heart, the offset island of an American nuclear aircraft carrier.

Closer, the warship assumed the profile of a dancer balanced one-legged on the edge of the stage. And soon after, a smug politician's hand cupped in an acknowledging wave. As the light strengthened and the giant steamed swiftly nearer, she seemed to float on middle ground between sea and sky.

The masts atop her island grew distinct to Greg's eye—and the island took on a ramshackle quality sprouting aerials, latticework antennas, reflectors, dishes, and fire-control radomes. She was growing tall and hard, the tapering pedestal spreading into a powerful deltoid that challenged the sky and plunged deep into the sea.

Greg turned around and gazed at New York. The tops of the World Trade Center and the mast of the Empire State Building were gleaming red and silver in the first beams of the sun. Dirty smoke drifted among them.

When he turned back to the aircraft carrier, she had become quite suddenly very, very wide. Still miles away, she seemed to fill the horizon, and he fancied he could see the fighter planes on her deck, bristling with rockets, and steam curling from the catapults that would fling them into battle. God only knew what Rudy had done with the meager hours Pat had bought him.

42

ADMIRAL TANG'S ELITE GUARD radioed for reinforcements, and a hundred heavily armed commandos marched Mayor Mincarelli, Renata, Ken, and Kate up to the street and into City Hall Park. A hint of morning light penetrated the smoke that hung over the park; high, high above, the sun itself shone on the tops of the World Trade Center.

Small-arms fire crackled in the surrounding blocks, but from what the mayor could see, Tang's troops had overwhelmed the police. As he stared around his war-torn city, Mayor Mincarelli's eyes locked on the Red Chinese flags flying atop both towers of the World Trade Center and from the dome of the Municipal Building and the cupola atop City Hall.

Mayor Mincarelli tried to ram new thoughts through his brain, new ideas to persuade Tang Li to surrender. The time for the American counterattack was drawing near.

The Chinese admiral spoke first. "Taiwan is only one small step toward the restoration of China's empire. Far more important is the recapture of vassal states and the establishment of new vassal states."

"*Vassal* states? What are you talking about?"

"China has always received tribute from her vassal states. Vassals 'kowtow' when they present gifts to the emperor."

"Admiral, you are taking leave of your—"

"The jewel in my crown of vassal states will be the richest city in the world—New York."

"*What?*"

"Tribute, Mr. Mayor. New York will pay annual tribute to the Emperor of China."

He's insane, thought the mayor. The helplessness that thought engendered must have shown on his face, because Admiral Tang said, "I'm not mad, Mr. Mayor. We are moderns. We live in a world of instant image. The image of China receiving tribute from the formerly most powerful nation in the world will bring into our camp every one of your country's enemies. They, too, will kowtow."

Shots rang out.

All eyes snapped toward City Hall. The Chinese flag was falling from the mast. Two New York City cops—one tall, one short—were silhouetted against the blueing sky, and as bullets screamed around them, they coolly clipped an American flag to the halyard and started to raise it.

"Just as I am saying," Tang said, "image is all. Faced with a hopeless situation, your brave police officers show a fine appreciation of image. In hopes they will rally their 'flagging' forces."

Mayor Mincarelli stood frozen, awed by the cops' courage. Tang murmured into his radio.

Twenty powerful flashlights illuminated them for the gunners. Their hats went flying. The taller officer was black, a tall black woman; her partner, a stubby little guy whose eyeglasses glinted in the blaze of light. A bullet knocked the woman down. She climbed to her feet, dragged herself up the steep pitch. The flag rose in jerky fits and starts. Then the wind caught it and flattened it against the sky as the gunfire drove home and both cops tumbled down the roof.

The mayor whirled on Tang, enraged. "How are you going to collect tribute once you've gone home?" he asked, too angry to conceal his scorn.

"We will accept your check," Tang replied blandly. "Backed, of course, by the gold which we will take with us as security."

"Gold?"

"From the Federal Reserve bank on Liberty Street. Half the gold reserves in the world, I am told. You are caretaker for minor nations. Now China will care for them."

"You're a criminal," said the mayor. "A murderer and now a common thief."

"China doesn't want your *money,* Mr. Mayor. We demand *tribute*—the symbol of power acknowledged."

"The United States will never allow that. The U.S. Navy will sink every one of your submarines before you and that gold are within ten thousand miles of China."

"The United States has no such option," Tang retorted coldly. He raised a radio to his lips. "I have mined your buildings, Mr. Mayor. My sappers have laid precision charges in the Federal Reserve Bank, the Stock Exchange, the Municipal Building, to name a few of the more prominent, and under both towers of your World Trade Center.

"I can destroy your entire financial district just as I destroyed your One Police Plaza. No one will prevent our voyage home."

"He's bluffing," said Ken.

"I've already demonstrated that I am not bluffing—by blowing up One Police Plaza. Shall I demonstrate again?" He looked up. "Shall we start with the North Tower of the World Trade Center?"

Mayor Mincarelli followed the Admiral's gaze, to where the sunlight rimmed the top three stories.

Admiral Tang said, "Those Islamic terrorists had the right idea a few years ago, but neither the means nor the imagination to succeed."

"*You* are the terrorist," Mayor Mincarelli shouted. "A cowardly, bloodthirsty terrorist."

Tang locked eyes on the mayor. "My soldiers have had the means, the expertise and fully eighteen hours in both World Trade subcellars to set the charges on precisely the right pilings. The towers will fall across your financial district—I will defuse the explosives when my last boat drops anchor in Chinese waters and New York pays tribute. Until then, your entire financial district is my hostage."

"He's bluffing," repeated Ken Hughes. "There are no explosives. We sank the ship carrying his explosives."

Admiral Tang just kept staring at Mayor Mincarelli, demanding his surrender.

Was it possible that he didn't know? wondered Ken. Or were there two ships of explosives? Or three? Had they landed more dynamite on the East River side of the island?

Tang spoke into his radio. The reply, which was a while in coming, led Tang to touch his ear. It was a quick, reflexive action and Ken wondered if his hand was ever so slightly trembling. But when the Admiral spoke again, he drew his radio to his lips, spoke firmly, sharply, demanding obedience.

At last Tang faced Ken, and as he did, his trim body seemed to sag like a birch bent low by the weight of ice.

"Was that you, too, Tugboat Captain?"

"He's bluffing, Mr. Mayor."

"Are you sure?"

"A bunch of old vets from the Intrepid Museum rammed his explosives ship with a decommissioned destroyer."

Tang squared his shoulders. "Tugboat captain, you are my nemesis."

"You murdered my crew and attacked my city. You expect me to walk away?"

Tang said, "I thought it was you, Mr. Mayor. Instead fate sends me a man and . . . a woman."

He looked at Kate. He looked at the mayor. His eyes drifted to his guard—the commandos seemed puzzled, sensing something was wrong, but were still eager to fight.

He beckoned their first circle, placed an arm around Ken, nodded to Kate and the mayor to follow, and started walking. Surrounded closely by the guard, they walked out of City Hall Park, across Broadway, toward an old church that occupied the block between Vesey and Fulton. The churchyard was protected by a wrought-iron fence. A section had been blasted open; the palings on the other side of the hole bent and twisted.

Tang walked Ken through it into the graveyard, among the headstones. A commando squad was waiting there. Tang spoke. The men removed their LED lights and dropped them on the grass in a red ten-foot circle. Ken eyed Tang's pistol, and surmised that he and Kate were headed to their execution.

"Do you recall, Captain, that because you saved my life you are responsible for my life?"

"I recall you said you owe me 'big-time.' "

"I've repaid you with your life, 'big-time.' And the life of your young lady. Have I not?"

"So far, we're still alive," Ken conceded.

"I now absolve you of your responsibility for my life. Forever. Will you do me a favor in return? Will you look out for my men?"

"What do you mean?"

Tang walked Kate and Ken into the circle of LED lights.

"There is a thin line between triumph and failure. I have come a long way and brought many good men with me. But I sense that the hairsbreadth between death with honor and lives wasted is about to disappear. That my sailors and my commandos are willing to die for me—and China—does not mean that they should. Do you understand me?"

He spoke clearly, so that even Rudy Mincarelli—between two commandos a step behind—heard what he had said.

"What do you mean?" demanded the mayor.

Kate saw Mincarelli's face harden into a lupine take-no-prisoners expression as he sensed capitulation.

"My men go home," said Admiral Tang.

"They throw down their arms," shouted the mayor. "They surrender to the police, like the criminals they are."

Ken cut him off. "Send them home."

"Stay out of this!"

"He's good to his men. He's a sailor's sailor. I guarantee you they will fight to the death unless he tells them not to."

"The criminal will stand trial," said Mincarelli.

Ken turned to Kate. "Can you. . . ."

Kate said, "I am a witness, Mr. Mayor. Admiral Tang has offered to stop fighting. Only you can save thousands of lives. I am witness to your response."

Mincarelli glared at the two citizens defying his will. They stared back, so sure of themselves he wanted to shoot them. Then the woman said to Renata, "Talk sense to him." And when he looked at Renata, she returned a brisk nod.

The mayor bowed his head. "Admiral, your men will surrender to my police; they will not be abused. And they will be sent home as prisoners of war."

"Don't let them scuttle the subs," Ken interrupted again. "They'll wreck the harbor worse than it is already."

"You heard him," said the mayor. "Agreed?"

*   *   *

Tang spoke at length into the radio clipped to his vest. When at last he looked up, he said in English, "It is done."

Then he turned to Ken, speaking in the same conversational manner as when he had explained the execution of Commissar Wong. "It was my original hope to tumble the World Trade Center's North Tower onto City Hall. It's a quarter mile high—as tall as seven city blocks on end—and two city blocks wide. Four million square feet of office space would have quite an impact on City Hall. But when my engineers measured it out precisely, they concluded it will reach only this far."

Tang indicated the red circle. Then he said, "You saw my munitions ship sink?"

"Last I saw, it was sinking."

"But did you see that one truck got off?"

Ken's heart fell. "I saw it."

"Step out of the circle, Captain. Take your young lady to shelter."

"What are you doing?"

"I will leave my mark on this city. All China will know that my armada brought it to its knees. The Chinese will rejoice and unite."

Ken stared up at the North Tower, one hundred and ten stories high. "You're committing suicide."

"Sacrifice. Not suicide. My sons will inherit a legend. And that legend will inspire Chinese to unite."

The boat handler again raised his eyes to the sunlit top of the tower. He traced the arc it would fall in, counting the buildings it would drive down through the pavement deep into the concourses and subways below, imagining the myriad invisible underground systems it would paralyze—transport, electricity, gas, steam, water, sewage, telephones, computer lines—visualizing the people hiding in those tunnels. He grew aware that Tang was watching him anticipate the effect, and he realized that at this moment he was the only person in New York who could change the admiral's mind.

"I gotta tell you, Admiral. In my experience, a son would rather have a live father than a dead legend."

"The legend of my China Armada will restore the Middle Kingdom."

Ken bored into Tang's eyes. He didn't look nuts, but appeared very, very sure. Maybe that was the same thing. "How many sons," Ken asked, "ever fill their father's shoes—much less their legends?"

"In *my* experience, grandsons do," said Tang. "Tugboat Captain, you're a seafarer. Did you know that hundreds of years ago, a great Mandarin of South China sailed a gigantic ship across two oceans to Africa? Neither Africans nor Arabs nor Westerners on that trading coast had ever seen a ship like it. When the great junk sailed home to China, the emperor ordered it broken up for firewood. China was the center, ruled he. The universe. There was no need to leave it. But, of course, Chinese ventured abroad again, by the millions. But never again as explorers. Not as bold traders. Not as warriors. But only as poor coolies begging to work like slaves.

"Until today."

The Chinese admiral signaled his commandos to escort the mayor back to City Hall Park. "Run, Tugboat Captain." And when Ken stood firm, Tang turned to Kate. "Take his hand and run."

Then he spoke into his radio.

Ken felt the ground heave under their feet. Kate grabbed his hand and they ran from the graveyard, leaped through the blasted fence to Vesey Street. At Broadway they looked back.

The North Tower of the World Trade Center shivered. The sunlit top swayed. Windows broke loose from their frames and rained down in a long, cacophonous, pealing, rumbling crash until the broad World Trade Center plaza was many feet deep in broken glass.

Naked as a skeleton, the tower began to tilt.

Admiral Tang watched it slant toward him, filling the sky with a crumbling bulk. He was a Mandarin of South China. He had sailed his armada under three oceans. He had shown the way.

The building leaned into the city and, gathering speed, fell straight as a mast onto the broad plaza. It buried the lower buildings, spread across Church Street, and thundered into the graveyard of St. Paul's where Admiral Tang Li raised his arms to greet it.

43

RENATA BRADLEY PUNCHED her speed dial. "This is Renata Bradley for Mayor Rudolph Mincarelli. Patch us into Mr. Jennings, now. . . . Peter, Renata . . ."

The news anchor sounded grave. Did he think he was about to broadcast Rudy Mincarelli's surrender?

She handed Rudy the phone. He was gaping, dazed and disbelieving, at the quarter-mile, two-block-wide mountain of rubble that had buried whole buildings.

She checked her watch and mouthed, "At five o'clock Wednesday morning in New York City, I, Mayor Rudolph Mincarelli, have accepted the unconditional surrender . . ."

Rudy put the phone to his lips.

Trains, power, communications. Thousands of people.

"I, Rudolph Mincarelli, duly elected mayor of New York City, have accepted the unconditional surrender of Admiral Tang Li's invading troops, submarines, and support craft at five o'clock Wednesday morning in New York City. Admiral Tang's soldiers will lay down their arms, and surrender to the police officers and detectives of the New York Police Department. His submarines will surface and anchor at—" He glanced at Ken Hughes.

"Gravesend Bay."

"At Gravesend Bay. The prisoners will be processed at—" He thought he would pass out, he was so tired. Where the hell were they going to put eight thousand prisoners? Most of them were downtown already. "At Battery Park in lower Manhattan.

"In the clear and necessary interest of not inciting new violence, I call upon all United States military forces to wait outside the confines of New York City until nine o'clock Eastern Standard Time, at which time they may come in to start the process of repatriating the prisoners. Naval forces may, at that time, collect the submarines from Gravesend Bay." Marty better get the President to back him up on all that, but whether the military waited or not, the important thing was that, in the eyes of the world, the mayor of New York City had set the agenda for a peaceful surrender, and no one could come in shooting.

"I call upon Consolidated Edison to get its power plants up and running, and order all police officers to report to their precincts. As Commissioner Stowe was killed while bravely defending Police Plaza, I hereby appoint as his successor the former acting police commissioner, Greg Walsh.

"Finally, to the people of New York, my fellow citizens, I say we have much rebuilding to do and many dead to mourn, and we will do both together."

Renata touched his arm. Brilliant!

He pushed END, gave her a weary smile, and said, "I'd like to see Greg get out of this one."

In one of the crowded cop wards set up at NYU Downtown Hospital, around the corner from City Hall, an exhausted nurse tapped Hector Sanchez awake. "We got a bed free for her now."

Hector, bandaged from his left ankle to his left shoulder, was lying on his back, with Harriet Greene nestled in his good arm. "That's okay," said Hector, gently stroking the fringe line where the unbelievably soft skin of Harriet's brow met her hair. "Give it to somebody else."

"Listen, Officer, she's been shot four times. She'll be a lot more comfortable when I move her into her own bed."

Harriet opened one Demerol-glazed eye. "Try it," she whispered, "and we'll kill you."

44

KEN HUGHES WAS sharing a cup of Red Cross coffee with Kate Ross under a bullet-riddled tree in City Hall Park when Mayor Mincarelli, who looked even worse than they felt, broke away from a gaggle of staffers to say, "I owe you one."

"Build a freight tunnel to Brooklyn and we'll be even."

"We're studying that," the mayor said, eyes flickering toward the five-block hump of wreckage that stretched from the base of the remaining World Trade tower.

"You've been studying it for twenty years, for crissake. Last chance to save the port before the new deep-draft ships make us a ghost town."

Renata Bradley edged closer, peering over Kate's shoulder. Her cheek was bandaged, her eyes blackened, and it hurt her to speak. But she asked Kate, "Is that Jose Chin's camera?"

"His or his station's. I'm going to give it to his brother."

"What were you watching on the screen just now?"

"Jose had his jacket-cam mini-module on. It kept video

taping after they killed him." The camera was blinking a low-battery warning. Kate hit Play and angled the monitor so Renata could see.

"My God!" breathed Renata.

"But that's not really how it happened," said Kate.

Jose's last tape, shot at an angle from the floor where he lay dead, made it appear as if Mayor Rudolph Mincarelli had punched Admiral Tang Li.

"He didn't punch Admiral Tang, he just shoved him," said Kate. "And it didn't change anything. Tang's bodyguard swatted him like a fly."

"Nonetheless," said Renata, "I wonder if you would give me that tape."

Kate said, "Jose told me you can make still photographs from video."

"Yes, I know," said Renata, reaching for the camera.

Kate hugged it closer and said, "Even though it didn't happen this way, Mayor Mincarelli looks so . . ."

"Presidential," Renata gritted through her teeth. "May I have that tape?" She cast an ominous eye toward the thousands of cops fanning out from their temporary headquarters in the Tweed Court House.

Kate said, "I see a firsthand account. Published in hardcover. I even see a title, *In the Bunker with Rudy*. Is it mine?"

"Naturally, your boss would be my first choice—"

"Naturally, my boss will shepherd my project after *I acquire In the Bunker with Rudy*."

"What kind of deadline?"

"We'll crash out the hardcover before the nominating convention. Paperback a month before Election Day."

"You got it."

"Eighty percent of the royalties to Jose's family, of course. Twenty to his mentor's, Arnie Moskowitz."

"Of course."

"If New York Yes! claims they own it . . ."

"They'll wish they hadn't."

Kate opened the camera, popped out the tape. "Oh. One other thing. You heard Captain Hughes. The harbor is a wreck. Sunken ships everywhere. Captain Hughes, with his experience and contacts, is unusually qualified to be New York City's salvage master."

"Done! Give me the tape."

Renata stuffed it into her deepest pocket.

Ken passed the coffee back to Kate. "Congratulations. You drive a hard bargain. But what makes you think I want to be salvage master?"

"You said you want to do salvage. Why not start at the top? Am I being pushy?"

"It has a vaguely familiar ring of 'Stop tugboating and take a job ashore.' "

"I didn't mean it that way. Oh, God, I wouldn't do that to you. I just wanted to help your salvage business."

Ken thought about it. Fact was, for a woman like Kate Ross, he'd be well advised to go ashore and hang by his ankles, if that would make her happy.

"Actually, from what I saw of the poor *Queen*, the first thing I'll be salvaging is her. I'm going to need a place to stay for a while."

"You can stay at my apartment. But only if you sleep with me."

"Like I said, you drive a hard bargain."